The Tercentennial Baron

by

Will Damron

To my family, without whom the Baron would never have had a chance to live.

And to Ray: as promised, the first copy is for you.

From the pages of D. H. Grimm's
Spirits of the Night and Twilight:

> *It has often been whispered, through the cloistered Scottish glens where his legend thrives, that to meet the Baron is to see how the veil between the realms is torn asunder: to feel the dread of darkness well up from your heart.*

> *It is, after all, from our darkest fears that these demons draw their lifeblood. And our darkness will always betray us.*

Scotland

The Present

The boy scrambled up the rim of the shadowy hill. His knee slipped on the grass and he cursed through ragged breaths, hands slashing the earth to find a hold. His panic flared hotter every second. If he didn't make the crest soon, his friend would die.

Down in the village behind him, a scream tore through the still night. *Let it go*, he ordered himself. *There's nothing more you can do for them. Get to the barn. Everything depends on the barn.*

With a rasping cry he swung his knees onto the hilltop and clambered to his feet. Towering before him, like a beast roaring to life in the dark, was the stone barn. It was engulfed in flame.

The boy swallowed hard. The barn had stood for centuries, an abandoned relic from the days of feudal lords and tartan-clad warriors. Now its stones were singed black, the roof gleamed angrily, and the doorway yawned into a blinding chasm, daring the boy to approach. His courage began to wilt—nobody could survive such a fire. *But the old man has seen far worse*, he reminded himself. He ignored the suffocating heat, and raced toward the door.

He was halfway there when he suddenly froze: a shadow had moved inside the barn. The boy peered closer, past the falling beams and roof thatching—and his heart leapt in his chest. A human form, silhouetted against the blaze, was rising from the barn floor. He wore a long, billowing coat, and grasped a saber that glinted with blood as he staggered to his feet.

The warrior propped himself on the sword and slowly lifted his head. His vivid eyes glowed through the flames, arresting the boy in a haunted and desperate stare.

The boy knew then that he might be too late. But he'd come too far to turn away. He swallowed his fear, drew a deep breath, and ran inside the barn.

Chapter One

Spirits of the Night and Twilight

P ercival Dunbar snapped awake with a sharp gasp, slamming his head into the metal lamp above him. A merciless clang resounded through his bedroom, and he swore as he rubbed the sore spot. His face had left an imprint in the book on his desk, the paper wrinkled around the words he'd been reading the evening before: "*Sunlight washes out the forms of ghosts. That is why they are best visible in the shadows, and at night...*"

Percival pushed the book away, hoping it would dry quickly. It was old and musty, its spine held together by two tattered strips of fabric. He'd dug it out of Granny's attic yesterday when she'd sent him up to lay mouse traps, and he dared to believe it was more ancient than she was. (He wished he knew; the copyright page had given up and left long ago.) But he did know this was a book he could never let Granny see, for she would think the subject too disturbing—too dangerous—to ever allow him to read it. It was called *Fifty-One Wraiths, Phantoms, and Creatures: A Compendium of Studies of Questionable Occurrences*, by D. H. Grimm.

"PER-CY!"

Percival bolted from his desk and snatched his mobile phone: 5:47 AM, almost sunrise.

"*PER-CYYY!*"

"I heard you, Granny, I'm up!" he called. Her voice was especially shrill and grating this morning.

Just then, a crisp breeze—colder than usual for late summer in Scotland—swept over Percival from the window in front of his desk, and he noticed how hot his skin felt. He patted his face from his nut-brown eyes down his pointed nose and chin, ran his fingers through his shaggy black hair: everything burned to touch, and not as though he'd just been dreaming of a fire. As though he really had just run headlong into one.

"*Percy!* You've thirty seconds to get your scraggy hide out to the chicken coop, or I swear I'll make you sleep there!"

A myriad of curses cascaded through Percival's mind, but he knew, after thirteen years with Granny, not to give her more ammunition than necessary. He peeled off his flannel shirt and jeans, tossed them into the old berry crate that served as a laundry bin, and tugged on fresh clothes as fast as he could.

He'd almost left the room when his eye chanced on *Fifty-One Wraiths*—and his empty stomach twisted. If Granny ever saw the book, he'd return to find it in pieces. He grabbed his favorite large, red-tasseled bookmark, which had "Barclay's Books and Inks" printed on the front. On the back, as he always did, he'd signed his name in sleek, dark letters. He flagged the page, eased the book shut, and wedged it into the hidden niche between his dresser and closet. Then he opened his door.

Percival spotted her as soon as he stepped out: Granny McGugan, shrouded in shadow across the living room, grey hair flying every which way like scruffy fur, eyes wild in the gloom. She was wearing her usual outfit of mud-caked boots, dark dress, and tattered jumper that smelled of mothballs and something like old, dry toast. Now that Percival was a teenager he'd gained a good six inches on her, but that didn't make him feel any more a man under her glare. She said nothing further. Just stood there, round and stormy like a cannonball, watching him as she sipped her tea.

Percival scowled back, and trudged through the living room. He had to duck to avoid the rusted meat hooks that hung from the ceiling, left from the bygone days of the McGugan farm when pork loins would be suspended to dry over the floor. He undid the four locks on the front door, and had just turned the knob when he heard: "An' don't think I didn't hear you shuttin' that book in your room just now."

Percival stiffened. He carefully turned back, his face devoid of expression.

"What, I'm not allowed to do homework?"

"It's nearly Festival weekend," Granny murmured. "You don't have any homework." She took one step forward in the dark room. "If I find you've been readin' another o' that books—"

"Well I haven't," Percival returned. He kept his body still and his eyes locked on Granny's. The best, and simplest, way to lie to her.

But just in case she wasn't convinced, he tossed out a challenge. "Search my room if you don't believe me." And he walked out the door.

Percival wrinkled his nose against the smell of cow manure that always permeated the morning air. He may have put on a good show, but as he tromped to the chicken coop and collected the eggs inside, his heart was hammering. He refused, no matter what, to lose another book to Granny McGugan.

Percival wasn't normally so attached to books, but he had a history with the works of D. H. Grimm. After all, he was no stranger to dreams like the one that had awoken him. And while other kids might shrug off such things, Percival hadn't ever been able to do so. The reason was simple: his dreams

5

never faded away. They never seemed surreal or fantastical upon waking. If anything, they felt more real than his day-to-day life with Granny McGugan.

And so, every chance he had, Percival immersed himself in the peculiar world of D. H. Grimm. For Grimm was the only author who researched, catalogued, and explained the sorts of creatures that came alive in Percival's dreams. Creatures of the supernatural.

This was also, Percival guessed, the reason that all of Grimm's works were banned in his town of Bonnybield.

Percival caught his first glimpse of Bonnybield that morning as he crested Granny's lane on his rusty bicycle, two cartons of eggs strapped to the rear fender. The town was built into the side of a glen that descended before him, and surrounding the tidy rooftops and scattered sheep pastures were acres upon acres of lush berry fields.

Bonnybield was one of the oldest villages in the county of Angus, and Bonnybielders knew berries. In fact, there was little else they cared to know much about. They liked to sigh and shake their heads at how so many "modern" farms nearby only grew one or two types of berries, for a good Bonnybield farm still boasted a variety of raspberries, strawberries, gooseberries, tayberries, brambles, redcurrants, blackcurrants, white currants... the list went on. They grew other things, of course, and gardened, and traveled when they felt they ought to. But a surefooted Bonnybielder never really left his snug little glen, and never felt at home without plenty of green fields around him, just ready for the final harvest.

As Percival coasted down the winding avenues of medieval stone, he saw flags unfurling from windows and banners being strung across the street, even heard the whine of bagpipes practicing. The decorations grew larger as he sailed into the frenzy of the High Street: a square overlooked by the church at one of the tallest points in town. A mercat cross topped with a nineteenth-century lamp towered in the middle. It was festooned with blue and red ribbons, and a massive banner hung behind it, proclaiming:

BONNYBIELD'S 399ᵀᴴ BERRY FESTIVAL
HERE'S TAE THE FARMER, AN' PROSPER HIS FIELDS!

The Berry Festival was the crown of harvest season: a weekend of tastings, games, music, and dance, while the town elders poked through one another's fields to find the ripest and grandest Prize Bunch for the yearly medal.

Percival couldn't have cared less who won the Prize Bunch. To him the Festival meant an extra day off from school and all the raspberry crumble he could eat. But as he walked the eggs into Camden's Grocery, and smelled the toasted sweetness of the first desserts arriving for the weekend, Percival felt a strange, cold feeling trickle through him.

He paused. It was something akin to fear, but not normal everyday fear as when his teacher yelled at him for turning in homework late, or he thought Granny might find one of his books. This was a deep, heavy fear, chilling each limb of his body, and the more he became aware of it, the more he felt it was somehow connected to the Berry Festival. As if something was... *off* about the coming celebration this year. He tried to keep moving, but it seemed all the blood had been pushed to his feet, and he ran into—bounced off of, more like—the oak-barrel torso of Jamie McCarra, the local butcher's son.

"Heh! Watch your step, Dunbar!"

The older boy shoved Percival back to make room for his belly in the grocery aisle. "God, I'll have to wash the stink off me before school, you dirty wee midden."

But Percival hardly registered the insult. All at once, a swarm of sensations rushed upon him: the oven-like heat on his skin, the dire conviction that he had to save somebody who was trapped... and, for a lingering second, the warrior in the barn flashed across his vision. Leaning on the crimson saber. Staring at Percival with trenchant, harrowing eyes, as if the world were about to end.

Get a hold of yourself, he commanded. No dream had ever followed him this intensely... *Just get through school, and you can sort it all out later.*

School, however, was no better. In fact, it was worse. Percival tried to distract himself by taking rigorous notes in history class, but only ended up producing a sketch of a fiery barn atop a hill. His teacher Mr. MacGillivray knew something was amiss when Percival Dunbar seemed to be writing so studiously, so he confiscated Percival's notebook and, upon seeing the violent image of a burning building, informed the boy he'd be visiting the headmaster after Festival weekend.

Later, as Percival ducked out the school door, he passed his classmate Danny Watson, who asked, "Where're you goin', Percival? The relay starts in half an hour."

"So?"

"So, we're Second-Years now, numpty! We've got to set up!"

Percival's stomach plummeted. The relay was the annual Carry Tae Yer Kin Relay, the informal kick-off to the Berry Festival. It took place on the secondary school's track field, where teams of family members had to carry something— literally *any*thing weighing five to ten pounds—in a relay-style race across a finish line. That was it. Prizes were given for Fastest Time as well as Most Creative Relay Item. One year, Jamie McCarra, his brother, and their father won while passing along a bottle of whisky. When Jamie crossed the finish line, he popped open the bottle and downed a healthy swig.

It was all harmless family fun.

But for Percival, that was just the problem. He had no family.

Granny McGugan would never deign to do anything so

social as the Carry Tae Yer Kin. She never even ventured into Bonnybield anymore.

And Percival had no memory of his parents at all. His mother had died giving birth to him, in Granny's own bedroom, and his father had left Bonnybield immediately after. Nobody had heard from him again. And every time Percival asked Granny about his parents—what they were like, why his father left—she gave him nothing but menacing silence.

So it was that Percival was finally forced to watch the Carry Tae Yer Kin Relay. Not only did he have to set up cones for the relay points, but he was tasked with recording each family's times. He saw the McCarras laugh and gallop along like a pack of donkeys, the Cormags pass a live rabbit between them (to the cheers of the gathered Bonnybielders), even old Mrs. Purdie waddle her eighty-five-year-old body across the finish line carrying her legendary blackberry pie. When she began slicing and serving it to the judges, Percival had had enough. He grabbed the nearest student, shoved the clipboard and pencil at him, and stormed off the field.

Ten minutes later, he'd biked back to the High Street and parked outside his after-school job at the town bookstore, Barclay's Books and Inks. He stood gripping the cashier's counter as he watched Mr. Barclay's dusty computer whir to life.

Percival knew somebody would yell at him for deserting his post like that, but he didn't care. Every other person there could laugh and joke and cheer, and Percival envied how easy it was for them. He felt the flare of a bitter, long-burning anger. Toward Granny, for never once attending a Berry Festival with him. Toward the mysterious, faceless man who had left him there, to grow up with her.

"Percival! That you, lad?"

"Aye, Mr. Barclay," Percival called, in a sharper voice than he'd intended.

Gordon Barclay wheeled his massive torso into view atop the steps beside the counter, which led up to the rear stacks and his office. His round, mustachioed face scowled down at the boy. "What're you doin'? You don't start for another twenty minutes."

Percival shrugged. "Aye," was all he said.

"Not much for the relay, eh?"

Percival didn't respond. Despite the fact that his boss almost never smiled, Percival had always liked him. When he'd turned ten and Granny demanded he find a farm job, Barclay had been generous enough to pay the boy a few pounds to sweep floors, stock books, and man his counter instead. Percival was beyond grateful. He despised berry-picking.

"Listen, laddie," Barclay said, teetering down the steps to the counter. "I suppose it's good you arrived a bit early…"

That was when Percival noticed Barclay was cradling a large, brown object against his paunch.

"You're, eh…" Barclay began. For a man who never had trouble getting right to the point, this was the longest he'd ever taken to say anything.

"This is your thirteenth Berry Festival, aye?" Barclay finally asked.

"I guess. I turn fourteen in October."

"Oh, aye? Well…" Barclay cleared his throat. Cleared it again. Then he just sighed and confessed, "I don't know how else to say this, laddie, but I've been keepin' somethin' for you."

As if he couldn't wait to get rid of it, he dropped the object on the counter. It was a paper parcel, slightly wrinkled and tied with twine, and covered in a thick film of dust. It was about the size of a hardcover book.

"Not long after you were born," Barclay continued, "I found this on my doorstep one mornin'. I only knew of you as the new bairn on the McGugan farm, and we were all still grievin' for your mother. She was such a sparklin' lass…" He paused, his voice softening. "So full of spirit. And then this… well, it was addressed to you."

That was when Percival noticed a large smudge on the top corner of the parcel. He picked it up—it was heavier than he'd thought—and blew away the dust.

The smudge, he realized, was writing. In a scratchy, uneven hand, somebody had left a message on the paper:

To Mr. Gordon Barclay -

I believe you to be an honest man. This book is the property of Percival Dunbar, currently residing in the home of Alice McGugan. I beseech you to keep it safely in your possession until Mr. Dunbar has surpassed 13 years of age. At that time, I ask that you convey it to him.

He shall be forever in your debt. As am I.

Percival looked up at Barclay. "That's it?"

"Aye!" Barclay harrumphed. "Bit presumptuous, don't you think? No name, no return address—I thought it might 'a been a bomb!" Barclay chuckled to himself, which he accomplished while still not quite smiling. "Whoever this loun was, I doubt he knew you'd wind up workin' for me!"

Percival smoothed his hands over the crinkling paper, felt the bumpy texture of the book cover underneath. "What is it?"

Barclay sighed. "Laddie, it could be a phone directory for all I know. Whatever it is, it's yours. And now I've given it to you." He patted his steak-like hand on the counter. "Happy Festival."

"Happy Festival," Percival replied, as Barclay waddled back up to his office.

Percival traced his fingers around the edges of the parcel. This dusty thing had been sitting in Barclay's office for thirteen years? Strange as it might seem, Percival knew why Barclay had agreed to the giver's request: if anybody asked a favor of a lifelong Bonnybielder using words like "honest man" and "forever in your debt," they were sure to get what they wanted.

But who would have left a book here for *Percival?* Why not entrust it to Granny McGugan, if it were so important?

Percival grabbed a pair of scissors from beneath the computer, and snipped off the brittle twine. He didn't know why, but he had a feeling that whatever was hiding beneath this paper, it was old and of great value. So he carefully popped open each edge of the wrapping, and unfolded it from the mysterious tome.

Two thoughts struck Percival in quick succession. The first was that this was definitely an aged, well-used book. The second was what the embossed letters above the title spelled out: *D. H. Grimm.*

Percival couldn't tear the rest of the paper away fast enough. *Grimm!* Another book by the one writer he was never supposed to read. He drew his fingertips over the cover: hard, gold-colored leather, with a swirling design of a blue eye in the middle. Over the eye, in more embossed letters, was the title: *Spirits of the Night and Twilight, and Other Studies of Questionable Occurrences.*

Percival had heard of this book. Most everybody had. It was the rarest of Grimm's works, his most harrowing collection of supernatural phenomena. It was not only banned; it was forbidden to be discussed.

Percival flipped open the cover—and the air in his lungs froze. There was another name, written in flowing black letters over the title page: a signature from the first owner of the book. *Elliot Dunbar.*

Elliot Dunbar. Percival's father.

Percival let out his breath on a burst of sound—somewhere between a shout of surprise and a laugh of joy—then clapped a hand over his mouth. He hurriedly shut the book, wrapped it back up, and buried it in his backpack. Neither Barclay nor anybody else on the High Street could know he possessed

Spirits of the Night and Twilight.

But there was one person he *could* tell. The only person he wanted to tell.

"Percival!" Barclay yelled from his office. "Look lively! Mrs. Cormag is on her way for the school order!"

"Right!" Percival called. He scrambled for his mobile, found the contact he wanted, and dashed out a text:

Meet me tonight. There's something you've got to see.

He pressed *SEND*, then retrieved a box of textbooks from under the counter. He had a good deal of work to finish before he'd be released, but he attacked it now with vigor. For the first time in a very long while, he was eager for the night ahead.

Miles away from Bonnybield, at that moment, a huge motorbike sped up the road in a blur of silver and grey. It weaved around cars like a sleek insect, disappearing from view as quickly as it emerged, until it attained a stretch of road for itself.

The motorbike's driver shifted gears and felt the humming beneath him settle into a comfortable rhythm. He looked around, drinking in the settling mist. He liked the mist; he felt safe in the shrouded nature it brought, and though he would have loved to stop and watch night fall, he knew it would only waste time and distract him from his purpose. If he kept going north at this speed, he could reach his destination by midnight. *He had to get there* and then he'd have time to slow down, center himself... as long as he didn't eat again along the way. Eating for him was a tricky endeavor, and something he had to plan carefully. It was better that he save his energy. He would need all of it for what lay ahead.

He switched on his headlight and settled into his seat, welcoming the chill of the evening air.

Chapter Two

The Voice on the Wind

P ercival whipped his bike around a puddle on Scobie Road above town. The day was sinking into orange twilight, and a rain spell had left the asphalt slick and treacherous as he pedaled back to Granny's.

He knew he couldn't let her see any of his hunger to shut himself in his room and dive into his father's book. So he'd have to play along with her—act humble, do whatever she asked without talking back—until he could quietly slip away. He swerved around two sheep wandering the road and turned onto Granny's lane, coasting toward the stone farmhouse nestled against the heather-capped hill. Stretching from either side of the lane were berry fields that once had supported the farm, but had now deteriorated into wild-grass abandon since Grandfather McGugan died, years before Percival's birth.

Percival rounded the small wooden workers' dormitory— the *bothy,* Granny called it, empty for a half-century now—and parked his bike under the eves of the house.

Just after he stepped off it, he faltered. The breeze was playing a delicate tune on the wind chimes by Granny's door, and something about the eerie, unresolved melody made his skin prickle.

He looked toward the darkening fields, the hills as they

flattened into shadows… and felt it again. Not the scorching heat from the fire, but the desperation to save the man within—and the dread. A raw wave of dread, seeping into his bones with the onset of night.

"PER-CY!"

This time Percival actually jumped. Granny had surely seen him arrive, and was wondering why he wasn't inside yet. He fished out his keys and opened the door.

The familiar smell of burnt sausages assailed him, as if trying to escape the dank house. Granny stuck her head out from the kitchen, the living room television flickering over her creased face.

"Hurry inside, lad! You'll get the cold."

Percival wiped his boots, shut the door, and fastened its four locks. Granny trundled past him to the TV, depositing a bowl in his hands. "Supper," she announced.

Bangers n' mash. Percival could tell from the scent faster than the sight. His stomach grumbled in protest; he was famished, but she'd made this meal so often in the past month he didn't think he could take any more of it.

"I think I'll eat in my room, Granny."

"No, you'll eat out here." Granny planted herself in her green plaid armchair. "You're spendin' too much time in that room as it is. Look." She thrust her mug of toddy at the game show warbling from the TV. "*Garlan's Challenge* is on."

"So?"

"You used to like it."

Percival gritted his teeth. *Act humble…* "Granny, I'm just really tired, and—"

All of a sudden, a rush of wind arose outside and rammed the front of the house, clapping the shutters against the windows. The window frames groaned as the gale began to grow stronger—when, quickly as it had come, it ceased. As if switched off. Not a whisper of a breeze remained.

Granny McGugan went still in her chair. She placed her bangers n' mash on the table beside her, and slowly turned to Percival.

"Did you latch the shutters on the windows?"

Percival braced himself. Of course there was one chore he'd forgotten...

"You are goin to bring me to my wits' end!" Granny pounded her fist, stood up, and charged over to Percival. "Are you goin' to pay to replace every window here? The winds are gettin' wild, like they do this time every year, an' still you forget to latch the shutters!" Then her voice sank lower, to a sinister purr. "Why is it you can't remember to do *one simple thing* for this house? What happens to folk that don't do what they're told?"

Percival lifted his chin. He knew what she expected him to say.

"They fall in with bad people. And they die young."

"An' what's the result o' that?"

It took all of Percival's resolve not to look away in fury. She wasn't letting him go easily tonight.

"They leave you no choice but to raise their child."

Granny's eyes revealed her smug approval. "Now. Awa' an' latch the bloody shutters."

Percival sunk his smoldering gaze into her a moment longer. This was the one detail Granny ever allowed him about his parents. His mother, Granny's daughter, had never listened to Granny's instruction. Never wanted anything to do with farm life. So she grew up to marry a bad man, a man not from Bonnybield: the dishonest, fickle Elliot Dunbar. And died having his child.

Percival dropped his bowl on the dining table and marched around to each window, throwing open the bottom pane and latching the creaky exterior shutters. Granny hummed to herself in a low, disjointed rhythm as she returned to her armchair: satisfied with the sense of duty she'd restored to her grandson.

Percival had just slammed the latch on the final shutter when another gust of wind buffeted the house, even stronger than the first. He stepped back, stunned at how violent the winds were this year. This one whined through the ancient seams in the walls, as if testing their ability to stand—and then Percival realized he heard another sound *within* the wind. Something that didn't belong there, but was clear as a bell to his ears.

It was a low, agonizing moan. As if some heartbroken person were crying many miles away. Percival tried to shake the chill that slithered up his neck... this had to be a trick of the air over the Scottish hills. But as the wind grew in power, so did the moan, swelling from a deep, mournful cry to a harrowing wail that reverberated through the house. Percival's breath felt locked inside him, and his muscles had turned to ice.

All at once, just as before, the wind dropped to stark silence.

"... Granny?" Percival's voice came as little more than a creak, and he noticed Granny was still slouched in her armchair. "D—did you hear that?"

But the old woman didn't reply. She just sat very still with her head inclined, as if lost in thought. *Did she even hear me?* Percival wondered. But he saw now was his chance to evade her for the night. He forced his frozen limbs into motion and slipped quietly around her chair. He was just about to open his bedroom door when, out of nowhere, she began to sing a high, lilting tune:

"*Once, twice shrieks the wind, the Baron will come back again...*"

Percival stopped, his fingers cold and tingly where they hovered above the doorknob. Granny's voice was softer than ever, a scratchy murmur that sounded all the more uncanny because everything else was so hushed. But that song... he'd not heard it since he was five or six. It was an old nursery rhyme she used to sing. Glancing back at her, it looked as if an unexpected memory had carried her away for a moment. Her gaze was distant, almost puzzled, as she went on humming.

Percival turned and shut himself in his bedroom, giving the knob the twist to the left that jammed it from the outside. *Alright. That was weird.* He tried to gather his wits, and had just felt his breathing settle when a sharp TAP sounded from the window behind his desk.

He tensed. The sound came again. *Tap, tap.*

Percival edged forward, pulse quickening. He recognized this could well be the worst time to open a window, and the eerie cry was still ringing in his ears... but he thought he knew what the tapping was. He climbed atop his desk, lifted the glass, and eased open the shutters.

The bracing air rushed upon his face. Percival saw nothing that would have made the sound: only Granny's lane stretching away like her own knobby finger, and the jack-o-lantern smile of the sun slipping behind the hills.

Without warning, something sharp and gelid sunk into the skin of his arm.

Percival looked down in horror and tried to jump backward, but he couldn't move. A strong, spindly hand had flashed up from beyond the window and seized him by the wrist.

He stifled a yell as he stared at the pale white fingers. He tried to pry them off, his mind scrambling to understand what was happening—and then he heard maniacal giggling.

"*Gotcha!*" A fiery-haired head popped up before him.

"For God's sake, Abi!" Percival whispered as he yanked his arm to his chest. "Your hands are bloody freezin'!"

"Woke you up, though, didn't it?" Abigail Sinclair grinned. She had a freckled face and turquoise eyes like a sun-dotted stream, and was wearing her scarf, jean jacket, and backpack. Adventure clothes. "Come on, the rain's finally stopped. You ready?"

"I might be if you'd just texted me! Why the tappin' on my window?"

"I *did* text you, numpty. Where's your mobile?"

Percival patted his jeans and realized he'd left his phone buried next to *Spirits of the Night and Twilight* in his backpack. "Never mind," he said. "Listen—a moment ago, in all that wind, did you hear anythin'? You know... unusual?"

Abi looked at Percival with vacant eyes. "Like?"

Percival stared back at her. Was he the only one who'd heard that sound?

"Are you comin' or not?" Abi asked. "It's just a bit o' wind, Perce. I've only got a few hours!"

Percival listened for any sign of another terrifying cry, but the air seemed calmer. Abi was right. It was nothing he needed to worry about now, and he was dying to show her his father's book. He flipped off the light and made sure his backpack was secure on his shoulders.

"And was that you I saw leavin' the relay today?" Abi whispered. "I got there late with my da'. Didn't think you'd be there..."

"Nor did I." Percival mounted the desk, swung his legs out the window, and dropped to the ground beside Abi.

She seemed to register that he'd rather not talk about it, and punched his shoulder instead. "So where are we goin' this time?"

Percival couldn't help the smile that cracked his face. He'd known Abi since their third year of primary school, and though she had many other friends in town, she was Percival's only friend. She'd taken pity on him when he showed up to school in the same clothes for a week straight. When he turned ten, she saved her allowance to buy him his first coat that actually fit him. And once it became clear that Granny would never allow

Percival to go to another kid's house, Abi had started visiting him in secret.

Percival's expression turned crafty. "Let's go to the stone." Before Abi could respond, he launched into a sprint away from the house.

Percival beamed as the breeze flung his hair back over his scalp. For a moment he forgot the dread he'd felt all day, for these had always been his favorite evenings: just after a rainstorm, when the wind was still panting from its effort, as if trying to conjure one more torrent from the clouds. Many times as a boy he'd snuck out wearing nothing but his old corduroy trousers, and let the lingering rain sting his skin, test him. That was when he'd first believed that this was the air that brought ghosts, and whipped up sprites and shrouded wraiths of the night. He thought it was their coy laughter he heard on Granny's wind chimes, that it was their eyes he felt as he crept outside. That secretly, they were longing to hurl themselves forth, unmasked, from the twilight breeze.

Abi caught up to him and they jogged the familiar path that muffled their footsteps: around the bothy, over the soft part of the gravel lane where the rocks wouldn't crunch, and across the dead field to the north. He glanced back at the house, a whisper of light in the gathering darkness. Granny hadn't discovered his escape.

"Don't tell me you'll let a bit o' cold slow you down!" Abi goaded as she sped past Percival. They clambered up a ridge at the end of the field, emerging at a mighty oak forest. Percival raced Abi along the trees toward the sunset, a cramp spearing his stomach. He tried to lengthen his stride for a final push, but Abi was already skipping her victory dance around their destination: a looming rectangular standing stone.

"Must be hard doin' a sprint carryin' a mighty napper like yours!" Abi sang.

Percival staggered to a stop with his hands on his knees.

"Least I don't run like a farm goose." He tapped his temple. "And my napper *is* mighty, thank you."

"That why you walk as if you don't know how to balance it on top o' your body?"

"Shove off." He straightened and approached the stone, which was so tall its peak was lost in the leaves overhead. The side that faced out from the forest was covered with flowing carvings reminiscent of the ancient Picts, and were dazzlingly intricate: a snakelike symbol had actual rounded scales, and another felt like tree bark if Percival ran his fingers over it.

Percival unslung his backpack and slid down the cool, lichen-covered face of the stone. Abi joined him, removing a thermos of tea from her pack. A steep slope with patches of purple heather curved to their right, toward the dying sun. Above them the land rose to the high crest of Balloch Hill; below lay the quiet lights of Bonnybield.

"So," Abi said. "What's this I've got to see?"

Percival took one more breath to recover from the sprint, and then recounted Barclay's story about the mysterious package.

"That's so random," Abi declared. "Somebody left a book with Barclay, for you, before you could even read?"

"Not just somebody." Percival drew the parcel from his backpack, and carefully unwrapped the golden-covered book.

Abi gasped, her eyes swelling in shock. Her fingers grazed the enigmatic blue eye, as if she couldn't believe it was real.

"That's *THE Spirits of the Night and Twilight?*" she whispered.

Percival nodded, and flipped open the cover to reveal the bold *Elliot Dunbar* inscribed within.

Abi lifted her gaze to Percival's, a mixture of sympathy and disbelief in her eyes. "Your *father* left you the most infamous book in the world?"

"Aye. And I found another Grimm book in Granny's attic

yesterday. Remember the first I came across? When I was seven?"

Abi's expression was guarded. "I remember what Granny did to it."

That book had been called *Banshees, Bellirolts, and the Bodach Man*, and young Percival had found it wedged at the back of Granny's bookshelf. But when he brought it into the living room to read, Granny gave it one look, sprang from her chair, and hurled it into the fireplace. She cursed Percival as a layabout fool for reading such rubbish, while Percival could only stand and watch as the book crumpled into flame.

Percival held up *Spirits of the Night*. "He may have signed this one, but what if the others were his, as well? What if he left them for me to find?"

Abi pulled her coat tighter. "Perce... I'm glad you've got somethin' of his. But there's a reason Grimm is banned. It's like his books *change* people. There was this one man: bought *Spirits of the Night*, said he was goin' off to hunt ghosts, came back carryin' a human head! He swore it was talkin' to him. Another took his family to find some 'magical cave' in the Highlands. They turned up a year later screamin' about demon children who tried to eat them. Spent the rest of their lives in an asylum."

Percival shook his head, and looked down at the mist creeping into the streets of Bonnybield. "Everybody's got things they choose not to know. They're afraid o' what knowin' might do to them." He glanced at Abi. "Remember those dreams I told you I have?"

Abi gave a short nod. "Aye."

Percival opened the book, and noticed Abi flinch. "They've come to me off and on as long as I can recall. I'll see people who died ages ago. Or strange creatures I've never heard of before. And this may sound mad, but they're *always* things I end up findin' in Grimm's books. Look: here he gives the three categories of ghosts. Or here: these are beasts that only come out—"

"Wait." Abi pointed to a page he was flipping past. "What's that?"

Percival looked more closely, and saw several sentences scrawled in the margin of the page.

"Your da' didn't just sign the book," Abi said, astonished. "He was takin' notes."

Percival nodded, his blood beginning to pulse with exhilaration. Whoever his father was, whatever had made him so abhorrent to Granny McGugan, Percival could now know this piece of the man's life. He had a window into his father's thoughts.

Did he have dreams like me, too? Percival wondered, as he flipped through more notes beside Grimm's text, with pictures, questions, even references to other books. *Like the Ghillie Dhu,* one said. *How often does this spirit appear?* asked another. *See BB, 47.*

Then he stopped. He'd reached a page with so many scribbles down the margins Percival couldn't decipher half of them. Elliot had underlined the title on the page, and when Percival read it, he angled his head curiously.

"Look at this." He passed the book to Abi.

Abi took it as if handling a loaded gun. She remained very still as the breeze fluttered wisps of hair around her temples. "*The Tercentennial Baron,*" she murmured.

"Aye. This was the most important thing to him in the book." Percival leaned over the page, and read aloud:

> *"Tercentennial Baron, The: [Also referred to as simply The Baron]*
>
> ** CLASSIFICATION: Unknown. Most likely a Type I Spirit or a Hominid Demon.*

23

* One of the most dangerous beings on record. If encountered, DO NOT APPROACH.

According to legend, this unnamed Baron was once a wealthy Scottish nobleman, most likely during the late 1600's. A curse was supposedly laid upon his family, which caused him to go mad and burn down his own castle. He was presumed killed in the fire. What is known, however, is that he reappeared at the Battle of Killiecrankie in 1689. A tall, broad man with long black hair and a dark scar on the left side of his neck was seen charging with the Jacobites that day. He was said to have 'eyes that glow'd greene like a man possessed,' a feature used to distinguish him ever since. Those who saw him refused to mention him by name, referring to him only as 'that Dread Baron.'

Whatever the secret to the Baron's past, he has proven a regular apparition, as a figure with his exact description has turned up in eyewitness accounts for three hundred years. He was reported striding across Culloden Moor after the fateful battle in 1746, attacking workers in Ireland during the rebellion of 1798, and fleeing scenes of murder in Barcelona, Florence, and Victorian London. His most recent sighting was in 1983 in Glasgow, when he slit the throat of a local man, then vanished.

All these accounts involve gruesome acts of slaughter, so the Baron has become a fixture in popular speech as the most sinister of curses."

"Good God," Abi said, recoiling. "Why would anybody want to know about this?"

Percival stared at the bottom of the page. "Because he saw him."

Abi narrowed her eyes and looked back at the book. Percival pointed to his father's final note:

9 Sept '97. Jade eyes, prominent scar. Sped off like a hawk.

And beneath that:

FIND HIS NAME. Means everything.

At that moment, something in the earth around them shifted. The trees ceased their rustling, the clouds encircling the moon grew still… and Percival realized the breeze had stopped. Not died down, just stopped. Everything felt too calm, too hidden, as though the night were holding its breath.

Percival rose to his feet. Abi shifted, as if from a prickle on her skin.

"I don't know, Perce," she said, closing the book and hugging her warm thermos. "Let's call it a night, yeah? Maybe tomorrow we can—"

"*Abi.*" Percival was staring past her, his body as rigid as the standing stone.

"What?"

"Somethin' just moved behind you."

"… What? Perce, if you're kiddin' me on 'cause of this Baron thing—" And then she turned and saw it, too.

A tall, lanky man was standing out on the slope by a patch of heather. He hadn't approached from nearby, but had just materialized, like an image on the TV. He was motionless, outlined against the purple horizon, gazing down toward Bonnybield.

"Oh my God…" Abi's words barely passed her throat. "Who is—"

"*Shh.*" Percival pulled her to her feet. No sooner had he done so than the man turned his head, and *disappeared.* It took less than a second: his entire body simply blinked away. He might as well have been a mirage.

"*Perce…*" Abi began haltingly.

Suddenly, the man appeared again—this time less than twenty feet away.

Abi jumped, and Percival's heart lurched in his chest.

Neither of them could make a sound. The man, however, couldn't be less concerned with them. He continued staring down into Bonnybield, as if waiting for something to happen. Even his attire was strange: he wore a dark greatcoat and tall hat like somebody from a Dickens novel, and his face was unnaturally smooth and delicate, like porcelain. He looked as if he'd stepped out of a nineteenth-century photograph.

Yet his eyes were not green, Percival noticed. Nor was there a scar—not even a mark—upon his skin. This was not the Tercentennial Baron. But it *was,* finally, the first supernatural being Percival had seen. His mouth quivered in a thrilled smile, and his limbs thrummed with adrenaline.

Abi's hand inched toward her coat pocket.

"A… photo," she breathed. "Otherwise nobody will believe—"

"No. No, we must leave him be." Percival didn't know why, but he felt that the hillside, for that moment, was not quite part of his and Abi's world. He became drawn to how focused the ghostly man's stare was on the town. Somehow, Percival was sure this was no spirit come to revisit a scene from life, as Grimm said many ghosts did. This man was *searching* Bonnybield for something very particular.

"I want to see what he's lookin' at," Percival whispered. He set the book in Abi's trembling hands and crept down the slope, trying to place himself near the man's sightline.

"*Perce!*" Abi hissed as she clutched the book.

Percival raised his hand to quiet her. He reached a point directly beneath the man and was scouring his eyes for some sign of intent when, without warning, the man's head flicked down—fast as a raven's—and fixed his gaze *on Percival.*

Percival jumped so violently he fell back on the grass. Everything inside him turned to ice: he saw now that the man's eyes burned bright yellow, like a panther about to pounce. Those eyes pinned him to the hillside, and the man's face took

on a look of wonder as he stared at Percival. Almost impercep-
tibly, his lips parted, and two whispered syllables escaped:

"*Dun... bar...*"

The air exploded. A brutal wind burst from atop the hill
and swept down the slope, knocking Abi to her knees. Percival
clung to the grass and felt his gut tighten when he heard, even
louder than before, a tormented moan pierce the wind. The
man's yellow eyes went out like a pair of lights, and he turned
and vanished, not even leaving a footprint in his wake.

Percival looked up and saw Abi's eyes howling in fear, her
hands clamped over her ears. He didn't have to ask her this
time. He knew they could both hear the moan still lingering
over the hillside.

Chapter Three

The Stranger on the Silver Bike

T he sun rose to a cloudless sky over Bonnybield the next
morning. A vibrant tide of orange spilled down the
avenues, seeming to rouse the medieval buildings before they
were ready for the day.

But to the old man who shuffled onto the street, earlier
than anybody else, the uncommon brightness of the sun made
perfect sense. It was even welcome. It told him the elements of
nature might be shifting.

The man was ancient and wiry, bent like a scythe, with a
great hooked nose and long neck. A tattered cap, faded trousers,
and two wool blazers hung off his bony frame. He plodded
along on a cane of dark, twisted wood, echoing with a *rap-tap*
through the streets, until he reached his destination: a lone
bench in front of the church. He eased himself down, steadied
his cane before him, and focused his eyes across the street and
up to the view he knew so well. Slowly, his lips began to move.

"*Whisper o' the night... just beyond the burnin' heath...*"

The first Bonnybielders opening their shops for the day
paid him no mind. After all, Old Man Crannog had been
performing this same ritual for over ten years.

"In arms there come two beasts... writes the sign o' knights alight..."

Some thought Crannog's lines were bits of a poem the rest of the world had long forgotten. Most thought him a harmless lunatic—maybe one who didn't know any other words—because when anybody asked him where he was from, why he had come to Bonnybield to sit on a bench and stare up toward the hills and mutter to himself, he never answered. He just continued intoning in his heavy brogue, the words creaking out in a seamless, incorruptible rhythm.

"The sun draws in its dragon breath..."

But Crannog was aware, as a sailor spies the first shadow of storm over a calm sea, that something in the air was different today. That images beyond the scope of other men were converging. That soon, he might finally be granted the vision he'd been seeking.

After school later that day, Percival lurched onto the High Street on his bicycle, his limbs tense with exhaustion. He and Abi had bolted away from the slope as soon as the man had disappeared, and Percival made sure she was safely home before he snuck back to Granny's. However, every time he closed his eyes, he saw the predatory gaze in that face, and was terrified he'd be wrenched awake by another wail. He felt knocked off-kilter, as if the world were tilting the wrong way, and a dark unease churned through him.

As he passed Old Man Crannog, however, Percival slowed his bike. Crannog's eyes were shimmering in the afternoon sun, and Percival was taken aback by how bright a blue they were—too bright, too clear for such a weathered face. He couldn't remember noticing them before. They were so riveted on whatever Crannog was watching, Percival forgot his fear for a moment, and stopped to marvel at them.

He'd always felt a kind of silent camaraderie with Crannog, for he was an outcast just like the old man. All the other

Bonnybielders thought Crannog stared at things that weren't there, but Percival had never believed that. Secretly, he suspected Crannog saw something that *was* there—something hidden to everybody else.

"Percival! Is that grimy bike o' yours needin' a push?"

Percival looked up to see Mr. Barclay leaning out from his shop door. He sighed and trudged through the swarm of Bonnybielders finishing last-minute preparations for the Berry Festival. In front of the mercat cross, a platform was being erected and adorned with ribbons and multi-colored hydrangeas. A member of the town council sang a ditty about the Prize Bunch as he checked a to-do list on a clipboard. The High Street hummed like an orchestra before a symphony.

"By the way..." Barclay said in a lower voice, as Percival leaned his bike against the outside wall, "be sure to lock both sets o' doors this evenin'. The Mochries are back in town." He practically snarled the name.

Percival went motionless by his bike. "I thought they were in prison..."

"They were. Again. Now they're on parole. Just keep your eyes open, eh? Hopefully they won't make trouble this year."

Percival's belly coiled into a knot. He hadn't seen the two Mochrie brothers since he was eleven. They used to throw cherry bombs at Granny whenever she came to town, and now she hadn't left her farm in years. *Loony McGugan,* they called her. The last time they'd been present for a Berry Festival, Inspector MacTaggart had arrested them on thirteen different counts of theft. And each time they'd been to prison, at least one other inmate had turned up dead. Nobody was ever charged for those murders.

"Come on then, laddie!" Barclay waved his arm toward the door. "It's our last day before the Festival."

As if Percival had forgotten. On top of that, the first words he heard upon entering the shop were:

"I told you, Balgair, it's been such a dry year an' the

midges so bad I can't point to one bush o' mine that'll yield a Prize Bunch!"

"There's aye a somethin', Macauley. Pity the harvest is ending..."

Two older men were sitting in the corner of the bookstore, sipping cups of afternoon tea—the *midyokin,* it was called—and munching on a plate of biscuits. The garrulous Captain ("Cap") Macauley, whose farm bordered Granny McGugan's, smiled and raised his cup to Percival. "*Fit like,* Percival?"

"Fine, thanks, Mr. Macauley," Percival replied, dropping his backpack behind the cashier's counter and sorely wishing he could steal a few biscuits. It'd been hours since lunch. He nodded to the man opposite Macauley: the Reverend Mr. Balgair of Hambledon Trinity Church (known as "Hambledon-on-High," for the trudge up the hill to it was an act of faith in and of itself). It was the same church that towered behind Crannog's bench.

"Hello, Percival," Balgair droned in his soporific voice. "The good captain has been regaling us with the saga of raspberry calamity in your corner of the valley."

"You can scoff at me, like," Macauley snapped, "but you've no record to uphold. This might 'a been my third Prize Bunch in a row! That wid 'a made number four on the four hundredth Festival next year! See Mrs. Gibbs? Now, *she* has a chance..."

Percival closed his eyes and gripped the counter, just as he'd done the day before. Like Barclay, Macauley and Balgair had always been kind to him—they often let him stay late and delay a return to Granny's, or drove him there so he wouldn't have to bike in the rain—but he couldn't listen to them a minute longer. Every blissful step his neighbors took toward the Berry Festival only heightened his alarm. Something was deeply wrong, and nobody else seemed to feel it. Whatever he and Abi had seen last night, Percival was certain it had appeared here, at this time, for a reason.

Enough. Fighting another flash of those unearthly yellow

eyes, and that rattling whisper of his own name, he woke up Barclay's computer and opened the internet browser. In the search field he typed: "*disappearing man with yellow eyes.*"

Not a brilliant start, he thought, *but there has to be something out there...*

There wasn't. That is, except for overblown descriptions of demons from the Bible, some truly bizarre pictures, and articles warning that if your eyes are yellow you probably have jaundice and should get to a doctor right away. Percival sighed and tried another search: "*disappearing man Angus Scotland.*" This turned up even less. He inserted other words, using combinations of "*ghost,*" "*paranormal,*" even "*wizard,*" but nothing online even came close to mentioning what he'd seen.

Percival dropped his head to his chest in frustration. His eyes went to the floor and he spied the half-open zipper on his backpack... and beneath it, the flash of something gold.

Did I really...? he thought, but then remembered of course he had! He'd returned the book to his backpack after he and Abi had run from the hillside, and must have forgotten to hide it in his room before leaving for school.

Percival glanced around the store for Barclay, but didn't see him. He cleared his search history from the internet browser (he'd made *that* mistake before), unzipped his backpack, and carefully drew *Spirits of the Night and Twilight* from it.

Balancing the book on a shelf beneath the counter so it remained hidden, he skimmed the table of contents, pausing when he found a chapter entitled "Spirits and Creatures Reported in the Twilight Hours." He flipped to it and scoured the text for anything resembling the tall ghost, the awful wail... Then he had it. Or thought he did—even his heartbeat seemed to hesitate as he pored over the page. Everything fit, the details were perfect; yet one piece was missing.

Percival hid the book away and dashed out a text to Abi: *Meet at B's ASAP. I know what we saw.*

❦

The sun had just set, and Balgair had left Macauley alone with a newspaper, when Abi strode into the store and tossed her messenger bag off her shoulder.

"Finally!" Percival yelled from the Bonnybield of Bygone Days section, where he was restocking books. "I texted you hours ago!"

"My da' and I were settin' up for the ceilidh this weekend, Perce, you know that," Abi snapped. "Then I was helpin' him take leaf samples for the people who've been worried about their crop—"

"*Has he been back to my fields yet?*" Macauley yelled from across the store.

Abi closed her eyes and ignored him. Her father, Dr. Sinclair, taught biology at the secondary school and was Bonnybield's resident botanist.

"Look at this," Percival whispered as he met her behind the counter. He opened the Grimm book to where he'd left off, keeping it concealed from the rest of the store.

"That thing last night? It was a *Watcher.*" He pointed to the page. "A Type III Spirit, meanin' it looks like a normal person but leaves no mark on our world. '*They stand still as stone... only observed in the time between sundown and total night... staring silently toward some concentration of human activity.*'" He indicated farther down: "'*The Watcher is a rare entity, and has only been seen when clashes between spirits rip through the pale curtain of the supernatural, and are visible in our world.*'"

"A... supernatural clash?" Abi asked. "It's just Festival weekend! What does—"

"Abi!" Percival's whisper grew more heated. "We saw a *spirit* that *recognized me!* And we both heard that last cry comin' through the wind!"

"I don't know what I heard, Perce! I was scared to death last night, but what if that was just one o' the *hundreds* o' ghosts we've heard about since we were babies? I mean, maybe it doesn't need some big explanation!"

Percival let out a frustrated growl and shouted to Macauley at the back of the store. "Mr. Macauley! Sorry to bother you, but have you ever felt the wind blast about like it did last night, and heard a terrible voice moanin' through it?"

Macauley looked up from his newspaper, barking out a dry laugh. "Oh, you mean like a banshee?"

"No..." Percival sighed, and mumbled, "A banshee's only heard by people in the same family. Never mind that: how about a strange, stony-lookin' figure who appears in the hills at twilight, and if you try to approach him, he disappears?"

Cap Macauley regarded Percival for a long moment before his grey eyebrows rose, and the newspaper drifted to his lap.

"Oh. *Them*," he said, as if he'd recalled something he'd forgotten years ago, and didn't know where to place it now. "I've heard o' them, sure. From my grandda'... but he'd only ever whisper about them. That was tales fit to feature the Baron. He even said he'd seen one o' that ghosts—"

"*Ghosts?*" a bear-like voice growled from the steps by the counter. Percival turned to see Mr. Barclay shuffling down from his office carrying a thick ledger. His scowl fell over Abi behind his counter, and she inched away from Percival.

"What are you botherin' old Cap about, Percival?" Barclay demanded. "Ghosts and ghoulies? It's not Halloween for two months yet, you know."

Percival looked away from his boss, pretending to gather his thoughts, but he was surreptitiously pushing *Spirits of the Night and Twilight* farther beneath the counter.

"There's... somethin' odd goin' on here, Mr. Barclay," he said. He knew he might sound mental, and had to be careful how much he revealed. "Last night, we heard... eerie sounds on the wind. Horrible cries, like somebody bein' murdered, and then it happened again, and it wasn't my—"

"Percival." Barclay leaned against the counter, looking at Percival as he would a child scared of a thunderstorm. "You've always been an imaginative lad. I like that about you. I thought the same things when I was a young loun! But you're gettin' a bit old for this now, are you not? Our minds can play tricks on us. You keep your head down: work, study, be diligent. That's all a lad can do."

Percival felt his neck and shoulders grow taut, and he couldn't help blurting out: "But I saw a man, and he *disappeared—*"

"No, you didn't!" Barclay's tone was suddenly forceful. "And even if you think you did, you keep it to yourself! This is an old town, those are ancient hills; we're awash with tales o' fairies and phantoms and God knows what else! They're not things we're meant to understand." He leaned over the counter and lowered his voice. "*And you don't go pokin' about for answers to the unnatural.* Now, back to work. You've only fifteen more minutes of it." Barclay snatched a pile of receipts off the counter and tottered back up to his office.

Macauley didn't say a word, just snuck his face back into his newspaper. Under the counter, Percival's hand lingered on *Spirits of the Night.* His father's book. He knew Barclay would never have kept it for him if he'd known what it was, but despite the shame his boss had just driven through him, Percival felt defiant. If Elliot Dunbar were here, he'd be asking the same questions Percival was.

Abi edged closer to her friend, and was about to say something when he pushed the book to her.

"Do me a favor," he said. Abi's expression was equal parts puzzlement and alarm. "Read the section on Watchers."

Abi shrank from the book, but Percival was insistent. "Please. I think there's somethin' missin' from it."

Abi creased her brow. "What?"

"Grimm says Watchers '*stare silently.*' Why did the one last night say my name?"

Abi's turquoise eyes widened for a beat, as if she'd forgotten. She stared anxiously at the book for several moments, shook her head, then slipped it into her messenger bag.

Percival watched Abi button her coat and open the shop door without a word. As she walked out, in the instant before the door closed, the night air that blew inside carried the echo of another grief-stricken cry.

The man lifted his head, every muscle locking as he scanned the dark hills around him. Something was wrong here. He'd felt a disturbance—a new presence with an anguished, urgent tone, sending a tinge of vibration through his ears... and suddenly it had ceased. As fast as the snuffing of a life.

The man leapt up from where he'd been meditating. The sound had been so faint he hadn't had time to identify it. But as he turned his head, he caught its discordant echo in both ears. *There.* It was coming from the town. The town in the next glen.

He normally wouldn't have followed such a signal. This one, however, was desperate, unstable—it demanded investigation. He strode down the slope and climbed aboard the silver motorbike waiting there. No headlight this time. Nothing to draw attention. His purpose in these hills was of the utmost danger, and he couldn't chance anyone knowing he was here.

He spurred his motorbike to life, and glided across the night-cloaked hillside.

Chapter Four

The Tercentennial Baron

T he summer light was hot upon Percival's face. Hotter still was the rest of his body, clad in layers of cotton with a cloak to ward off rain showers. He rose and fell gracefully, a sword clacked against his side, and he realized he was astride a horse. He felt... determined. He was bound somewhere for battle—a plan of war was crystallizing in his mind—and then up ahead, he spied a castle.

But something was amiss about the castle. A large shape was perched on a stone ledge near a window, much farther up than any man could climb. And yet it *was* a man: a short man in a hooded cloak, crouching and watching Percival. The hood concealed any features, but Percival was gripped with the certainty that on that face was a wide, cruel smile. The man lifted a hand, and his unnaturally long fingers waggled in a teasing wave—

"*That's all, then, you budding young scientists!*"

Percival jolted as his eyes opened, and he scrambled to sit up in his chair. But class was already over. His pencil had left a graphite trail down the middle of his notes where he'd dozed off.

Dr. Sinclair—Abi's thin, energetic father—was wiping a slew of biology terms off the blackboard. "Don't forget chapters two and three, and have a smashing Festival weekend!"

Percival crumpled his notes into his backpack, and darted from the classroom without even zipping it up. He clambered upon his bike outside, and didn't stop pedaling until he'd reached the corner of Butcher's Lane and the High Street. He could hear the din of gossip and laughter around the corner at the mercat cross, where the Festival Parade was minutes from beginning. He took advantage of the deserted lane, and leaned against the cool stone of the butcher's shop.

What is happening to me? he thought. Seeing ghosts, *hearing* ghosts, having yet another dream with things that made no sense: a horse, a castle, being somebody else hundreds of years in the past... and as before, his last memory from the dream lingered. He still felt the prickling alarm of the figure on the ledge watching him.

"Perce."

Percival turned to see Abi approaching from up the lane. She glanced around to be sure they were alone, then gave him a look that seemed oddly helpless. Nothing like the bright, plucky Abi he knew.

"I'm sorry for what Barclay said yesterday. I know you can't help bein' curious."

Percival thrust his hands in his pockets and shrugged. Abi came closer, dropping her messenger bag.

"I read it."

Percival's eyebrows leapt up. "About the Watcher?"

"Aye, but I didn't find anythin' about them speakin', like you said. I did find somethin' else."

Percival still thought Abi looked oddly vulnerable—almost shell shocked—as she pulled a world history textbook out of her bag. It took Percival a moment to realize he was looking at a textbook jacket over *Spirits of the Night and Twilight*, and his lips curved in a small smile. Abi had always been more adept at stealth than he.

She flipped to the end of the section on Watchers, and showed Percival the book. "Read the bottom. The footnote."

Percival peered at the small type, and read: "'*Though Watchers are almost always sighted alone, their presence has been known to accompany that of the unmistakable* Wailer—*a creature of dire portent. The Wailer's long, plaintive moan warns of murder where it is heard.*'" He looked up at Abi, his body suddenly humming with fear. So they had the name of the second creature. He continued: "'*Here are the most recent instances of Watcher and Wailer being recorded simultaneously: London, UK: 26 September 1841. Naas, Ireland: 21 May 1798. Culloden, UK: 13 April 1746. Killiecrankie, UK…*'"

Percival snapped up straight. "Oh no…" He tore back through the book to where his father's notations were thickest, and pointed to the page. "Do you know what this means, Abi?" he asked breathlessly.

"It means, apparently, somebody here is about to be murdered."

"Not just that. Listen: '*What is known… is that he reappeared at the Battle of Killiecrankie, in 1689.*' Then, '*He was reported striding across Culloden Moor after the fateful battle in 1746, attacking workers in Ireland during the rebellion of 1798, and fleeing scenes of murder in Barcelona, Florence, and Victorian London.*'" Percival snapped the book shut so hard the textbook jacket flew off. "The Tercentennial Baron."

Abi's lips parted in disbelief. That was when it clicked: Percival had grown up hearing Macauley speak of tales "fit to feature the Baron," Granny's "the Baron will come back again" nursery rhyme… Yet he'd never thought to ask who this Baron was.

His words came faster as he explained: "Every time a Watcher and Wailer have been reported together in the last, oh, two-and-a-half centuries? The Baron was there. And remember how Watchers only appear when a supernatural battle bleeds over into our world? The Baron is only ever seen killin' people! What if he's *part* o' that battle?" He looked toward the teeming High Street. "Abi, he's comin' here."

"Perce, that's mad!"

"Look at the signs! Most places he's shown up have *been* famous battles—"

"The 'signs' are tellin' us that somebody here is about to be murdered, and that Watcher *said your name!*"

Percival felt as though his body had been sheathed in ice. Abi was right. What on earth was he going to do? He had no idea how to face anything that had happened in the past three days, and now his *life* might be in danger? Abi was shaking her head.

"I don't know what's happenin' here, Perce, but it's scarin' me now, too. We... we should talk to my da'. Or Mr. Barclay. *Somebody* who can help us figure out—"

"I don't know that we can tell your da', Abi." Percival's voice was low and solemn. "Or Barclay. Or any of the grown-ups. They'd be more scared than we are."

If only my father were here, he thought. Elliot Dunbar had been the first person to question the Baron legend. He'd be able to guide them.

But he wanted me to have this book. Percival gazed into the sphinxlike eye on the cover, and remembered his father's note inside: "*FIND HIS NAME. Means everything.*"

The Baron was coming. But if Percival and Abi could uncover who he was...

"... We'd know what he was about to do," Percival murmured.

"What?" Abi asked.

He looked up at her. "There's another thing missing from this book. Why was the Baron at all those places? The Battle of Culloden, London... I think there's a reason for where and when he strikes. If we find that reason, we could stop him."

"Stop a three-hundred-year-old killer? That's impossible!"

"Abi, we've got to do *somethin'!* Everybody here is in danger, and they have no idea!" It was then, knowing how dire things truly were, and hearing the simmering excitement from the High Street, that Percival realized how he wanted to protect these people. These frustrating, *normal* Bonnybielders, with their berries and midyokins and disdain for his books... they were still the only home he'd ever known, and they had been his refuge from Granny McGugan. They might be blind to what was happening, but they didn't deserve to get hurt.

"Look," he said, "if we can find a way to warn them, lie if we have to, then—"

"*Percival Dunbar.*"

The sudden voice was so deep, the tiger-like growl in it so menacing, that Percival was petrified to face the source of it. When he finally turned, he saw two young men lumbering up the street. It was the shorter one who'd spoken: mid-twenties, tautly-muscled, sporting a military-grade outdoor jacket and a crew cut. A feral spark glinted in his dark eyes.

"What's 'at in your wee hand there?" the man drawled in a heavy brogue. Percival looked down and mentally cursed: the golden cover of *Spirits of the Night* was shining like a beacon in the waning sun. He tried to stuff it into his backpack, but it wouldn't fit. A low chuckle dribbled from the second man, who was taller, with a belly like a sack of oats and a witless grin plastered to his face.

Percival felt the hairs on his neck prickle to life. Barclay had been right. The Mochrie brothers were indeed back in Bonnybield.

"This, Jim?" Percival asked the shorter Mochrie. He tried to shrug nonchalantly, but it came off as too forceful. His hands were already sweating around the cover. "It's a book. People read 'em sometimes."

"'At's not just any book. It's a *banned* book. An' you're

flashin' it about like you're proud of it." Jim furrowed his brow as if genuinely puzzled. "Tell me: what's a pish poor loun like you doin' wi' *Spirits o' the Night?*"

"Just found it." Percival took a slow step backward. "It's just some bloomin' pages; I don't know what—"

Jim lashed out and seized the spine of the book. Percival's heartbeat spiked, and he noticed the bright ink of a new tattoo flex on Jim's hand: a grinning black and green demon, dancing as if to celebrate some sinister accomplishment.

"They're not just *bloomin' pages,* nancy-boy, an' you know it." Jim leaned closer, his snarl hot against Percival's face. "I bet you know, too, there's been some *michty strange things* happenin' around the town. Aye?"

Percival struggled to pull the book back, but he was no match for a fully grown man. And what "strange things" would a delinquent like Jim Mochrie know about?

"Come on, Dunbar, I'm not Loony McGugan; you can tell me." Jim grinned in his best imitation of affability. "Been seein' things? Hearin' things? Things nobody else wants to talk about?"

Cold needles raked across Percival's skin. He wanted to believe the treacherous gleam in Jim's eye was mere ridicule, but it couldn't be. It was the shine of knowledge.

"I don't know what you mean," Percival argued desperately.

Abi stepped forward to grab the book with him, but Frank, the other brother, stopped her with a hostile glare. Jim whispered, through smiling teeth, "You're a liar. There're ghosts in the hills. The twilight lady is cryin' wi' the wind. An' now I see you wi' this book. I have to admit, it makes me wonder: *what do you know?*"

At that moment, a chorus of bagpipes from the High Street blared the opening strains of "Scotland the Brave," and Jim loosened his grip on the book for half a second. It was all

Percival needed. He tore the book away, grabbed Abi's shoulder, and ran to where he'd left his bike against the wall.

"Take this and go!" he implored her. He shoved the book between her jacket and jumper, just out of view of the Mochries, and helped her mount the bike. Jim was cursing several yards behind him.

"No, Perce—"

"I'll meet you at your house in an hour. I'll be fine! Go!"

Abi scrambled for the pedals, but Percival gave the bike a firm push, and her feet found purchase at the last second. She rode furiously, whipping out into the High Street and flying down the slope of the glen. There was no way the Mochries could catch her.

Percival didn't look back at Jim or Frank. Terrified and wondering how, on top of everything else, his father's book had earned him the wrath of Bonnybield's two most violent men, he shot out of Butcher's Lane. He pumped his legs up the High Street toward the church, ignoring the stares of other Bonnybielders, who were trying to enjoy the kilted pipers marching the opposite direction. Old Man Crannog had left his post for the day, and Percival ducked around his bench into a tiny alleyway.

He cloistered himself in the shadows, waiting for Jim and Frank to rush past. But they didn't appear. All Percival saw were rows of kilts parading past, followed by the local Highland dancers, policemen in their crisp uniforms, the Bonnybield Rugby Club… nobody noticed him pressed against the dark wall.

Percival took a long, stuttering breath, and decided it would be smartest to stay where he was for now. He was shaking as he recalled the gleam in Jim's eye, that the man knew about the Watcher, the Wailer… The Mochries were brawlers and bullies, who'd only ever tormented Percival out of amusement. Now *they* were the only others aware of what was happening?

Percival sank to a crouch against the bumpy stone, and watched the endless parade march by. He stayed there even longer as the crowd followed it—people laughing, children licking ice cream cones topped with berries—and waited as the High Street emptied. He didn't rise until he heard the pipers stop several blocks away at the Town Hall, and then the head of the town council speak into a microphone and welcome everybody to the ceremony. Berry Festival weekend had officially begun.

Percival crept forward, his gaze sweeping the High Street before he left his hiding place, and walked briskly up the avenue. He needed to get to Abi's as soon as he could, but she lived far from the center of town, and—he suddenly realized—the Festival crowd was blocking the straightest route. Percival cursed and broke into a jog. He followed his mental map of town as best as possible, using side streets and alleys as shortcuts, but it wasn't long before he became disoriented. He'd only taken one or two routes to Abi's on his bike, and this wasn't either of them. Even his mobile phone wouldn't help: in this part of town, it had zero signal strength.

Percival growled, doubled back, and tried a different street. When that one ended in a fork, he knew he was in trouble. He glanced up, saw there was almost no light left in the sky. Percival gritted his teeth, made a snap decision—left—and sped up to a run. He turned down another alley, was racing the deepening shadows on the walls—when suddenly the feeling that he'd made a mistake whipped through him.

"*Wee Dunbar...*"

The words came in a low, thick drawl, sloshing off the stones of the alley. Percival's heart seized, and he spun back the other way, but a sturdy hand flashed out and knocked him into the wall. Out of the shadows sauntered the two brothers.

"What do you want now?" Percival yelled. This was beyond anything he'd thought the Mochries would do. For the second time that day, he tasted the metal of adrenaline.

"For you to come wi' us," Jim purred. "Nice and quiet-like."

Chapter Five

The Jolly Pair

P ercival tried to inch along the wall back toward the High Street, but the lumbering form of Frank Mochrie—still with his big, stupid grin—blocked his way.

"Come with you?" Percival repeated. "Is this about my book? Honestly?"

"There's no way that book is yours, nancy-boy!" Jim barked. "You've no idea the meanin' o' what's written on that pages. *That* is a book o' the Otherworld."

Percival was about to demand again what Jim was talking about, when a cold understanding seeped through him. When Jim said *Otherworld*, it wasn't with disdain or doubt like others would in Bonnybield. He said it with intrigue. Even reverence.

"You... so you want the book for yourself."

"What would *we* want wi' your stupid book?" Frank sneered, his voice like an overgrown child.

"The book just proved that you're our man," Jim said, edging closer. "Seems to me, Dunbar, you've been meddlin' in things you ought to have left alone."

It took all Percival's nerve to force his pounding heart back down his throat. "Do you know what's happenin' here?" he asked, half-pleading. "Do you know about the Tercentennial Baron?"

"The green-eyed Baron?" Jim smirked. "Aye, we know all about the Baron…" But he didn't seem interested in explaining further. Frank was lumbering closer like a bear, and Jim's eyes were fixed, unblinking, on Percival's face.

Percival was fed up with being cornered. Just before the Mochries pinned him to the wall, he feinted toward Frank, then slammed his booted heel into Jim's shin. Jim howled in pain as Percival bolted past him. Frank, however, was faster than he looked: he caught Percival in two steps, his trunk-like arms locking the boy's behind his back.

"Hold him there, Frankie!" Jim snarled, shaking out his leg. On seeing Percival trapped, his eyes widened to a mask of terrible glee. "Ooh, you're more of an eejit than I thought, nancy-boy."

Percival squirmed against Frank's hold, but couldn't budge. He was suffused with panic and bewilderment. "Just tell me what's goin' on!" he yelled.

Jim's response was a quick flash like electricity. Before Percival could take another breath, a long flick knife glinted before his face.

"That's what's goin' on." Jim cocked his head as he held the knife inches from Percival's eye. "Oh, I'm sorry—was that the end o' your bleatin'? You're *ours*, Dunbar. See, Frankie and me, we're the best bounty hunters outside the Highlands. Servin' only lords o' the occult." This time he turned his hand to make sure Percival saw the dancing demon imprinted there. "They call us the Jolly Pair," he said. "You've no idea the war that's comin' to this wee glen. We're just the vanguard. And we're to collect anybody who knows anythin' about the voices on the wind, or the men in the hills: anythin' like what's written in that book." His lips arced in an insidious smile. "But now that I think about it… I'm not sure our client cares if we deliver you alive, or dead. So since you've been such a bloody pest to me, what do you think? Shall I take my chances?"

figure was there, darting through the shadows as Jim rose and slashed at its torso. The figure leapt around the knife, caught Jim's hand, and swung his entire body into the air, impaling him on his own blade. Just as before, Percival glimpsed a crimson flash beneath the figure's hand, but it vanished in less than a second, and James Mochrie fell to the ground with his flick knife protruding from his chest.

Percival climbed to his feet and felt the tremor of his flayed nerves, but he kept himself up. The figure stood only a few steps away, its thick shoulders heaving with a strange kind of exhaustion. It wasn't breathing hard; rather, it seemed to be stretching itself, as if transferring some kind of energy through its limbs. It rolled its neck and lengthened its fingers… that was when Percival saw a single dark claw, almost an inch long, extend from each fingertip.

Without thinking, he stepped forward.

"Hey. You."

The figure's head flicked to the side, and it flew into the alley shadows.

"Wait!" Percival called. "Don't go—" He tried to follow, but his knees turned to putty and he staggered against the wall. He looked to the cobblestones to steady himself, and saw they were rimmed with Jim's blood, the broken corpse inches away. He couldn't help but be fascinated by how hypnotic the man's blank stare was. A minute ago it had been full of so much fury and fear… now he just saw the absence of the soul in a human face.

Percival's head shot up. *The soul…* He put a hand on his forehead to slow his thoughts, but the truth was undeniable. He knew exactly what he'd seen—what this *creature* was—because he'd read about it years ago.

A quiet footfall sounded in the shadows ahead.

"Are you injured?"

The voice that boomed from up the alley was deep, its

smooth, deliberate tones sounding more English than Scottish. Percival did his best to stand without the aid of the wall, and peered into the recesses of the buildings. He couldn't see his rescuer.

"I'm not," he said. "Show me your face."

There was no response.

"I know what you are," Percival said, his voice beginning to falter. "What are you doin' in my town?"

Still no response. Just then, he heard the two-tone whine of sirens from across town. The police would arrive in seconds.

Percival caught a flurry of movement into a side alley, and he sprinted after the figure. "Don't leave, please!" he cried, and skidded to a stop when he saw the man pausing beside a pair of bins. He knew he was mad to ask any favors of this creature, but it *had* just saved his life, and he still needed help.

"Look, I'm sure you don't want to be found by the police, but neither do I! You don't know Inspector MacTaggart, and he'll never believe me about what happened here. Just help me get away from this street, please!"

The sirens were only blocks away now, and Percival heard tires screech as they neared the alley. The figure's massive shoulders turned toward him, and his long mane of hair gave a single shake, as if cursing the situation. Percival was about to plead again, but the figure suddenly charged toward him, looped one arm around his waist, and draped the boy over his shoulder. In the same movement, he leapt up from the alley floor—a leap so powerful it propelled them over the eaves of the next house. With a thrilling rush, Percival realized this man was *soaring over* Bonnybield. He bounded along the rooftops, each step sending him and Percival twenty yards, though his feet hardly made a sound as they hit the shingles.

Percival raised his head to see where he was going, but they were moving too fast and the bitter wind stung his eyes. He'd just realized they'd flown clear to the outskirts of Bonnybield, when the figure slowed over an empty street. He glided down, gently as a feather, to the ground near a flickering lamppost.

He shrugged Percival off his shoulder and let the boy stumble onto the cobblestones. He turned before Percival could see his face, and approached a giant object parked just beyond the reach of the lamplight: a long, silver-colored motorbike.

"Is that yours?" Percival briefly forgot the Mochries as he gazed at the vehicle. It was twice the size of a normal motorbike, with a graceful body that swept back in a plow-like shape from the front and curved to a point at the rear. There looked to be a compartment behind the seat that could hold a full suitcase.

"Naturally," the man muttered, pulling a set of goggles from his pocket.

Percival stepped closer. He was not about to let this stranger leave.

"Hey! Who *are* you and why are you here?"

"I'm protecting you. All of you," the deep voice said. "Leave it at that."

Protecting us… Percival was riddled with confusion, but if a supernatural creature like this was protecting Bonnybield, there could only be one reason.

"The Baron," he said. This caught the man's attention. He stopped before donning his goggles, and his head inched back toward Percival.

"You're protectin' us from the Tercentennial Baron! He's on his way here, fightin' some supernatural war. There have been signs for the past two days."

The man finally turned to face Percival. Most of his features were still hidden in shadow, but his head raised to its full six-foot-plus height, and his broad chest and shoulders were outlined by the lamplight.

"How do you know of the Baron, lad? Who are you?"

Percival tried to keep from scoffing. This was not a man he

should offend. "Everybody's heard *some*thin' about the Baron. But if you mean the signs, I read about them in *Spirits of the Night and Twilight*. And my name is Percival. Percival Dunbar."

The man's head tilted back, and his voice became quiet, almost awestruck. "Dunbar, did you say?"

Percival nodded, surprised his name had such an effect.

"Who was your father, lad?"

Percival's heart kicked up inside him. Everybody in Bonnybield knew the disgrace of his father's departure; nobody had ever discussed him with Percival.

"His name was Elliot," Percival said, "but I never knew him. I'm the only Dunbar in Bonnybield."

The man was silent for several moments, then gave a small nod. "Well. I must apologize for not introducing myself sooner."

He stepped into full view of the fluttering lamp. He was hardly dressed for the Scottish cold, with only a long brown coat over a V-neck t-shirt, and jeans with brown buckled boots of well-worn leather. The shirt and jeans were peppered with clean holes from Frankie's shots, the coat dotted with the Mochries' blood. But his face was what struck Percival the most: he had a taut, angular chin and high cheekbones, with a strange, sunken nature that implied he'd been weathered far beyond his years.

"You see," he said, parting the long, wavy mane that fell to his shoulders, "you are no longer the only one of your kin here. My name is David Dunbar, Third Baron of Haddington, born in the Year of Our Lord 1665."

He lifted his chin, and a pair of vivid, jade-green eyes shone in the lamplight.

"I am the Tercentennial Baron."

Chapter Six

The Bellirolt

P ercival felt all the blood sink to his feet. He had the sudden urge to turn and flee, yet was so stunned he couldn't move.

"You..." His voice stuck in his throat. "*How?* You just saved my life!"

The Baron's eyes flashed with amusement. "Quite."

"But—I've read about you. You're a cold-blooded murderer! You've been killin' people for three hundred years!"

The Baron raised a cautionary finger, and his voice turned hard as steel. "That is but a scrap of the truth. I would advise you to hold your—"

He broke off when Percival unexpectedly twisted his head to the side. The cut on his neck was beginning to burn, and upon dabbing it he saw it was still trickling blood.

The Baron's eyes flared in alarm. "Was that my doing?"

"Aye," Percival bit out. "Your bloomin' claws."

The Baron stepped toward him. "Lad, I need to tend to that wound."

"You *what?*" Percival snorted and backed away.

"Percival, that cut, if not treated right away, will fester. And when that happens you will begin to see things no boy your age should witness."

54

"Oh, like two men killed right in front of me? I told you: *I know what you are.*" Percival leveled his head at the Baron. "You're a bellirolt. You're a demon creature."

The Baron was about to interject, but Percival said: "I mean, look at you! It makes perfect sense. You're not dressed for Scottish weather, 'cause cold temperatures don't bother you. I bet you live out o' that motorbike, which would be hard if you needed what normal people do, like food, or water—but you don't, 'cause you don't eat or drink anythin'! You feed on souls, *human souls*—that's your lifeblood, isn't it? That's what gives you your strength, that's how we flew over half of Bonnybield just now, how you survived those gunshots, what makes you age so slowly—why you're over three hundred years old and hardly look fifty! And I'm supposed to let you patch me up?"

"If you want that wound to heal, then yes!" the Baron replied. "I understand you're in shock, Percival, but I came to that alley to help you."

"You were *murderin'*," Percival fired back. "That's what bellirolts do! The Mochries, you *ate* their *souls...*" He recalled with gut-churning clarity the crimson lights he'd seen beneath the Baron's hand, and the pitiful, empty look left on Jim's face.

"They would have killed you, lad," the Baron said.

"Well thanks, then. But we've had enough supernatural rubbish here, and *you're* the reason for it. I don't know what your fight is, but kindly take it out o' my town. And I'll take my chances with this wee scratch." Percival turned and strode down the street.

All of a sudden a sheet of wind flew up in his face, stopping him like a wall. He spun to see the lamplight shudder and dim as a cloud of invisible weight filled the street. The air seemed to tremble around him, and even the stones beneath his feet felt tense, as if in panic. The Baron stood in the middle of it all, hands turned away from his sides, virescent eyes blaring.

Awe and terror surged through Percival like current.

The Baron's voice pervaded the street as if speaking from the walls themselves. "*PERCIVAL. If you leave here alone with that wound after encountering those men, there are much darker forces of the night that will not let you return home, believe me.*"

The force rattling the street began to subside as the Baron relaxed his hands, confident he had Percival's attention. "Yes, I am a bellirolt. But though you've read quite a lot, I'll give you that, you know nothing of my so-called 'fight,' nor of who I truly am. At this moment I'm the only man who can help you. Now will you accept?"

Percival didn't feel he had a choice any longer, as the burning in his neck was swelling to hot flares of pain. He nodded, still quavering from the Baron's power. "Fine."

"I recommend we find someplace indoors. Outside of town, if possible."

That wouldn't be easy. Percival couldn't exactly bring the man into Granny's living room. "We could try my Granny's bothy."

The Baron gave a nod toward his motorbike. "Hop on Maggie, then. Quickly."

Percival approached the colossal machine. "Maggie?"

"It's her name," the Baron said simply. He climbed on and gunned the engine, which sounded nothing like a normal motorbike—no rumble, no bone-humming growl. It gave only a delicate whir, like the whistling of wind over snow. Percival mounted the seat behind him, noticing a logo emblazoned on Maggie's side: a coat-of-arms with a tall white star in the center of a blue shield. Underneath was the lettering "*Vaslor Nimarièl.*"

"Hold tight, lad!" The Baron spurred Maggie forward, and they rocketed up the street. Percival felt as if he were riding on air. The wind streaking past and pavement droning underneath now melded with the sound of the engine, as though the earth itself were pulling them along. Percival directed the Baron down Granny's lane, and in moments he'd parked in front of the bothy and killed the engine, the whirring fading like the volume on a stereo.

"Let's get inside," Percival said as he scrambled off the bike. "Before my—"

Just then he heard the creak of a hinge, and spun to see Granny McGugan standing in her doorway, her baleful eyes shifting between the Baron and his bike.

The Baron turned his body to hide the bullet holes in his clothing. Percival sputtered, "Granny! Listen, this... man is from out of town. He just needs to use—"

Before he could say another word, Granny charged out past him, straight to the motorbike. Her eyes were set not on the contraption itself, but on the blue and white coat-of-arms on its side. *Does she recognize the logo?* Percival wondered. She must have, because she gave it two kicks of pure wrath, leaving smudges on the polished body, then faced the Baron.

"*I know where you come from,*" she snarled, thrusting her finger in his face. "Think it's the first time I've seen that, do you? *Do you?*" She kept pointing at the coat-of-arms, and Percival was beyond perplexed. Here was a menacing stranger speckled with blood, and Granny was angry because of his motorbike?

The Baron looked equally confused, and spread his hands in a gesture of peace. "Madam, I assure you I've no idea what you're talking about. I'm a relative of young Percival's father, and I merely wanted—"

"*Never mention that lad's father to me, you bloody snake!*" Granny's voice cracked like lightning through the night. Percival had never seen her so ferocious. "He was a two-faced scoundrel who left Percy as a bairn an' vanished like a shot in the wind! I'm the only one who's cared for the lad! Ever!" She leaned closer to the Baron. "Now you'd best be off. Far away from here. You're not welcome to set one foot on my land."

With that, she turned and marched back to the house. "Come now, Percy," she barked as she passed him. Percival didn't budge.

Granny stopped by the door and turned. "Percy! Why are your clothes torn? Come inside!"

But Percival had seen far too much that day to step back into Granny McGugan's cave. His town was under siege by supernatural phenomena, and the Tercentennial Baron—the most legendary monster in the world—had arrived and *rescued* him. He needed answers. And the Baron was the only person who could give them to him.

"No."

Granny stepped toward him, shoulders hunched like a gargoyle. "*What* was that?"

Percival faced her. He did his best to ignore the pain that flashed again in his neck. "Are you goin' to tell me how you know where he comes from?"

The old woman stood rigid, a wall of defiance.

"How about why my father was such a scoundrel?" Percival couldn't stop his voice from rising. "Or why he left, anythin'?"

But Granny's face was fixed in an iron scowl. The breeze slapped the hem of her skirt against her boots. Without moving a muscle, she declared: "I'd rather fall into my grave this instant than tell you a thing about him."

Percival nodded and looked away, finding he had to force a hard lump down his throat. There was nothing more to say. He turned, and climbed the steps to the bothy.

"Percy, I know what's best for you!" Granny insisted. "Now be a good lad an' come inside. You don't even know this man! *I don't want him here!*"

"Then call the bloody police," Percival muttered as he unlatched the bothy door. He knew Granny would do no such thing. She'd never trusted the Bonnybield police.

"I'm not leavin' my house 'til he's gone, Percy!" Granny's voice was gaining a dark tone of resentment. David Dunbar cast one final look at the woman, in which he seemed to decide he didn't care if she tried to stop him. He waved a hand over the back of his motorbike, and the luggage compartment popped open. From it he pulled a leather duffel bag, and followed Percival into the bothy.

"Percy!" Granny was screaming now. "You can't listen to that man! There are things—*dark things*—you don't know about the world! Come back here! *PER-CYY!*"

Percival shut the bothy door behind them, bolting its iron lock.

⁂

Twenty minutes later, Percival was sitting on one of the eight cots in the musty bothy, his shirt off and a wool blanket draped around his shoulders. A small lamp had been placed on a stool next to him, and its naked bulb cast a flat, uncompromising light around the room. David stood a few feet away, stirring a mixture he'd concocted in a small basin. The medley smelled of cloves and a sharp, thyme-like herb that reminded Percival of the meat pies Granny made when he was younger. David had cleaned Percival's neck, and said he would apply a salve to ease the discomfort and close the wound, but Percival would forever have a small, black scar on the spot.

He felt his mobile vibrate, and suddenly realized he hadn't spoken to Abi since he'd sent her away on his bicycle. She'd texted three times, asking where he was, if he was safe, and did he know the Mochries had been murdered?

Percival paused, phone in hand. Did he dare tell Abi he'd been there when the thugs were killed? How much had the police deduced on their own?

Percival didn't want to lie to his only friend, but he knew she wouldn't just accept that he was seeking medical treatment from the Tercentennial Baron. *I'm alright, Abi*, he wrote back. *I found somebody who might know what's been going on.* He thought for a moment. *An old man,* he clarified. *I'll text you as soon as I know more.* Her mention of the Mochries brought that violent memory pouring back, and he added: *Pls keep the book hidden. Don't trust it with ANYBODY else.*

Percival's hand quivered briefly as he pocketed his mobile: his nerves were still buzzing from his near-murder and the confrontation with Granny. Her shriek, like a bird of prey, rang again in his ears. He looked to David.

"How did Granny recognize your motorbike?"

David shook his head. He'd donned a clean button-down shirt, and Percival saw he wore a little arrowhead-shaped stone on a chain against his chest. "I've no idea, lad. She must have been mistaken. I built Maggie myself, and I've never been here before."

There was an uneasy silence as he continued stirring the mixture. Percival was confused: the man had just revealed he was the Tercentennial Baron, had even offered to help Percival, and yet he suddenly seemed withdrawn.

"Let me see your claws."

David paused and sighed. He approached, wiped off his hands, and put forth his right. His fingers looked normal and uncorrupted, but he extended them to their full length and a thin, dark claw emerged noiselessly from each. The claws were hooked and gleamed like talons in the light. Percival reached out to touch one, but David relaxed his hand and they drew back inside. Only a faint white slit on the tip of each finger remained.

He wagged his now innocuous finger at Percival. "I wouldn't, if I were you." He returned to the salve. "Bellirolt claws are designed to kill, and they can maim without our meaning to. Obviously." He nodded at Percival's neck. "They're not weapons of nature; they're dark tools given to beasts, and they leave an indelible mark. A poisoned wound.

This balm will draw out any toxins." He sat beside Percival with the basin, and whipped the mixture into a paste before dabbing it on the boy's neck.

"This will sting for a moment," David said. "And I'll have to apply it down your shoulder, as well, for good measure."

Percival felt a pinching sensation in his neck, as if his skin were trying to reseal itself. David was shaking his head.

"I am sorry for this, lad. I only wanted to save your life and leave."

"You weren't out for a meal?" Percival challenged.

"Well, I happened to find one, didn't I? Unlike most of my kind, when I must feed I do it on people who are set to harm others."

"That doesn't make it right."

"Quite true, Percival. But if I don't eat, I die. And if I hadn't been there tonight, you would have died. So tell me honestly how sorry you are that I happen to be a savage, soul-eating killer." He threw a sharp look before returning to his work.

Percival winced as his skin grew tighter. "How old were you when you became a bellirolt?"

David's lips thinned. "Twenty-four."

"Do you ever regret it? Becomin' one?"

David paused and lifted his gaze. Burning in his eyes was an air of such disbelief it bordered on betrayal. "You think I sought this life?"

Percival was scared to answer. David placed the basin on the floor and gave the boy a hard look. "I have killed a great many people. In ways far more gruesome than what you saw tonight. Bellirolts are the plague of humanity, lad. We live to claim the souls of men, to touch them in their moment of death and so gain our strength. But it is a *terrible* strength. Never one I would seek for myself. We are all corrupted by this force within us. This hunger to destroy. And once you cross the threshold I have, there is no return."

"So you can't be transformed back into a human?"

David inclined his head. "Percival, do you know what a bellirolt truly is? It's a demon, with no corporeal form or feeling except to kill, that inhabits the body of a human. If its host is dying, the demon will seek to transfer itself to a new one. That can only occur if, at his moment of death, the host *touches* a living human. Then the infection proceeds. Once inside the new body, the demon entwines itself with that person. They become inseparable. You cannot transform *back* into a human. This is the proof."

David turned and lifted his long hair to reveal a thick, black knot on the nape of his neck. It was about the size of half a golf ball.

"That is the Black Swell," David said. "The only weak spot on our bodies. You could put a bullet through my head and the wound would close in seconds, but puncture that Swell and the demon's blood seeps out of me, and my life is finished."

"And if you can't transfer the demon to another person before you die?"

"Then it dies, as well. That's the only way to kill a bellirolt: open the Black Swell and leave the poor beast to die alone, far from the reach of any man or woman."

Percival pulled the blanket tighter around him as the cold of night set in.

"So this *mark* that I'm to have…"

"We call it the Sable Scar." David picked up the basin and stirred the aromatic paste again. "Some bellirolts enjoy Scarring their victims before they attack them. Marking them for death, as it were."

Grimm's words surfaced in Percival's mind. "You have one, as well, don't you?"

David looked at Percival with a hint of annoyance, yet nevertheless pulled aside his left collar. Running straight down his neck, below the ear, was a long, charcoal-black scar. He smeared a final bit of salve on Percival's shoulder and then sat back, studying the boy.

"You know an awful lot for such a young lad."

"I read it. In D. H. Grimm books that belonged to my father." In the hollow of his belly, Percival felt the hopeful spark he'd known since he was young: the tease of a chance that somebody could point him toward his father. "That's all I know about him: he was obsessed with the supernatural. He saw you, you know—back in the '90's, I think. It changed everythin' for him. He wanted to know who you really were."

David's lips curled in a sly smile. "Doesn't everybody."

"Well, did he ever meet you? I mean, are you and he actually related?"

"No, I never met the man, Percival." David's eyes darted away for a moment. "And I am sorry to hear of how he forsook you. It is... difficult not to know our parents."

Percival tilted his head, suddenly curious about David's parents. But then David's gaze returned, with a warmth—a pride—Percival had not yet seen from him.

"However, I *can* tell you something about him," David said. "You see, I've followed this branch of my family for many generations. Elliot Dunbar was the son of a Bryan Dunbar, from East Lothian. Do you know where my home of Haddington lies?"

"In East Lothian."

"Indeed. You are, in fact, directly descended from a certain Robert Archibald Dunbar, who died in 1750."

"Did you know this Robert?"

"Of course I did. He was my younger brother."

Percival nearly choked on his own breath. "You can't be serious! So..." He stood up, shaking his head. "That makes you my, what—?"

"Great uncle." David's eyes flickered in the light. "Well.

Several times over."

Percival snorted, and folded his arms beneath the blanket. "My uncle, the Tercentennial Baron, from the seventeenth century." He felt as if all his notions of reality had been turned inside out. "So have you followed any other—"

Without warning, a fierce wind pounded the wall beside Percival, and he jumped away from it. The glass in the single bothy window clattered like an old man's teeth. The wind crescendoed, and lancing through it Percival heard, yet again, the spine-chilling cry of the Wailer. It sounded more sorrowful, more dire tonight than ever. Or perhaps that was because he now knew what it meant.

"*Percival.*"

Percival spun to face David. A hint of the voice lingered like a spectral bell.

"Did you hear that Wailer?" David's eyes were bright and urgent.

Percival had to breathe before he said, "I've heard it for the last two nights."

David rose to his feet in a nimble, catlike move Percival had never seen from a human. "For *two nights?*"

"Aye," Percival said, unnerved by the sudden silence around them. "The signs o' you and this supernatural battle, like I said."

David squared his jaw. "Tell me the others."

"Just that my friend and I saw a Watcher on a hill above town."

"Where was it looking?"

"I don't know exactly... down toward Bonnybield."

"And the Wailer. When did you hear its cry these two nights past?"

"Around this time, mostly..."

"Mostly? Percival, I need to know the exact hour."

"I don't know the hour!" Percival cried. "I wasn't lookin' at a bloomin' watch—"

"Then *think*, lad! What was happening the first time you heard it?"

"I was… standin' in Granny's living room. The sun had just begun to set."

"Good. And last night?"

"It was right after sunset. I was at work at the bookst—"

"Great God." David strode across the room, consumed in thought. "That was it…"

"That was what?" Percival asked.

"I too heard the Wailer last night," David said. "I was nearby, and wasn't sure at first what it was, so I came to your town to investigate."

"Well?" Percival stepped closer to him. "What's all this mean to you?"

"I can tell you for certain *one* thing it means," David said. "You, my dear boy, have a remarkably potent Second Sight."

Percival blinked in confusion. "You mean… I can see the future?"

David shook his head. "Seeing the future is very different, and *very* rare. No, Second Sight is the ability to feel signals from other realms."

Chills of anticipation began to crawl up Percival's neck. "What other realms?"

"I think you know." David's eyes seemed to glow with a hue that was at once meaningful and mysterious. "Somehow I think you pay attention to signs that most people tend to ignore. Not everybody, for instance, can hear a Wailer." He swept his hand to the window. "I'd wager you've known all your life there are more than just shadows and mist surrounding us now. There are other planes of existence beyond this one. Together, they're called the Otherworld. Most humans are not in tune with them; we're all taught we have but five senses. Yet every man and woman is endowed with Second Sight. You just happen to be more cognizant of yours than most."

A smile fluttered to Percival's lips. So there was a *name* for the connection he felt to the supernatural. David was right: in a way, Percival had always known.

"Wailers, then," Percival said, "they're part o' some other realm?"

"The physical Wailer does not inhabit our day-to-day world, correct."

"What about Watchers? They just appear and disappear at random."

David began to pace, as if trying to sort out something else while he spoke. "You'd do well to remember, Percival: if a creature or thing 'disappears,' it's merely a trick to your earthly eyes. Watchers move so swiftly through the twilight that they're invisible unless they stand still. We call them Boundary Figures; they never involve themselves in our affairs."

"Then why did the one I saw speak to me?"

David stopped midstride. "It… the Watcher *spoke* to you?"

"Aye. It looked at me and said, '*Dunbar.*'"

A dark wave of concern swept through David's face. He snatched up the salve basin and marched to a sink in the corner of the room.

"Wait! Why would it do that?" Percival asked.

"I don't know." David scrubbed out the basin, his tone cold and removed.

Confused, Percival followed him. "Look, Watchers only appear when some supernatural clash bleeds over into our world. So this one was sayin' our name—"

"What have I just said about Second Sight?" David flung a caustic look before turning back to the basin. "These things don't 'bleed over' into our world; they're *part* of our world. All the realms are interconnected. We feel them, we just don't see them."

Percival didn't understand why David had turned so bitter, but he was certain he could provide an answer. "Fine, then it said 'Dunbar' 'cause it knew you were on your way here to kill more people—"

"Percival, do you honestly believe that every town I've ridden into for three hundred years also heard Wailers and saw Watchers?" David turned and faced the boy. "I've been fighting *for* something, and these omens have only appeared at dark turns, when there was some... disruption in the fabric of nature. Something the entire supernatural world was anticipating."

"Fightin' for what?" Percival asked. "You're a bellirolt. Murder is your nature."

A flash of deep wrath, the sort that could only have burned for centuries, shone in David's eyes. "That is a reputation I have borne because, clearly, there is no way this world can stomach the truth."

Percival almost retreated from David's stare, but he stood firm. "What truth?"

"That bellirolts are more numerous than you can imagine," David said with severe calm. "That there are armies of them. Fostering and feeding off of every human war. And that I have been battling, all these centuries, to destroy them. My own kind." He cocked his head. "You see, things are not always as they seem at first glance. Did you not consider that '*The Baron*' could be more than what you read in D. H. Grimm?"

Percival wanted to deny it, but knew he couldn't. His eyes fell to a cot nearby.

"You know that some of what's happening here has happened before," David continued, with the same intense stillness. "In my experience, however, it's not *that* it happens again, but *how*. History has patterns that reappear."

David's words suddenly jostled loose an image inside Percival. *History has patterns... A baron from the 1600's...* "The castle," he murmured.

David's eyes narrowed. "Pardon?"

Percival looked up at him. "Did you ever own a castle?"

An abrupt, tormented look passed over David's eyes. He didn't respond.

"I had a dream in class today," Percival said unsteadily. "I was on a horse, approachin' a castle. Wearin' old-fashioned clothes, and a sword, like I'm sure you used to have back in Haddington. But there was somethin' odd about the castle: a wee man, in a cloak, was perched in a window. And he was grinnin', and wavin' at me."

David's mouth fell open, as though a gruesome, hated ghost had suddenly appeared. "*MacBain...*" he said, his voice thick.

"That was your life I saw." Percival could barely speak he was so unsettled.

David looked nothing like the hardened warrior of a minute earlier. He was in pain, and exposed. "What you saw," he said, "was how I became a bellirolt."

They were both silent for a long minute, until David rolled his shoulders back and reassumed whatever armor he'd just misplaced.

"Do you want to learn more, Percival?"

"About the bellirolts?"

"Not just that. I must discover what is afoot here, especial-ly what that Watcher was trying to tell you. It could well involve both of us."

"Well if it does, what brought *you* here?" Percival asked. "I mean, I know you didn't come for the Berry Festival..."

David's lips lifted to a near-smile. He shook his head. "I was merely passing by on my way north, preparing to camp in the hills, when I heard the Wailer last night."

Percival creased his brow. That didn't make sense. "But Wailers cry to warn of murder, and you've already killed the Mochries, so why did we just hear another?"

"Percival... Wailers do not cry to warn of just murder.

They betoken death on a much grander scale."

Percival felt his chest contract. "Like a battle. Or a... massacre."

"Possibly." David nodded. "We must discover the threat before it's too late."

"How long do we have?"

"There's the rub. Based on what you've told me, the Wailer's cries have been occurring roughly an hour later every night for three nights in a row." David's gaze turned leaden. "It's a countdown, Percival. I cannot tell when the zero hour will be, but it is fast approaching."

"Then what are we goin' to do?" Percival stepped forward. "Do you have a plan?"

"We're going to follow the signs," David affirmed. "Beginning with that Watcher. Watchers, you must remember, see all. And you..." He crossed his arms, his trenchant eyes scrutinizing Percival. "You also have a talent for seeing things. However, you're ill-equipped to use it."

"How? What am I missing?"

"The history of this war. You've dug as deeply as you can for a mortal boy; I admire that. But there is more to this fight than Watchers and Wailers. There are soldiers and magicians and spies, all working to annihilate the bellirolts."

Excitement began to crackle like electricity in Percival's chest. "Then tell me about them. Tell me your story," he implored. "I want to know what you were doin' at Killiecrankie, at Culloden. I want to know why my father was so curious—"

"I *shouldn't* tell you anything of the kind," David said sharply. "But I need your help. You know this town, and you've witnessed the signs thus far. More important—" his voice lowered to a fierce quiet— "you have *no notion* of how I've fought, of what I've suffered, to bring our cause this far. That is why I shall speak of my deeds. And when I do, I want to know what you *see*. Together, we might be able to find out what's happening here."

A fire began to flow into Percival's limbs, as this new, dangerous purpose took shape in him. He was making a pact with the Tercentennial Baron.

He felt as if he'd grown an inch taller. He nodded. "Right. Agreed."

David returned his nod. "Good. Then we shall begin tomorrow morning." He strode past Percival to the door.

Percival spun to follow him. "Wait—tomorrow? I mean *now*, let's begin now!"

"Now is the time to rest, lad," David said, unbolting the lock. "Come find me at daybreak. We have a daunting task ahead and our minds and bodies need to breathe. Well—" He caught himself with an ironic smile. "*Your* body does, in any case."

Percival didn't see what was so funny, but his argument was quickly withering. He felt his legs begin to give out as the events of the day flooded back to him. Still, he remained standing stubbornly with the blanket draped around him.

David rolled his eyes and crossed to the boy, handing him his shirt and coat. "Keep the blanket. I'll walk you to your door."

As they stepped into the raw night, Percival burrowed deeper into the blanket. He felt his mobile vibrate again, and saw another series of texts from Abi: *Who are you talking to? Of course I'll hide the book, but tell me what's going on. I want to help...*

Percival looked away. There was no way he'd risk involving Abi in what he and the Tercentennial Baron were about to do. It was perilous enough for him, and he was sure David wouldn't be keen on introducing yet another person to the secrets of his world. He took a deep breath, and texted back: *I'm sorry. I can't tell you more yet. Please trust me, Abi. I'll call when I can. STAY SAFE.* Then he switched off his mobile.

As for safety, the last thing Percival wanted was to spend the night in Granny McGugan's cold, creaky house. What was to keep him from being attacked again?

"I shall be resting, but I'll watch over your house tonight," David said, as if sensing his concern. "When one knows the Otherworld, one can see into it even when unconscious. Though I doubt anything will try to harm you whilst I'm here."

"The Mochries didn't seem to get that," Percival mumbled beneath the blanket.

"Well, you're right on point there. And I even gave them two warning cries."

Somehow Percival managed a weak smile. For the moment, at least, he was able to think not of the horrible scene in the alley, nor how terrifying David's bellirolt cries had been, but that David had been there, and that Percival was still alive.

It took Percival what felt like hours to fall asleep that night, but as he finally gave in to fatigue he found himself sinking into a world of dark warmth, far from the harrowing alley in Bonnybield. A bit of light bloomed ahead, and he was standing on a mist-shrouded hilltop, with a large black stallion cantering toward him. The stallion had a white stripe down its muzzle, with a little matching beard on its chin, and as it turned its head it revealed a long horn that gleamed like ebony. For such a colossal, dangerous-looking creature, the black unicorn was as playful as a child, rearing and jumping around Percival. He found himself laughing. The standing stone with the carvings was also there, and it was when Percival ran with the unicorn to the grassy crest, and peered over the hill, that he fell into a sleep deeper than any dream could enter.

Percival blinked awake as a gentle sun peeked through his window. He was still in his trousers and socks, wrapped in the fusty blanket from the bothy, and lay for a moment thinking of nothing except how his left arm was asleep. His body ached, but he forced himself up and away from dwelling on it. He had a story to hear.

Percival changed clothes, and on his way out remembered the new scar on his neck. Stepping to the mirror, he pulled aside his jumper collar and there it was: a thick, charcoal-black mark, barely an inch in length. He touched the Sable Scar, twisting his head this way and that. There was no pain whatsoever. It felt raised and cold against his fingers, as if it weren't part of his body.

"For the rest o' your life..." he mumbled, and stepped out of his room. He looked across to Granny's door and saw it was closed. She wasn't awake, or was still too angry to speak to him. Either was for the best. He had no time to argue with her. He poured himself a glass of water in the kitchen, grabbed a few scones, and snuck outside.

The sun was setting a peach-colored fire to the morning mist, and the crispness of the water mirrored the bite of the air. The scene was disarmingly placid, like the surface of the sea on a still day. There was not even a hiccup of wind.

"Top o' the morning, Percival."

Percival started, nearly spilling his water. David was reclining on the bothy steps in his brown coat, his newly polished boots stretched out on the gravel, a carved wooden pipe in one hand issuing a tendril of smoke. Maggie gleamed in the mist beside him.

"Mornin'. David." Percival drew near, catching the sharp, sweet scent of tobacco.

"How are you feeling?"

Percival inhaled slowly. "Overwhelmed."

David gave a grim smile and nodded. He rose in his fluid,

catlike way, and his eyes seemed to peer straight into Percival. "I must tell you this. Not only are you barely an adolescent, you're also my kin. I feel an even deeper responsibility to protect you. Whatever is coming for this town is something not even I have foreseen. So please: consider one last time. Once you know what I'm about to tell you, you will have quit the realm of innocence. In three hundred years, I've never simply told my story to anybody."

Percival fought the smile that tugged at his lips. "I'm not scared o' your story."

"Not yet." David's face was as eerily still as the morning around them.

Percival didn't break David's gaze. He knew the bellirolt needed to see strength. "Neither of us can solve this alone. And I've *got* to know what's happenin' in my town."

David studied him for a moment more, then straightened and puffed on his pipe. "Do you remember your dream?"

"Aye." Percival had had a host of dreams, but he knew David meant the one with the castle.

"Then we shall start on that day. And whilst I talk: would you be so good as to take me to where you saw the Watcher? I want a look at the place myself."

"Aye. This way." Percival deposited his water glass by the bothy door, and led David toward the northern field, along the route he and Abi had sprinted just three nights earlier. "That day from the dream: that was when you became a bellirolt?"

"Just before," David said, his voice settling into the rhythm of their walk. "I was a young baron then—headstrong, arrogant... and longing to leave my mark on my country. Yet little did I know that was to occur in a way I'd never imagined."

He gave the boy an earnest look as they crossed the driveway and stepped into the field. "We're going back over three hundred twenty years, Percival. Prepare yourself."

Chapter Seven

1689

G alanforde was the name of the castle. It stood at the crest of a subtle hill that rose like flexed muscle over the plains of Haddingtonshire. The red sandstone walls glowing in the afternoon sun, with the soaring parapets and Northeast Tower, conjured the image of a rust-colored falcon scanning its domain.

David Dunbar, Baron of Haddington, lowered his head and tightened his grip on the reins. He spurred his chestnut stallion Pompey faster as his castle came into view. It was early July, and the muddy roads had slowed his journey more than usual. He followed the curve of the River Tyne, past the sloshing mill wheels in Haddington town, and turned onto Old Nungate Bridge. As Pompey's hooves clopped upon the worn stones, David pressed a pouch of sweet herbs to his nose: the rotting body of a horse thief hung from an iron hook off the side of the bridge, the baron's warning to future wrongdoers.

He passed the decrepit St. Mary's Church, where generations of Dunbars were buried, and reached the lane that led to Galanforde. He nudged Pompey into a gallop, beaming as the wind whipped back his long hair. His cloak billowed out over the stallion's back, ripples of sunlight glinting off the red and silver Dunbar coat-of-arms on its surface. He slowed in front of the stables, and dismounted as a groom ran over to him.

David strode through the stone archway into his castle, grasping the smallsword at his waist as he leapt up the winding steps two at a time, until he arrived at his chambers. A washbasin of lilac-scented water awaited him, and he eagerly plunged his hands into it. He felt, rather than heard, his steward enter the room behind him.

"Glass of Canary, Douglas." David splashed the road from his face and neck. "And tell the dressers I'm ready."

"I've just sent for them now, sir." Douglas's deep voice reverberated through the room. David saw Douglas was already carrying the wine, and he seized it and a towelette without looking at his steward.

"And how was Your Lordship's time at Craigvaran?"

David wiped his face and considered the pale gold of the wine in his glass. "Invigorating," he said, taking a swallow. "Nothing compares to the sea air upon your face in the summer."

His personal tower, Craigvaran, ten miles away on the coast, served as his only escape from the demands of the barony.

"I also received news from Edinburgh." David took another draft.

"Indeed?"

David finally allowed his gaze to meet his steward's. A slow smile drew across his face. "Everything is unfolding precisely as I would want. The battle drums are sounding, Douglas. We shall soon see our king restored to the throne."

Douglas's eyes grew cloudy with concern. "I see Your Lordship is well pleased."

"But you are not." David strode to the window as a noise outside caught his ear.

"I merely urge you to use caution, sir. This is a precarious hour—"

"They're here." David turned with a grin and finished his wine. A red-framed coach covered in black leather, drawn by a team of four horses, was gliding to a stop before the castle. On its door, christened by a recent rain spell, was the Dunbar coat-of-arms.

Three servants bustled into the chamber with David's clothes for the evening. All of a sudden, before they could shut the door, David heard a low, plaintive cry echo into the room. It sounded as if somebody were moaning in hopeless agony, high above them in the castle.

David thrust his wine glass into the chest of a servant and stormed out of the chamber, gazing up the staircase that circled away into the darkness. The cry rebounded off the shadows like a hollow, dissonant chord.

David spun to Douglas. "I gave you specific instructions to make certain—"

"Of course, My Lord; I beg your pardon. I shall see to the tower myself." Douglas bowed and lowered his eyes, as he hurried past David up the stairs.

Below them outside, green and silver embroidered coats glimmered in the sun as two young men stepped from the coach.

David returned to his chamber, and allowed his dressers to remove his coat and smallsword. "Quickly, lads," he said. "Your baron and his cousins have a war to start."

Two hours later, David rose to his feet in Galanforde's High Hall, as the rich, smoky aromas of mutton and tench filled the air.

"A toast, dear Dunbars!"

His four companions turned to face him down the table. David's father had called the hall the Eventide Room for the swath of orange and gold that bathed the windows behind his chair. David caught some of the sunset in his crystal goblet as he said:

"First, to our guests. A hearty welcome back to Galanforde, Sir Evander and young Master Tippler! I rejoice to see you at my table again." He nodded to his newly arrived cousins, bedecked in wigs of long, curly hair and cocked hats with feathers. "Master Tippler" was Calum, barely twenty, with soft features and large brown eyes that looked upon everything with perpetual wonder. He sat with his hat tilted and wig askew, grinning dazedly through his wine.

Seated across from the cousins were David's younger sister Eliza, plump and bright in her emerald gown, and his brother Robert, ten years old and echoing the look of their deceased father. Already the boy had the same slender jaw and dark features, and his hair hung straight around his temples.

"To this fine, rousing Canary," David saluted the wine, "to the health of all present, and to our beloved country. May we preserve and defend her always!"

The toast was repeated with gusto as David seated himself. He pushed aside his fingerbowl and ivory toothpicks and faced Sir Evander beside him. Born within a month of each other, he and Evander had been raised almost as brothers. They'd learned to ride, fence, and hunt together. Evander was taller and leaner than the baron, but he had the same commanding voice, and a paler version of David's green eyes.

"So, have you visited Edinburgh of late, David?" Evander asked. "Heard the news at court?"

David gave a small snort. "I've no interest in that stinking city."

"You'd adore the playhouses, David," Eliza hummed. "All those men declaiming upon the stage…"

David shot her back a teasing glare, then leaned closer to Evander.

"I am informed of the affairs at court, and *yes,* I am outraged. But attend me well, cousin: I've already devised a plan. You see—"

At that moment, another tortured howl—just like what David had heard in his chamber—floated through the stones of the High Hall, and hung like a frigid cloud over the table. David thought he felt it slinking up his skin.

All the Dunbars stiffened in their seats. Evander eyed David with caution and asked, "Is that—"

"No." David's tone was sharp, but confident. He smiled. "The wind has played odd tricks of late. Summer breezes have eerie effects on an old castle. Nothing to worry about." He could feel the critical stares of Eliza and Robert, but didn't meet them.

"Well," said Evander, snatching up his goblet, "as we are drinking healths: Long Live our new sovereigns. Here's to our noble Queen, and God Save the King!"

David's heart thudded to a stop. Under normal circumstances a man would always toast the king after a meal... but these times were different. The "king" to whom Evander referred was little more than a puppet. A fraud. Worse still, Eliza, Robert, and Calum were all echoing the toast.

David raised his eyes to the tapestries that adorned the walls: Roman deities and emperors reclining at the edge of the light. He saw his Julius, his Augustus, his Bacchus and Apollo—figures of glory that were cowed by nobody. He looked down to his fingerbowl, candles flashing on its dark water, and slid it closer. His hand tightened around his goblet and, glancing around the table, he passed it slowly over the fingerbowl.

"God Save the *true* King," he said. "The King Over the Water."

A thick silence settled in the wake of his words. All eyes were on the baron as he took a measured swallow of wine. Even Calum seemed to have lost his hearty glow.

Evander shook his head in amazement. "So. This is your 'plan,' David? To join the rebellion? To think, all this time we've been supping with a Jacobite."

David narrowed his eyes and sat up straighter. "Do I surprise you, cousin? *James* is your rightful king. In Scotland alone his family has ruled for centuries. Now his throne has been stolen by this Dutch fop William and his counterfeit queen—"

"Who were invited by Parliament."

"The *English* Parliament. Those fools are meddling in the affairs of God and kings, and I shan't have a horde of Englishmen telling me who my king is!"

A tense stillness pervaded the room. David put aside his goblet and said, more softly, "Evander, you and I know that Viscount Dundee has raised his standard in support of King James, and is marshaling an army in the North. Well, this morning, I received news at Craigvaran. The commander of William's government army has just arrived in Edinburgh, and his forces are impotent. His lieutenants are ignoring orders. His plans are stagnating. And—lo, behold—support for William and his litter of usurpers is crumbling. We have a chance, coz, to combine our powers and strike the enemy before they leave Edinburgh. With your wealth and my title, we could field enough regiments to pummel them and join Dundee's army. *We* could shape the destiny of Scotland, of all Britain." He sat back in his chair. "Not to mention, secure the name *Dunbar* as one of the mightiest families in the country."

Evander was quiet for a moment, then reached for his dessert plate. He carved a careful sliver of cheese with his knife. "David, I'm well aware what is afoot in Edinburgh. Calum and I came by way of there this morning."

"Well why didn't you say so?" David smirked. "Did you drop a chamber pot on William's general before you left?"

"That would've been rather rude, seeing as we breakfasted with him."

David's heart constricted even more than before. "You *breakfasted...*"

"Yes. He invited us."

No, David thought. *No, this cannot be happening...* "And how was your breakfast with the traitor general?"

Evander paused to make sure he had David's full attention. "David, you've been lord here for—what's it been, nigh on a decade?"

"Well-nigh, yes. Since the year Robert was born." David could feel Robert look away at his corner of the table.

"And in that time, you've never failed to be vocal about your opinions of the Privy Council, or the ministers of Parliament..."

"I am permitted my opinions, Evander. To whom must I answer? Both my parents are in their graves."

"And God rest them, so allow me to tell you what I know they would. Your tongue has grown loose in recent months, and the Privy Council is listening. *Stop.* You're a lowly baron with a good name and a sizeable estate. See to the business of your lands, and leave the war to men of experience."

"I shan't be reproached," David said in a low voice, "by the same boy I used to duel with sticks in my courtyard—"

"Consider it a friendly warning." The look Evander shot David was sharper than his tone. "Believe me, coz, you don't want to tempt the army of King William."

David felt as though his chest were imploding. All he wanted was to make a difference for his country, savor the glory of restoring his king to the throne—and Evander was supposed to have been his lifeline. The man had enough money to build five Galanfordes, *and* he was David's blood.

So this is what it's come to, David thought. *My own cousin is willing to betray me to the English.*

Evander glanced around the table and tried to relax the mood. "Well—I trust we'll all meet at the games on the morrow? Yes?"

"I invited you to the martial games; I expect you to attend," David bit out. Suddenly, he spied a tempting opportunity. He tilted his chin at Evander, throwing out a challenge. "And I've long awaited your participation in one."

Evander nodded, though he looked confused at David's tone. He stood, and Calum, Eliza, and Robert followed suit as they all departed for their chambers. David felt no obligation to rise with them. He only stared at the long, empty table.

An hour later he was plodding through the Armory Hall carrying a partially lit candelabra, the flames playing upon the trellis-work of polearms, claymore swords, and muskets that bedecked the walls. He still couldn't believe how quickly his dream to join Viscount Dundee and retake the country had withered. He paused as he neared the end of the hall and the candlelight revealed a portrait: a nine-year-old David Dunbar, lavishly arrayed in a miniature suit of armor and grasping a spear.

There was such dignity, such composure in that boy's face. Where had it gone? When had he become this buffoon whose visions of glory were doused by his own family? David stared at the poise of his youth looming over him, and decided he would never be blindsided by one so close to him again. Evander's betrayal ate through him like a disease.

He fished a ring of keys from his waistcoat pocket and unlocked a small door opposite the portrait. He trudged up the steps beyond, brocade shoes clacking intrusively on the cold stones. This was the Northeast Tower, highest in all of Galanforde, and its staircase seemed to spiral up forever in the thick dark. Finally David reached another door, with a faint light emanating from the keyhole. There was another clink of keys, the snap of a lock, and David entered the tower chamber.

Two figures were already present in the airless room: one standing at a table with a single candle, the other crumpled in a canopy bed. The standing figure was a tall, spindly man wearing an apron and securing a stoneware jar.

The man bowed as David approached the bed. Stale sweat and urine rankled his nostrils. He sniffed the bag of herbs from his pocket, and brought the candelabra closer to the bed-figure's face. The face turned, with aching sluggishness, toward the warmth. David saw its eyes were open.

"Hello, Grandfather."

Edward Dunbar, First Baron of Haddington, fluttered his sunken grey eyes, trying to discern what was before him. His skin seemed to have thinned even more over his skull, making the outline of his long forehead visible, and his cheekbones jutted out horribly over his jaw. He still had his powerful chin and nose—characteristic of Dunbar men—but they were so distorted he looked like a waking cadaver.

"Who's there?" Grandfather demanded, as David seated himself in a wicker chair and set the candelabra aside.

"It's David, Grandfather."

"David?" The man creased his impossibly tight brow. Then his eyes widened in relief. "David! Oh, good. How is Rebecca with the pregnancy, David? She's still with child, is she not?"

"The *other* David, Grandfather." David sighed. It was foolish to think the man had for once recognized him. "You conveyed the barony to him when I was born, remember? When you first took ill." *Ill* was a kind euphemism by now. Grandfather was demented—possessed by evil spirits. He'd started following demonic voices and faces through the castle just before David's birth. Eliza and Robert had learned not to mention him to David, and they never visited the tower. David and Douglas kept the only keys.

"Oh… oh yes, of course," muttered Grandfather. "You do look so alike… It's important, lad, that you send him to visit me again—"

"Yes, well he's dead." David looked back at the spindly man. "Any improvement?"

"Bled him twice this week," the man said. "Fever not as bad as it was, but it comes in surges. Doctor believes the critical days are upon him."

"Well you can rest the leeches now; his color is diminished." David leaned forward and inspected his grandfather's jaw, turning it over like a dead fowl. "And no sign of those hellish spots. Good." The old man's skin felt like wet vellum, a repulsive sensation, and David had just pulled his hand away when Grandfather's cold fingers brushed his forearm.

"David... wherefore did they turn on you?"

It felt as if those fingers had chilled all his blood. "What do you mean?"

Grandfather had now wrapped his hand around David's wrist. "You've been robbed of something very dear. And you would have vengeance for it. Why?"

David slid as far back in the wicker chair as he could, but wasn't able to wrench free from the old man's grip. How did Grandfather intuit these things? No way could he have overheard their supper from the Northeast Tower.

Witchcraft, David told himself. *This is, in fact, what witches do...*

"Listen, Grandfather—" He finally pried himself from the bony shackles. "I'm hardly of a mind to share my woes with you this evening. Unless you can tell me why you saw fit to wail in agony *twice* today, when I told you—"

"Your father was speaking to me, David."

David caught himself. Despite what he knew about Grandfather's affliction, an old, cavernous longing got the better of him.

"My... Really. And what was he saying?"

At that, Grandfather's dark eyes deepened like the nighttime halls of the castle, and he seemed too overcome by terror to answer.

I am the fool of my family, David thought bitterly, and stood with the candelabra.

"David—" came the weak voice again.

"*Silence from you!*" David spun and slammed the candelabra onto the table so hard that two of the flames went out. He barked at the servant: "We need another doctor. Somebody who can truly rid this man of his demons. At times I think they'll keep him alive forever just to torture us!"

But the servant was no help. He remained silent at his table, staring at the unhappy noblemen. David turned back to the shriveled man on the bed—and flinched as he recalled the last figure he'd seen in such a bed, with this clammy chill to the air... It had been many years ago. Somewhere in the castle a baby was crying, a newborn named Robert, who was not supposed to survive due to his early birth and his mother's death soon after. David was standing, much like at this moment, before his prostrate father, who'd fallen from his horse and had been coughing up blood for days. The elder David beckoned the younger close, saying, "*You must heed your grandfather, boy. I should have, but I did not. Now I fear what lies ahead, and I would that I could counsel you... but you may find me through him. There is truth in what he sees. Stay with him. Go not more than a day's journey hence from him. Promise me you will do this.*" And young David promised, though all he could focus on were the sickening red stains on his father's sheets. Two days later the elder David died, and was buried beside his beloved Rebecca. Young David inherited the baron's title, and pledge. He was barely fifteen years old.

"Nobody, Grandfather..." David murmured. "Nobody, not even my own cousins, will give me permission to leave you. Am I to be chained here 'til I die?"

The thought was unbearable. But he was a Dunbar of Haddington, a man of honor, and as rash and cruel as his pledge was, he could not give it back.

"David…" The voice rose yet again from the bed, gentle in its infirmity. "Your father comes, time and again, as an angel. He has no wings, but I know he is an angel, for he *flies*." Grandfather's waxy skin tightened in a smile. "He wears a shimmering stone about his neck, and carries a great sword like the knights of old. And he comforts me. And allows me to sleep."

"Oh?" David said mordantly. "He flits about like a cherub? Cherish your good dream, then. I've no time for fantasies."

"Oh, he is real, David—but the dreams are *ghastly*. In the dreams comes the green-eyed demon, with a black mane like a lion, talons like a hawk. And he jeers at me, and… *eats* my children in front of me. Without the angel I would have no courage." His head shot up and he looked at David with flaring, bulbous eyes: "Let go your vengeance, David. Your father sends a warning: *let it go*."

David stared impassively at the old man. He yearned to believe his father's spirit was reaching out to him, but as a shiny angel warning of sin?

And I shan't dampen my vengeance to spare my cousins, he vowed. *Nobody betrays David Dunbar.*

David turned to the servant. "See to it he's bled again next week if he's too flushed. And for God's sake, keep him quiet. We have guests now."

He snatched the candelabra and turned without another word to his grandfather. The tower lock clicked assuredly behind him as he left.

Chapter Eight

Savage in the Dark

The next day found a brilliant sun blanketing the green behind Galanforde, where a buzzing, boisterous crowd of East Lothian's elite was gathered. This was the annual Haddington Games, devised by David to show men's skill in single combat: fist-fighting, wrestling, broadsword, saber, smallsword... He never failed to attract a robust crowd, as there was no spectacle like it in his corner of Scotland. And as with all spectacles, no gentleman would dare miss the chance for a good wager.

Metallic clangs rang out from the middle of the green. Two men in medieval armor were locked in a heated battle, wielding broadswords that flashed in the sun. The silk-adorned observers perched on tiered benches, drinking wine and cheering or gibing with every blow. David leaned forward in his chair on a dais at the end of the green as the fight reached a climax. Eliza stood clutching several ladies' hands off to the side.

In a sudden, dexterous blow, one combatant smote the other across the back, dropping him face-first to the grass. Raucous shouts erupted from the benches as two squires ran to remove the fighters' helmets. The standing champion, a man named MacBurie, shook out a mass of red hair and grinned at his fallen adversary.

"Just a touch short of my helm there, eh?" he bellowed, and turned to the crowd. "If he knew how to wield a broadsword, I might well be headless!"

The other combatant tugged off his helm, revealing an exhausted Sir Evander. Calum, his brother's squire, helped him to his feet and the two hobbled off the green. David watched them with calm satisfaction, then stood and descended the dais.

"A rematch!" he called to the gentlemen tallying their debts.

"Oh come now, Haddington!" Lord Belhaven, a stout man with a haughty, round face, shouted from the benches. "The man is bested. We have a new bout to see."

"I'll double your wager then, John." David swept back his burgundy coat and placed a casual fist on his hip. He wore a silk waistcoat with threads of gold and blue stitched with pearls, under a long black wig and cocked hat. He glanced at Eliza's friends nearby, flashing a roguish smile. The ladies giggled as he called back, "I'll stake twenty pounds Sir Evander wins in another round."

Evander grabbed David's shoulder and hissed, "Are you mad? You told me this MacBurie was a slack-armed lily from the country!"

"He *is* a slack-armed lily from the country," David retorted in a low voice. "If you'd watch his backstroke he wouldn't be plowing the green with you!" He pulled his cousin close. "*You are carrying our family name. Fight like a Dunbar.*" He clapped Evander and Calum on the shoulder and returned to the dais, draping himself in his chair.

"Well lay on, MacBurie," David called. "If you can take the strain."

MacBurie's eyes darkened as he bowed. "I am Your Lordship's humble servant."

The men's helms were replaced, and they squared off again. Evander swung first, MacBurie parried; Evander swiped at MacBurie's legs and the man sidestepped him, landing a resounding blow on his side. The crowd roared as Evander staggered, but after David's gibe, MacBurie made certain he hit Evander's arm, chest, and then finished him with a blow to the side of his helm. Once more, Calum rushed to his brother on the grass.

"It must be said, these Dunbars have no lack of fraternity!" MacBurie called as he removed his helm. "What next, My Lord? Shall we duel with broomsticks? Perhaps he could wield one o' them better!"

A few chuckles dribbled from the crowd, but David sat stone-faced in his wooden throne. He knew he mustn't show it, but inside he was grinning. *There, Evander,* he thought. *How does defeat taste to* you? But David wasn't finished yet. There was one final act to his performance, his reply to Evander's warning from the night before. He stood and strolled onto the green.

"What about smallswords?" he asked. MacBurie looked at him, puzzled. David nodded to the man's outfit. "You must be sweltering in that armor. Perhaps you can discard it and we'll try your hand at the smallsword. Against me."

All sound on the green evaporated. Evander was motionless with his helmet in hand, and MacBurie stood agape. Lord Belhaven tried to lighten the mood.

"You can't be serious, David," he chortled. "Are we doubling the stakes again?"

"No stakes from me, Belhaven, just a friendly duel with MacBurie. An exhibition match, before the next bout. Though I shan't preclude any wagers amongst yourselves."

All the guests seemed to be holding their breath while thinking the same thing. Finally it was MacBurie who said it.

"My Lord," came his hesitant voice, "this is most improper..."

"Is it? This is *my* castle, MacBurie. You shall abide by my rules at my games, and the lord of Galanforde may insert himself into the display if he sees duly fit."

David snapped his fingers and Douglas was at his side, slipping off his coat, wig, and hat. The baron shook out his long black hair in the midday sun, while MacBurie's cuirass was unbuckled and a gentleman's smallsword was brought to each man.

"There, now," David murmured, as he stretched his broad shoulders and tested the weight of his weapon. "First cut, shall we say, MacBurie?"

MacBurie's eyes kept shifting to his patron Lord Belhaven, who looked just as flabbergasted as he. "My Lord..." MacBurie implored again.

"No, no." David wagged his finger. "We are now just two men with swords. Come. Let us see if you're as fearsome without that armor."

Calum and Evander retreated to the dais. MacBurie, spurred by David's jeer, began circling him. David studied his movements: how he stepped without his heavy armor, how his big hand clenched the thin smallsword—then David sprang into attack.

MacBurie was hardly prepared for the speed with which the baron fought. He struck like an adder, thrusting his blade in such a tumult that the champion was thrown off balance again and again. It soon became obvious that he was toying with MacBurie: beating his sword away, then retiring, nudging him just enough to shake his focus before striking from a different angle.

Finally MacBurie responded how David hoped he would. He got angry. He fought back with animal-like fervor, and the air broke out into a cacophony of sword-clangs. MacBurie had many pounds of muscle over David, and he used them now, forcing the baron back almost to the dais. Just when it seemed David would be skewered at his cousins' feet, he found a hole in MacBurie's feverish sword-strokes, and thrust his blade in a swift lunge. The battle halted, and David heard a collective gasp from the crowd. MacBurie looked down to see David's sword buried a fingernail's length into his abdomen—not quite a wound, but enough for blood to show. Another few inches, and he could have claimed the man's life.

David retracted his blade as a dazed MacBurie wiped a speck of red from his shirt.

"A touch." David let his tone be flippant, and he cocked an eyebrow and swaggered comically off the green. The spectators broke into applause—most simply relieved that MacBurie was still alive—and David tossed his smallsword to the master-at-arms.

"I shall see to it your winnings are paid to you, Belhaven," he said. "Your champion has a fair hand with the blade."

Lord Belhaven made no response. His face reddened as he collected his manservant and MacBurie, and exited the green.

The Baron of Haddington resumed his seat and dabbed sweat from his forehead. He accepted a cup of wine from Douglas, then looked up to see Evander glowering over him. They shared a flinty stare, both grasping what David had proved. If they took opposing sides in the Jacobite rebellion, David would cut his cousin to pieces.

"You know, David," said Evander, "if you keep tossing away wagers like this, you'll find yourself bereft of a castle."

"Not I, coz." David took a leisurely draft of wine. "A gamble or two lost is nothing to me. The battle of fortune is paltry compared to that between gentlemen-at-arms, and when I play at the latter I play to *win*."

Evander's expression hardened, and David's gaze drifted back to the green, where two bare-chested fighters were squaring off with raised fists. "One thing you ought to know about me, Evander: I shall bleed my purse dry long before my pride." He threw a final glare at his cousin, who blinked and looked away.

"And so it will go down in history," he murmured, as one fighter's punch shattered the nose of the other, and blood sprayed to the thrill of the crowd.

As the afternoon waned, David tried to ease his mind by strolling along the canal in his walled garden. The fragrant blossoms and the meandering fish in the water usually cooled his temper, but he was still seething over his cousins' duplicity. Evander had disappeared after the games and Calum was playing pale-maille with Eliza, while the other guests were scattered over the grounds resting, drinking, or fishing. Robert was probably tucked away in his chamber, immersed in one of David's books.

David flicked rocks out of the path with his ivory-tipped cane as he walked. He had made his point to Evander, he was certain of that, but now he worried for his own safety. All Evander had given him was a warning, yet what if he were intent on *spying* on David, reporting everything back to the general in Edinburgh? Would Calum—innocent, wide-eyed Calum—stoop to such a level, as well?

One of the rocks David flicked landed with a PLUNK in the murky canal. Something about the twinkling light on the water drew him closer for a moment. Specks of sun played upon the ripples he'd just created, and the more he watched, the more he found himself aware of nothing *but* the water. It was a blissful, calming feeling: his vision seemed to expand into one complete sense of this long, wet ribbon. He swore he *felt* the cheerful little pops of the bubbles on the surface, the lazy swaying of the green growth on the rocks beneath... in an involuntary movement, the fingers on his free hand fluttered.

The water looked, just for an instant, as if it rippled with them.

David thought of the dark water in his fingerbowl the night before. He smiled in irony at the daring toast he'd made, and turned to leave the canal. As he did, the fingers at his side suddenly prickled with a furious heat. He jerked his hand up in discomfort, whereupon a great swath of water—a thick brown sheet—*followed* his hand, leaping up from the canal and drenching the entire side of his body.

David stood dumbfounded, blinking water off his face. What on earth had just happened? For a moment he thought this was a very intense daydream, but the water that flew from his nose as he snorted convinced him otherwise. His wig, his coat, even his stockings down into his buckled shoes were soaked in the smelly water. *What the blazes did I just do? - No,* he corrected himself, *it attacked me.* A fish must have jumped as he'd turned to go. That was the only explanation.

Right then, David felt the sharp alarm of eyes on his back. He spun and scanned the garden, but saw nobody. Was it a guest? Had somebody seen this little event? The feeling continued to hang there, like a whining insect over his shoulder, until he decided he'd had enough strangeness for one afternoon. He walked rapidly away from the canal, and had Douglas bring him a plate of sweetmeats and fresh clothes in his chamber. By the time he'd endured supper with the remaining guests, he was more than ready for bed.

But try as he might, this was to become a night without sleep for him.

The moon was tremendous. It reminded David of a pale cat's eye, staring unapologetically through his open window. It appeared several fathoms closer than the night before, as if suddenly taking a keen interest in Galanforde. David was lying under a single blanket, frowning back at the moon, when he realized he'd been doing so for hours. His body was fatigued, yet his mind refused to rest. He rolled over to face the wall and thought of the duel, wondering if there were anything else he could have said to Evander, to further prove he was not a man to be crossed...

Just then, he heard a sharp tap somewhere behind him, as if a stone had struck the outside wall. He stiffened, and listened. The sound didn't come again, but the hairs on his neck began to bristle. Something didn't feel right.

Another sound—a subtle thud, like a book being placed on a table—reached David's ears, and his tingling hairs turned to chills. He'd heard this sound in *both* ears, meaning it had traveled up from the floor, as well. It had come from inside his room.

David didn't breathe. He knew he could roll over and have a plain look at whatever had entered the chamber; after all, it might be a wayward bird or a loose shutter thrown by the wind... But there was no wind. There was no fluttering of wings. There was only the soft glow of the moon on the wall he faced—and suddenly something moved across it. A shadow, quick and stealthy. It was long... a *person?* No, his door was locked and his chamber was four tall stories above ground. No man could climb that height.

David heard the thud again, louder. *Footsteps. Roll over,* he said to himself. *Roll over and face it! - No, I must retain the element of surprise.* He slid his hand from beneath the pillow he'd been clutching—one muscle contraction at a time—down the side of his mattress, to the dirk he kept hidden there. *Douglas always called me over-cautious,* he thought. *But I shan't be caught unawares, you silent devil...* He drew the slender blade from its sheath.

The shadow passed over David's bed. Now was his chance. Pivoting quickly, he swung the pillow in one hand to parry any oncoming blow, then thrust the dirk at the dark shape beside his bed—but it never hit a thing. Instead, it vanished from his hand, and David heard it clang against the wall across the room. Something quick as a whip flew over his face and stung the left side of his neck, biting him like a viper. He cried out and flailed at the shape in front of him, but it was gone as fast as it had appeared.

David flung off his blanket and brought a hand to his neck, fingers tracing the line of blood trickling down his skin. Terror-stricken, furious, and confused, he was about to launch himself at whatever moved in his room—and then he spied the dark shape again, perching on his windowsill. It was a man, with wild hair and a long cloak with a hood that had fallen over his back. The moon encircled his small form as he crouched like a goblin, gazing at David with invisible eyes. Ever so slowly, he raised five long fingers in a flirtatious wave across the room. David's blood froze: gleaming in the moonlight was a hooked claw extending from each fingertip.

"*Dun - bar...*" the man hissed, flooding the room with demented pleasure. He turned his body away, and just as David sensed that a grin was emanating from that hidden face, the man grabbed the tail of his cloak and dove into the night, disappearing beneath the moon.

Chapter Nine

Great Suspicions

"*WATCH! DOUGLAS! Call the damned watch!*"

Cradling his neck with one hand, David bolted to the window. His heart was pounding so hard he didn't even feel his feet strike the floor.

He leaned over the windowsill and scoured the dark grounds for some sign of the intruder. *Is this a nightmare?* He'd had dreams this powerful as a boy, sleeping in the chamber where Robert now was, wondering what might slip through the window to torment him before the relief of dawn... but the stinging pain in his neck was real. In fact, it was getting worse.

David scanned the shadows of the walls beneath him, the trees, the outbuildings... then he saw it. The attacker was gliding across the silver landscape into the woods—completely uninjured after leaping from David's window. In seconds, he had vanished.

A rap on David's door nearly halted his thundering heart.

"Come!"

Douglas entered in his dressing gown, and David ordered him to dispatch every watchman to search the woods for a cloaked intruder. The men combed the property for hours but found nobody, so David armed ten servants and set them on a rotating patrol around the castle. He ordered the spindly servant who attended Grandfather to examine him instead, and persuaded Eliza to sit up with him. Douglas brought several cups of soothing hot rum, so that when morning finally arrived, it found David snoring on a daybed in his antechamber in a fitful, alcohol-induced slumber.

Both the servant and Eliza assured David that his wound was nothing more than a scratch, running from beneath his left ear to his collarbone, and posed no threat whatsoever to his life. It was, though, developing a raised black outline that none of them could explain. David hadn't told anybody his attacker had wounded him with a claw, but what troubled him equally was why this *thing* hadn't tried to kill him. It was lightning-swift, agile… why had it climbed—*jumped? flew?*—up to his window, just to scratch him on the neck and leave? Was this some bizarre threat? Then David thought, with a sinking chill: *Was the attacker sent by Evander?*

The next day, the pain from his scar grew worse… then excruciating. The stinging quickly swelled to burning, as if he were being scalded with hot coals—which soon spread to his arms, fingers, chest, and legs. The burning would dissolve as fast as it had come, then reappear moments later in a different place. It was maddening: he couldn't predict where he would feel it next. David decided he required a real doctor, and dispatched to Edinburgh for several right away.

He awoke many hours later to Douglas's deep voice murmuring about an arrival, and turned his head to see a figure being led into the antechamber—but it was no doctor.

It was Grandfather. Lurching, reaching, his features even more sunken than when David had last seen him, eyes receded into two sockets that shone with pale lights. He staggered toward David wrapped in a yellowing sheet, a look of desperate sorrow carved into his face. Pinned to the daybed, David could only scream—until the face drew nearer, and it transformed into another, unfamiliar: a pudgy, middle-aged doctor staring in alarm. David saw there were three different men in the room, in addition to Douglas, Eliza, and Evander. He had to meet each doctor twice before he was satisfied they were real and Grandfather had been a mirage, but their diagnosis of his scar did nothing to comfort him.

"It's a wound," said one, "but unlike anything encountered in my twenty year. Reacting to some foul presence in Your Lordship's body, which needs to be expunged."

"It's a mark of the devil," said another plainly. "Whatever this intruder was, it was not of the common world, and has implanted a demon in Your Lordship. My Lord has better need of a man of the cloth than one of us."

"I say 'twere the Devil hisself!" The third stamped his foot, not to be outdone. "Note the shape o' the wound, how it festers an' grows dark despite constant care—if this be no harbinger o' terrible fevers an' sickness to come, then may the Lord strike me down here an' now!"

"Seeing as none of you bloated sacks of intestines can agree on my condition, can one of you at least offer a remedy?" David didn't open his eyes as he spoke, for a hot twinge had erupted across his forehead.

"Aniseed," said the bulbous-faced man whom David had mistaken for Grandfather. "Chewed with honey, and at the proper time of day, mind you—"

"Rubbish," said another, this one with a long neck and bulging eyes like an ostrich. "My Lord—" he glanced at the third doctor, "I believe my other colleague and I agree this is beyond the realm of treatable maladies. We fear you have been possessed. Your scar resembles that described in the final chapters of the *Demonology*."

The doctor produced from his bag a heavy, well-thumbed book, with a lion on a shield engraved on the cover. David knew the book well: the authoritative volume by King James VI of Scotland (grandfather to the exiled James) on witch-hunting and protection from evil spirits. The doctor flipped to a page toward the end and read:

"From the appendices to the third volume, concerning the Devil's Marks:

> *Finally, as to the most heinous class of marks: those inflicted by the non-human. One among these stands out as the most ill-favored, that being the Sable Scar, often found in the most conspicuous place on the body, and being a cut of varying length or shape, but rarely deep enough to be of serious injury. It is characterized by a raised black mark around the scar itself, and the victim, now surely possessed by that spirit Satan, suffers attacks in the body and burning pains of fire, as well as visions of the Devil. Such victims must perforce be guarded with caution, for they descend then into fits of rage, which signals their ultimate, terrible demise."*

He closed the book. David stared at the doctor in horror. "What do you mean 'demise?'" he demanded.

"Death. Everybody who is found with such a mark soon meets a brutal end, and oftentimes those close to them, as well."

In the corner of the room, Eliza's face grew pale as ivory. David snatched a towelette and dabbed his forehead and neck. Sweat continued to roll off him.

"My Lord…" The third doctor—an impish, balding man in dire need of a better tailor—leaned forward. "We must needs find you a holy man—one who can drive this demon from Your Lordship's body. That is my humble counsel."

David glowered at all three men through the beads of sweat on his face. "There is no *demon* in my body. I shan't submit to exorcism; it's beneath my station—"

The ostrich-man cut him off. "But My Lord, the *Demonology*—"

"*Hang the* Demonology!" David slammed his fist on the daybed. "I am no witch, nor am I possessed. I was *attacked* by a savage in my own bedchamber! And all I hoped was that one of you bundles of lard would be able to ease my pain. But as you insist on reducing me to the abuses of a peasant, I'm dismissing you from my castle. At once."

None of the doctors budged. They stared at David like a tiger about to leap.

"*Be gone!*" David bellowed. "And tell nobody what you've seen here!"

The doctors bowed and scampered from the room. The door clicked shut behind them, though the sound reverberated between David's ears with a maddening clang.

Two days later, David's pains miraculously began to subside, and he shakily ventured to his study. He was trying to occupy his mind with a request for a mill repair in Haddington when he heard a familiar knock on the door.

"Come, Douglas."

"My Lord..." The steward's voice quavered uncharacteristically as he entered. David turned to him. "I've just come from your grandfather."

"And?"

"He *insists* on speaking with you, sir. He told me of his visions, of his... gruesome..." Douglas blinked, and swallowed. "I cannot speak of what he described. He claims there are dark, eldritch things coming for Your Lordship, and—forgive me—I must say I believe him."

David buried a cringe as a burning spot flared in his chest. He looked down to his desk, trying with all his might to focus on the papers before him. "Grandfather is possessed, Douglas. Don't be taken in by his fantasies and riddles."

Douglas shifted on his feet. "There is one other thing, My Lord."

"Speak."

"It's come to my attention that the Edinburgh doctors

have not kept to themselves about your... condition."

David felt all the color drain from his face. "Continue."

"Rumors have been swarming throughout that city, and have now reached Haddington, about this castle. Some call you a raging Jacobite, others an outright witch. My Lord, the people of Haddington hear your grandfather's cries—they know he's been ill for years, but few now doubt he is bewitched. And many would think it was by Your Lordship."

David gathered a breath and looked up at the painted ceiling. He was so overwhelmed he almost had no voice. "*Great God...* What is happening, Douglas? I am Lord Haddington. A Dunbar. Not some shadowy devil-worshipper..."

As if in response, a tormented wail echoed through the window and into the study. David pounded his hands on the desk and stood up.

"Oh, *confound it all!* I am losing my senses!"

But Grandfather's cry continued, and David even thought he heard a lower, more mournful cry join it, rising to a discordant pitch that was sure to cleave his skull in two.

"*Auugghhh—ENOUGH!*"

And suddenly, all was silent. David gripped the desk and tried to take hold of his frayed mind. Something slammed in a passage above him. The clack of footsteps upon stone echoed down the wall, growing faster, until they neared the study. A white-faced, panting servant appeared in the doorway, and straightened upon seeing David.

"My Lord," he said between breaths, "Your grandfather..."

"Now what?" David groaned.

"He's dead, sir."

David swayed where he stood. "What?"

"He screamed just now, called out for you, and then... passed on."

David turned, feeling as if the floor had disappeared beneath him.

"My Lord…" Douglas stepped forward, but David raised a hand to stop him.

"Make the… necessary arrangements with the body," he said, rubbing his face. "I am leaving for Craigvaran."

"But sir," Douglas protested, "the household—"

"This household is not where I care to be right now. Grandfather is dead, I am under attack… and I cannot trust my cousins." He looked up to the servants, who hadn't moved at all. "Are either of you deaf? You, see to the body; and you, Douglas, tell the groom to see to my horse. I shan't be gone long."

Both men bowed and exited the room. David stumbled out after them, denying the pangs of sickness he still felt. He wanted his riding clothes, he wanted Pompey, and he wanted to leave. He needed a place where he felt safe. He needed the open sea.

An hour later, the life-giving scent of salty air enveloped David's body. He reigned in Pompey to a trot as they skirted the cliffs of North Berwick, and stopped at the door of his medieval stone tower, Craigvaran. A young red-haired servant stepped outside.

"Cameron, show Pompey some oats and a clean stable; he's earned a rest." David dismounted the stallion in a bound.

"Yes, My Lord. Welcome back," came the cheerful response. David smiled and inhaled the ocean breeze. He disposed of his riding cloak and hat within the tower and brought a fresh cup of wine to the edge of the cliff. He looked to the nearest promontory, where the great ruins of Tantallon Castle stood, and swept his eyes across the wide, blue Firth of Forth. Beneath him the grassy cliff dropped nearly a hundred feet to the water, which lapped against dark boulders on the beach. The wind whisked his coat around him in fond greeting, and as he sipped the golden sweetness of the wine, he found he was able to ignore the sting that flashed in his neck.

Thank God for happy escapes. He toasted the afternoon sky.

At that moment, almost without his noticing, his skin prickled on the back of his neck. He flicked his head in annoyance, but felt the same sharp unease he had in the garden after the water incident. Was somebody indeed spying on him? He scanned the open grass, the cliff, the tower... nothing betrayed a hint of movement. The breeze faded, and all became eerily quiet.

All at once, the burning spots erupted over his chest and neck, paining him so much he couldn't focus on his surroundings. David dropped his goblet and backed away from the cliff. He felt certain—beyond all logic—that somebody was standing right behind him. But just as in his bed on that horrific night, he dreaded turning around.

"Cameron?" David called. No answer. He heard a soft click, like a door being shut. "*Cameron!*" The wind had abated; why couldn't his servant hear him?

"*CAMERON!*" That was when rapid footsteps sounded behind David. He spun, his hand shooting to his smallsword— and he was seized. A dark shape, smelling of foul stables and cheap tobacco, collided with his body, and before he knew it he was lifted off the ground and the sword was torn from under his coat. He held his breath, bracing for a rough collision with the earth... but it never came. The ground had disappeared beneath him, and when David looked down all he could see was the deep blue of the water.

He was flying. His captor had his chest in an iron grip, and they had soared off the cliff and were gliding, borne by no natural force David knew, high over the Firth of Forth. Every ounce of courage drained from David as scratchy, hot skin approached his ear, and a voice growled with stomach-turning breath: "Good day, *Yer Lordship.*"

His captor spoke with a thick Highland brogue, and David

could feel a wicked grin forming along that face. "Fine-lookin' scar ye hae there…"

Twisting his head, David saw a pair of dark, pitiless eyes; an unkempt face; thick hair that whipped about as they flew; and a black outfit with a long, hooded cloak. A shiver convulsed his body as he recognized it: the same cloak from his bedroom. This was the monster that had scarred him.

"Bin waitin' for this moment a long time," the kidnapper hissed. "I'm no sure if ye heard o' me? They whisper my name all o'er Inverness: *Peadar MacBain, Scourge o' the Nobles*. I'm gonnae take yer soul in that bonnie wee castle o' yers. One by one, I'll devour the Dunbar clan. How dae ye think I'll look as Lord o' Galanforde?"

Suddenly a sharp CRACK blasted out from the cliff, and MacBain lurched in the air. His grip on David loosened, and David began to fall toward the water. Howling in terror, he latched onto MacBain's boot at the last moment.

MacBain had stopped flying and was now hovering in midair, as he cursed and held his hideous skull in pain. David's arms were locked around his attacker's leg, and he twisted to look back at the cliff. On the edge, not sixty yards away, a short, dark-haired man stood with a smoking carbine in his hands. He, also, looked to be a Highlander, as he was dressed in a kilt of red tartan. *Not only am I abducted by flying beasts*, David thought, *but Highlanders are traipsing around my tower?*

The Highlander discarded the carbine and whipped forward a longer-barreled musket from his shoulder. David looked up and realized MacBain was recovering. Had that carbine shot actually hit him *in the head?* And he wasn't even injured?

"Let go, My Lord!" the Highlander yelled from the cliff. David looked at him, panic-stricken. *Let go? Are you out of your mind?* He dared to let his eyes drift down, and recoiled when he saw the azure waves far, far beneath his dangling boots. He groaned in agony and clung more tightly to MacBain's stinking leg.

"Let go!" came the Highlander's voice again. He fixed the musket to his shoulder and took aim at MacBain. David was aghast: was this man really trying to blow the monster out of the air? From that range, with David so close?

A second blast rang out from the cliff—and to David's amazement, it hit home. MacBain's body rocked in midair, and the musket ball seemed to explode in black streaks behind his neck. One of the streaks fell and singed David's shoulder. He winced and tried to shake it away—then realized it was blood. MacBain was bleeding a dark, vile blood, thick as molasses and pungent in odor. His hovering stance in the air faltered, and he raised a hand to the back of his neck where the shot had gone through. The viscous substance gleamed on his fingers. He looked down to David. His lips curled into a guileful smile, and mouthed the name *"Dun - bar"* once more. Then he fell out of the air.

David lost his grip on MacBain's boot. He plummeted, with the monster following him, down, down, gathering terrifying speed as the water rose to meet him. He lost the sound of his scream in the wind howling past his ears, and tried to cover his face, as if he could break the hundred-foot fall about to end his life. But in the split second before he hit the water, his mind seemed to slow—as if his descent were slowing—and MacBain shot down behind him and latched onto his torso. Locked in a sickening plunge, both men crashed into the sea.

David felt himself sinking, as millions of bubbles squeezed the air from his lungs. He had no idea how he was still conscious, but he fought with every particle of strength to pry free from the monster's grip... then MacBain went limp. A scorching pain, like a fiery spear from each of MacBain's hands, stabbed into David's body. Every vein and bone felt as if it were bursting, and a hot, magma-like presence crawled up his spine—turning his organs in on themselves—then settled in his neck. His throat swelled and choked him, as if something were emerging from the skin at his nape, and the pain in his limbs shot out his fingers in a blinding light that sapped his strength.

David's mouth opened in a silent, gurgling wail, and the water consumed him, and he remembered no more.

Chapter Ten

The Bell of St. Mary's

S omething was stroking David's outstretched hand. He had the vague sensation he'd been floating through clouds of voices that cried in agony, terror... but he only heard them as if through a haze. Their faces were indistinct, their words lost, and soon only a chilling echo remained. He shook his head to clear it, and opened his eyes.

He forced them shut again.

He'd thought he was in his bed, in the warm halls of Galanforde, but that couldn't be right. There was something odd about how his muscles moved, how slowly his head responded when he shook it... then he felt hair drift and tickle his scalp.

He was still underwater. Moreover, the soft padding he had supposed was his feather mattress he now noticed was squishy and grainy. It was *mud*—thick, cold mud—and it continued everywhere he groped around him. David's hands froze as he realized the truth: he was lying, spread eagle, at the bottom of the Firth of Forth.

His eyes opened to the hand that had awakened him. All was pitch black—he could do nothing but feel his surroundings—and as he stretched his hand it brushed something slim and leathery. *Seaweed* had been waving over his skin. He patted his entire body, making sure everything was still in its proper place. What on earth had just happened? How was he still alive?

David sat up in the dark void, a move requiring much more effort than he'd anticipated. No man could survive being unconscious on the sea floor, so he couldn't be breathing... He tried inhaling, and felt nothing. Just cold, salty water filling his nose, mouth, and throat. It wasn't the most pleasant sensation, but it wasn't lethal. So what was keeping him alive, if he wasn't breathing?

It's curious, David thought as he raised himself in slow motion from the muddy floor, *I don't miss the air. I don't even feel the need for it.* The idea was both terrifying and exhilarating. He felt *free,* as a dull current moved over his waving clothes and made him stumble. *Maybe this is death: I'm now a spirit doomed to wander all ends of the earth... though this doesn't feel half-bad.* The agonizing pain after he hit the water must have been the end of his life—so now what? He ought to find the surface first, and get his bearings.

He picked a direction where the sea floor seemed to be inclining, and heaved one foot in front of the other. Immediately he stumbled upon a large lump, and a thick piece of fabric fluttered against his leg. He went rigid. This had to be the monster, MacBain, and his horrid cloak. *The sea can have you, scum,* he thought, and continued around the body.

Before long David saw a bit of light break to his left, and he followed it. The sea floor became steeper and rockier, and David scrambled on his hands and knees until he saw the sun through the shifting waves, and with a final lunge he broke the surface and felt cool air on his face again. Right away he knew he needed to cough, and he hacked up mouthfuls of tepid seawater, sputtering onto the dark stones around him. The process was disgusting, though he felt better afterward—even rejuvenated, ready for a good meal and a bottle of Canary. He could taste the crisp, salty air on his tongue, yet still was not inhaling it. He found if he made the effort he could do so, but his lungs seemed to have forgotten how to breathe on their own. It was bewildering, this absence of the basic sign he was alive… Even so, what did he care? Alive or no, he was still David Dunbar; he had his body and his mind. And apparently, he could survive being drowned.

The sun was grazing the rim of the tall cliffs above him. He must have been unconscious for several hours. He slipped and clambered along the wet rocks, out of the flowing tide— and then stopped. A movement ahead seized his attention.

It was the Highlander who'd killed MacBain, advancing out of the shadow of the cliff. He clutched his musket in one hand, and along with his red belted plaid he wore a white shirt and leather jerkin, with a sporran at his waist. He looked like a walking battle machine: a carbine over his back, basket-hilted claymore at one side, dirk at the other… David felt naked in his wet clothes before this impressive warrior. He'd never actually seen a Highlander before.

"Oh God," the Highlander said, in a voice much younger and higher than David had expected. A look of horror overtook his face. "It has happened."

David stumbled closer and saw the Highlander was no older than twenty, about a head shorter than David, with an unruly black mop framing his face. His skin seemed carved of glossy marble, so distinct and pure were his features, and he shared the wide-eyed, awestruck look of Calum—though this man's eyes gleamed a keen, sapphire blue.

"Speak your name, Highlander," David commanded, as the terrified expression remained etched on the man's face. "And what the devil you're doing on my land."

"William Cardross, My Lord, your most humble servant." The man made an awkward bow. "I do beg your pardon, but I've been followin' that bellirolt for some time now, tryin' to kill him, an' I finally tracked him here. Alas… I wasn't quick enough to shoot him afore he flew off wi' you!"

The world suddenly began to turn circles over David's head. He realized he was intensely hungry—it'd been hours since he'd eaten—and he could hardly focus on the young man's words.

"My Lord, I owe you a prodigious apology," Cardross went on. "If I'd 'a thought you'd end up as you did in the sea, wi' MacBain… *Oh,* but I don't know how I was so foolish!"

Tears began to well up in poor Cardross's eyes. David was only aware of his hunger mounting further—not a deep, guttural hunger, but an exhausting, pervasive one that drained every muscle in his body. He felt he couldn't think of anything else until he'd satiated it. He placed a hand on his head and tried to steady himself.

"You've… been following *what?*" he asked, closing his eyes.

"The bellirolt, sir," Cardross repeated. "MacBain, that madman, that's what he was. A seethin', blood-lustin' bellirolt."

"What in God's name are you talking about?"

Young Cardross looked taken aback. "Why, the bellirolt demon. That's what was infectin' MacBain's body. That's how he could fly, had his claws an' all. He killed nobles, see, that was his specialty. You were his next prey."

"His prey?" David's hand brushed the now painless scar on his neck.

"Aye, I see he scarred you. But rather than kill you, he did what's worse…"

"Worse? What could be worse than killing me? I thought *you* killed *him.*"

"Oh, I did! Yes sir, I succeeded in that." Cardross nodded emphatically. "But I fear in the process, he has turned you into one o' his kind!"

David couldn't believe the audacity of this young man, but Cardross seemed so certain of what he said. "One of his— what?" David demanded. "Demons?"

"No just any demon, sir: a *bellirolt*." Cardross nodded toward the sea. "You've been in that water for near five hours now. Any other man would 'a died. But you… well, you don't look much the worse for wear!"

"This is impossible," David growled. "I am finished with people hurling the word 'demon' at me. I ought to clap you in irons and haul you off to prison."

"A fine noble gesture that would be, seein' as I saved your life." Cardross's bright eyes flashed across the rocks at David. "I told you to let go—if you'd done as I said you might 'a been safe!"

"That's enough—silence!" David crossed the remaining rocks in a few long strides, his anger building like a blinding storm. "I am in no mood to be lectured to by an insolent, feeble-minded peasant!"

To David's surprise, Cardross dropped to one knee, and laid his musket on the shore. He even unsheathed his claymore and held it up to David in a show of complete deference.

"My Lord, please forgive me: the fault is mine for your condition. I would that I had acted sooner afore MacBain had taken you… but now I shall do what I can. I pledge my life to your service."

David snorted and tried to interject.

"I beg you hear me, sir!" Cardross's voice was firm, though he didn't lift his eyes to David's. "Not all men who become bellirolts lose their true humanity, their *goodness,* an' I might help you…"

"*For the last time, Highlander, I am no demon!*"

Cardross slowly lifted his gaze, which looked hollow with sadness. "What's on the back o' your neck?" he asked.

David narrowed his eyes and raised a hand to his wet neck. To his shock he felt a large, warm lump had formed on the nape, firm to the touch, but not painful like a bruise.

He said as casually as he could, "Must have hurt myself when I fell."

But the Highlander shook his head. "It's the Black Swell. All bellirolts have it. A mark o' the demon's presence in your body. You an' it are one now."

David stared at the impish figure kneeled before him, and felt fear creep up his spine for what seemed like the hundredth time that week. It wasn't abject terror like before; this was the sinking suspicion that this stranger might just be the only man speaking the truth to him. *But he's a rough Highlander*, David found himself thinking. *What can he know of me? I feel no devil in my body. He is pathetically deluded.* David straightened himself and dropped his hand.

"I shall spare you my wrath for your insolence," he said coolly, "because you killed my attacker. But I've no need of an uncouth servant such as you. I shall return to my castle and I bid you farewell. I suggest you see your way out of my lands, and soon." He strode toward the narrow path that zigzagged up the cliff.

Cardross turned on his knee and continued to plead as David walked away: "My Lord, please hear me! I know these creatures—I know what you're about to endure! I can help you, keep you from becomin' one o' the Dark Legion! *Do not return to your castle!*"

But David marched on, his boots squelching as they climbed the path. "I am no demon, Highlander," he said, surprising himself with his calm. "I am no demon."

He repeated the words to himself all the way up the cliff.

David never had such difficulty saddling Pompey for the ride home. The stallion neighed and reared up as David approached him, and once mounted it was all he could do to not be thrown before he reached Galanforde. He was glad to shove Pompey into the hands of his groom.

It wasn't until he stood naked before his mirror that David was forced to see what a dramatic transformation had taken place on the sea floor. His arms, chest, and legs had gained several pounds in muscle, and his belly—usually slightly round from a healthy diet of beef and wine—now clung to his ribs, as he felt the same draining, raw hunger he had on the shore. The effect was too staggering for David to grasp. He pushed it from his mind until he could eat. He pulled on some garments and descended to the High Hall.

Night had settled around Galanforde by the time David rose to his feet with a silver goblet before the family.

"A toast."

Four other solemn goblets rose in response. David cleared his throat.

"To His Lordship…" A wave of fatigue pounded him, and he shut his eyes. Despite his crippling appetite, he hadn't been able to eat a single morsel during supper.

"To Edward Dunbar, First Baron of Haddington." David swallowed. "A great man… an ambitious man. Who restored Galanforde to her present glory…" He could feel his family glaring at him in revulsion. His shirt was un-tucked, his waistcoat unbuttoned, and he wasn't even wearing a cravat. He didn't care. Anything around his neck felt too constricting. "A *persistent* man. May God keep his soul, amen." He thrust his cup in an obligatory manner and collapsed in his chair, throwing a leg over its wooden arm.

A seething silence pervaded the table. Finally Eliza leaned over to him.

"David, you are not well. I think you ought to retire."

"I shall do no such thing, sister; I've not had my meal. I desire something else. This course doesn't suit me." He motioned for the nearest footman, and as the man approached, David sipped his wine. The sweet, wildflower flavors bathed his tongue, but the feeling lasted only a second. When he tried to swallow, the wine turned bitter and rancid in his throat, and he twisted his head in disgust. As far as he could tell, not a drop had reached his belly.

As the footman took hold of David's plate, David snatched it back and held the man's hand on the table. "Are you certain the food is properly cooked?"

"Qu-quite so, sir!" the footman stammered.

"Qu-qu-qu-quite so?" David mocked him. "Did you see the cook roast it?"

"Well, n-no, My Lord, that was in the k-k-k... the kitchen."

"Well, get you then to the damned k-k-kitchen, and tell the c-cook that His Lordship requires a new dish to satisfy his delicate palate. And tell the fat old imbecile to produce such a course in the next half-hour, or it'll be *his* loins I feast on next!"

The footman fled the room.

Eliza glowered at her brother. "You're being horrid, David."

"Really," Evander chided from across the table, "is this how a gentleman behaves on the eve of his grandfather's death?"

"The man has been dying my entire life, you halfwit. Nobody has borne him as I have. I thank God he's in a contented place. We may all sleep now." David had no patience to give thought to his words. They only lashed out of him like whips.

"I, for one, would be happily kept awake if I knew Grandfather were still alive," came a soft voice from down the table. David's eyes shot up to see Calum tracing the rim of his wine goblet.

"And what would you have done to *keep* him alive, Calum Dunbar? Hm?"

"Nobody here is attacking you, David..." Eliza said.

David swung his leg off his chair so fast he didn't even see it move. He leaned forward. "Nobody is attacking me?" He looked around the table of poised, elegant gentry, with their rigid backs and dainty fingers upon their goblets, and felt sick. Were they so perfectly mannered they couldn't see what was right in front of them?

"*Nobody* is attacking me?" David let out an absurd laugh. "Do you not recall what happened the night after I declared my support for the Jacobite cause?"

Evander stared incredulously at David. "How could we forget?"

"Yes, how indeed could you forget, Evander? Let me ask: what do *you* know about cloaked men who can scale castle walls?"

Evander stiffened. "You suggest that I would ever—"

"I don't suggest, I *accuse*." David stabbed a morsel of meat with his knife and pointed it at Evander. "You've aligned yourself with the wrong side of this war. And you, too, Calum Dunbar—" David turned his knife to Calum— "what part have you played in all this?" There was something about Calum's silence until tonight that was unsettling David. *He secretly fears you*, he found himself thinking, *so he won't say it aloud, but he has more sinister designs for you than Evander.*

"Tell me, Master Tippler!" David pressed Calum. "Master Wide-Eyed, Lily-Livered Imp: do you also think you'll gain favor with the lords in London by spying on me and sending men to kill me—"

"For the last time, David, I've sent no man to kill you!" Evander yelled. "And if you slight my brother once more—"

"Then what? You'll fetch a broomstick to duel me?" David thrust the meat in his mouth, but just as with the wine, it turned bitter and vanished as soon as he tried to swallow it. He gripped the table in frustration, and tossed another gulp of wine into his mouth to clear the taste. Again, it evaporated into filthy air at the top of his throat. He hawked, spit, and hurled the silver goblet, which bounced down the length of the table.

"What is *wrong* with this damned wine?" he demanded of the remaining footman. The young man dove after the goblet and cleared it from the table. "Another bottle!" David called as the footman rushed from the room.

"David, you've become a vile host," Evander said, shaking his head at his plate. "Truly vile. And I was so looking forward to another week at Galanforde…"

All David could focus on was a broad, throbbing pain spreading through his head. He rubbed his face with one hand, and was dully aware that Calum—all the way down the table—gasped as he did so.

Calum had been the only one to notice that as David drew his hand down his face, five dark claws had extended from his fingertips, glistening in the candlelight. They disappeared before David could see them.

"David." Eliza pushed her plate away. "You must make amends with your cousins. I know you're upset from this attack, whatever it was, but—"

"*I shall not make amends!*" David roared, slamming his hand thunderously on the table. "You don't understand. None of you do. I've been thwarted at every turn in my life. Well, no more!" His anger began to rush like a mad river through him. He felt powerful, free—and dangerous. "*No more, I say!* No more shall Grandfather, nor any treacherous kin, stand in my way. I am the Baron of Haddington. If I want to ignite a war, I'll do it. And I'll cut down every weed that springs in my path."

His words were met with yet another silence. *Look at them eyeing you with contempt*, he thought. *They want none of this for you. They'll see you hanged first…*

Finally Evander spoke. "David, if ever you find yourself with a kinsman's blade in your breast, it shall only be the fault of your own arrogance."

There it is, David, a thought as clear as a bell rang through his head. *They hate you. And oh, how you shall make them pay for such hatred!*

David leapt from his seat and hurled the platter before him against the wall. Evander and Calum rose in protest, but that only inflamed David's aggression. In fact, the more he became aware of it, the more it fed him with a magnificent, unstoppable strength. He flung chairs aside as he advanced on his cousins. Eliza shrieked at him to stop, Evander warned he would lock the baron in his own dungeon, and Calum snatched a meat knife and tried to hide it by his side. At that, the hunger reared inside David like a snarling bear. *You picked the wrong day to threaten me, coz.*

With one hand he overturned the entire supper table, the last barrier between him and his family. Food and silver scattered, and the candelabras bounced to the wall, where they ignited the base of the Augustus tapestry. Eliza and Robert fled the room screaming, and David saw true fear flash in Evander's eyes as the tapestry crackled alight.

"*Fire!*" Evander called. "Bring the buckets! Servants! *The buckets!*" He ran out the door.

David found himself laughing, and jeered after him, "Afraid of a little heat, man?"

He and Calum moved toward the door at the same moment, whereupon Calum jumped and brandished the knife.

"What now, boy?" David snarled. Every muscle in his body was taut and poised to attack. "You draw a blade on your own host?"

Calum eyed David in horror, backing away as if facing a coiled serpent. He glanced at David's hands. "You are... not David..." he choked.

The baron cocked an eyebrow. "Do you doubt me, Calum?" He stalked closer, reveling in the power of his presence, the way the flames behind him danced in Calum's dark, terrified eyes...

"If you draw that knife, you'd better use it!" David swung his arm at Calum, who dove out of the way. David wasn't prepared for the strength of his own limb arcing through the air, and it almost sent him somersaulting. Calum readied the knife again, trying to inch his way around David to the door. David yanked off his waistcoat and swung it to try to disarm Calum. Again his cousin dodged, and bolted for the door. David bounded across the room, grabbed the overturned supper table, which was streaked with flame, and heaved it across the space toward the door. The great mass of wood crashed to the ground in a cacophony of splinters and sparks, blocking the exit. Calum crouched in terror and frantically looked about. The fire was licking its way across the tapestries, consuming Apollo's arm and Bacchus's head—there was no way out except through one servants' door in the corner. David circled Calum, savoring the vision of this man poised to do battle with him. He felt a hot thrill as he sprang into the air.

The next few moments passed in a flash. David's hand connected with Calum's shoulder, and they rolled on the ground. David saw the glint of Calum's knife near his arm, and backhanded it across the room. Calum scrambled to his feet but David caught him round the neck with both hands, and hurled him to the floor. It was the moment of impact, when Calum's body crashed into the hard wood, that David felt the most exhilarating rush of his life.

Beautiful, saccharine warmth filled his veins. It shot through his hands, arms, shoulders, down his back and into his toes, then rose and burst in the crown of his head in a shattering firework of ecstasy. He forgot who he was, where he was: he only writhed in pleasure as he was carried to a sweet, blissful place far away.

It might have been an hour later, it might have been five minutes, but David was only aware of coming to his senses as he stumbled into the Armory Hall, staring at his hands. They were smeared with blood. It couldn't have been *his* blood; he felt no wound nor remembered any injury. He staggered and realized how lightheaded he felt—he was hungry again.

Hungry? Did you not just eat? he asked himself. *Of course I didn't; I had no supper...* Then he was sure his eyes were playing tricks on him, for he saw what looked like black talons emerging from his fingers. He turned his hands and they were gone. He stretched his fingers, and they were there again. *Talons and blood... Am I going mad?*

A voice echoing from the passage behind him brought his head up.

"DAVID! DAVID!!"

As David turned, memories of the night trickled back. Supper. The argument. The fight. *Fire.* He could feel the warmth of the blaze all around, burning through the rooms on the other side of the walls... he even saw a tendril of flame slip through the ceiling above him. The fire was spreading rapidly.

Evander appeared in the doorway of the Armory Hall, fury and anguish contorting his face. *"David."* He jabbed an all-too-sinister finger at the baron. "Where is my brother?"

David stared at him. "How should I know?"

"David, the High Hall is ablaze and I cannot find Calum! Where is he?"

Suddenly, as if on instinct, David hid his hands behind his back. *Blood, and not mine... Have I killed Calum?*

"What was that on your hands." Evander's words were less a question, more an accusation. "Show me your hands. What have you done with my brother?"

It was then, as Evander took an authoritative step toward David, that the snarling desire for dominance lurched to life in him again. He saw Evander the same way he'd seen Calum—a treacherous, subhuman threat to his happiness—and found himself thinking: *Oh yes... your brother. The one who would have stuck me like a pig with a supper knife. The weak little urchin who had the gall to challenge me.*

"I know nothing of your brother." David spread his arms innocently and shrugged. Evander recoiled in horror.

"*Great God!* Is that Calum's blood?"

David looked at his hands and discovered, for the first time, he was not repulsed by what he saw. "Oh my..." he murmured. "I'm afraid so. Dear Evander." Remorse felt as foreign as the seas of a distant world.

Evander cried out in rage and clipped David across the face, which only sent him staggering and laughing.

"God curse you for a kinsman, David." Evander's voice dripped with grief.

David's laugh continued, and it propelled him to his weapons display on the wall, where he snatched the first basket-hilted claymore that met his grasp.

"Where's your broomstick, coz?" David jeered. Evander grabbed another claymore from the opposite wall, and both Dunbars charged across the room toward each other. Just as they were about to meet, the ceiling gave way with a loud SNAP, and a flaming wooden rafter crashed to the floor between them. David didn't waste a moment worrying about his Galanforde; he only wanted Evander all to himself. He grinned at his cousin across the fiery debris before darting off in the opposite direction.

David heard Evander clear the burning rafter behind him. He glimpsed his childhood portrait, with all its nobility, being consumed in flame at the end of the hall. Any affection for it felt like the memory of a forgotten body. He turned up a winding staircase to his right, as the portrait slid from the wall and crashed face-first to the floor.

He sped up the steps, around and around until he ducked out onto a parapet that ran the length of the castle. He welcomed the night air on his hot skin, and just had time to register that the roof at the end of the parapet was catching fire, when Evander's footsteps drummed up the staircase behind him. David wheeled about, blade ready, as his cousin pitched himself onto the parapet. He locked eyes with David.

"Let's end this, you dog."

"Lay on, coz," David growled through a smile.

With cries that made blood ring in their ears, they launched into battle. Rampant vengeance poured through every stroke of their swords. The duelists were silhouetted by the orange flames on the roof as David forced Evander back along the parapet, until Evander's sidestroke caught him across the forearm. David's shirtsleeve sliced open in a long line of blood. However, no sooner had the wound appeared than it began to *seal itself up,* an unseen force stitching the skin back together. A moment later, David looked and felt as if the injury had never occurred.

Evander's horrified eyes rose to his cousin's. "What *are* you, David?" he asked in a choked voice.

All David knew, as he stood upon the blazing parapet, was there was no creature on earth that could best him at that moment. He felt like a lion.

"I… am more than human." David grinned. "I am smoke, and lightning." His sword flashed twice, and Evander lost his grip on his weapon. With a sudden lunge, David thrust his blade deep into Evander's chest. Something told him he needed to be close to Evander right then, to *touch* him, so he grasped his cousin's face as he sank to the parapet.

"Goodnight, Evander." David found his voice high and unfeeling, and he watched the last light fade from Evander's eyes.

Again the wondrous feeling of ecstasy bloomed in David's body, as if pure energy were pouring into him. He thought he saw a faint crimson glow beneath his hands as he loosed Evander's body—sword-pierced and all—over the edge of the parapet. David felt full to the brim, *alive* in the crackling night… And then the feeling passed like a breeze.

David heard screaming. He looked around and realized the entire roof of the castle was on fire. *Galanforde! My Galanforde!*

What had he been thinking? He rushed to the edge of the parapet, and was met with a sight that would be seared into his mind forever.

Chaos, gruesome and terror-stricken, reigned on the grounds around the castle. Evander's body had fallen at the base of the wall, and a young kitchen maid was trying to drag it away. *People,* dozens and dozens of people, were running back and forth beneath the red, roaring building, carrying fire buckets and injured servants. A woman's burning dress had just been put out; her skin was covered in black, festering burns. The groom and head cook were stockpiling valuables. Horses sped in all directions... had the stables been spared? Was Pompey there? Then he saw Eliza and Robert running into the night, a manservant behind them bearing Evander's body. None of them looked back—not at their beautiful home being reduced to ash, not at the solitary baron who stood shrieking their names atop it.

Shame—base, throat-rending shame—clawed David's insides. This was all his doing. His fault. He couldn't bear to see the tragedy before him, yet couldn't tear his eyes from it. He screamed, in a childlike plea for help, "Douglas! *DOUGLAS!*"

Suddenly, like a hammer splitting his skull, the gong of a bell resounded in the night. David looked out: it came from St. Mary's Church near Nungate Bridge, the one bell left in the roofless tower that David had never heard in his life. Every soul in Haddington would now be roused, summoned to lend whatever aid they could to their lord. A cluster of torches began to gather across the bridge. *They cannot find me here*, David thought; *I won't let them see me like this...*

Every time the bell of St. Mary's tolled, David felt his skull and bones shudder as if they would break. This was the judgment laid upon him. His barony was forfeit. His title—his livelihood—was destroyed. With the burning of Galanforde, there could be no more Baron of Haddington.

Overwhelmed with grief, unable to tolerate the pounding righteousness of St. Mary's any longer, David ran to the far edge of the parapet and dove into space. He plummeted feet first through a tree and landed with a harsh CRACK on the ground, but any pain dissolved as his body employed whatever new mechanism it had to heal itself. He staggered up and, without another glance back at his beloved castle, tore off into the night.

Chapter Eleven

The Helm
of Bonnie Dundee

B ack in Bonnybield, grey clouds had shrouded the morning sky. David and Percival were walking along the edge of the oak forest, toward the standing stone where the Watcher had appeared. The slate-colored buildings of the town sprawled through the valley to their left.

David's pipe had grown cold long ago, but he still cradled it by his side, as if protecting it. Percival felt in shock, and uttered the only words he could find:

"I just... I can't believe you killed them. Especially Calum... he seemed so kind."

"He was." David's voice sounded thin and scratchy. "Not a day goes by I don't think of them. It is one thing to murder a man; it is another to murder a kinsman. But to murder *two* kinsmen, in cold blood, whilst they are guests in your house..." He broke off, a glassy film covering his eyes.

Percival's steps slowed as he watched David. This sadness was not at all what he'd expected from the bellirolt. In David's halting voice, he heard the echoes of centuries of regret. "Well, the demon was controllin' your thoughts, aye? You even said you *felt* it enter you from MacBain—"

"Percival." David looked down at the boy. "Nobody, and no force, moves our hands without our allowing it."

They continued in silence for a moment. David finally seemed to register his smokeless pipe. "The great irony, of course," he said, emptying the pipe bowl, "was my grandfather had somehow seen it all coming. I never heeded his warnings. I wish I had."

"What happened to Eliza, and Robert?" Percival asked. "Did Douglas survive?"

"Sadly, I don't know. I found records of a Douglas who secured employ with Viscount Irwin a year later; I pray it was the same man. As for my siblings, I learned only traces of their stories. I had arranged Eliza's engagement to a baronet in Galloway, near Evander and Calum's home, but it was called off. She did eventually find a husband, though not a man of her station. I had robbed her of that." He looked away at the patches of heather sloping to the west. "After that night, I knew I could never return home. The bell of St. Mary's cracked whilst alerting the town to the fire. The rubble of Galanforde was cleared—even the foundations were dismantled—and used to restore the church later." David smiled in wry amusement. "I heard it was said in Haddington that 'The lords had spent so lavishly on their palace there was naught left to do but reduce it to ashes.'"

"But you said the burnin' of Galanforde meant there could be no more Baron of Haddington? I don't understand."

"Galanforde was the caput of my barony, Percival. The legal anchor of my authority as a lord. In those days, if your caput was destroyed, your title went with it. Thus I am—I was—the last Baron of Haddington."

Percival felt a stab of pity for David. Being a baron had meant something to him, and he wondered what David might have been able to do if he'd never met MacBain.

Percival recognized with a start where they were, and

grabbed David's sleeve. "This is it."

"This…" David stopped, and stared up at the standing stone at the edge of the wood. He drifted toward it with a curious, reverential expression, and placed one palm flat against the Pictish-style carvings.

"A great man is remembered here," he said in a quiet voice.

"Who?" Percival asked. "You know what those carvings—?"

David silenced him with a hand, and gave a reassuring smile. "A story for another day. Tell me about the Watcher."

Percival narrowed his eyes, irritated, but showed David where the Watcher had been standing on the slope of Balloch Hill, and where his gaze had been directed. David mimicked the spirit's stance, peering into the Bonnybield glen.

"Are we goin' to find the Watcher?" Percival asked.

David smiled. "No. But we are going to follow his clues. These spirits know what they're awaiting; our task is to decode their riddles. Come."

Percival approached and stood beside David, trying to draw himself up at least close to the man's height.

"Do you notice anything, Percival?"

David's voice was low and calm, as if drawn from the earth beneath them. Percival shrugged. "I see Bonnybield."

David ticked his head back, and glanced down at the boy. "Are you really going to fail our quest so soon?"

Percival turned to respond, but David snapped his fingers toward the valley.

"No, keep looking. You must remember all I said before about Second Sight. Everything you've felt throughout your life—the images perched on the corner of your vision, the instincts you've sensed but were told to reject—it is all real. The Otherworld is ever-present. I'm sure my little display on the street last night confirmed that."

"You mean when you made the lamp flicker? That was your bellirolt power."

Percival thought he could feel David's eyes gleam beside him, and he sensed a mild admonishment from the man.

"Oh, no. Percival, that was magic."

"Well, clearly *some* kind of magic…"

"No, no—bellirolts do have powers, just as any wraith or demon has abilities beyond the human reach, but they are limited. What you saw was magic. The Great Science. It is elemental, woven into the fabric of nature. It's what allows us our Second Sight. *Accept* that, and tell me what you see."

Percival sighed, feeling ridiculous. How was he going to just *see* what was obvious to a Type III Spirit and a three-hundred-year-old demon? All his revelations so far had simply appeared to him, unbidden, simple as a shifting breeze. He closed his eyes in an effort to clear them. Upon reopening, he was greeted with the same view.

Percival shook his head. "I don't—" Even as he spoke, one building below them grew into sharper focus than anything else around it. Like a sudden optical illusion, it seemed to lean toward him, and he *felt* its presence like a tilting weight.

"The Old Steeple…"

"Is that the ruin there?" David asked.

"Aye." Percival nodded to it: a decrepit stone tower on the High Street rising like a crooked finger to the sky. "It used to be the town hall. Damaged by lightning two hundred years ago. Probably the oldest building in Bonnybield."

David nodded, satisfied. "Then that is our next purpose."

They had no sooner started down the slope than an image flashed across Percival's periphery, like a racing sparrow. He stopped, his heart thudding. He knew what he'd seen—but what on earth was it doing here?

"Percival?"

Percival saw David was eyeing him with interest.

"*MacBain*," Percival whispered. His bewilderment was mirrored on David's face. "I saw… the same thing from my dream. MacBain perched on your window—or, the silhouette of him. It just… flew past me."

"MacBain is dead, Percival."

David's tone was so harsh and final Percival felt as though he'd been slapped. He swallowed and did his best to compose himself.

"Aye, o' course…" Hadn't David wanted to know what he saw?

David turned without saying more, pulling a silver case and lighter from his coat. He drew out a cigarette and ignited it as he snaked his way down the hill.

Percival stumbled to catch up. "So what happened after you left Haddington?"

David looked out briefly into the glen.

"I went to join the Jacobite rebellion. I felt I was being lured, as if by a sweet smell many miles north, to the place where Viscount Dundee's army was about to face King William's troops: Killiecrankie Pass." David twisted his head, as if the memory stuck like a foul taste in his throat. He glanced at Percival. "This was before I met the men who taught me the truth of magic. Who taught me not to be subservient to my bellirolt demon. For at that moment, arriving to join the Jacobites, I was thirsting—desperately—for battle. Part of it was certainly the demon within. But I also thought I knew something every other man in that army didn't."

"What was that?" Percival asked.

David exhaled smoke, and a hint of savagery twinkled in his eyes.

"I knew I could not be killed."

The acrid smell of burnt gunpowder filled David's nostrils. He peered down the line of kilt-clad men to his left and saw splinters fly from the trees, as a musket volley from down in the pass struck the forest. A few Highlanders lobbed insults in

Gaelic at the government troops, but most—having played this game all day—just stood, and breathed, and eyed the red-coated mass below.

David's body pulsed with anticipation. He'd been standing on this hillside since early afternoon, watching the government army ooze like spilt blood through a cornfield beneath them, baiting the Jacobites to attack. But the Jacobites were facing the setting sun, and would blind themselves if they charged now. So they waited, and it took all of David's patience to wait with them, for what did his eyes care for the paltry sun?

He shivered in response to his throbbing hunger. This was a different feeling than the draining emptiness he remembered after Craigvaran. No, this was a hot surge every few seconds from a place behind his nose and eyes, some new organ that reminded him of the ecstatic power from the last time he was satiated.

The tip of the sun brushed the opposite ridge of Killie-crankie Pass. David loosened and re-clenched his fingers around his claymore and round targe shield. He'd stolen the weapons from a drunken carter he'd killed at a tavern, a meal that had amounted to a mere drop of water on a parched tongue. His entire journey north he'd felt his body was saving itself for a grand feast, that he had only to follow his mysterious new sense to reach his prize.

Suddenly, the bearded Highlanders beside him exploded with jubilant cheers. David looked left and saw a grey-brown horse turn between the trees and canter along the front line of men. Astride the horse was Viscount Dundee, looking like a modern Achilles in a gleaming cuirass and a helmet adorned with bright feathers.

"I charge you all to remember," he called over the cries of his men, "that upon this day rests the fate of your king and country! I see you before me, MacDonnells; and I hear you, Camerons, and the Clanranald; but shining on the breast of this hill we stand as one people, as true Scotsmen, as God himself has made us!"

David's hands were quivering with suspense now. He recalled that very morning when he'd arrived and knelt before the viscount, and spun a tale of how he, Lord Haddington, had seen his castle ransacked by English soldiers, and was pledging his sword to Dundee's cause. Dundee reminded him that the cause was not his but that of King James, to which David nodded and said he'd sworn allegiance to James upon William's coronation, and thereby came the fate of his home. David could have proven his title by reciting his lineage back to Alexander II, but instead Dundee took David's hand in his own, and said to his officers, "He has the soft hands and face of the nobility. This man was certainly a baron."

Was certainly... David's blood roiled upon hearing his title in the past tense. Now he stood listening to this viscount give the speech *he* ought to be giving, rallying these men to battle who might have been his... "MacLean, Second Battalion," had been Dundee's orders for David's placement. "I'm putting you with men who will keep an eye on you, Haddington, for this is a most unusual circumstance," he'd said. *Let them try and keep their eyes on me*, David thought, as the sun sank lower over the western hill. *I'll kill ten men before these Highlanders have lifted their swords.*

"... And all good men," Dundee cried from his horse, "and King James among them, shall crown you with laurels for your valor today! Long Live our noble King, and long live the church and the people of Scotland!"

A thundering cheer resounded from the army, and David joined them with all the vigor in his trembling body. Dundee took his place at the head of the cavalry line, and then all sound ceased, as if a curtain had been drawn across the hill. As one silent mass, the army began to advance down the hillside.

David followed the example of the men beside him,

crouching behind his shield as he walked. He heard orders barked from the sea of red beneath them, and then a barrage of musket fire crackled through the remaining trees. Men screamed down the line to David's left, but the Jacobites continued their downward march. Another volley exploded, and another. David felt his shield pop and waver as a musket ball embedded itself in it, but this only heightened his desire to charge. By now the front line of Highlanders was nearing the edge of the forest, close to the bottom of the hill, and David could see the wide, sweat-laden eyes of the redcoats staring toward him.

"Ready pistols!" the captain to his right called.

David heard a chorus of clicks as each Highlander drew a pistol and cocked it.

"*Fire!*"

A thousand blasts erupted from the Jacobite line, and on their heels came the hot-blooded roars of the Highlanders. They smacked their sword hilts on the edges of their shields and thrust their blades skyward, as a great pounding of hooves shook the earth. David looked back to his left to see Dundee's horsemen break through the trees, the viscount himself in the lead. The last rays of sunlight shimmered in brilliant orange and gold off his helm, a victory beacon for his men.

"*CHARGE!*"

With a whooping cry, David rose to his full height and plunged forward with the wave of Jacobites. They stormed from the forest into full view of the setting sun, flying toward the enemy. The redcoats, having just fired a volley, were scrambling to affix a new device, the bayonet, to the muzzles of their guns—but they were out of time. The two soldiers facing David were just able to scream and thrust their half-ready weapons forward before he was upon them.

He cleaved his sword once, twice, saw blood arc through the air, and his momentum toppled him over his slain adversaries. The same compelling need to *touch* them surged through him, he obeyed it... and felt the same euphoric rush as when he'd killed Calum and Evander. This time, however, it lasted only a second before subsiding, and he was left charged, stimulated—but not sated. *If I take but a few more, surely the feeling will last longer...*

He was on his feet again, sword and shield ready, and fell upon the next redcoat. Two strokes, and the man was down; one, two, three, and he had another—each time David clutched their falling bodies and received his rejuvenation, but it wasn't enough. *More.* The redcoats were already falling back, trying to run in terror down the pass, but David pursued them, feeling more invigorated with every swing of his blade. He ignored the lancing pains when a bayonet or musket ball ripped his flesh, for his wounds closed as quickly as they appeared. He hurled his round shield like a discus, knocking a captain clear off his horse. He vaulted over the bodies between them and impaled the man with his claymore.

"*Haddington?*"

The word jerked David from his blood-frenzy. The redcoats on foot were in full retreat down the pass, their bayoneted muskets doing little against the axes and swords of the Highlanders. David looked around for who had spoken; the voice was so familiar... then, astride a horse in the government cavalry ahead, he recognized Lord Belhaven.

"*John!*" David roared with laughter. "Where's your champion now? Shall we settle the twenty pound I owe you?"

"What have you *done?*" Belhaven yelled, horrified.

"Off your horse, then!" David approached Belhaven, sword at the ready. "Do you deny your country, you bloated rat? *Off your horse, coward!*"

But the horse, it seemed, had made up its own mind. As David moved toward it, his skin tingling with fire, his sword caked in blood, the animal neighed and whirled, speeding down the pass. David bellowed after it, and charged headlong into the line of enemy cavalry.

※

An hour later, the last glimmers of purple light were receding behind the hills of Killiecrankie. The field of the first charge had grown still, as a horrific tapestry of mangled bodies spread across the earth, and scattered moans floated up into the night.

Mingled with the sounds of agony was a high, giddy voice that wavered in the air, as if singing drunkenly. The voice drew the attention of a pair of Jacobite Highlanders, their bristly faces crusted with blood, dirt, and sweat, and they poked through the bodies until they found its source. Lying on his back, staring up at the first stars of night, was the tall, handsome nobleman—somebody had mentioned he was a baron—who had joined their cause at the last minute. His shirt had been completely slashed from his body, his breeches bore several bullet holes, and though he was streaked with blood, they couldn't see a single wound on his skin. In his right hand he clutched half a claymore, bathed in crimson.

The Baron smiled upon seeing the Highlanders' faces over him. It was a gleeful, intoxicated smile.

"We won... did we not?" he asked.

"Aye..." one of the Highlanders responded. "Lord Dundee has fallen, though. Shot right thro' the breast as he led the charge."

"Dundee... oh..." The Baron drifted away for a moment. "*Bonnie Dundee.* He was so grand... his helm was like fire..."

The Highlanders looked at one another, and then the Baron's hand shot up and grabbed one of theirs, pulling it toward him with startling strength.

"We *won*, lads. We cut them to pieces."

"Aye, certainly." The Highlanders both nodded, trying to appease the madman. He nodded in return, a wicked light in his green eyes that neither Highlander would ever forget. The

Baron settled back, and began to hum a discordant tune with a dazed grin.

"That man is richt unco," one Highlander muttered, shuddering, as they backed away. "I saw him cleave five horsemen tae bits single-handedly—*mounted horsemen,* mind ye! He must 'a killed forty men today…" When they regrouped with their victorious comrades the next morning, and even when their army disintegrated in battle a month later, the Highlanders did not see this Baron in their number. And they were glad for it. *Perhaps he was but a ghost,* they thought; *strange things happen to your senses on the battlefield…*

They both did remember that they heard the Baron laughing deliriously as they walked away into the night.

Chapter Twelve

A Noble Man

David's head snapped up to the speckled light of the forest. He saw muted hues of orange and blue through the trees; it must be late afternoon. *Or morning?* The recent days had spun around him in a blur. He often came to his senses in strange places he thought he'd seen before, and just as he was about to recognize them, he'd find himself somewhere entirely different. As he moved, he noticed he was walking bent over. He looked down and saw his hands were full: under one arm he carried a thick fur cloak, dotted with blood, and under the other... *under the other was somebody else's arm.*

David retched and flung everything to the forest floor, scurrying away from it. The second object was indeed a man's arm, severed at the bicep, a claymore locked in its grip. Judging by the red trail behind him, he'd been dragging the limb for some time. He staggered against a tree, ignoring the blood he smeared as he cradled his head. That was when the images returned: a dozen Highland cattle—big, shaggy beasts with hair over their eyes—and the five men in plaid who were herding them along a moor. Then a band of Highlanders appeared and charged the group, brandishing axes and screaming *"Death to the Campbell!"* David felt a familiar tingling sensation behind his nose and eyes: the sweet, stimulating scent that meant food.

He saw talons grow from his fingertips like an eagle swooping as he set upon the attackers, felt the rapture that meant he'd achieved his kill... and then he'd ended up in this forest. With a fresh claymore for his empty scabbard, and a cloak to cover his fraying clothes. David kneeled and shoveled dirt with his powerful hands until he'd made a shallow hole, and buried the severed arm in it. It was a pitiful gesture. But he wanted to somehow make amends.

A few hours later the sun had set, and David settled himself against a mossy tree. He adjusted his new claymore so he could draw his legs up to his chest, and wrapped his body in the fur cloak, which smelled of wood smoke and charred meat. It was not a position for warmth, as frosty weather bothered him little; rather, it gave him a small sense of comfort. An involuntary shudder rocked him, as he tried to stifle the memories he knew were coming. Times like this, alone in the wilderness, all the thoughts he'd kept at bay under the daylight flooded mercilessly to his head. He thought of looking out on Haddington's plains from Galanforde, Eliza singing to him while he was ill, a smile his mother had shown him once, learning to ride with his father, smelling the air at Craigvaran— and, hard as he might repress it, the final, horrid night. The fire, the anger he couldn't control, the sight from the parapet... He couldn't grapple with everything he'd destroyed. He couldn't even grapple with where he'd been and what he'd done since then. He felt like a small, rotten piece of his former self.

Suddenly, he lifted his head. He'd heard something— something *musical...* was it singing? He strained his ears, not wanting to move from this position of solace. Was this another of the voices he'd been hearing for weeks? Another eerie screech or wail that floated through his head at night? Then he heard it again. It *was* singing, somewhere behind him in the forest. It even seemed to be happy singing.

David clambered to his feet, curiosity outstripping his fear.

He'd seen too many strange lights hovering in these woods, or bodiless eyes watching him by night, to be frightened by singing. The forest was black as tar, but his vision had adjusted to making his way in the dark. He crept toward the sound, and after a few moments he smelled smoke. A bit of light appeared ahead, flickering from a clearing. David scoured his surroundings for any sign of movement, but this didn't feel like a trap. It was a man's voice singing, and it echoed shamelessly to the high canopy of trees:

> "*Oh, Bessie Bell and Mary Gray, they were twa' bonnie lassies!*
> *They biggit a bower on yon burnbrae, an' theekit it o'er wi' rashes!*"

David stepped in his ragged boots to a tree near the clearing. A small campfire was burning, over which a rabbit was roasting on a makeshift spit. Various items had been strewn about the fire: a satchel, musket, and targe shield. Sitting cross-legged before the fire, his back to David, was a short man clad in a kilt and armed with a claymore. David couldn't see the man's face for his ratty mop of hair, but he was amused at how the Highlander swayed back and forth in song, oblivious to anything else in the forest.

> "*Fair Bessie Bell I lo'ed yestreen, an' thocht I ne'er could alter;*
> *But Mary Gray's twa' pawkie een gar'd a' my fancy falter!*
> *Oh, Bessie Bell an' Mary Gray, they were twa' bonnie lassies...*"

David couldn't help but think there was something familiar about the voice and the odd little figure, though he didn't look like one of the Highlanders from the skirmish that day.

David crept from behind his tree to get a better look. Just as he did, his torn boot slipped on a patch of moss.

"Bessie's hair's like a lint-tap, she smiles like—"

The Highlander's singing broke off, and he froze. Hardly a second later, he'd jumped to his feet, spun around, and brought a carbine to his shoulder. David hadn't even noticed the second gun.

"Who goes there?" the Highlander called. "Speak now!"

That was when David remembered: it was the Highlander who'd appeared on his cliff at Craigvaran. The man who'd killed the flying beast MacBain, who'd tried to pledge his life to David. *Cardross*, David recalled. *That was his name.*

"Lower your weapon, Cardross," David said softly. He stepped forward until he could feel the campfire light upon him, and raised his hands. He remembered the man's deadly accuracy at Craigvaran, and didn't feel like suffering the painful—albeit temporary—wound to the head.

"You halt right where you are." Cardross's voice was firm and sharp. "Identify yourself, as I said."

"Your name is Cardross, is it not?" David's mouth felt distant as he spoke, his voice scratchy and unsupported. He couldn't recall the last time he'd spoken to anybody.

"Aye..." Cardross replied. "What's it to you?"

"You once saved me from a flying beast. Do you remember?"

Cardross's eyes narrowed, then flew wide open.

"Lord Haddington?" he choked.

David had barely started to nod when the young man leapt back behind his campfire for protection. He kept the carbine trained on David.

"Stay where you are!" he yelled. "Not one step closer! I can hit your Swell from right here!"

"Hit my what? What the devil is the matter with you, man?"

"*You're* the de'il, is what! Are there any more wi' you? Here in the wood? *Are there?*"

"Any more what? Put that gun down, you imbecile! *Put it down, I say!* I want to talk to you."

Cardross's head jerked back in surprise. "*Talk* to me? What the blazes for?"

Suddenly a spike of flame shot up between the two men, and Cardross looked down and howled in dismay. His spitted rabbit had caught fire and was charring by the second, and he looked torn between keeping his gun pointed at David and saving his supper. He tried to snatch the burning animal with one hand but yanked it back in pain. David realized this might have been his best meal in a month.

"Look, let me…" David strode to the fire and plucked the flaming rabbit from its clutches, ignoring the burn that seared his hand for a moment. He smothered the flames on the meat, leaving a crusty black shell that looking anything but appetizing, and offered it unceremoniously to Cardross.

Cardross's gaze flashed from the rabbit to David and back again, until he finally stepped around the fire and snatched his supper. He kept a wary eye on David.

"You are David Dunbar, Baron of Haddington, and a bellirolt, are you no?"

David's stomach plummeted upon hearing his old title again.

"I don't know what I am, Cardross," he said. "I… I hoped you might help me."

Cardross cocked his head. The rabbit, all but forgotten, dangled by his side. "Oh. Well… I'm sorry for the gun, then. It's just that I saw you get turned into a bellirolt. And I hunt bellirolts, see?" He shrugged as if to say, *Well, what can you do?* "I thought you'd come to kill me. If you just want to talk, well… I suppose you can take a seat. Sir."

☙❧

They sat without speaking for several minutes, the fire crackling between them. In its fluttering light, before another human being, David quickly became conscious of his appearance. He pulled the cloak tighter around his miserable clothes, and rubbed his jawline out of habit. He'd been amazed at how smooth his skin had remained since Galanforde; only a few whiskers met his touch.

Cardross was munching his charred supper as best he could. He glanced up.

"I heard what happened to your castle."

David nodded dourly. "Has word gone round about the mad baron who burnt down his home?"

Cardross's eyes widened in fear of having offended David. "Oh no! Just that Lord Haddington's beautiful castle had burnt to the ground, an' he with it. An' then I heard tell o' Highlanders who saw you at the Battle o' Killiecrankie. Well, they described somebody wi' the *look* o' you, but I knew. I said to myself, 'Aye, that'll be him.' It makes sense: you bellirolts are drawn to battle."

"Cardross, what is this creature you say I am, and how do you know so much about it?"

Cardross swallowed and smacked his lips together. "A *bellirolt,* sir, like I told you at Craigvaran—"

"And please—" David cut in, "stop calling me 'sir.' Any fool can see I am no baron."

"Well, whether you have the title or no, sir—beg your pardon—you're a man o' the finest breedin'. No bellirolt can take that from you." He paused as if for emphasis. "Very well, then, Dunbar—"

David cringed. *Nobody* had called him that before. "*David,* Cardross. Just call me David."

"Very good, David, then. An' I am William." Cardross set his mostly-eaten rabbit aside. "A *bellirolt* is a kind o' demon. Lives inside your body. Feeds upon your most violent energies.

An' the only way a bellirolt is passed from person to person is through touch at the moment when the old host dies."

"Well if it lives inside a person's body, then somebody must cast it out," David concluded. "Through exorcism."

Cardross chuckled. "What, like the Lord Jesus in the Gospels? The Son o' God might 'a had that power, but you won't be seein' no man today exorcisin' no demon. Never mind what ol' James VI blabbered about in his *Demonology*. No, the only way to kill a bellirolt demon is to kill its host, an' no let it touch another man as it lies dyin'."

"And that's what that man—MacBain—was? A bellirolt?"

"Aye, sir. *David*, sorry. He was a bit of a madman afore he was turned, though. A good many bellirolts meld into society, so nobody knows the difference 'twixt them an' a normal man or woman, but no MacBain. He lived like a vagrant, fancied himself 'Scourge o' the Nobles.'"

David recalled MacBain's putrid stable smell. Given his life now, he could hardly blame the bellirolt for it.

"I'd wager that's why he was after you," Cardross went on, "why he scarred you: to mark you for death. It's an old bellirolt ritual."

"But how did you kill him? I've been shot and stabbed many times, and the wound merely vanishes. And *why* did you kill him whilst he was holding me in midair?"

"Oh, aye…" Cardross's blue eyes darkened in a way that reminded David, torturously, of Calum's expression that last night. "That was a grave mistake o' mine. See, I come from Inverness. As did MacBain. My family had a farm there— mither, faither, four sisters—an' one day MacBain an' his gang o' bellirolts arrived an' killed 'em all. Lookin' for a feast, I'm sure. I hid in the stable. I was eleven years old."

"Great God," David said. A deep ache for Cardross heaved through him; losing his parents at fifteen now felt trifling. "William, I'm so sorry."

"Thank you." Cardross's eyes fell. "But I decided, on that day, I was goin' to learn about this menace—these brutes that murder anybody they please. I was goin' to find every one that attacked my family, an' kill them. So I read, traveled, talked to town elders. An' I trained myself to fight. I found out what these bellirolts were: deadly supernatural beings, who look like humans and move in our world, for they all used to *be* humans. But once turned, they have prodigious strength, keener senses, claws that infect all they touch—an' they gain more powers as they age. As you saw wi' MacBain, some can lift objects, even *themselves,* off the ground wi' their minds. An' their bodies— includin' yours—are impervious to harm, save one spot: the Black Swell."

David recalled the searing pain he'd felt in the water when MacBain died. *So that* was *a demon invading my body.* The thought felt like it should have come from somebody else's life. David had been destined to be a grand general, not a murdering vagabond. He touched the thick knot on the back of his neck.

"This?"

"Aye." Cardross nodded. "Filled with the blood o' the demon. That's why I shot MacBain how I did: one to stop him movin'—an' I hoped he'd drop you, or you'd let go—an' another to hit his Swell an' finish him. What I didn't foresee was that he'd still be holdin' you as he died. A bellirolt's death grip is an impossible thing to break."

David stared at his hands as the firelight quivered across them. Every line was creased with dirt, from places he couldn't even name. He remembered them bathed in blood on the last night at Galanforde.

"So I am cursed, then," he said in a hollow voice. "Doomed to… live violently the rest of my days."

"Oh no, David…" Cardross leaned forward. "That's just the thing, see. That's why I pledged my life to you at

Craigvaran—why I'm still willin' to do so. You have this demon within you, aye. Naught can change that now. But you don't have to let it *overcome* you. You don't have to end up like MacBain."

"I don't know, William..." David rubbed his face. "These past days—weeks, I can't tell how long—my mind has not been my own. Just today I came to my senses stumbling through the wood, after throwing myself into a clan battle on the moor."

"As I said, bellirolts have an innate sense o' where and when combat is to happen. You can't help it. What clans were fightin'?"

"I don't know. The defenders were Campbells, I believe."

"Ah..." Cardross raised his eyebrows. "The other might 'a been the MacDonald, still avengin' Glen Coe."

"Glen Coe?"

"Aye. Campbells massacred MacDonalds there, back in '92."

David's chest froze. "'92? Cardross, what year is it?"

Cardross's eyes swelled larger, again evoking the memory of Calum. "Oh David, you don't know... it's the Year of Our Lord 1699."

David felt as if his brain had sunk to the back of his skull. "I've been out here, on my own... for ten years?"

Cardross seemed to search for encouraging words. "How much time did you think had passed?"

"*Weeks,* maybe a month, I don't know! How the devil could I have been wandering for a decade? I hardly feel a day older!"

"That's part o' bein' a bellirolt. They call it *demortisation,* a changin' o' the humors in your body, as everythin' adapts to the demon. Bellirolts age prodigious slow, see. It might be five or six more years afore your hair grows another inch."

David remembered the lack of whiskers on his face. Would it really be that long before he'd have to shave?

"William, how many years am I to live as this creature?"

Cardross shrugged. "Hundreds. Most bellirolts are killed, o' course, afore they die of old age. It's the nature o' the warrior life. Like as no, there are some over a thousand years old."

David's eyes fell shut in anguish. "Cardross... I cannot live for hundreds of years. Not like this. I killed my own cousins, do you know that? That's how my castle burned. I cannot control this force inside me. It demands satisfaction: it's only at peace when I've killed, and afterwards I'm revolted by myself."

David looked up to see Cardross's brow knitted in sympathy. "There is hope for you... as you're no proud of all you've done."

"I couldn't be. Not when I only feel sated killing people."

"Well..." Cardross was struggling to be delicate. "That *is* what's sating you. The lifeblood of a bellirolt is no food nor drink. You'll never need them again. If you are to survive you must take human lives, an' touch them as they perish, so you bring them into you. Your cousins' souls are feedin' you right now."

"My..." David's mind felt numb. "So they will never be at rest?"

Cardross shrugged again. "If one day you die, without passin' on your bellirolt to another, their souls will be released. At least that's what most folk believe."

David's eyes fell to the glowing wood of the fire. As the flames split it into a checkered red, it looked like a disease.

"Then I am the devil."

"*No,* David. You're an ordinary man who was turned into a monster against his will. You have an awful curse, aye. But you also have incredible abilities. You're a near-invincible warrior! Think what you can do!"

David shook his head. "I shan't live a life of murder."

"Well you're goin' to have to!"

"I don't *have* to do anything, Cardross!" David exploded.

"My destiny—all my ambitions have been stolen from me! All I ever wanted was to make a difference for Scotland—"

"Then you still can! There are *thousands* o' bellirolts all over the world, armies o' them. An' right now, as we speak, they're killin' innocent people—people like my family! These are the most dangerous, savage creatures on God's earth, an' what better service can you do than to help bring them down?"

David wanted to believe Cardross, but all he could feel was hate for every moment his existence was prolonged. A thought flashed in his mind: *I ought to maul that little wretch—it's his fault this happened to me...* But he shook it from his head.

"This is not the life I choose to live," he said resolutely.

Cardross smiled. "David... somethin' tells me you haven't seen enough o' the world to know which life you choose. An' certainly not enough to know which life has chosen *you.*"

David stared at the brash little man. How did he know what David had and hadn't seen?

Cardross rose and walked around the fire, kneeling at David's side. "The reason I am here, in these woods, is that I seek somebody. I've sought him for years, since afore I met you at Craigvaran. He's a teacher, from an ancient order o' warriors that's only whispered of these days. But their order was founded to fight the bellirolts."

"Then I can only hinder your quest, William."

Cardross shook his head and smiled again. "David, this order is legendary. They're thought to be descendants o' the Druids, the old keepers o' lore an' magic. An' I finally know where this teacher can be found. It's several days' north o' here, through dangerous country, an' I could use your help. An' it certainly seems you could use mine."

David continued to be amazed at the audacity of young Cardross. He presumed to know what David needed? *He does know far more about my condition than I... What if this teacher could tell me even more?*

"Allow me to renew my pledge," Cardross said, eyes blazing with eagerness. "Allow me to help you, David, as I am responsible for your bein' a bellirolt. If we can find this man, together, I warrant you we can make the difference you speak of. We can't make you human again, but we can make certain nobody else has to endure what you have."

We can't make you human again... The miserable words echoed in David's head. He studied the Highlander, trying to see past those bright sapphire eyes.

"How do I know I can trust you, Cardross?"

"David Dunbar..." Cardross settled back on his haunches. "I am swearin' my life to a bellirolt. You think *you* are worried about trustin' *me?*"

David's lips fluttered. It was as much of a smile as he would allow.

"Well. Who is this teacher we seek?"

Chapter Thirteen

Doneval Graven

D avid awoke the next morning to birds trilling overhead. He could smell the ashy remains of the fire beside him, and heard Cardross's placid snores a few feet away. He felt unusually well rested, and for a moment he supposed it was thanks to the new cloak he'd used as a pillow. Then he remembered he was due to begin a journey with this young Highlander. For the first time in ages, he was waking up with a purpose.

David rose and buckled his sword belt around his waist. He realized it must be late autumn, as the trees were almost barren, and the mist hung heavy and unyielding. Cardross was curled like a cat near the last smoking log, wrapped in his kilt.

Graven, David thought. *That was what Cardross said this teacher's name was.* The notion of seeking out some old Druid buried in the Highlands seemed more desperate the longer David thought about it, but what else could he do? He was without family, friends, or a home, and so far this eccentric Highlander was the only man who'd shown him any sympathy. He just prayed that when his need to kill arose again, he could stop himself from turning on his companion.

When Cardross awoke, he donned his weapons and scattered the ashes. David realized how underprepared he must

146

look: he carried only a sword and cloak, while Cardross still had two guns, a claymore, a targe, and a satchel brimming with supplies.

"I must needs live on my feet!" Cardross beamed. "Off we go!" And they started forward.

According to Cardross, they'd spent the night a few miles outside of Torcastle in southern Inverness-shire—a revelation to David—and this Graven fellow lived in the mountains of Kintail, nearly sixty miles to the northwest. The pair emerged from the forest as the mist was melting, and mounted a ridge stretching away from the rising sun. Farmsteads appeared on either side, nestled into whatever corner of arable land they could find.

David was impressed by the swiftness with which Cardross's short legs carried him. When they did stop to rest, Cardross would plop down upon the earth, not shedding a single article he was carrying, and swig water from a sheepskin pouch. David was content to stretch on the grass and observe the clouds ambling across the sky. He no longer thought twice about the lack of a parched feeling in his throat.

And so they traveled, bellirolt and Highlander, following the curves of the ridges as they wound their way north. They crossed barren hilltops on which no man could live, jumped through gullies mottled with rocks, and skirted the edges of lochs with glassy waters, where David felt the air penetrate him, calm him. For at least those moments, he didn't feel so far from human.

They stopped only in secluded areas where Cardross judged they were safe. He preferred to avoid roads so as not to draw attention, and chattered while they walked about any topic that landed in his mind, from bawdy jokes to legends of clan war to his experience hunting bellirolts.

"I don't know how many I've killed," he said, chewing on a hunk of cheese. Night had fallen and they were sitting by a fire on the shore of Loch Quoich, near a stone bridge whose parapet had crumbled. David was puffing on a clay pipe that Cardross had dug from his satchel. The tobacco was far from quality, but the comfort of doing something familiar—something human—helped him relax.

"You'll find, David, you must be careful who you ask in these parts about bellirolts. Everybody knows about them, but few will speak o' them. An' many that do make 'em into ghost stories. See, so few people know what a bellirolt truly is an' how to fight one, they never think one might be your neighbor, or your bedmate in an inn, or—"

"The noble in the next castle," David finished. He removed the pipe from his mouth and shook his head. "William… if there really are more bellirolts like me, who populate the world alongside humans, killing constantly, how has there not been an all-out war against them? I'm an educated man—I've never once heard of them."

"Oh, there *has* been a war." Cardross nodded. "Problem is, society hasn't noticed it. Most o' the time it's hidden in the wars o' men. As long as there 'a been legions o' bellirolts, there 'a been folk who dare to oppose them."

"Like this order you mentioned."

"Just so. Look around you, now." Cardross nodded to their surroundings. "All is quiet. All is still. Most people don't know what really lurks in the darkness, beyond the fire. Oh, they know deep down, but they would never admit it. So they tell jokes and stories, sing songs—anythin' to ward off that unsettlin' feelin', the one that just doesn't make sense."

David shrugged. "It's natural for man to fear the dark."

"Perhaps. But nobody questions *why*. Nobody suspects that maybe there are other *worlds* that come alive when we sleep, other battles that occur in the shadows of our own."

David snorted. "Battles nobody would notice? Come now."

"Often they occur in places like this, my friend. On the fringe: in glens, forests, where any who dwell have heard o' strange creatures all their lives."

"So you'd have me believe every fairy tale I've been told," David surmised.

"Fairy tale?" Cardross lifted his thin black eyebrows. "Have you actually looked around you since you've been on your own? Have you *observed* the night?"

"It's dark, William. There's nothing to see."

"Wrong." Cardross popped one last morsel of cheese into his mouth and settled back on his elbows. "Try again."

David furrowed his brow. He was tired, and not in the mood for games. He looked at the loch, saw the dark infinity of the water, and shrugged.

"Again," said Cardross. "You have bellirolt eyes; you can see much better than I. Try over yonder. By the bridge."

David had to turn around to see the bridge, so he forced an agitated sigh from his lungs. As his eyes adjusted he could make out the vague outline of the stone, with several arches over the water… exactly like Nungate Bridge in Haddington. He cringed and turned back to the fire.

"It's a simple bridge," he said, and shoved the pipe back in his mouth. As he did so, a sensation rushed over him, distinct as a blast of cool air, prickling from the base of his spine to the nape of his neck. His first thought was that something was approaching him from behind, but that made no sense.

Across the fire, Cardross hadn't moved a muscle. "Again."

David scowled, but turned back, as slowly as he could, toward the bridge.

"What if I told you," Cardross said quietly, "there was once a creature—an otherworldly, humanlike thing; we'll call it a fairy—who used to hover about this loch on autumn nights. Many, many years ago."

As the bridge came back into view, David let his eyes

adjust to the dark. He saw the water, the long shape of stone…
and then, under the first arch, something moved.

"The fairy was lookin' for its lover, see. A beautiful lady
who'd been cast out by her laird. Love is no limited to
humanity, you know. Well, it so happened the lady was
banished for bein' with another fellow—not our fairy friend.
An' thus, the fairy succumbed to despair. An' despair *changes*
such creatures."

As David continued to look, he saw the outline of a
rounded back beneath the first arch. It was as if something—
some*body,* deformed and grotesque—were hunched on the
bank, digging half-heartedly in the mud. Every now and then a
bulbous head, far too small for such a thick, rotund body, rose
and looked about. A glassy eye flashed in David's direction, and
his spine went rigid. But the eye took no more than a moment's
notice of its visitors, then turned back to the shadows.

"That's what they call a troll, David," Cardross went on.
"A creature, mutated by its sorrow, doomed to scavenge by
night under a bridge on Loch Quoich. This is the nature o'
creatures o' the night. We feel them, but we pay them no mind.
We tell ourselves it's only our imagination. What we fail to
accept is that imagination *is* intuition. The troll is real: we can
see him if we only look."

David continued to look, entranced. The fire popped
behind him, Cardross settled down to rest, but David kept
watching the outline of the troll, as the moon-brushed water
glistened behind it. It was like trying to hold onto a dream
while he hovered on the brink of waking, so he fought to go on
watching, until the pipe grew cold in his hand and his body
sank into sleep.

The next morning Cardross had already scattered the ashes by
the time David pried open his eyes.

"Evenin' red an' mornin' grey, help the traveler on his way! Up wi' ye, David!"

It was indeed a smoky, grey morning, which did nothing to rouse David. He stood and rubbed his eyes, casting a surreptitious glance back toward the bridge. Only hints of its stone outline were visible in the mist, and there was no movement beneath it. The troll had disappeared with the coming of day.

Cardross said they were about to pass the last village where any goods could be bought, and he needed to replenish his food and gunpowder.

"Then buy what you need," David said, "and I'll meet you on the road afterward."

Cardross smiled. "I think you ought to come with me, David."

David paused as he was tightening his sword belt. "I shall do no such thing. I'm following you to find this teacher, not to fraternize along the way."

"At some point you're goin' to have to talk to people aside from me."

"I am not ready, Cardross—"

"You can start—" Cardross drew a small bundle from his satchel— "by bathin'. Once in a decade wouldn't hurt you." He tossed the bundle to David, who unfolded it and found several small, soft rocks inside.

"What's this?"

"Lavender soap." Cardross grinned. "Pilfered it from a lass down in Greenock." He nodded toward the mist-laden loch. "Go on, then!"

David shot a severe look at Cardross, but peeled off his ragged clothes and waded into the frigid water.

An hour later, feeling invigorated and refreshed, David accompanied Cardross into the village of Kinloch Hourn between the hills. After so long in the wilderness, the lavender scent that now clung to him was overwhelming, and he thought he might be more self-conscious than if he hadn't bathed at all. The villagers they saw were clothed in little more than muddy rags, and David hid as much of himself in his cloak as possible.

Cardross finally found a pair of tottering old men who were kind enough to help, though they answered his "Good day, sirs" with a string of nonsense-words.

"You're in luck, David," Cardross said over his shoulder. "They only speak Gaelic here." Thankfully, so did Cardross, and he continued the conversation in a rolling, lilting tongue David had never heard. Cardross exchanged some tools from his satchel for bread and salted beef, then pointed to the hills where he and David were headed. All of a sudden the old men began speaking with great urgency and shaking their heads. Their eyes grew wide with terror.

"*Ayr-henégan!*" one said in a hoarse whisper. He pointed at the road leading out of town. "*Ayr-henégan a Cinn Tàile!*"

"They say the 'Shaman Graven'—that's what they call him—lives in an old fortress in the mountains o' Kintail, a few miles east of Loch Duich," Cardross said to David. "But they also say bellirolts rule those mountains."

"*Ayr-henégan:* that's Gaelic for 'bellirolt?'" David asked.

"That's what it means, but it's a tongue much older than Gaelic. No the sort o' word you hear often."

David glanced around and noticed they were garnering suspicious stares from the other locals. Some looked as though Cardross had just cursed the entire village.

"*Tapadh leat,*" Cardross thanked the two old men. "We'd best be goin', David. They'll no be trustin' us now." He sealed the food in his satchel and marched through the mud past the last little huts, David at his heels.

The next day the pair entered the mountains of Kintail, cresting a windy ridge topped with thick yellow grass. Though they were both on their guard after the villagers' warning, David felt rejuvenated by the climb, and gloried in the view around him. Stark, barren peaks undulated for miles in every direction: a stunning, dramatic beauty compared to the sprawling greenery of Haddington. *This*, he thought, *was where my Galanforde should have been.*

Cardross tied back his thick hair, and pointed at a glassy reflection in the distance.

"That there is Loch Duich," he said. "And we're due east from it now, so we ought to be within a mile o' this fort. Trouble is—" he surveyed the hills around them— "I don't see one measly sign o' life anywhere."

At that moment, the sharp tingling sensation exploded behind David's nose and eyes. He shook his head reflexively, but it persisted. His gaze was suddenly pulled to a swath of trees off the side of the ridge.

"Something is happening," he muttered to Cardross. The deep, anticipatory feeling of hunger began to spread through his body.

"What is it?"

"Down the hill there..." David recognized the signal now: his body told him it was food, but food meant *battle*. Dread lanced through him. Somewhere beneath them, any moment now—

"Somebody is about to die." *And by God, if I can stop a murder this time, I will.* He'd barely had the thought, and he was off.

He plunged like a battering ram down the ridge. He heard Cardross urging him to stop but ignored it. The Highlander was a good tracker; he could follow. David dove into a thick pine forest, heading toward a ravine. His left hand clutched his claymore in its scabbard; his right grabbed his cloak to keep it from snagging on branches. He plowed on, letting his feet find the ground they needed, until the tingling behind his face shifted in tone—as if vibrating at a different frequency—and his head flashed to the left. *There.* He dashed to a rocky ledge and peered over.

He was standing above a path that snaked through the woods along the side of the slope, and on this path two adolescent boys were walking. They were dressed in ragged kilts and cloaks, and led a sturdy chestnut horse pulling a cart of chopped wood. All three moved in silence, heads bowed as they watched the ground before them.

Suddenly the horse's ears pricked up, and it tried to yank its head back from the boys' grasp. A second later, David saw why. Two dark-looking men rocketed forward from the other side of the path. They sprang from tree to rock to earth like David imagined jungle cats might, and let out horrible roaring sounds as they landed. *Those can only be bellirolts,* he thought, *and in no way can these boys stop them...*

David's legs reacted before the thought had reached them. He took a running leap from the ledge, soared twenty feet through the air, and landed between the startled travelers and the bellirolts. He drew his claymore.

"*Leave them be,*" he snarled.

The bellirolts, standing with claws spread from their grimy hands, looked at one another in confusion. Their hair was long and unkempt, and they wore matching black robes with dark fur vests and claymores at their sides.

"Who's yer captain?" growled one. "Are ye loyal tae the Dark Legion of Orgeron?"

"I don't know what you speak of, and I care not a *fig,*" David spat. "But you will leave this instant. Both of you."

At this both bellirolts reared up and unhooked their claymores.

"Curse ye for a traitor!" yelled one. All David saw was the

flash of both blades, and they flew into the air toward him.

One boy behind him screamed. David found himself doing the only thing that made sense: he stepped forward under his attackers and skewered one straight through the groin. There was a screech of pain, and the bellirolt fell to the ground on top of him.

"The Swell, David! *Aim for the neck!*"

Cardross had arrived on the ledge above them. David realized that the bellirolt he'd stabbed was not dead; he was writhing like a fish on top of David, trying to wrench his body away from the claymore. In one violent kick, David jumped up and freed himself and the sword. The other bellirolt was on him in an instant, swinging his claymore at the exact point on David's neck that Cardross had indicated. How had David forgotten this? Thinking now that it was a miracle he'd survived Killiecrankie, David ducked the blow and cleaved the bellirolt's sword-arm from his body. He then thrust his own blade straight through the bellirolt's neck. The effect was instantaneous, and the creature dropped like a stone to the ground.

Inky liquid from the punctured Black Swell dotted the path. The horse was rearing and trying to back away, as the boys did their best to calm him. The bellirolt David had skewered had recovered now, but rather than attack David, he arched his neck and let out a thundering roar to the forest that rattled every bone in David's body. David raised his sword again and advanced on the bellirolt, but the creature was too swift and flipped backward out of David's reach. Again, he roared.

"The game's up, David!" Cardross skidded down the slope to David's side. "There'll be more on their way any moment— get these lads out o' here!"

David nodded and ran around the panic-stricken horse to the cart. He cut the horse's harness, grabbed its bridle, and sheathed his sword.

"Up you go!" He hoisted the two boys upon the horse's back. "Ride for your home. Don't stop or look back! And don't follow this path again! *Heeah!*" He slapped the horse's hindquarter, and it tore off down the path.

The first bellirolt, however, was not finished. He ceased his roaring and bounded after them, almost matching the speed of the galloping horse.

"William…" David said, but Cardross was ready. He'd already un-slung the musket from his shoulder, cocked it, and took half a breath to aim. There was a blast of smoke, and the bellirolt crumpled to the grassy path. The horse with its riders galloped around the corner of the hill and disappeared.

It was the total stillness that permeated the forest that told David they were not out of danger. The strange spot behind his face was tingling again, but now the signal was coming from all directions, and his head rose to the woods around him. He nearly choked at what he saw.

The forest was full of bellirolts. They had appeared noise-lessly and stood as still as the trees, staring down at the unfortunate pair beneath them. All were dressed like the two warriors David and Cardross had just killed: black robe, fur over-garment, and a sword at the hip. Not a single one stirred or made a threat. *There must be over fifty of them*, David thought. *Dear God, we are finished.*

"We dinnae see many travelers in these parts. An' certainly not ones who are so *good* at killin'."

David and Cardross spun to see who was addressing them. From up the hill, beyond the cart that lay abandoned on the path, one of the bellirolts stepped forward. His black robe was finer than the others, with gold trim and an ornate, embroidered sword belt. His face was covered in a thick black beard, and his eyes—almost equally dark—shone with malice. David had to fight the urge to shrink beneath his gaze: this was as fearsome a Highland warrior as he'd ever seen.

"An' whilst I admire an able swordsman any day, ye must understand, lads: I take great offense at ye murderin' my lieutenants."

David edged closer to Cardross, his right hand on the grip of his sword. He was scanning both ends of the path for an escape, but he'd seen how these creatures moved. As if in response to David's thought, the lead bellirolt flicked up his hand. His dark robe fluttered, and from its folds a long, silver dagger shot toward David and Cardross. They were about both to draw their claymores when the dagger halted in midair, poised with its tip just beyond David's head.

David's jaw dropped in horror. He'd seen MacBain fly through the air—but this was what Cardross had spoken of that first night in the woods. Bellirolts moving other objects *using their minds.* Could this one stab them without lifting a finger?

"*Ye* are a bellirolt. A young one, from the Lowlands; 'at's plain as day," the leader said to David. "But ye…"

The dagger shifted in midair to point at Cardross's head.

"Ye look tae be human. In fact…" the leader crooned, "ye're the one they call the Hunter, aye? The little weasel wha fancies himself protector o' humanity. Word has it ye killed MacBain at North Berwick."

Cardross was staring a hot stream of hatred up the hill.

"I take it from yer silence I am correct!" the leader bellowed in triumph. "This is quite a find, is it no, lads?" He flicked his wrist, and the dagger flashed by David's face again before speeding back up the hill to the leader's hand.

"As you have correctly identified us, Master Scholar," David said in his most blasé voice, "perhaps you wouldn't mind introducing yourself?"

A chorus of chuckles echoed from the hillside, and a few of the bellirolts muttered insults. But the leader raised his hand, and the sounds ceased. He spoke in a steely voice, abandoning all mirth now that his identity had been questioned.

"Ye shall remember me, here an' in the afterlife, as Arran Deuchar. Lord o' Kintail." David noticed Cardross stiffen even more, keeping his baleful gaze fixed on Deuchar. The bellirolt lord continued: "An' though yer ignorance tries my patience, I shall offer ye one chance for mercy. Ye ken the ways o' war, I see that. If ye swear fealty tae me an' the Dark Legion, I'll only kill yer human lackey today. What say ye?"

David glanced over the dark-robed warriors perched on the slope like vultures—more creatures of carrion than human beings. He felt something like a glow of excitement in his chest, as if his own demon were tempted by the offer.

"*David.*" Cardross spoke in a whisper, still keeping his eyes on Deuchar. "You remember I told you I was intent on findin' all the bellirolts who'd killed my family?"

David nodded, and Cardross squared his jaw. "I've repaid their kindness in turn. All of 'em. Save one."

David looked at his young guide, and understood now the fire that burned in his stare. A wave of guilt heaved through him. Cardross had only wanted David's help to find the teacher Graven, and now David had led him into a deathtrap.

"It seems I owe you a grim apology for this, William."

Cardross broke his stare to look at David, and his face softened. "You were tryin' to save those boys' lives…"

"I pray we did save their lives. Together."

Cardross's eyes brightened for a moment.

"And now," David said, "I am going to help you honor the lives of your family." He stepped forward, and drew his sword.

"I was wondering, *Lord* Deuchar," David called out, "if you might be able to assist me. You see, I'm frightfully inexperienced at spilling the blood of another bellirolt." David raised the tip of his blade, examining the inky liquid on its surface. "So far, my count is only one. Would you be so kind as to offer yourself for practice?"

The bellirolt lord smiled: a sinister, heart-stopping curl of the lips.

"Yer folly disappoints me, Lowlander. But yer limbs will dae nicely tae hang at the corners o' my dominion. *Legion!*" He raised his dagger high. "*CHARGE!*"

A collective roar shook the slope. At the same moment, fifty bellirolts lifted themselves into the air, drew their swords, and flew down toward the path, hair and robes whipping behind them.

"We stand together, David!" Cardross yelled. David raised his claymore, heard Cardross's carbine explode beside him, saw a spatter of dark blood—and the bellirolts were upon them.

David had never fought so furiously. The spot behind his face now flared with vigor as he unloosed a maelstrom of instinctive moves: cleave, parry, slash, disarm, kill, cleave, block, thrust... He knew he was hungry, so he grabbed each bellirolt he killed—but there was no euphoria. There was no feeling at all. It was as Cardross had said: David could only devour *human* souls. He could never sustain himself by killing bellirolts. His courage began to falter as he felt his hunger more intensely with each sword-stroke. *It's not fair—I can only feed on the lives of men...*

Just then Cardross was ripped away from David's side and thrown to the ground beneath two bellirolts. David roared with rage and hacked away the attacker in front of him, but three more appeared in his place. He had to get to Cardross before he was killed, before his soul was consumed—then he saw his comrade expertly slice the neck of one bellirolt before the other forced him back down, and they rolled, locked in a death-wrestle, off the path and down the slope. They vanished from sight.

David's body screamed for food. He felt the ripping stab of a blade in his side and he grunted; then felt another in his leg, but he battled through the pain. The wounds would heal, he was not dead yet, he had to get to Cardross...

Suddenly a blue light flashed in front of David, and he

stumbled and blinked. Two bellirolts in front of him were jerked backward, before crumpling on the path. Another who was poised for a kill shrieked, as he too was yanked back by a strange blue light, leaving him motionless on the ground. The fighting ceased as David and his attackers looked up to the ridge.

Standing on a bare knoll above the battle, directly opposite Deuchar, was a figure wielding a long staff of dark, twisted wood. As David looked more closely he saw it was an older man, with a dirty-grey mustache and beard that draped across his chest, wearing a deep brown, hooded robe. Tied across his torso was a plaid of dark tartan held in place by a metal brooch. As far as David could tell, the man had no weapon other than his staff, which he swung and pointed in David's direction.

"*Loách-Tà!*" As the man thundered the words, more blue flashes of light erupted from his staff, speeding like arrows at the bellirolts beside David. The light engulfed them, pulling them off their feet and drawing screams of pain from each one.

"*Ventum-Cerél!*" This time the old man swept his staff in an arc before him, and a blast of wind—mightier than any David had known in his life—whipped down from the knoll and scattered the remainder of Deuchar's force like bowling pins. Several bellirolts ran for cover around the corner of the ridge.

"*GRAVEN!*" Deuchar roared from his place on the hill. David looked upon his rescuer with new eyes: this was the great teacher they'd been seeking.

"I've long hungered for the day when ye'd show yer face in my lands again, ye white-livered beggar," growled the bellirolt lord. His face burned with wrath.

"*Your* lands?" The man called Graven spoke with a rough, gravelly voice that was nonetheless as resonant as an ancient cavern, echoing over the slope. He sounded like a Highlander to David's ears, but possessed a slower, more refined lilt than David had ever heard. "Deuchar, you hold no claim whate'er to the lands o' Kintail. Too long now have you tortured our country, hiding like a worm in your mountain. You know where I dwell, yet you wouldn't dare face me without your Legion to cover you."

Deuchar roared with laughter, and drew a ruby-hilted claymore from his side. "I need none o' my legion tae cut ye tae bits, ye foul monstrosity! Ye trollop's son! *Lay on!*"

With that, Deuchar raised himself into the air and sped like a bullet over David's head toward Graven. Graven waved his staff in a quick flourish, and he too lifted into the air, hurtling to meet the raging bellirolt. The two seemed destined to collide above the trees when Graven suddenly whipped his staff forward, and a sapphire light engulfed Deuchar. The bellirolt screamed and plummeted to the ground. The effect only lasted a moment, however, as he wriggled free of Graven's strange power and raised his sword. Graven lowered himself smoothly to the sloping earth, and flung more bursts of blue light at Deuchar, but the bellirolt proved himself far more agile than his followers. He bounded from tree to tree like a gigantic insect, almost too quickly for David's eye, and landed with his blade swinging at Graven. The old man blocked the attack with one end of his magical staff and returned with the other, moving with the dexterity of a warrior in his prime. Graven thrust his staff up into the hilt of Deuchar's sword, knocking it skyward out of his grasp, then blasted the bellirolt across open space into a sturdy pine, where he fell and groaned.

Graven now turned his attention to the ruby-hilted claymore spinning above his head. He aimed his staff at it and concentrated for a moment, whereupon the sword shuddered in midair, and fell back toward the earth. David realized that Graven actually *had control* of the spinning weapon, for as he whirled his staff around his head and pointed it at Deuchar, the sword followed the same motion. It spun toward its owner as if fired from a cannon, and Deuchar was just rising from the ground, the beginnings of a sneer on his face, as the blade collided with his neck and severed his head. The claymore embedded itself, still quivering, in the ink-spattered tree behind him. Deuchar's body thudded to the forest floor.

Graven breathed a deep sigh and planted the staff beside him. He cast his eyes around for other bellirolts, but the few that remained scampered off like hurt animals into the trees. He then turned to David.

"Kintail has not been a place warm to travelers of late," the old man greeted him. *You don't say?* David wanted to reply, but Graven's dark brown eyes didn't match the irony in his voice. Instead, they seemed to pin David like spears where he stood.

"What brings you, a Lowlander bellirolt, to these hills?"

David stepped forward, wavering a little.

"In truth, Graven, we seek you, sir."

Graven strode down the slope to David, who saw that the man's face was not only wrinkled, but disfigured. His skin was carved with the evidence of many lifetimes' worth of travails: a broken nose that had healed crooked, one eyebrow that sagged lower than the other, and *two* Sable Scars across his right cheek. His grey hair was pulled into haphazard braids as it came near his face, and his eyes looked as deep and dark as a forest on a winter's night.

"*We* seek you?" Graven echoed. "With whom do you come?"

David froze in alarm as he remembered his companion.

"Cardross!" He rushed to the edge of the slope where he'd seen the Highlander fall, jumping over the bodies of bellirolts. The forest descended in a steep decline from the path, leveling off to a ledge twenty feet below David—and there Cardross lay, shuddering and groaning as if he had a fever. Sprawled beside him was the stiffened body of a bellirolt, his Black Swell slashed and mangled.

"Oh, Cardross..." David's stomach began to turn. The dead bellirolt's hand was clamped around Cardross's forearm. Protruding from the nape of Cardross's neck, just visible as he writhed in the leaves, was a thick black knot.

Chapter Fourteen

The Augury

A s the sun faded to a red glow over the mountains of Kintail, David and Graven lumbered into a glen blanketed in verdant grass. David was carrying Cardross (with all his extra weapons) over his shoulders, and though the Highlander was a light burden, his continued moaning and stirring were not making for a smooth journey.

Graven was leading David to his "outpost": a stone structure he'd carved from the remains of a fortress that lay at the top of this glen by a stream. Graven's face had darkened in sympathy upon seeing Cardross turned into a bellirolt, and he said he could help the Highlander if David could carry him to the outpost. As long as they moved swiftly, before Deuchar's forces could regroup, they'd be safe inside.

"This is the place, Dunbar," Graven called over his shoulder. David could see the wide stream trickling across their path, and just beyond it the thick circular wall of an old keep. The keep seemed to rise from the natural rocks of the hillside, surrounded by the remains of other structures, all so covered with moss they looked as much a part of the landscape as the trees.

Graven strode to the stream and waved his staff in a spiral over the ground. Five large rocks raised themselves into the air, lightly as petals on a breeze, and formed a narrow bridge over the water. Graven crossed his magical ford in a few graceful steps, but David approached with more caution. He didn't have Graven's powers; was this even safe for him? On the other hand, he felt too weary to jump the stream carrying Cardross.

"Well come along, now," Graven said. David placed one foot on the hovering bridge, surprised at how sturdy it felt. He made quick work of walking over the stones, but as he reached the last one, he felt it quiver in place. He cried out as his knees almost buckled and Cardross swayed on his shoulders. Then he looked up to see Graven standing by the door of his outpost, a mischievous gleam in his eye. The old man let out a small grunt—a tickled sort of "*Hm*"—and turned toward his home.

David shook his head. *So the old codger enjoys practical jokes, does he?* He was ashamed that Cardross was now a bellirolt, not to mention he was starving after such a battle—this was no time to be toying with him. He hurried onto solid ground, and felt a thud as all five stones replaced themselves neatly along the stream bank. David glared at them. What would they do next, leap up and dance a reel? He trudged over to Graven.

The oaken door to the keep was affixed with a curious iron lock, in the shape of a crooked question mark. Graven withdrew a slender metal rod from his robe and traced it through the outline of the lock, muttering something as he did so. The lock hissed, popped, then the door swung open. Graven ducked inside, and David followed.

The interior looked like a cross between a medieval strong-hold and a professor's library. David had never seen so many *things* crammed into one space. He was standing in an enormous stone room that stretched upward at least forty feet. Papers and books were piled high all around him, some leaning against each other as they teetered a story and a half into the air. David was astonished by the sheer volume of books: he'd had a library of some two hundred back at Galanforde, and that was considered a luxury. Graven had many times that number. No wonder the old man sounded different from every other Highlander. He'd probably read his way across several continents.

David also saw prints hanging lopsided on the stone walls: maps of the British Isles, Europe, the New World, and even a new Dutch illustration that showed all the planets revolving around the sun. A few simple wooden chairs stood near a hearth opposite David, and the only other furniture were tables that dotted the room. On the tables lay bones and skeletons of woodland animals, jars of strange-looking herbs, and—resting innocuously among them—claymores, daggers, broadswords, a Spanish rapier, a spear, a ball and chain, and a large shield that looked as though it had survived since the Dark Ages. There were no windows except high above David's head, and leading to them were zigzag wooden staircases that, like the towers of books, looked as though they could barely support themselves. Dangling from the staircases was an array of musical instruments: a guitar, a lute, several tabors, and a well-used set of bagpipes.

Graven had leaned his staff near the door and was coaxing a peat fire to life in the hearth. Its smoked-dirt scent began to mingle with those of old paper and rock. Once Graven had a small blaze, he stretched out his hand and said in his gravelly voice, *"Fiesum-Cerél."* This time David was sure his fatigue was tricking him, but when he blinked and looked again he saw that a small ball of fire had risen from the hearth and was floating toward Graven. The old man flung the fire out into the room, where it split into several smaller flames that ignited half a dozen candles around the space, giving the center of the keep a hearty glow.

"Now then, Dunbar: bring your friend and I'll have a look at him." Graven was rolling up the sleeves of his brown robe and pulling a tray of bottles from under a table. David left the weapons he was carrying by the door, letting them clatter to the dirt floor. Graven turned his head.

"And mind the animal parts by the wall!" he called. "I'm comparing the hoof and snout designs of boars and deer."

"The—*what?*" David jumped when he saw what Graven meant. On a stand by the door were the heads of a wild boar and a stag, gleaming with a paste that David assumed was a preservative. A lower leg of each animal was placed beside the heads, along with some measuring instruments.

"Dear God."

"Oh, it's fascinating, I assure you, Dunbar!" Graven hadn't looked up from his bottles. "I have a theory, you see, that there was once an ancient animal with the traits of a boar *and* a deer, and over thousands of years its children were separated by land, food, climate… and in time bore the creatures we know today. Come along there with Cardross; we haven't much time."

David brought his companion to the growing warmth of the hearth and laid him before Graven. Cardross's skin looked clammy, and he was muttering nonsensical words as his head lolled about on the floor. His body didn't appear different to David, who remembered his own muscular transformation after Craigvaran. *Then again*, he thought, *Cardross has probably been in robust condition for years given his lifestyle.*

Graven spent the next half-hour dabbing Cardross's brow with a rag soaked in a sweet-smelling solution, sprinkling fine green powder over his face and hands, and muttering an incantation over and over. He explained the key right now was to keep Cardross calm, to pacify the new bellirolt in his body so that when he awoke his first instinct wouldn't be to kill Graven and David.

Finally, Cardross moaned and opened his eyes. When he saw the men's faces above him, he closed them again. David's stomach sank in remorse.

Then, a weak smile appeared on Cardross's lips.

"It seems you an' I are trapped with each other as long as we can stand it, David," he said.

David let out a stuttering, emotional breath, relieved Cardross was speaking to him. "You once pledged your life to me, William. I now owe you the same."

Cardross held up two fingers in David's direction. "*Twice* I pledged."

"How are you feeling, Cardross?" Graven asked.

Cardross's body tensed. "I—I'm no breathin'...."

Graven patted his shoulder. "You no longer need to, lad. Focus on relaxing your body. Your demon will want food in time, and we'll cope with that when it comes."

Cardross's eyes suddenly bulged, and he sat up. "You... you're Doneval Graven!"

Graven gave a small bow of the head. "Iain Kenneth Doungallas MacGregor Doneval Graven, your servant."

"My heavens, man," David said. "You've near as many names as a prince."

"Well, names are important things, are they not, Dunbar?" Graven slung a sheepskin blanket over Cardross's shoulders. "They connect us to our past. My mother was of Clan MacGregor; my father was a warrior named Graven. And *he* was one of *your* kind." He nodded to Cardross and David.

"One of—a *bellirolt?*" David was baffled. Cardross, however, recoiled.

"You're a shadeling!" he said. Graven nodded.

David shook his head in confusion. "What is a shadeling?"

"Offspring of a bellirolt man an' a human woman," said Cardross. "You don't see many o' them who are actually, well, *humanlike...*"

"Cardross is right," said Graven. "Bellirolt women cannot bear children; they're barren on account of the demon. Bellirolt men, however, can and do procreate, often with grisly results.

Most shadelings enter the world as deformed infants who live no longer than a few days. Any that do grow beyond weans are often killed owing to our witch-crazed world. I was fortunate enough to inherit only benefits of my father's nature."

"*Benefits?*" David sputtered. "To being one of us?"

"Certainly, Dunbar. I, like you, age more akin to trees and hills than men and beasts. And since I was a wee boy, I've had a keen bond with my Second Sight."

"Your *what?*"

"How old are you, Graven, if you don't mind my askin'?" Cardross said.

Graven smiled. "Shame over one's age is a birdbrained way to wander through life, lad. I shall be four-hundred-forty-five come January."

Cardross let out a bizarre squeal of amazement, and looked to David for the same response, but David couldn't muster it. There were too many questions swimming in his head.

"Graven," he said, "we have sought you because of your prowess in fighting bellirolts. Now if you please, sir, I must understand *what* this world is that I have entered."

Graven studied David with his earthy eyes and settled back against the stone of the hearth. "Well, Dunbar, that story must needs begin with you, for I'm not certain what 'world' you feel you have come from. You were raised in… Edinburgh, by your accent?"

"Haddington."

"Haddington!" This piqued Graven's interest. "Ah, well I was close. And you were turned whilst there?"

David nodded, and related as much as he was comfortable sharing: being scarred in his bedroom and transformed at Craigvaran. As for Galanforde, he only said he had accidentally set the castle on fire and fled it.

"But you ought to have seen him in that pass just afore you arrived, Graven!" Cardross chimed in. Learning that he was speaking with a four-hundred-year-old warrior seemed to have kindled his spirits. "Regular Robert the Bruce he was! Slew near two dozen bellirolts himself, an' all to save two poor lads!"

"Yes, I was about to press you on that very point," Graven said. "I saw a horse galloping out of the wood with two riders, and assumed the cause was Deuchar. I traced their steps as fast as I could. Were they friends of yours, Dunbar?"

"Who, the boys? Certainly not!" David shook his head. "But if I hadn't done anything they'd have been slaughtered by Deuchar's minions."

Graven furrowed his weathered brow. It felt as if an ancient tree or rock were regarding David with a human face. The effect was humbling.

"You are a brave man, David Dunbar. You might have lost your life today."

"I hate these creatures," David responded, before he could think. "I *hate* what I have become—what I have allowed Cardross to become. I'd much rather rid the earth of them than save my own rotten life." Despite his best efforts, David's voice was beginning to tremble.

"I would caution you against hating what you are," Graven said, as if such hate were a foreign concept. "You've toppled headlong into a brutal war, sorely unprepared, so I'm sure you must be bewildered. It's a war that's been raging for centuries, and humanity, of course, is brilliant at denying it. They all learn the wrong things: that there are people deemed *good*, crossing themselves and serving their king (whoever they decide he is), and there are people deemed *bad*, serving the devil and called witches.

"The truth is far more intricate. Our world—this Land of Seasons, with its cycles of birth and rebirth—is but one of many realms that exist, and there are just as many beings who dwell in other realms, whose presence shapes our own. The universe is one great web of different worlds: some echoes and shades of ours, some entirely unique, but all intertwined. And the common property linking these realms is magic."

"Magic." David's tone was as neutral as he could make it. He almost said *"Devil's stuff,"* but after seeing what Graven could do with magic, he couldn't very well belittle it. "And this 'Second Sight' you mentioned connects us to magic?"

Graven nodded. "Every human is endowed with it, be he Pope or pagan."

"So every human can be a magician? Do all the... spells and tricks that you do?"

"Ah, but for it be a trick it would have to be an illusion, aye? There is nothing illusory about magic. And yes, every human can practice it. It's a scientific art. And like all science, it must be studied, with care and discipline, before it can be put to use."

"Have there always been men here who study it?"

Graven raised his grey eyebrows. "If not always, close to. It's an ancient tradition, and the beginnings of magic in this world go hand in hand with the beginnings of the bellirolts. You see, eons ago, before our forefathers trod these isles, this land was inhabited by a race we call the Sorcerers. They were human in form, but not natives of this realm. They spoke their own language, the Sorcerer's Tongue, which we use to this day to harness the magic around us. They lived in perfect harmony with the natural forces of the world, in a way impossible for us to grasp in this modern age, and so they left almost no mark of their presence here.

"But with the spread of our Celtic ancestors, the Sorcerers decided their time in this realm had come to an end. They bade farewell to their home of many thousand years, and set sail for an island off the coast of Scotland: a place rich in magic, known as Eralan. From there, they disappeared into their own realm. But before they left, they passed on secrets of their magic to the new lords of the land, so their ways would not be lost. You've heard of the ancient Druids?"

David nodded. "Certainly. The heathens."

Graven exchanged smiles with Cardross. "Call them what you will, Dunbar; the Druids were but the priestly class of Celtic society, and they were the first to perfect their own method of the Sorcerers' magic.

"Many centuries later, things changed again: the First Bellirolt rose to power in Scotland. To this day we don't know from whence he came, or how he attained his abilities, but he built an army that devastated those early kingdoms. Thousands died at his hands, almost all the Druids among them. Men of magic had to go into hiding... until one of the Gaelic kings found a way to summon the Sorcerers *back* to this realm. For with their magical prowess, humans might stand a chance against the bellirolts."

"An' he built the Ring o' Pillars! Like it says in the Augury," Cardross cut in.

"The Augury?" David asked. "Like a prophecy?"

"In part, yes." Graven crossed his legs in a very un-genteel way before the fire. "This king journeyed to Eralan, where he constructed a ring of nine pillars, freestanding in the middle of the isle, as a magical gate for the First Sorcerer's arrival. The king took on a symbol for his cause—a black unicorn, for the indomitable spirit of his fight—as well as a new name for himself: Nimarius. In Sorcerer's Tongue that means 'guardian of man.' Hence, the band of knights he founded to practice magic is known as the Order of Nimarius.

"Once the First Sorcerer was summoned, he helped the Order defeat the First Bellirolt, but by then thousands more had come into being. The First Sorcerer died, another arrived to take his place, and still the bellirolt hordes fought and multiplied. So it was that after Nimarius's death, his bard recorded the verses we now call the Augury. It chronicles Nimarius's deeds, and foretells the one chance to annihilate the bellirolts for good."

"Tell it to me," David implored. "Please, Graven."

A subtle light bloomed in Graven's eyes, as if he'd been waiting for David to ask. "You'll have to forgive me for not singing—the tune is long forgotten. Listen closely." He cleared his throat and looked to each bellirolt as he spoke:

"Once and final for the Unicorn King:
Nine pillars risen in a ring,
Borne and built by Man's own hand
On the enchanted Isle of Eralan.

These are the words of the Unicorn's Sons—
The Clan of the King, the Gifted Ones—
Who recalled the beings that once walked our land:
The Ancient Sorcerers of Eralan.

When came the fury of the Devil his Beasts,
Who rose and ravaged our homes from the East,
'Twas the King our forebear, the Unicorn Lord,
Who sought then the aid of Eralan's shore:

'O Islands of the West, pray lend thy might,
And guide our ships with wisps of light,
That through dark furrows we may row
To Eralan, dock of the Sorcerers' abode!

Isle where the Jade-green Zephyr coils,
Isle of the Unicorn's Toil:
A Ring of Pillars as posts to the sky
To bear the first Sorcerer nigh.'

Now heed you well what this mage prophesied:
That he would fight for the King, and after he died,
Another would come, and so on in kind—
But like the stone Pillars, there would only be Nine.

And, behold, there shall rise a Beast with such might
As to all the forces of Darkness unite,
And march on the lair where the White Phantoms sing,
To crown himself Lord: the Mortairian King.

And seek not relief from the mysterious Isle
As passes the Seventh Sorcerer's trial,
But know when the Last of Eralan appears,
For he is all the Mortairian need fear:

He shall come forth from woman's womb
At the ground of the Bravest Guardian's tomb,
And rise, first Marked by the Demon's hand,
From the blood of Beast and Eralan.

So you who rise and to battle ride
When the hour of fate is nigh:
Beware the Ninth of Eralan,
Born of the flesh of Man."

Chapter Fifteen

The Name
of the Sorcerer

After Graven finished, a tranquil silence hung in the room. David sat motionless, letting the words resonate in his head.

"So the only one who can actually destroy the bellirolts is this 'Ninth of Eralan?'" he asked.

"In short, yes," replied Graven. "Only the final Sorcerer—who will *not* arrive from Eralan like every other before, that is key—will be able to defeat the bellirolt called the Mortairian, as well as the Mortairian's Legion."

"And how many Sorcerers have arrived thus far?"

"Eight." Graven breathed deeply. "And the Eighth proved to be the shortest-lived Sorcerer of all. He barely survived a year after appearing from Eralan, upon the death of the legendary Seventh. And that was hundreds of years before I was even born."

"So it's been centuries now that there's been *no* Sorcerer to fight the bellirolts?" David found it hard to believe that any resistance to these creatures still existed.

"Just so." Graven nodded. "We still await the arrival of the Ninth."

"Who is to be born human, aye?" asked Cardross. "'*From woman's womb.*'"

"Not just born human, but one who will rise with the blood of a bellirolt *and* that of Eralan in him," Graven said. "Which means…"

"One of the Sorcerers… fathered a bloodline?" David finished his thought.

"Right again. The prevailing theory is that the Eighth Sorcerer was the forebear of that line."

"So what does it mean, then, that he must '*come forth… at the ground of the Bravest Guardian's tomb*'? Who is this Bravest Guardian?"

"By all accounts, the Seventh Sorcerer. He died being tortured by bellirolt lords, as he refused to give away the Order's hiding place. His bravery gave his comrades time to escape and ensured their survival. That's why the Augury warns to '*seek not relief from the mysterious Isle as passes the Seventh Sorcerer's trial.*' No help was to come from Eralan during his ordeal."

"But the Mortairian…" Cardross asked, "he *is* on the rise, is he no?"

A dark cloud settled over Graven's face. "You refer, my young friend, to Claudius Orgeron. We fear he shall be the Mortairian, though he's not yet claimed his crown. The story goes, Dunbar, that the First Bellirolt left a magical crown in a cave somewhere in Scotland: a place called Tor Bellorum. The crown could only be claimed by the next bellirolt who amassed an army mighty enough to warrant the opening of the cave. As the Augury says, the cave is guarded by '*White Phantoms*': Snow Wraiths, who split the skulls of humans that hear their cry. Naturally, any expedition to discover Tor Bellorum has been unsuccessful, and that is surely for the best! There's no telling what manner of power that crown will bestow upon the bellirolt who claims it. And the one who right now commands the Dark Legion of bellirolts, who will become the Mortairian if he finds Tor Bellorum, is Orgeron. He is the oldest, therefore the most powerful, and by far the most cunning. The last time the Order faced him in battle was twenty years ago, and his Legion cut through the knights' army like a scythe at sun-up. The Order is now a shadow of its former self, and Orgeron's whereabouts are unknown. Deuchar was merely a captain of his."

"There's still one piece of the Augury that puzzles me." David rubbed his eyes as his energy drained even further. He was hungry—very hungry—but felt he could ignore it as long as he had this riddle before him. "At the end it says '*Beware the Ninth of Eralan*.' Why should anybody fear the man who is to deliver them from the bellirolts?"

"Why, because he is to *be* a bellirolt." Graven's eyes shone with a kind of crazed wonder. "The Ninth shall rise '*from the blood of Beast and Eralan*.' Only one of the bellirolts' own can bring them down. 'Beware' does not perforce mean *fear;* it means *be cautious.* This Sorcerer could be a very dangerous man. And he will, like as not, be the man you least expect."

The trio sat in silence for a moment more before Cardross piped up. "Graven, are *you* one o' the Knights o' Nimarius?"

Graven smiled—a motion distorted by the Sable Scars on his face—and gestured around his home. "My dear lad, you are sitting in one of the few surviving outposts of the Order of Nimarius. I've been a knight since I was sixteen."

Cardross squealed in excitement again, and jostled David's shoulder. As if in response, a set of musical chimes rang out in the vast room, and David looked up to see a small box of blonde wood resting on a mantle above the hearth. The box played a gentle, whimsical melody twice before ceasing. Graven waved a hand toward it.

"Mind not the music box; it will do that from time to time. I suppose now you'll both need some sustenance, aye?"

David glanced in horror at Cardross. Was Graven going to offer them some sort of human sacrifice? To his relief, the old man pulled two vials of bright green liquid from the tray he'd used to treat Cardross.

"Swallow, and think not of the taste."

David accepted one of the vials, but he and Cardross exchanged dubious looks.

"Graven, we cannot swallow anything. Believe me, I've tried. Everything vanishes on the back of the tongue—"

"This will not, Dunbar, I assure you. It's Mooradian's Elixir—*Moora-Juice,* we like to call it. An Order engineer fashioned it back in the sixteenth century to pacify bellirolts he was trying to interrogate. It won't stop your feeding, but it will stem your hunger. Sile it down your throat like whisky, go on!"

David uncorked his vial. It was the color of grass on a fresh spring day, but smelled like the brew of a crooked apothecary. It didn't even look like liquid: if anything, he would have called it "liquid-smoke." He closed his eyes and downed the vial.

A rancid taste filled his mouth, but only lingered for a second before he felt it being sucked back into his throat, up into his nasal passages, even under his tongue—and the hunger was gone. He didn't feel the euphoric rush that accompanied his feeding; rather, he simply had no desire to eat. It was a calming sensation.

Graven was flitting about the room like a bat, waving his hands and sending objects flying like some sort of demented circus. Two sheepskin beds were landing before the hearth, a twenty-foot stack of books was moving itself to make way for them, and a large wooden basin full of water was lowering in front of David and Cardross. Graven spoke as he moved.

"You would do me great honor by staying the night, lads. These hills aren't safe for two lone travelers after dark. In the morning we may talk more, and I'll lend what counsel I can. For now, rest. You've both had a trying day, and—" he finished his whirlwind of preparation and turned to them— "you're lucky to be alive. There's some water to refresh yourselves." He snatched a kettle from near the hearth and moved away.

Cardross leaned over the basin, about to splash himself with water, but stopped. His face seemed to grow long and gaunt, as if something in his reflection were changing him from the inside out. He slid his fingers down his cheek.

"Is this… the face of a monster, David?" he asked. David's heart twisted yet again, and he searched desperately for words of encouragement.

Cardross shook his head. "It's odd—I just… never thought I'd be one."

Graven had paused his business with the kettle and was looking back at Cardross, the creases in his face heavy with pity. David wondered how many men, over four hundred years, he'd seen in the same condition.

"William…" Everything David wanted to say sounded feeble. Truth be told, Cardross hardly *looked* changed, and certainly not like a monster. But then, David's eyes returned to the water in the basin, and an idea bounded into his head.

"William, would you like to see a trick?"

Cardross's mouth opened in confusion. "A trick?"

"Stand back. This is my homespun attempt at Graven's magic. Watch closely!"

David stared at the dark water, trying to recall the sensation from that day, ten years ago, when the canal in his garden had attacked him. He found himself breathing—an odd choice for his body, but the circulation of air helped him concentrate. He focused on the water: its surface, its depth, its swaying feeling as it poised on the edge of the basin—and his fingers tingled again by his side. It was as if he could feel the water without touching it: it was cool, supple, ever-changing, and just when he sensed the liquid begin to ripple with their connection, he lifted his hand and a plume of water sprang from the tub and splashed over Cardross's cheek.

David clapped his hands in triumph and let out a deep laugh. It was the first joke he'd ever played on anybody. But his mirth ceased when he realized Cardross wasn't laughing at all. Instead he was staring at David in stunned surprise and wonder. David turned to Graven. He bore the same expression.

"David Dunbar..." The old man spoke slowly. "How long have you been able to do that?"

"Do what?" David was annoyed at their response. He'd only wanted to cheer Cardross up. "Play with water?"

"No, *manipulate* water, David! How long have you been able to do it?"

"I've... only done it one other time, back in Haddington. But that was before I was turned into a bellirolt, over a decade ago."

Graven's eyes seemed to deepen like two caves. "David, the ability to control water is one of the few signs of somebody with *prodigious* magical ability." His long grey hair shook on the emphasis of the words. "Water is a mutable substance: very difficult to influence. Only Sorcerers have ever been known to innately do such a thing."

A river of ice ran through David's chest. This was all wrong...

"You remember the Augury, and what it said about the Ninth of Eralan?"

David nodded dumbly.

"You were born of a woman's womb, you were scarred—*marked*—before you became a bellirolt, and..." Graven's disfigured face began to transform with a look of radiant triumph... "you were born at your castle at Haddington?"

"Galanforde?" David's voice was halting. "Certainly. I lived my whole life there."

Graven absently raised a hand to his cheek, touching his Sable Scars. "David, the Seventh Sorcerer, the Bravest

Guardian, is buried in a tomb not half a mile from Nungate Bridge—a stone's throw from that castle. You were a baron, so you know your lineage?"

David almost forgot he was being asked a question. He nodded again.

Graven flung out his arm toward the ceiling, and David turned to see half a tower of books making way for a faded green tome that flew through the air. It sailed like a falcon returning to perch in Graven's hands.

"This is the Book of Calmorran," he said, turning the thick, groaning pages. "It records all the branches of Scottish families descended from the line of Eralan."

"Hold there." Cardross stepped closer, his face still dripping with water. "If you don't know which Sorcerer fathered the line, how can you tell who's descended from it?"

"You don't until they die," Graven replied. "If a body carried the blood of Eralan, you'll see a host of tiny, white flowers with red centers sprout above the grave. The flower is called the Ilsinora. It was first seen by Nimarius himself on the Isle of Eralan: proof that the dead person was kin to the Sorcerers."

He found the page he sought and thrust the book at David. "Look here," he commanded, his voice clipped with anticipation, "and tell me if you recognize a name."

David accepted the heavy volume into his hands. *Tiny, white flowers with red centers...* Somehow he couldn't pry the image from his mind. His eyes swam over the small letters on the page, and it took a moment before he could read them.

"*Maclellan*" was the first name that looked familiar; one of them had married a Dunbar years ago. He scanned the thin fibers of the family tree across the page, looking for a full name he might know... and stopped. His head began to sway over his body.

"*Arthur Fergus Dunbar,*" David said, and looked up at

Cardross and Graven. "Of Mochrum, in Galloway. Died 1603. My great-great-grandfather." His hands trembled as he returned the book to Graven. "And frankly, those white flowers—I remember them on my father's grave."

Cardross's jaw looked like it had dropped past his neck.

"It's you…" he whispered, staring as if David had transformed into a king before his eyes. Suddenly Cardross exploded into the air like a firework, waving his arms and crying: "*All hail the Ninth Sorcerer of Eralan!*"

Graven laughed out loud, his scarred face creasing with joy.

"*ALL HAIL DAVID DUNBAR!*" Cardross sang.

The words were still ringing in David's ears the following evening as he sat on the grass-carpeted roof of Graven's keep, watching the last rays of light disappear. He'd been perched there for most of the day, and didn't budge as he heard the old man approach from behind.

"It's amazing," David murmured. "My eyes suffer no damage from the sun. I've watched it ride across the afternoon clouds, plunge to the western ridges…"

Graven's voice rumbled over him. "Are you well, David?"

"… I don't know."

Graven settled himself beside David, bringing his distinctive smell of pine, wool, and earth. "David, the Augury only *names* you as the Sorcerer," he said. "It doesn't spell out what shall occur. You don't have to embark upon this path."

"Don't I?" David looked at the old Highlander, startled for a moment by how deep and weathered his scars looked this close.

"No. If you take the Knight's Oath and begin training, you are pledging your life to this cause. The way of the *magian*—a man of magic—is a path you choose out of devotion, free from vengeance and pride. So if your heart is not open, do not begin the journey."

"But I'd be a fool not to!" David said. "Look at me. What else am I? Not a baron… sometimes I don't even feel like David Dunbar." He looked at his hands, recalling the foul, slippery blood that had glistened on them in the burning halls of Galanforde. "I've not told you what happened the last night at my castle. After I'd been turned, all my wrath came screaming to the surface. I didn't know what was happening. I couldn't plug my rage, and I killed both my cousins. They were guests there. I started a fire during the fight, which might have killed five, ten, *twenty* others—I don't know. I don't know what sort of life I've brought upon my sister and brother. I don't even know where they are."

A look of deep concern clouded Graven's eyes, but David continued. "And I realized, when I saw those bellirolts threaten the boys in the wood, that they didn't feel this remorse. It was foreign to them. It was foreign to Deuchar." He held Graven's gaze, and the ancient warrior's focused look seemed to draw him out of himself. "*I know* I'm not like these other bellirolts. And I shan't be able to live with myself if I don't make the most of this… *ability*. So you see, I have no choice. Because I shall never choose inaction. I don't even know what a Sorcerer is—based upon what you've told me, I'm terrified to be one. But I believe I was born to do something of import in this world. If I can stop others from suffering the way my family has… I'll join whatever cause there is."

Graven was silent as he studied David. His scars were thrown into sharp relief by the retreating sun. "I warn you, David," he said, "this is no life of glory in battle. Scotland, and all the world, will most likely never know your name."

David felt a flicker of sadness. A decade ago, such words would have devastated him. "Then I shan't fight for laurels. I've always wanted to make a difference for Scotland. Now you tell me I am your Ninth Sorcerer. Please: *teach me* what that means."

A light evening rain began to drizzle over them. Graven's dark stare relaxed, and he laid a hand on David's shoulder.

"There is somebody I'd like you to meet." He pulled David up with him.

Two hours later, in a wet little village near Loch Duich, David and Graven approached the door of an inn. They both wore fresh clothes: Graven had donned a dark blue robe with his plaid wrapped around it, and sported a bonnet with a hawk feather. David felt like a new man in a clean shirt, breeches, and boots, and he used the hood of his fur cloak to shield himself from the rain.

The inn was a haggard lump of a building, whose second story looked as if it were sinking into the first. A cracked wooden sign by the door bore some creative drawings of whisky and bread, and a few small windows hinted at candlelight within.

"This is the place," Graven said with a touch of amusement.

Upon entering, a barrage of laughter fell upon David's ears. At a table by a roaring hearth, several older men were sharing a bottle of whisky and guffawing. A grimy serving boy ducked between the other tables, clearing cups and sneaking the final drops of liquor from each. But it was the man at the head of the main table who commanded the attention of the room, bellowing in an English accent:

"I do not jest! The chap had been in his cups since eight in the morning, and he insisted—nay, *declared! Proclaimed, lads!*" —more snickers dribbled from the table— "that he would have his post to Stirling by dinner that afternoon. So he sets out—the packages aren't even strapped atop the coach, mind you—and within an hour—*one hour, I say!*—he'd toppled clean off the post and lay snoring in a ditch. And the best part: the coach kept pressing on to Stirling! Had it not been stopped by the constable, I warrant you his horses would've made it there by the time he said, though he were dozing by the road the whole time!"

"And you shared a tankard of ale with him afore he'd even risen from the ditch, eh, Cecil?" Graven's gruff voice broke through the laughter and set every head turning toward the door. He smiled at the rotund, rosy-cheeked fellow named Cecil, whose eyes narrowed to thin slits upon seeing him. "Or was that wee Tavish MacRan I'm recalling, outside the grog shop in Fife?"

A nervous silence hovered in the wake of Graven's interruption. For a moment nobody seemed to know how to address him. Finally, a man beside Cecil let out a chuckle.

"*Haud yer wheesht,* old man," he sneered at Graven, and turned back to the table. He'd hardly reached for his cup when Cecil pulled a long dagger out of nowhere, and plunged it between the man's fingers in the liquor-soaked table.

"*Do—not—EVER—speak to Doneval Graven that way again.*" All jolliness had vanished from Cecil's face. He now appeared as cold and deadly as a sharpened axe. Cecil held the man's horrified gaze a moment longer before withdrawing his blade and turning to Graven.

"Been a long time, old chap," Cecil said, jerking his chin up. "Thought maybe you'd forgotten what good spirits tasted like. Unless you've fashioned a still in that mountain hovel of yours." He grinned rakishly.

"Even if I had I'd be loath to share it with the likes o' you, you blellum rascal," Graven replied. "Why don't you leave this company in peace and join my friend and me for a private drink?"

"And why in St. George's name should I do that?" Cecil spread his arms. "The Duke of Loch Duich is holding court, and we've half a bottle of whisky yet before us!"

"*Mir-tynach ny-gurh, Vamboldich,*" Graven intoned. His calm demeanor remained unchanged, and though every head at the table turned, trying to ascertain what language they were hearing, Graven's eagle-like gaze was focused only on Cecil.

"*Vyer-grum bedech. Sho fellech grum-gaird fall'Eralan.*"

Cecil's eyes flew wide like two windows. For the first time, he looked at David, who'd been standing in the shadow by the door.

"*Shur vlyer-falch?*" Cecil asked. Now his companions were shifting their eyes back and forth between the two men. David guessed this was Sorcerer's Tongue they were speaking; he only wished he knew what they were saying about him.

Graven nodded to Cecil. The Englishman rose from the table, as if in a trance, and made his way around his companions. He muttered, "Finish mine, Rabbie, there's a good man," and lumbered across the room until he was almost nose-to-nose with Graven. David now saw that Cecil was well into his middle years, with azure eyes and an unshaven face that looked to have been devilishly handsome in his youth, but age and drink had rounded it and reddened the veins in his cheeks. His salt-and-pepper hair was shoulder-length, and he wore a brown suit and greatcoat that framed a well-padded body.

"*Nos-mye-irum, Gravendich,*" he said. Where Graven stood erect, Cecil hunched to meet his gaze, and the old Highlander tipped his head toward David. Cecil turned to him, his eyes still wide in the dim light.

"You are the Ninth Sorcerer?" he asked quietly, his breath thick with peaty liquor.

David nodded and lowered his hood. "I am, sir. David Dunbar, of Haddington."

Cecil's face took on a look of grateful recognition, as if meeting a friend he hadn't seen in years. A smile pulled at his mouth.

"Then I am your most humble and obedient servant Cecil Wambold. Of the Order of Nimarius." He gave a slow bow from the waist.

"Cecil is a fellow knight of the rank of Paladin," Graven said, his voice now betraying a hint of admiration. "He is my oldest friend. And now, you lecherous reprobate, we need call a conclave posthaste. There is much to be done, and the Court of the Order must be re-formed. We have a Sorcerer to train."

Chapter Sixteen

The Order of Nimarius

D avid paused his story as he finally seemed to realize Percival had been standing in the same place, staring at him, for several minutes. The two Dunbars were winding their way into Bonnybield via alleys where they wouldn't be seen, and were still many blocks from the Old Steeple. Percival gaped at David with narrowed eyes.

"You're a *Sorcerer?*" Though he didn't quite mean to, his tone sounded utterly skeptical.

David nodded. "The last of them."

Percival gave an incredulous laugh and ran his hands through his shaggy hair. He'd felt a gripping chill when he realized he'd dreamed of Nimarius's symbol the night before: the black unicorn. Yet another vision his Second Sight had granted him.

He faced David. "So that's the supernatural war, then. You and this 'Order,' versus every other bellirolt in the world. A couple o' humans against *thousands* o' bellirolts. Perfect! We're doomed." He shoved his hands in his pockets and leaned against the nearest wall, just as his stomach gave a low rumble. He cringed. What he wouldn't give for a steaming hot Forfar bridie from the bakery right then…

David seemed not to notice, and smiled. "You don't yet

know what a Knight of Nimarius is, Percival."

"Oh, aye? You mean they're not all old men and drunks? What were the others like?"

"Well, I wasn't allowed to meet any more right away. That conclave Graven mentioned was only to reconnect with his surviving brothers. I was kept in seclusion to train for my knighthood: a *ten-year* process. I thought it would all be swordsmanship, levitating rocks as Graven did... as if magic were but a skill."

David shook his head, his expression somewhat sheepish. "I couldn't have been more wrong."

On a heath above the outpost, a deafening CRACK blasted apart the stillness of the summer afternoon. A host of birds erupted from the trees as a scorching wind shot past them. David's voice bellowed after it:

"*DAMN THIS CLAY-BRAINED, NO-GOOD, TWO-PENNY SPELL!*"

David was facing an eight-foot-tall standing stone, clutching his head in frustration. Cardross and Wambold sat nearby. The first was polishing his claymore, the second polishing off a cup of ale.

"You're not focusing, David," Graven said from the side of the heath.

"I've *been* focusing for the past four hours!" David yelled.

"And how does that warrant your wee tantrum now?"

David roared again and ran his hands through his wavy hair. He shot a trenchant look at his teacher. "For a year-and-a-half, Graven, I've done everything you've asked of me. Cardross and I spent near a week atop your muddy roof in the pouring rain, sitting, focusing, *not thinking*, just *being*—going from one insipid exercise to another, and all you tell us without end is that 'our minds are not in the right place.'"

"They aren't," Graven stated.

"*Well what the devil* is *the right place?*" David heard Cardross sigh in irritation, but he focused on Graven. "I'm trying to lob a spell at a big stone. Had I a pistol, a sword—a knife, even—I could strike the same inch of it every time, but *no,* I'm to use *my mind* to direct it there, and apparently I'm such a beef-witted lump that nothing is coming *out* of my blasted mind!"

"David..." Cardross gave up pretending something else was occupying him. "Graven *has* told you how to focus; I heard him—"

"You shut your gob." David jabbed a finger at Cardross. "You've not been able to do this, either."

"David, you're a *Sorcerer;* you know you can do it..."

"I never asked to be a Sorcerer."

"Great Gabriel's Hounds, Dunbar," Wambold moaned.

"I didn't! What makes me the Ninth Sorcerer? In part, the fact that I'm a bellirolt, which was forced upon me—entirely out of my control. And now I must—"

"*Control, David?*" Graven's voice clapped like thunder over the heath. "Control? Do you *ever* control what abilities you need in life? Do you control which men wander across your path whose souls you take? Did you control whether you met Cardross there, and found me? The face of humanity is pockmarked by the pretty fools who live for *control.* Let your past lie where it is, my friend." Graven stepped closer and softened his tone. "The question is: what will you do with what you have now?"

It was all David could do not to roll his eyes and turn away. He was tired, he'd lost his focus—why couldn't Graven let him be for the day?

"David, I've seen you experience your connection to your Second Sight. But if you are to *sustain* that connection, you must give yourself over, so the self may know this air, the stone, the grass, the stream... and act in harmony with them." He returned to his side of the heath, keeping his dark eyes locked with David's.

"By giving up control," he said, "you gain control. Try again."

David groaned, and muttered, "Why can't I just see the spell book where all this is inscribed?" To his surprise, Wambold burst out laughing.

"Only after you find me three newts' eyes, five frogs' toes, and a big black cauldron!" Wambold roared. "A spell book indeed…"

"I'm a half-step away from having you stand and face me like a man, you cup-shot rogue," David said. But Wambold only laughed harder.

"Peace, Cecil." Graven raised his hand. "I think you owe David an explanation."

Wambold sighed and wiped a tear from his eye. "There's no such thing as a spell book, Dunbar. How can you *write* a spell? You might as well give a recipe for an ocean wave, or a summer rain. Explain how a violinist transports you with music. Impossible! It is different for every person. Spell books are jokes." He gulped the last of his ale.

"This is why our spells are learned orally, David," Graven said. "The tradition of our teaching never has been and never will be written upon paper. You must *live* what you are taught. A spell is drawn from the inmost soul, the *spark* of a person, and will behave differently depending on where it is conjured, and the knight conjuring it."

"Hence why bellirolts can almost never practice magic!" Wambold added. "True magic goes against their nature. A Knight of Nimarius shares knowledge and trust with his surroundings. Bellirolts seek to dominate their surroundings."

"So my demon might be barring my abilities," David surmised.

"Wrong." Graven replied. "You might be, though."

David sighed and cast a forlorn eye up to the sun. There was no way Graven would let him rest as long as daylight burned. He squared his shoulders and faced the standing stone again, feeling Cardross's keen eyes on him as he had every time. He appreciated the support, but at the moment he could do without the pressure.

He closed his eyes and focused his mind. This spell was called the Disabling Fire: the first he'd seen Graven perform at the battle with Deuchar. It was the primary spell a magian was taught to use against a bellirolt, for whereas the monster could heal from a sword or musket ball, a direct hit from a Disabling Fire would stun one for hours. Wambold had demonstrated a minor version on David: he'd felt as if he'd been struck by a battering ram, sapped of all energy. He understood now why Deuchar's forces had fled upon seeing Graven.

David opened his eyes, assumed a fighting stance, and stretched out his hand. He stared at the center of the stone, and shouted, "*Loách-Tà!*"

Nothing happened.

"Remember, David," Graven said, "*intention* is everything. The Sorcerer's Tongue is only used to focus your energy. *Connect* to the power driving you, and send it forth."

"That's what I thought I was doing," David said through gritted teeth.

"You know, you've hardly been at this a pissing-while, Dunbar," Wambold said, cleaning his fingernails with a toothpick. "You and Cardross have not even stood your foot-ale yet."

"Our *what?*"

"You're still squires! All of this is probably far too advanced for you."

"The devil it is! *LOÁCH-TÀ!*" As David barked the words, a blinding burst of azure shot from his hand toward the standing stone. There was a deep, guttural BANG, and the face of the rock blasted into a hundred pieces. David dove and covered his face, and saw that Wambold had generated some sort of blue-green protective bubble around himself and Cardross. Graven had done the same for himself.

A mischievous look of triumph spread across Wambold's face.

"And *that*," Cardross said after a silence, "is why the fangs of a young viper are deadlier than those of a seasoned one!"

Meditation, reading, exercise, combat practice—these became the cycles of David's life. During breaks in training he would watch Graven's eccentric routines: the old man dove back into his studies of animal skeletons whenever he could, and several mornings David awoke to him bounding outdoors, throwing off his robe and plaid, and splashing in the stream like a child. The purpose of the mad-looking staircases in the outpost was soon revealed, as Graven would scurry up them as the sun was setting, or during the night, to observe the stars through a telescope and make notes in a dense ledger.

Matters grew more serious when Wambold brought reports that Orgeron's Dark Legion had attacked two villages to the south, supposedly looking for Tor Bellorum. But no matter how David begged Graven, his teacher refused to let him leave the outpost.

"Orgeron has discovered our Sorcerer exists, and is trying to draw him out," he said. "But that hour is not yet upon us. Orgeron is like a shadow in the night, David: the more you reach for him, the faster he'll slip away. We must wait for him to make a mistake."

And so the years passed, though they had little impact on David. For him, Cardross, and Graven, a year meant simply a cycle of seasons. Only Wambold, being neither shadeling nor bellirolt, showed signs of growing older. He was due to live longer than most men, Graven explained, because he'd spent so much time in the practice of magic. But David noticed him grow slower, saw more gray hairs sprout along his rosy scalp… it was an odd reminder of how long David would have before such things happened to him.

One of Graven's primary concerns, as he and Wambold mentored the two bellirolts, was teaching them to pay close attention to their need for human souls. They were to accept their demons, rather than reject them: to listen and know when they really needed sustenance, and when they were simply itching for violence. David and Cardross developed their own "code of honor" to keep them from killing at random. They took no women or children, never allowed a victim to suffer, and when possible they sought out those intent on harming others. Marauders and highwaymen became their grisly delicacy.

Before long, Cardross succumbed to the disorienting process of demortisation. He tore out of the outpost at night with ugly, throaty roars, consumed by the need to kill. David tried to calm him with Moora-Juice, but the effect was too temporary. Cardross would be gone for days, return looking nothing like himself and sleep for weeks, then repeat the cycle again as his body slowed to the rhythm of bellirolt age. Wambold did his utmost to involve the young Highlander in training, but Cardross became notorious for giving up after five minutes of effort.

"The little churl is costing me more sleep than a caterwauling banshee," Wambold grumbled one day. It was spring, and David was sitting with him and Graven on the roof of the outpost, around a stump that served as a table. The latter two munched on Graven's own baked bread and sipped a warm drink of steeped herbs he'd concocted—his version of what the English were calling "tea." David puffed on a wooden pipe he'd fashioned for himself. Cardross had bolted from the outpost shrieking for food the previous night.

"Cardross puzzles me," Graven said, sounding more troubled than puzzled. "He is eager to fight, but not to learn. You've seen how he enjoys watching *you*, David."

"Mayhaps he's sweet on you, old boy." Wambold nudged David.

Graven disregarded him. "I simply don't think he understands what is required to become a knight. His demon is feeding on some great abyss of hate within him. We can only assume it stems from the murder of his family."

"All the same," Wambold said through a mouthful of bread and butter, "you cannot discount his loyalty to our Sorcerer here."

"I do not for a moment," Graven replied. "His devotion is… unusual."

"He's shown me more devotion than anybody I've ever known," David said.

"What others have been devoted to you?" Wambold gave David a look of complete puzzlement. David swept aside the smoke between them and sat forward.

"I beg your pardon?"

Wambold shrugged. "I merely wonder whose devotion you compare his to."

"Are you saying you can't imagine anybody else being loyal to me?"

"Peace, both of you," Graven's voice rumbled across the roof.

"Peace?" David barked. "Graven, how am I supposed to train with this bloated English swine lying about? He has far greater love of the bottle than he does our cause. Why else did we have to dig him out of an alehouse when he could have been defending his neighbors from bellirolts, like you?"

"David…" Graven tilted his head. "Why must everything be a personal insult to you?"

David stared at both men—who'd adopted passive, reclined postures—in total confusion. In his day, in Haddington, he'd be meeting Wambold with swords at dawn for offending him like this. And Graven was questioning David?

"*Why?* Because I've suffered insults my whole life. Always from lesser men, *weaker* men."

Graven kept his cavernous stare fixed on David. "Leave us, Cecil."

Wambold grumbled, but stood up. "I'm taking the tea," he said with a note of triumph. He moved to the edge of the roof and muttered, "*Marghensiù.*" He gently rose into the air, and glided down off the keep, out of David's sight.

Graven placed his tea on the stump before him. "You've spoken to me, at times, of your grandfather."

David tensed, though he didn't know why.

"You've mentioned he was the reason you stayed so long at your castle. Why you never left earlier to join the Jacobites. Could you describe him?"

David didn't know what the old man was driving at, but he was ready for this lesson to end. "He was ill, always. Feverish. Delusional. Never did I see him so much as walk to the window and smell the breeze."

"Would you say he was weak?"

"Of course he was! The man never *did* anything. Never tried to make himself well—he only complained, constantly, of his ailments!"

Graven shrugged. "From what you've told me, his 'ailments' were naught more than his Second Sight reacting to a disturbance in the Otherworld. You were his grandson, the first Sorcerer to be born a man. And your turning would mean the murder of your kin and the ruin of your noble name. Did his 'disease' not parallel your life? Folk who are close to death often find themselves very *aware* of such things."

David grimaced. Graven might have a point, but what right did he have to talk about the ruin of David's name? Could he even understand what such a thing meant?

Graven pushed on. "Do you fear ending up like him?"

David was about to thunder "*No*," when he realized it wasn't true. He looked away to the stream.

Graven's voice was gentle and easy, like the creaking of trees in a summer breeze. "David, do you realize that what you fear in yourself is what your bellirolt is feeding upon? Even now? I believe you when you say you always wanted to fight for a great cause, to be a warrior. And yet you never set out to do that whilst you were a baron."

"I had made a *pledge* to my *family*," David explained. "I was to stay by Grandfather's side, and look after him. It was my father's dying wish."

"And did you truly look after him? Did you make his final years more comfortable? Did you help bring him joy? Or did you shut him in a closet, with a 'doctor' to bleed him and poke at him 'til there was nothing left for a disease to eat up? Tell yourself what you will, David—I say you did *not* honor your pledge. You chose to be ruled by a promise you made *as a boy* to a dying man. You denied yourself the life you wanted, 'til you were forced from the life you had."

There was so much David wanted to say—to yell—in response, yet he couldn't find the words for any of it. So he stood, stuffed his pipe in his pocket, and charged off the roof in the opposite direction Wambold had gone.

He hardly looked at or spoke to Graven for days afterward, until he stood upon the heath again, this time facing not the stone, but the dark-robed old man.

Cardross had returned, in better spirits, and was observing with Wambold once more. David wore only his breeches; he liked the sun spreading across his chest and shoulders. He watched Graven standing as still as the trees behind him, a flutter of wind waving his braided hair. David felt no need to move, either. He was studying his teacher.

Without warning, Graven sprang into action.

"*Loách-Tà!*" The Disabling Fire flashed toward David's chest like a lightning bolt. *Predictable*, he thought, as his bellirolt legs flipped him over the spell.

"Don't just *dodge*, Dunbar," Wambold called. "Return it."

David had heard the advice before. Graven began to circle him, and lobbed another Disabling Fire, this time in an arc. David spun out of the way. He could sense Wambold's vexation, but ignored it.

A second later, Graven attacked again, this time with a Fire so hot and quick it felt like a cannonball speeding at David. *This* was the kind of spell he could respond to. His mind latched onto the oncoming energy, and he pulled it above him with his left hand, sending the blue orb arcing over his shoulder and away from the heath. David paused for a second, eyes locked on his opponent—when he suddenly realized Graven's spell hadn't disappeared into the forest behind him. Instead, David *still had control of it,* and Graven was none the wiser. Just as Graven prepared another attack, David pulled his left arm forward, and the Disabling Fire streaked back toward his teacher. Cardross squealed with glee, and Graven barely had time to deflect the spell before returning one of his own. A real battle had begun.

David and Graven traded blows from their spells, each using the energy of the other to send the next attack. The air became so heated that a shrub near Graven crackled into flame, and he waved his hand over it while crying, "*Fiesum-Cerél!*"

David knew this spell: the one that summoned the properties of fire. A tongue of flame sped toward him, but he harnessed it before it reached him. His arms and face were nearly scorched as he spun the fire around his body like a slingshot, and hurled it toward Graven with such power that there was nothing the old man could do but dive out of the way. A great channel of fire now flowed from the flame on the heath, up around David's arms, and into a hot ribbon in midair. The more David fed the flame, the more it continued to pour around him: he could do anything with it.

"Hold onto it, David!" Graven called. "*Control it!*"

But David already had control, and it was invigorating. He raised the ribbon of flame so it shot like a fountain to the sky, and when his limbs began to shake he drew the last of it up from the heath and launched it into the air. It disappeared in a flash among the clouds, and in its wake a peal of thunder boomed over the mountains of Kintail.

At first David thought he heard screaming, but then realized it was Cardross crying out: "*You did it, David!* That's one o' the hardest spells there is! Od's bud, did you see that, Wambold?" He was jumping up and down like some sort of mad ape. Wambold was laughing.

"Hear, hear, Dunbar! Well done, man!"

But David was looking at Graven. The old man did not laugh, or even smile. He just stood on his side of the heath studying David with a curious face, and something like a twinkle in his dark, weathered visage. Finally, he gave a single, approving nod.

It was two weeks later when the four men arrived on a vast plain, their gazes set on a tor silhouetted in the twilight. Graven, with his gnarled staff, led the way. He and Cardross wore plaids pulled over their heads like hoods, while David and Wambold were clad in cloaks that whipped about them as they walked. The travelers crossed the squelching flatland called Mòine Mhòr, as Graven guided them toward the ruined fortress at the peak of the tor: a place known as Dunadd.

For centuries, Graven explained as they climbed the path up the tor, Dunadd was the stronghold of an ancient Gaelic kingdom. At its summit was a footprint worn into the flat rock, where new kings would step upon accepting stewardship of their land. This, Graven said, was the first Court of Nimarius, as established by the Unicorn King. And this was where the Order would begin again, with its final Sorcerer.

As soon as they had all gathered around the ghostly footprint, Graven raised his arms to the blue-grey sky, and proclaimed:

"*Gar-ylich, miell-tuboor linn duluch! Venyndrum gal-callas!*"

At first, nothing happened. Then David spied movement at the edge of the tor, and the outlines of several figures appeared around the rocks. They approached on silent feet from all directions, and in minutes forty of them stood atop the tor, facing Graven.

Graven swept his staff toward David. "*Sho limbech lassan-gaird fall'Eralan.*"

All heads turned to David. There was an awestruck pause, and then each figure in turn stepped forward, grasped David's hand, and knelt before him. They all gave him a curious salute: drawing the index finger of the right hand down the forehead, around the left eye, and bringing it to a fist over the heart. "Welcome, Sorcerer," many said, or "*Decurren umilonh*" ("I am honored and humbled"). To David the moment was surreal, the stuff of his wildest fantasies back at Galanforde: standing atop a mighty tor in the bracing wind, the land laid out beneath him, being greeted like a secret prince by followers he never knew existed.

Once everybody had saluted David, Graven stepped forward into the stone footprint, and intoned: "*Irlimm-baich grum-teynas.*"

The whole surface of the tor shuddered, and the stone beneath Graven's foot began to separate. The old man leapt back as the slab of rock holding the footprint sank several inches, and then swung down into the earth. David realized with a dizzying sensation that he was standing over *hollow* ground, for a great cavern was now visible beneath the rock.

"The First Legion of the Knights of Nimarius salutes you, David," Graven said, "and bids you welcome to your new fortress."

Chapter Seventeen

1746

A series of tinny clangs—sharp and staccato—echoed through the stone chamber. Young squires lined the walls, keenly studying the center of the room. Between two bright torch stands, their Sorcerer was drilling a pupil with a smallsword.

"Now, parade in the first position," David said. "Yes, good. Second, third, fourth... Bravo, now return with thrusts. Mind your posture, lad; relax your shoulders..."

"*David!*" A familiar boyish voice spilled into the room.

"Not now, Cardross. I want you to attack in the first position, lad."

"David, our scouts 'a sighted Orgeron."

Every student spun to look at Cardross, and David's sword dropped to his side.

"Where?"

"At the mouth o' the River Spey. He's hidin' in King George's army."

The squires murmured excitedly to one another, and a victorious smile pulled at David's lips. He sheathed his sword, patted his pupil on the shoulder, and dashed with Cardross out of the chamber, pounding up a cramped stairwell. Dunadd was a maze of little stone avenues like this, winding throughout the tor and making for a castle bigger than any David had seen above ground.

David threw open a heavy oak door, and he and Cardross ran out into the Great Hall: the void David had peered into the night Graven had reopened the fortress. In the center of the Hall was a long stone table at which several older knights were sitting with Graven and Wambold. All these men had attained the rank of Paladin, highest in the Order, and their twelve-man Court of Paladins had elected Graven the previous year to be Chevalier Superior—the wartime commander of the brotherhood. Adorning the high grey walls around them were shields bearing the coats-of-arms of noble families who'd supported the Order for centuries. A dim fire hissed beyond the table.

"It is true?" David called to Graven at the head of the table.

The old magian didn't look up from the message he was scratching with a quill. "Is what true, David?"

"That you've found him."

A growl escaped Graven's throat, and he paused his writing. Beside him, Wambold coughed into a filthy handkerchief. He was well into his nineties now; his eyes looked eternally bloodshot, and he was constantly hacking up something from his lungs.

"Pack away, you foul rotten sneak." He scowled at Cardross.

"Squire Cardross," Graven said as he laid down his quill, "if you spy on our Court one more time, I shall chain you in the dungeon so long that Dunadd will have been weathered to a stump ere you emerge."

Cardross mumbled something behind David, but David stepped forward to cover him. Cardross had yet to advance beyond the rank of squire, as he still hadn't mastered a single spell. Technically he wasn't even allowed in the Great Hall.

"All he told me was that Orgeron is with the government army. Is it true?"

Graven nodded, the slightest possible movement of his beard. "'Tis."

A hot fire swelled in David's gut, a mixture of thrill and anticipation.

"Great God! We've found him! When do we leave, then?" But Graven's expression was unmoving. "Oh, Graven—you can't keep me here whilst the Mortairian himself has finally—"

"*David.* We've not yet formed a plan as to how we shall engage Orgeron in the midst of a several-thousand-man army. And before I send you into this fight, I must be certain of something. You know who the government army is chasing?"

"Of course. Prince Charles and his Highlanders."

Graven lifted his chin. "The Jacobites." His eyes took on the effect of dark seas about to swallow David whole. "You fought for these people once before. I must know, before you leave Dunadd, that you do so for us, and not the Jacobite cause."

Somehow David had known this was coming. He needed to tread lightly here.

"You know I serve the Order first and foremost."

Graven, as usual, was unyielding. "Try again."

David hated these moments, when he was taken to task before he was ready.

"Very well. Why must I forsake my country because I fight for the Order?" A few heads shook around the long table. "Gentlemen, this is a Jacobite army that near marched into London several months ago! Scotland has never seen anything like this!"

"It is not your fight," Graven stated. "If you wanted to join the Jacobite cause, you ought to have made that your priority back in 1689, but you did not."

"Understood." David spread his hands. He didn't want to

endure this lecture again. "Then I'll prove it to you. You need a plan? Here it is: Cardross and I will embark first. We're bellirolts; we travel more swiftly than other knights. We'll meet the magia already at the Spey, conduct reconnaissance, and await your arrival. That is all."

Graven breathed in the proposal, and David felt every battle-ready muscle in him tense. The Chevalier pointed a long, knobbed finger like a tree branch.

"You are responsible for Cardross."

David nodded.

"Then be off."

David and Cardross waited until they'd descended two floors before clapping each other on the back and shouting in triumph. They slapped kisses on the cheeks of a group of ladies they passed, who worked as everything from cooks and seamstresses to blacksmiths and armorers—many of them wives or daughters of the near-one-thousand knights who lived at Dunadd. The women groaned and chided the two friends, but neither cared. They were taking their first step toward finding the Mortairian.

David had hoped Graven would offer some parting words for their mission. Instead, as he and Cardross were saddling their horses in the stable outside Dunadd, he saw Wambold hobbling through the grey spring morning on a cane.

"Oh good, you're still here," he coughed.

"Never thought I'd hear those words from you." David slipped a bridle over his horse's ears. "Graven is not coming to see us off, then?"

Wambold shook his head. "Too busy."

David looked hard at Wambold after he fastened the bridle. "What did he expect me to say about the Jacobites? Am I to suppose, after nearly five hundred years, the man's severed himself from the rest of Scotland?"

"Dunbar…" Wambold leaned against the horse stall, which creaked under his weight. "Do you know why I've pushed and prodded you all these years? You're like a carriage stuck in the mud. You need to move along, but you can't seem to without a hefty shove. Now, you've accomplished much, but you still forget who the true enemy is. Graven's not severed himself from Scotland: he *serves* Scotland. He serves all mankind. This *little war…*" He closed his eyes and shook his head wearily. "It is the very depth of horror. Families will be ruined. Children will starve. And you will see it happen many more times before you die. What you must seek is the *root* of hate, and those who feed upon it. Mind your pride, Sorcerer." He pointed his cane at David. "I don't want to see you undone by it. Now…" He rummaged in his greatcoat. "I have parting gifts for you."

On "gifts," Cardross appeared beside his horse. Wambold held out two bluish-grey stones shaped like arrowheads that shimmered in the dark stable. Each was just over an inch long and had a thin leather neckband attached.

"What are they?" Cardross asked.

"Sydaeon talismans," Wambold said, coughing again. "Sydaeon was the Second Sorcerer, and he brought knowledge of how to create these out of the minerals of the earth. Every knight has one." He patted his chest. "If you wear it round your neck, it connects you to every other magian within range of you wearing his. We can communicate by grasping them and speaking in Sorcerer's Tongue. Here." He offered the talismans to the bellirolts, who slipped them over their heads.

"Now, this is very important: if you find yourselves in danger, all you need do is clutch the talisman, and utter the words '*Sydaeus-Mir.*' Every other magian will feel his sydaeon burn against his chest, and if he grasps it, he'll see what you did when you summoned him."

David turned the little rock over in his fingers. It looked as

if stars were embedded in its surface. "Thank you, Wambold."
It was the first kind thing he could remember the Englishman
doing for him. He and Cardross walked their horses out of the
stable.

"One last thing, Dunbar," Wambold called. "Orgeron is
not poised to be the Mortairian for nothing. The man's as
crafty as a fox. There's a reason our scouts have just now found
him."

David wrinkled his brow. "Meaning he planned it?"

"Meaning he *wants* to be found. Tread very carefully as
you near that army."

David was unsettled by Wambold's words, but he gave a
terse nod. He and Cardross mounted their horses and trotted
off.

As they followed the Great Glen northeast, the pair chatted
about the Order, about what to expect with the Dark Legion,
and about the Jacobite army. David revealed what he'd kept
from Cardross and Graven for months: that he'd been
following the Jacobites' progress since the previous year, that
he'd kept every dispatch regarding their movements and
victories, and most importantly, that he still thought they could
win. That a Scottish king might rule Britain again.

At least that was until they stopped at a tavern outside the
city of Inverness, seeking cover from the rain. They ordered a
few drams to blend in, and sat above a floor littered with
broken lanterns and bent utensils, to learn the latest about the
Jacobites.

"No very happy tidings!" A frosty-eyed man in his mid-
forties, with an angular face and hooked nose, leaned across the
table to the travelers. "Government men outnumber Prince
Charlie's force, an' they're fresh tae the fight. That Prince be no
commander, if ye ask me—" he spat on the muddy floor—
"marched his boys near tae London only tae have 'em turn back
again! I heard half his force deserted already!"

"That's what I was thinkin' earlier, David," Cardross said in his ear. "The Jacobites are an army o' tacksmen an' tenants. Most o' them only fight 'cause their clan chief tells 'em to. It's family honor." He turned to the frosty-eyed man. "Where are the armies now?"

The man adjusted his lopsided wig, making it look even worse. Wigs were now tied behind the neck, with ridiculous, effeminate curls on the sides, rather than draping elegantly down the shoulders as they had in David's youth.

"Jacobites left Inverness today," the man said. "Word is they were headed east. Shouldn't be too hard tae find." His eyes—the clearest ice-blue David had ever seen—flashed across the table for a moment before he guzzled the rest of his beer.

David said in a low voice to Cardross, "They're making for the king's army! If we find the Jacobites, we find Orgeron in battle—he wouldn't dare miss such a feast!"

"Graven is goin' to skin your hide..." Cardross said with a devious smile.

At that moment David didn't care about appeasing Done-val Graven. Wambold wanted him to look for the "root of hate"? Here it was: too many years of rule by a king that wasn't Scottish. *If we take on the government army, we take on Orgeron.* The opportunity was too good to let pass. And Cardross needed no convincing. They left their drinking companion, paid the stable to keep their horses, and slipped into the night.

However, the rain continued, slapping across their path in cruel sheets, and the night was the blackest David had ever seen. He and Cardross soon realized they couldn't tell the difference between the mud-choked roads and the fields beside them. What was more, they were so used to being guided by their hyper-developed Second Sight that neither had thought to bring a compass.

When morning dawned at last, it brought an even worse omen: eerie moans floating on the wind, as if old women were wailing over loved ones many miles away. The cries were so sudden and fierce they battered the bellirolts' senses, confusing their route even more, and by afternoon they'd still seen no sign of the Jacobites. Worried, David hailed a boy in a nearby field who led them inside a farmhouse. A pretty young woman with ebony-black hair greeted them and offered them fresh milk.

"My husband joined the army last autumn," the woman explained, as she, David, and Cardross sat sipping the thick milk. The boy had gone back outside to feed the cows with his grandfather. "Our Laird threatened the farm if he didn't. Now, after all these months, everythin' that's happened—I was overjoyed tae see him come marchin' home the other week! An' yet he couldnae stay. He'd returned, but was still with the army." She gazed out the window. "The war is not over."

David swallowed his milk, cringing at the rancid feeling as it evaporated behind his tongue. He'd forgotten how to look as if he enjoyed human food. Cardross was doing a much better job playing the act.

"Ye're soldiers, then?" The woman nodded at the swords and shields the bellirolts had leaned beside their chairs. David and Cardross glanced at one another.

"From whose lands?" the woman asked.

"I hail from here, madam, just the other side o' the city," Cardross said.

"Do ye, now? Seems ye've lost yer accent a bit!"

Cardross frowned, but the woman grinned good-naturedly and looked at David.

"And ye, sir?"

"My name is Dunbar, madam. I come from Haddington-shire." David saw no reason to hide his name in these parts—his story had to be foreign to these people. But the woman cocked her head in curiosity.

"Dunbar?" she repeated. "How odd... you're the second man o' that name I've met this week."

David's head ticked back, surprised. "Indeed? Who was the other?"

"Well, he were michty kind… my husband brought him round afore they marched out. No from these parts, neither… *Robert* Dunbar, that were his name."

David felt as if his heart had been thrown back through his body. He clenched his cup as he tried to sound only mildly interested.

"Odd indeed, madam. Did he resemble me at all?"

The woman smiled. "Hardly. He were much older than ye. But come tae think of it… he did hae the same nose, an' eyes. Though his look were a bit sadder."

I'm sure it was, David thought. Robert would be in his late sixties by now, older than anybody who should be serving in the army, but the Jacobites might take any man. Could he really be fighting for them? At this critical moment? A thousand questions assailed his mind, but he couldn't focus on one to ask.

"Do you have any news o' where the army is?" Cardross asked.

"Would that I had!" The woman glanced again out the window. "Mistress MacNeil cam round this mornin', sayin' they were tae engage the king's army at Culloden. I heard terrible sounds no long after—I couldnae tell if they were cannon blasts or thunder claps from the storm. I was thinkin' o' sendin' my boy tae see, but thought better of it."

"Wait—you heard cannon?" David sat forward. "Are you sure it was cannon?"

"At *Culloden?*" Cardross repeated. "You mean the moor there, madam? Why the de'il would Prince Charlie choose that? It's naught but a broad, boggy plain! There's no shade nor cover to be found on it! You can't do a Highland Charge over Culloden Moor!"

David looked at Cardross, who lowered his voice. "David,

this does no bode well. If they've been tryin' to engage a superior force on that field—"

"Right," David whispered. It was time to leave. "These cannon blasts, madam: when did you hear them?"

"Oh, nigh on two hours ago, I suppose…"

"Two hours…" David said. "If it was only two hours, they may yet be fighting!"

"I think no, David," Cardross murmured, gazing far off.

"Cardross, we did not come all this way just to be—"

"*No,* David." Cardross turned to him with eyes as hard as steel. "Look." He nodded at the window. When David followed his gaze, his blood turned heavy and cold.

Approaching on the road from the east were several figures clad in red—not marching, but strolling. As they drew closer, David heard they were singing. The truth seared like an iron in his chest: the battle was over, and the king's men had won.

"On your feet," he said to the other two. *How? How in hell could the Jacobites have let this happen?* Cardross already had his claymore at his side and his shield over his arm. The woman leapt to the window and yelled to her son in the barn.

"*Andrew, haste ye tae the house! Andrew!*" She turned with stark, wide eyes to the bellirolts. "I cannae see my boy! I'm goin' tae find him!"

"No, madam!" Cardross stopped her. "He need only hide in the barn; he'll be fine. Stay here an' lock the door! Don't trust the redcoats!" Turning to David, he said, "The last thing the lady needs is two Jacobites in the house. Come, there's a back window!"

A moment later, David landed beside Cardross on the slick grass behind the house. They crouched with their backs against the stone, listening. The redcoats were indeed singing a drunken tune, and now seemed to be passing in front of the house.

David suddenly noticed that the searing heat in his chest

was his sydaeon talisman. He dug it from beneath his shirt, and saw Cardross was already grasping his.

"Graven is summoning us," Cardross said in a low voice. But David shook his head. He knew he'd reneged on his deal with Graven. He would answer for that later.

"Ye three: have a look at the barn. The rest wi' me!"

Rage spiked in David. The soldiers weren't passing the house by. What was more, their captain was a Scot. He prayed they wouldn't find the boy…

Just then, David was blinded by the tingling sensation behind his face, vibrating more strongly than he'd known in decades: his bellirolt signal that death was near. He heard pounding on the door of the house.

"Open up, in the name o' the king!"

David could feel Cardross looking at him for a decision. His eyes flashed up to the paper-white sky—so bland, so uncaring for such a foul day.

"Open up, I say, or by God we'll torch yer home!"

"Ye'll step awa' from my home if ye've half a wit between ye, sirs!"

"Ohh…" The captain whistled. *"Ye hear the tongue on that trollop, lads?"*

David's hand flew to his sword hilt, and fifty ways of cutting these redcoats to pieces blazed through his mind. *It's only the demon*—he told himself, closing his eyes—*you'd be a fool to reveal yourself if they end up leaving her in peace…*

But these soldiers were intent on doing no such thing. The next thing David heard was drunken cheering as several heels slammed against the woman's door, and then the burst of splinters as the mongrels entered her house.

"Where are yer Jacobites?" came the captain's sharp voice.

"AWA' from my house! I dinnae have any Jacobites! Do I look like a traitor?"

"Ye look like a Jacobite's trull, that's what. Where're ye

keepin' 'em, lass? In yer barn? Under yer petticoat?"

Cheers of agreement echoed from the other men. The woman screamed.

In less than a second, David had turned and dropped his shield. His bellirolt-sense was tingling so furiously he felt his face would burn off. Before he could raise himself back up to the window, Cardross caught his arm.

"*David.*" David could tell by strained look on Cardross's face that he had the same sensation. "They won the battle," he whispered. "We might have an entire army upon us, with Orgeron—"

David leaned in so he was nose-to-nose with the Highlander. "*To hell with all of them,*" he snarled, and launched himself through the window. His entrance was so swift nobody noticed at first, but a corporal gave a startled "*Heh!*" that set all heads turning.

There were nine redcoats in the room, all armed with muskets and swords, and stinking of brandy and rum—their rewards for a speedy victory. The captain was obvious to David: the tallest of the bunch with a bloodied epaulette on his right shoulder, he'd backed the terrified woman into the opposite corner. Her eyes cried out to David, and he felt the tingling begin to pulse like a heartbeat through his body.

"Well, well..." the captain crooned, flashing a black-toothed grin. "Dinnae have no Jacobites, dae ye, lass? This yer hussie, ye wretch?" He grabbed the woman's wrist, who twisted out of his grasp and tried to kick him, so he snatched her by her hair instead.

"*Unhand her.*" Without planning to, David had somehow made the walls of the farmhouse shudder with his words. A few redcoats looked to be losing their nerve.

The captain wasn't one of them. "Ye goin' tae fight for her? Ye dinnae look tae 'a been tae the battle, ye lily-livered dog. How about this, lass?" He leaned in to the woman. "Ye watch yer Jacobite die, an' then we'll teach ye tae shelter rebels. Munro, do the honors!"

The soldier nearest David drew his sword and stepped forward, but David halted him with a look. "Lay one finger on me and you won't get it back, I promise you."

"What are ye waitin' for, chub?" the captain yelled. "Have at him!"

Munro stepped forward and thrust his blade at David's torso, but David swept it aside with his forearm and seized the man's wrist. Suddenly he felt a fierce pain in his left side, and saw that another soldier had thrust his bayonet deep into David's abdomen. A chorus of laughter echoed around the room, and the soldier withdrew his blade, grinning. His face darkened, however, when no blood poured from David's wound. Instead, the hole in David's shirt showed his skin sealing itself up, good as new.

All eyes in the room now looked with horror upon their Jacobite enemy, and David relished the smile he cast back at them. Without warning, he let out a roar that made the wooden chairs rattle against the floor, picked up Munro by the wrist, and swung his body against the stone wall. David felt the man's spine shatter with the impact—and the life-giving rush of elation, as his soul flowed into David. David had fed in past decades, but not like this. *This* was his bellirolt rising back to life. In a flash, his years of magian training vanished and he was the world's most powerful warrior again, yearning only to kill. He drew his sword, lunged forward, and in seconds he'd cut down six more soldiers. He heard the door bang open behind him, and turned to see two flashes of red pass through it.

"Finish those two off! Ye, bring the company!" the captain yelled outside.

Only the woman remained alive inside the house. She was huddled in the corner where the captain had left her, trembling with a paralyzed, unhinged look on her face.

David helped her up with one blood-soaked hand. "Madam, is there any place on this farm you can hide? Who knows how many more—"

"My son!" the woman cried. "Andrew—he's outside!"

God, no... The boy and his grandfather were still out at the barn.

David raced outside, and was just getting his bearings when he sensed movement behind him. He spun to see Cardross tackling the captain not three feet from his head. The captain's sword passed so close to his face he felt the sting of metal on his nose.

"*The barn, David!*" Cardross readied his sword as the captain recovered. David turned toward the barn, where he saw three soldiers with bayonets fixed, circling behind the little boy and a stooped old man. Both prisoners were being forced to their knees.

In that instant, the storm of vengeance building inside David exploded outward like a hurricane. He ran forward, sword toppling forgotten from his hand. His throat burned with a savage roar, and just as the soldiers turned toward him he was lifted into the air, buoyed above the earth by his fury. This was no magian spell he was using—he'd gained the same bellirolt power MacBain had used at Craigvaran. He sailed fifteen feet above the earth and slammed his boots into the chest of the first redcoat, sending them both to the ground. Then another was upon him, trying to stick him with his bayonet, but David snatched the musket out of the man's hand and *snapped* the entire weapon in half—stock, barrel, and all— over his thigh. Gunpowder sprayed on the wet grass. David swung the butt of the musket into the soldier's temple, smashing his skull and dropping him to the earth. He didn't even try to touch him as he died.

With the bayonet end David stabbed the two remaining soldiers, then hurled the splintered weapon into the road. He turned to the boy and his grandfather, who were crouched in the grass with faces of baffled terror.

"I'm sorry," David said, his throat ragged, "but you'll never be safe here again. You must find new shelter, or this army will destroy you!"

"*DAVID!*" Cardross called from the house. "*David, come now!*"

David gazed at the victims in despair, knowing they were frightened, wishing he could help them more. "I'm sorry," he repeated, "I'm sorry! Flee, hide!" He left them huddled in front of their barn beside the three dead soldiers.

David saw as he approached the farmhouse that Cardross had killed the remaining soldier who would have brought help, and was standing over the body of the captain. Though the captain's face was contorted in pain, there was no blood around his corpse.

"Look at this," Cardross said. He turned the captain partway over so David could see his back. Sliced in half on the nape of his neck was a Black Swell.

"*My God,*" David whispered.

"That's not all." Cardross rolled the body back over and used his claymore to separate the front of the captain's shirt, revealing a black tattoo in the middle of his chest. The design was of a thick circle with an imperial crown in the center.

"A crown with a ring?" David asked, perplexed. But Cardross shook his head.

"Not a ring, David—an 'O'. For Claudius Orgeron. *That* is the sign o' the Dark Legion. And then there's this." He reached beneath the captain's shirt beside the tattoo, and unveiled a small, square letter pinned to the fabric. David tore it out.

The letter was sealed with a circle of black wax, and there was a name written in flawless script on the front: *Dunbar, Baron of Haddington.*

David slowly broke the seal and read the interior:

So sorry to miss you, dear Baron. I shall host another soirée
soon...
> *Yours,*
> *Claudius Orgeron*

Chapter Eighteen

The Colonel
on the Black Boar

R age. Humiliation. Foreboding. They all pounded through David's veins upon reading Orgeron's message. Had the bellirolt lord known this whole time that David would end up at a random farm outside Inverness? How?

Graven's fury as it reached David via sydaeon talisman was expected, but stung nonetheless. David had made a promise to conduct reconnaissance, to not involve himself for the sake of the Jacobites, and he'd failed. He hadn't even contacted a single knight in the area. Graven spelled out in clipped, gruff phrases the messages that had been sent while David and Cardross were wandering in the rain: *Orgeron posing as officer in king's army at Nairn. / Graven and battalion from Dunadd en route. / Battle imminent on Culloden Moor. Magia: seek Orgeron before armies advance. / Jacobites have been routed; Orgeron visible on the field. Many members of Dark Legion wearing red coats.*

And finally: *Ninth Sorcerer not present.*

To David, however, nothing compared with the gut-mincing truth he now realized. The Jacobites were finished. Failed. Just as he had that day. Scotland—at least the one in which he'd always believed—was now truly a vassal of England.

The feeling struck him most harshly when he and Cardross wandered the bloody roads away from the farmhouse, looking for some sign of Robert Dunbar, praying he hadn't been killed. They saw Highlanders fleeing, government soldiers riding them down like animals… and then they reached the battlefield.

It was rain-swept heather and swamp plastered with thousands of dead bodies. The sort of sight that didn't seem real, that should only be read about in books, but had exploded like a disemboweled carcass over Culloden Moor: a vision from hell.

Packs of redcoats scoured the field, looking for still-breathing Jacobites they could bayonet. Round shot smoked near the crimson kilts it had dismembered. An old woman and a young redcoat officer wrestled over a locket from a dead Highlander. A bearded man missing an eye called to David in faint Gaelic as he passed. David wanted to end his misery, but lost the stomach to do so. How many of these dead were scraps of a gory feast for Orgeron and his minions? David understood then what the Wailer he and Cardross had heard had been lamenting.

The battlefield reflected the dim sunset in a cruel, nauseous beauty, and David knew there was no point. It would take him days to discover if his brother lay on Culloden Moor. He had to accept that Robert and Eliza, like these Scots, were either dead or dying. He had outlived them, and would never see them again.

He and Cardross left the field. They returned to the Order, who decided that with the advancing wrath of the government army, it was no longer wise to remain in their fortress. So they left Scotland.

Fifty-two years crept by. On a narrow, winding street in the Irish town of Naas, a fierce-looking man dashed from behind a house, a letter clutched to his chest. The night air splashed his hot cheeks as he sprinted between the buildings, glancing behind him with wide, defiant eyes. He'd just rounded the corner where his horse waited when a small, wild-haired man flew down from above and slammed him against a wall.

"Not so fast!" Cardross jeered as he held the bellirolt to the grey stone. "Helmonite, now!"

David swooped down from another rooftop and clamped a pair of black shackles to the man's wrists. In one swing, his bellirolt arm nailed the shackles' chain to the wall above the prisoner's head.

"Well done, Cardross." Graven's rough voice echoed down the avenue as he and twenty other knights approached. All the magia (with the exception of Graven, whom David had never seen without his plaid) wore simple, dark suits with standing-collared coats and tall hats. They circled their new prisoner. Cardross, grinning with his boyish pride, snatched the bellirolt's letter and handed it to Graven.

David gave Cardross an encouraging nod. His friend had been the one to summon the knights to Naas, saying he'd found Orgeron's personal courier. After the Battle of Culloden, the Court of Paladins and most of the Order had relocated to the Irish countryside, to further build their army. One week after they'd arrived, Cecil Wambold died in his sleep. Graven was desolate, and mourned his friend for months. It didn't matter the centuries he'd lived; David saw him suffer loss as deeply as any other man.

Graven broke the seal on the letter and moved into the moonlight to read it. As he did, David glimpsed a circular posted on the house adjacent—a picture of the Irish harp with a laborer's cap, and the words: "*Equality: It is new strung and shall be heard.*" This was the motto of the United Irishmen, a secret army of some two hundred thousand intent on taking back their country from nobles and Englishmen. The Order of Nimarius wasn't the only hidden force in the British Isles anymore.

"What's this?" Graven turned to the prisoner, eyes wide with alarm. "This letter says the government troops in Dublin have been told of the uprising. And nothing is to happen there. How did you come by this?"

The bellirolt prisoner leaned forward against his shackles and bared a yellow grin. "You can stuff your skull, you shadeling filth," he purred in an Irish brogue.

Graven didn't so much as twitch a muscle, but Cardross stepped close to the bellirolt's face. "He asked you a question, you worm!"

"Peace, Cardross," David admonished him.

"David, the whole Order is in Dublin because that's where this rebellion is supposed to begin, *tonight,* the twenty-third o' May." Cardross turned to the prisoner. "If there's no uprisin' there, where is it happenin'?"

But the bellirolt only smiled again, reveling in the havoc he was creating. "You poor, poor magical halfwits… A gale of retribution is beginning this night, like no other in history. Our Legion has seen to it. From both sides!"

Graven was about to interject when Cardross drew his sword and slashed the prisoner's chest—twice—then used his newly perfected bellirolt power to pull the man forward without touching him, so his arms were straining against the shackles. The chains were made of helmonite, a magically enhanced alloy forged in Dunadd—one of the few metals a bellirolt couldn't break. The wounds on his chest were healing, but he trembled against Cardross's power, which, if Cardross pulled hard enough, would tear his arms from their sockets. *This* was torture for a bellirolt: constant pain the body couldn't heal fast enough. David had never seen such viciousness from his friend. He looked to Graven, whose hand was tightening in fury around his gnarled staff.

"*Where is it happenin'?*" Cardross demanded. "*Where is Orgeron? Tell me, or—*"

He was cut short by Graven flinging him back against the far side of the street and pinning him there with his staff. "You've just earned charges of criminal misconduct before a full Tribunal," Graven thundered, "you *impudent* brute—"

At that instant, a loud BOOM echoed from down the street. David's bellirolt sense began tingling like fire. *Here.* This was where the uprising was beginning.

Graven released Cardross and peered like a hawk toward the explosion. Another pounded through the night after it.

"*Magia!*" he barked above the rising noise.

"*Chevalier!*" all the knights responded.

"That's the High Street yonder. I want two squadrons to approach from the east and west. Sir Fraser, guard the prisoner. Sirs Aidan and Connor, you know the town—each lead half the company present. I'll go with Aidan, Sir David with Connor. Find Orgeron's men, capture or kill. *Valirr deconh!*"

"*Valirr deconh!*" echoed the magia. *Virtue and honor.* Another knight cried "*Vaslor Nimarièl!*"—*Strength of Nimarius*—as the detachments set off.

David kept the rebellious Cardross by his side as they neared the sounds of screaming and musket fire, and smelled the acrid bite of saltpeter. They wound through a maze of stone and shadow until Connor motioned that they needed to scale the buildings before them. A chorus of "*Marghensiù's*" sputtered forth, and the knights rose into the air en masse and touched down on a three-story roof. They leapt again to another roof and crouched behind its apex, then peered out over the main street of Naas.

David was unprepared for the maelstrom of violence raging beneath them. Companies of redcoats were scrambling into formation near a jail, as a thousand rebels converged on them from not one, but three different directions. Their eyes burned with manic fury, their collars flew open, and their swords and guns gleamed in the torch light.

So this was Orgeron's next "soirée", David thought. He and Cardross had each endured a month of solitary confinement after their misconduct during Culloden. If he wanted to restore himself in Graven's eyes, now was the time.

"Cardross and I will take to the street!" he yelled to the others. "The rest of you remain here and await our signal. Keep your sydaeons close, and look to the pike-men, or men with swords! Bellirolts have no use for muskets. Protect yourselves first!"

Cardross joined him as he jumped down into the bloody chaos. *How the hell did the Order not know of the uprising here?* The thought stabbed like a needle through his mind. There was no way the Order's scouts should have missed a thousand Liberty Men descending on Naas. How would he find bellirolts in this mess?

Just as he formed the question, he saw them. Two men with short, straight hair— "croppies," the Irish called them, for their statement against the longhaired aristocracy— charged the front line of redcoats with no concern for their safety. They pulled government soldiers into the fray with superhuman force, taking them down far too easily for men who looked unarmed… and then David saw thick leather buckles around their necks. He indicated them to Cardross.

"Collars?"

"To protect the Swells. That's them!" Both friends charged. The bellirolts gave one look in David's direction, and fear engulfed their faces. They barreled through the mass of rebels to the other end of the street, David and Cardross on their heels.

"It's your eyes, David!" Cardross yelled as they ran. "They glow green like a cat's in the dark!"

Fine time to tell me, David thought. So his eyes were a dead giveaway. No use hiding in the battle now. He leapt above the fray and launched two Disabling Fires that sent the croppies tumbling to the ground.

Now the word was out. The blue flashes of Disabling Fire were unmistakable, and in moments David had taken out two more bellirolts that appeared from the crowd ahead. Shouts of "*Vaslor Nimarièl!*" alerted him that both detachments of knights were now converging on their position. The bellirolts knew their game was up. David saw ten rebels break off from the crowd at the far end of the street and leap astride horses that had been waiting for them. They took one look back toward the battle, and upon seeing David, one of the gang nodded. They turned and galloped down the street.

That street connects with Dublin Road, David thought. *That's where Orgeron is!* If these bellirolts were going to inform him of David's whereabouts, he had to stop them. Cardross and the Order could handle Naas. He sprinted away from the battle.

As he saw the riders disappear ahead, David pumped his legs faster and allowed his mind to connect to the stones beneath him, the air around him. When he felt the energy build from his momentum, he shouted, "*Marghensiù!*", and soared fifty feet into the sky. Sure enough, he spied the bellirolts galloping out of town on Dublin Road.

"*Ventum-Cerél!*" David summoned a burst of wind to propel him forward like a rocket. He glided down above the racing horsemen, who were none the wiser for his presence, until he drew the saber from his side and sliced the neck of the nearest one.

The bellirolt toppled from his horse. The others drew their weapons as David slid into the empty saddle, but the horse was startled and veered off the road.

"*Ride, you fools!*" one bellirolt screamed. "*RIDE ON!*"

The rest of the gang charged off while David tried to get control of the poor horse. When he finally sped after them, the bellirolts had vanished into the darkness.

David rode for forty hard minutes, but only got close

enough to hear hoof beats of the bellirolts far ahead. His mind flashed on Orgeron's sickeningly precise script on the note from Culloden... he refused to let the Dark Commander get the better of him this time. Suddenly a wooden sign appeared to his right that read "DUBLIN CITY," and he dug his sydaeon talisman from under his shirt, gazed at the sign, and murmured "*Sydaeus-Mir.*" At least the Order would see where he was going.

David reached the scattered homes of Dublin's outer streets. All was as silent as a cemetery. He left his weary horse at a trough; in this quiet the animal would only give him away. There was no sign nor sound of the bellirolts. Perhaps they'd hidden inside? A heavy fog was creeping in from the sea, so David focused his hearing and smell, drew his sword, and snuck forward. Houses and shops gave way to taverns and churches, and still he heard not a whisper of life on the street. The British government had declared martial law, so all Dubliners were under curfew, but were there no patrols out? What about the knights already posted there?

The smallest touch of light was breaking the horizon as David reached a wider street—and froze. A large animal was taking shape in the mist ahead of him. David raised his sword and squinted: it was a tall, oddly shaped beast, moving as slowly as the fog around it. As it ambled closer, though, David saw it was not all *one* animal. There was a man, and a giant black boar upon which he was riding.

David was so baffled he forgot about his blade, and it drifted to his side. The boar's head alone was the size of David's torso, and two thick tusks gleamed from its mouth. Its shoulders were the height of a horse's, heaped with fur, and behind them sat the bareback rider, a gloved hand on a set of reins. It wasn't until the beast sauntered closer that David saw the rider wore the uniform of a British colonel, with two gold epalettes. He was the most polished officer David had ever seen: his boots shone like glass, and his breeches, waistcoat, and scarlet jacket were perfectly tailored to his athletic figure. At his side the colonel wore a diamond-hilted saber, on his head the tall shako hat of the modern army, spouting a dark plume.

The colonel halted several yards from David, resting a fist with an ivory-tipped riding crop on his thigh. That was when David noticed the ice-blue eyes, the long face and aquiline nose, and the curls of white powdered hair peeking out from beneath the hat. This man looked so familiar... yet David couldn't place him.

"Well, well, well..." the colonel sang with wonder. His accent was that of one who'd spent his life in an English palace. "*David Dunbar.*" He tasted the name in his mouth. "The one they call 'the Baron.'"

Suddenly the face registered in David's mind. It was those eyes like a choking frost... "You're the man from the tavern! Outside Inverness, fifty years ago!"

The colonel chuckled. "Well, I'm flattered you remember. Honestly that heartens me, because at the time I was rather put off that you never bothered to *ask my name.*" He inclined his head, fluttering the plume of his shako. "Claudius Orgeron, Marquess of Dublin. Your humble servant."

David felt as if drops of ice from those eyes had touched his skin. *This is the man.* The Mortairian. Heir apparent to the mysterious crown of the First Bellirolt. *Or is he?* David thought as he stepped forward, raising his sword point.

"We've been searching for you for a century," he said. "How do I know you're really Orgeron?"

Orgeron's lips quivered a little. "Because if I weren't, we wouldn't be speaking on the public street. I own this city now, you see. So you're meeting me at my court, Dunbar. Or— forgive me—the *Baron of Haddington.*"

"I ceased being a baron years ago; you know that. I put that life behind me."

"Oh, don't flatter yourself, Haddington. The only thing you put behind you—along with your Highland lackey—is a trail as plain as carrion to a hound. It takes all the fun out of the *chase* in this game."

"Game?" David snorted. "We're playing games, then?"

"But of course!" Orgeron gave a magnanimous smile. "It's a grand bout of chess, between two all-powerful creatures. Or has the festering old fool Graven not told you that?"

"Mind your words," David said in a level voice. "You speak of my friend."

"He's a shadeling, my darling baron; he is no one's friend." Orgeron's tone was of the utmost condescension. He swung a leg over the giant boar and slid down to the street, pointing the animal toward a puddle so it could plod over and drink.

"You know, Haddington," Orgeron mused as he watched his pet, "I really had hoped we could have met at Culloden. What a breathtaking duel we could have had. But alas..." he turned his glacier-like gaze on the Baron, "you were slow, you killed one of my soldiers, and that was all."

David stared at Orgeron. *This* was the feared general of the bellirolts? The butcher responsible for the deaths of countless magia and civilians? He seemed to care no more for war than he might for brandy or hawking. Perhaps it really was all the same to him.

I could kill him right now, David thought. *His Black Swell is one swift advance from my saber. I could sever his head and this would all be over...* And yet he felt no desire to do so. His bellirolt lust for death couldn't have been more subdued. It was as if he were on a stroll with an old friend, not meeting his archenemy. He winced as the sydaeon talisman burned against his chest. He ignored it.

"So you were trying to lead me into battle? At that tavern? Why not just declare yourself and face me then, like a true warrior?" David asked.

Orgeron laughed. "Because this is *chess, Haddington!*" His face suddenly morphed into that of a wolf about to kill: eyes blazing, teeth flashing. Just as quickly, he softened again and sang blandly, "Oh, Haddington, my dear little baron, I've been a warrior since before your meager title existed. And your innocence," he flicked his riding crop at David's nose, "though charming, is woefully transparent. I gave you an open move: I *pointed you* to where I'd be, I even remained upon the field—and you lost your way, then wasted your time defending a Highland wench. You disappointed me." His eyes brightened yet again. "Did you like my Scots accent, by the way? I've been perfecting it for years. I find that *blending in* can be prodigiously useful. Word to the wise: you ought to polish the skill yourself. You're known all about as the Baron. You're the most conspicuous magian of them all."

"Says the man riding a giant boar. Who fancies himself an officer."

"Oh I don't *fancy* myself anything, young man. I earned this rank through my service in His Majesty's army. It's a fetching uniform, isn't it?" He turned about as though David were his mirror. "I adore the cut of the suit."

"Your men slaughtered Scottish farmers back in '46," David said, seething. "It's rumored you killed as many off the battlefield as on. There is no honor in that uniform."

"*WAR is not about honor!*" Orgeron roared without warning, his voice rebounding off the misty stones. "*Honor* is a vulgarity, conjured by weaklings to civilize the acts of angry men. It's a fool's notion. Men are animals, Dunbar. There is no code in the kingdom of beasts."

"Then I ought to run you through this instant," David responded, raising his sword again, "though your blade isn't drawn. I ought to kill you just as you deserve."

"Oh, pray do not tease me, Haddington."

"Stop calling me Haddington!" David couldn't help the anger that lined his voice.

"Come now, man, you think because you burned your caput you're no longer a baron?" Orgeron said, his words gentle. "Deep down, you've always been nobility. I see it in your eye. These Highlander, these *Irish* peasants we raise our swords with... you and I are not for this lot. Nobility is in the blood, dear David. Look at you: you can't help but make a legend of yourself. The terrifying, green-eyed warrior who fights for the Jacobites. Very romantic; well done, indeed!"

Orgeron regarded David for a moment, that gaze encircling him like a gelid cloud. "You know, I used to be rather altruistic, just like you. I was an alchemist, studying under the patronage of King Edward I. After moving for years in the circles of these strange arts, I happened upon the world of the bellirolts. And, yes: your sacred Order. I, like you, sought more than the... mundane routines of these mortals." He flicked his riding crop around him. "So I laid a cunning trap for a bellirolt I found, killed him, and made myself the successor to his demon. I gathered lieutenants—men who, like me, strove for true *knowledge* of the Otherworld. We wanted to understand its properties, not just toy with them as the magia do. *We* do not shy away from the darker roots of our nature."

He nodded at the boar, who had drunk its fill from the puddle and was nipping at a fly on its leg. "It was about that time that I took on this servant here. He was a man then, his name was Brocklesby, and we were dwelling in the hidden caves of Petros halfway round the world, as I studied the waters that flowed there. They ran a brilliant green—rather like your eyes, Haddington—and had *transformative* qualities. But this Brocklesby... he was beginning to prick at my nerves a bit. Questioning my orders. Undermining my authority. So one day in a fit of rage I threw him into a Petrorian pool. And this is what emerged. Stronger than a horse. Shows no signs of yielding to age or disease. And now he does whatever I say, without question. Fascinating what effect a little *shove* can have sometimes."

David stared at Orgeron warily. For a moment, despite the force of his conscience, the urge flashed through him to seize the bellirolt's hand in companionship. He steadied himself—the feeling couldn't have been his own.

"Are you trying to recruit me, Orgeron?"

"Oh, 'recruit' is such a plebeian term, Haddington. We *recruit* underlings to serve in our armies. With you, all I need do is open the door. You know, even at this moment, there's something about the bellirolt within you that is not at ease with these *knights*. Because, in the end, it is their mission to kill you. You are one of *us,* my good man. When I find Tor Bellorum—and I shall—the day of reckoning in the Augury will have finally come to pass. The Crown of the Mortairian, in the rightful hands of us bellirolts, will endow us with power hitherto unseen in this world. You are the Ninth Sorcerer, David Dunbar, Baron de Haddington. The road forks with you. Why would you hinder my quest when we could help one another?"

Orgeron's eyes widened like two hypnotic pools: tempting waters of destiny that swirled before David. Then, the colonel blinked the moment away and snapped his fingers at the boar, who came trotting over.

"Just give it a thought," Orgeron said with his greatest air of insouciance. "God knows we have time, ha! And give my regards to old Doneval, would you? I do hope he heeds the fashion of the day and cuts that vile beard of his. Lest I use it as a handhold to behead him."

"What about your courier we have chained to the street in Naas?"

"Oh kill him, please," Orgeron replied, as if it were a favor. "If you don't I will." He mounted the boar in a spry leap, and looked down at David with something like fascination in his eyes. "It's so… *satisfying* to meet a true warrior again. I look forward to our next promenade together."

David indicated the boar with his sword. "I suppose *that* is the treatment I can expect if I don't join you."

Orgeron's brow wrinkled in disdain. "Oh no, Haddington. I wouldn't turn you into a giant pig. No, I have much better plans for you. They would involve the..." he rolled the idea around in his mouth like fine wine, "*slow incineration* of everyone you hold dear. I notice that, despite your rough-and-reckless exterior, there do seem to be those who wiggle their way into your cold heart. So I would have to mutilate you from the inside out." He smiled brightly. "A possibility like you does not saunter into my life every day, David Dunbar."

Orgeron turned his boar back in the direction he'd come, and twirled his riding crop over his shoulder. "*A bientôt*, Baron de Haddington..."

On a hot impulse not to be outdone, David fixed all his concentration on Orgeron's back, and hurled a sharp blue Disabling Fire at it.

But Orgeron had been expecting the move. In a motion almost quicker than David could follow, Orgeron flew up from the boar's back, disappearing into the faint canopy of the city. David's Fire landed with a loud SMACK on the boar's rump, sending the animal squealing away down the street. In seconds, as the first of rays of dawn pierced the heavy fog, it was as if neither beast nor rider had ever been present.

Chapter Nineteen

At the Court
of the Grand Duke

"W ait!"

Percival grabbed David's arm and brought him to a stop. It was early afternoon, and they'd just arrived in a dim alley alongside the Bonnybield Steeple.

"You mean," Percival said, "that was the first time you met the Mortairian, you're supposed to be the only one who can defeat him, and all you did was *talk* to him?"

David's expression turned rueful. "I wish I knew how to explain, lad, the kind of power he wielded in that moment. It was as if he'd bewitched my bellirolt demon, and all my warlike instincts were snuffed out."

"And drawin' on your demon was the only way you could fight?"

David pointed a long finger. "*That* was my error. I'd come to rely upon it. You can imagine Graven's response when I told him..." He turned toward the Steeple, looking for some clue as to what had interested the Watcher.

"Aye," Percival snorted, then stopped again as something struck him. "You never found Robert, did you? My ancestor."

David paused, his eyes falling. He slid his hands into his

pockets. "No, Percival. I did discover he died a few years after Culloden, and left children, but that is all."

Somehow it was at that moment, watching David with his thick, deadly hands stuffed in his trousers like a child, that understanding finally stirred in Percival. *This* was why David had chosen, on the street the previous night, to reveal his identity to a stranger for the first time in three hundred years. Not just because Percival was a Dunbar, but because Percival was his youngest, and probably closest, living relative. He wanted to connect with the family he'd never seen again.

"That must have been hard," Percival said with sympathy.

David drew a breath. "It was. But I found a new brother in Cardross."

Percival nodded. "Did he really never learn a spell? He'd been so eager to find Graven…"

"Cardross wanted to kill bellirolts." David raised a hand and ran it over the stone of the Steeple wall, streaked black from centuries of rain and dirt. "The secrets of magic have never much interested him."

Percival followed David along the wall. "What are you doin'?"

"Trying to discover what marks this building as so *special.*" David was nearing the front of the Steeple, which faced Hambledon Trinity Church on the High Street. "It's nearly as old as the town, I can sense that—plenty of human echoes here. But no traces of the Otherworld."

Percival glimpsed, in the thin gap between the Steeple and the next building, Old Man Crannog on his bench in front of the church. His hands were steadying his cane before him; his bright, clear eyes trained on something over David's and Percival's heads; his mouth still reciting the same verses. Percival smiled. His world might be spinning apart, but Crannog's bizarre routine would never change.

"Let's have a look inside," David said. "I'll need you with me, Percival."

Percival suddenly felt uneasy as he neared the High Street. "How do we know nobody saw either of us last night? Do you really want to be showin' your face here?"

"Percival, there is something key about this place, and if we don't—"

Right then, a piercing yell rang out from the High Street. David spun, as did Percival, thinking somebody *had* recognized them. But they were still in the shadows between the buildings, and when they looked out they saw every person in the square staring toward the church, where a thin man was jumping up and down in a fit of glee.

Percival went slack with amazement. It was Old Man Crannog.

"*It has happened!*" he yelled to the High Street, waving his cane at the afternoon sun. A magnificent smile radiated from his face, and he tore off his cap and seemed to paint the air with it. "Look, it has happened! Now is the time to go! All of us! Look!"

The High Street stood dumbfounded. After a moment, snatches of voices reached Percival's ears:

"*He really is mental!*"

"*Didn't know Moray Crannog had it in him...*"

Crannog, however, didn't seem to hear or care. He hobbled around the church and away from the street, as if to share his news with the rest of town.

"It's not for us to see! You must leave, all o' you!" he cried as he disappeared.

Percival stared after him, the voices of the High Street blending into a warbling cacophony. *Crannog is connected to the Watcher.* Percival didn't know how, but he *felt* it was true. Both had been observing something in the same area... or one had been observing the other. People had always told Percival that Crannog had lost his mind, or was so traumatized from some incident that all he could do was talk to himself. But the first time he'd laid eyes on the man, Percival had been seized with the notion that Crannog saw something nobody else did, and in order to really observe it, he had to avoid speaking to anybody at all. Until the time was right.

"This is, perhaps," David murmured, "the oddest town I've ever visited."

"He was lookin' for somethin'," Percival said, staring at Crannog's empty bench. "That man's been sittin' there, starin' at the top o' the Steeple, for over ten years. He wasn't mad or anythin' else—he was waitin' for somethin'. A sign."

David looked at Percival dubiously, but gazed up the wall of the Steeple to its half-crumbled spire. It was a stark, jarring shape against the blue sky. "I'm not detecting any such thing. What do you see, Percival? Tell me."

Percival was about to respond that he had no clue, when something in David's tone made him pause. It was imperious, as if he expected Percival to solve the whole puzzle then and there. And all of a sudden, Percival recalled Crannog's words.

"What could be about to happen that's not for us to see?"

David narrowed his eyes. "I just asked you—"

"I know what you asked me. And I know you want to get to the bottom o' what's goin' on here. But you're actin' like you're totally clueless about how these omens fit together. And for a three-hundred-year-old man, I don't buy it!" Percival saw indignation flare in David's eyes, but he didn't stop. "There's somethin' you haven't told me. Some bigger reason this place— and my help—is so important."

"Try the reason of saving mankind. Saving Bonnybield, and every semblance of peace in this world—"

"No, it's somethin' else." Percival paused as David's intention began to crystalize before him. "You were never just passin' through here. You lied. You came here on a mission, didn't you? One you can't fail at, like you did at Culloden and Naas."

David's eyes were roiling like tempests, a look all the more fearsome because the rest of his body was so still. He finally seemed to decide he couldn't deny it.

"My purpose here is of the strictest confidentiality, and in no way can—"

"Ach, rubbish!" Percival said, stepping as close as he dared. "You said you'd tell me what I needed to know! You don't get to use me for my Second Sight. Whatever secret you're hidin', it's part o' what's happenin' here."

"Percival, a *warrior* does not reveal a *secret mission,*" David said with finality. "I could be hauled before a Tribunal and banished from the Order for such a thing."

Percival snorted. "As if they'd banish a Sorcerer."

David parted his lips as if to say more, but held in the words. Percival noticed his eyes seem to deepen in that moment, swallowing yet another secret. The same eyes that had marked him through history, that were supposed to be signals of terror. To Percival, they seemed to penetrate everything before them, probing and studying, while retaining their own mystery. They reminded him of the green ocean, which saw all but would never speak.

He was determined to scratch their surface.

"I won't repeat a thing," Percival said, his tone softer. "But you've got to be honest with me. This is my town we're talkin' about. Please."

David's eyes closed for a moment, and Percival felt the wall behind them begin to crumble. When they opened again, their look had grown cold, forbidding.

"We've discovered that just outside this town is the hideout of Orgeron's field marshal—his lead general. I am to rendezvous tomorrow with a troop of knights, and we shall ambush him. He... took something from me."

Percival nodded. "So this all became personal for you. What did he take?"

David looked at Percival a moment longer, and turned away from the High Street. His voice came in a cutting whisper. "I never intended to share this much with you."

He then stalked into the shadow of the Old Steeple. "After Naas, we lost Orgeron. He might as well have evaporated that morning. The Irish Rebellion was strangled, of course. Just like the Jacobites. Scotland, Ireland... they all now knelt to the king in London." Percival could hear the grimace in his words. "Afterward, I remember watching smokestacks taller than churches appear on the horizon. I felt as if my bellirolt senses were being assaulted—I could *smell* the rise of the factories, how the world was changing. Cardross and I were given a mission then: take advantage of the new peace in Europe, venture forth, and reconnect with the old sects of the Order. France, Prussia, Spain, Italy—all these countries and more had had their own battalions of knights, before Orgeron severed their ties in the 1600's. Our purpose was to see if their courts still existed, and if they did, bolster them. If they didn't, rebuild them. I was to be the ambassador of the Order of Nimarius: the living proof of the truth in the Augury.

"For ten glorious years, Cardross and I sailed Europe. We built courts in seven countries, created an international network like the Order had never seen. It was the summer of 1841 when, for our final objective, we landed on the shores of Viareggio, in Tuscany."

David paused and glanced back at Percival. His jade eyes flared in the alley: two fervent warning lights.

"No matter what you think of what I'm about to tell you... do not judge me."

"Five hours!"

Cardross waved his new pocket watch from the dock, while David reclined against the mast of their boat and stared into the evening sun over the Ligurian Sea. A gentle beach curved to one side, while sharp mountain peaks cut the sky on the other. David was convinced that this part of the world lived under a different sun than that of Scotland. The oranges and reds of the sky over the deep blue water were bold, effortless—not hazy and hidden like at home—and they made him feel buoyant with energy and opportunity. He was *aware*, not just of the scene around him, but of its magical presence, which danced upon his skin with invisible fingertips.

"We sent his *own messenger* back to retrieve him *five bleedin' hours ago!*" Cardross stamped his foot. David smiled: he'd trained his friend to refine his Highland accent during their journey, and he remembered the days when an irate Cardross was almost unintelligible. "And the man said he's not two miles away! Is he arrivin' on the back of a snail?"

"*Eiiii! Buona sera!*" came a call from the shore. David stood and stepped onto the dock as their Tuscan contact approached. The late arrival was a long, wiry fellow with large eyes and a meticulously trimmed, waxed mustache. He wore a hideous pair of green-checkered trousers and an even more alarmingly green necktie, with a brown overcoat and tall hat. In one hand was a long, thin cane upon which he never leaned, but rather waved about like a drunken orchestra conductor.

"*Benvenuti!*" The Italian clapped his hands together. "Massimo Gallina. That is my name. And you must be—" he thrust his cane at David's chest, "*Lo stregone!*"

"I'm sorry?" David said.

"The Sorcerer." Signor Gallina sounded as if David were illiterate for not knowing the word. His thick eyes popped down to Cardross, to whom he nodded in approval. "*Perfetto!* I see you 'ave brought your servingman. Well—"

"Not my 'servingman'—" David corrected him, "my *friend*. This is Mr. William Cardross, of Inverness."

Cardross bowed in the manner David had taught him, but

Gallina only looked at the Highlander like some sort of mutated insect. "Car-dro," he said. He did not have a high opinion of the name.

"No, Car-*dross*. With a—never mind. Signore, we are pleased you've finally decided to arrive, but we must tend to the sale of our boat, which we were assured—"

"*O sì, sì*, the boat will be sold in no time. You will 'ave good price for it." Signor Gallina looked behind him, where several young men were bustling out to the dock. "These boys will take your things. We 'ave a long ride to *bella Firenze!* You will love Florence, Signor Stregone, where our outpost of the Noble Order still stands!"

"What of Signor D'Argenio?" David asked, fighting for patience as chattering Italians swarmed around him. "The gentleman who is to rebuild that outpost?"

"Ahh, Signor D'Argenio you shall meet tomorrow evening, when we 'ave something *molto speciale* planned for you and Signor Cardro! Leopoldo is entertaining at 'is *palazzo* in Florence, and Signor D'Argenio 'as invited both of you."

"Leopold… as in, the Grand Duke of Tuscany?" David was astounded.

"*Ma certo!*" To Gallina this was yet another obvious question. "*Vi prego, venite,* come—we have such work to do!"

Cardross trotted to keep up with David behind Gallina's long strides. He grabbed David's arm. "*He's wearin' a corset, David! Did you see?*" he whispered.

David nodded, suppressing a smile. "He might speak a bit slower were he not in such discomfort. Anyway, let's see how this one plays out. It's not every day we get to sup with a Grand Duke, now is it?"

The next evening, after they'd all survived a stifling night in Pisa, their rambling coach crested a hill and afforded the bellirolts their first view of Florence. The city was nestled into a gentle valley full of red-tiled roofs that shone in the sunset, with the pointed head of *Il Duomo*, the cathedral, soaring above them all. *Bella Firenze*, as Gallina called her, stretched out like a beautiful woman luxuriating in the hills.

The coach stumbled down into the city, rocking on the furrowed roads like a boat in a squall. David and Cardross were allowed minutes to change at D'Argenio's private palazzo, then were thrown into another coach. They rattled across the medieval cobblestones thick with mud and people, nearly toppled from the vehicle as Gallina hopped out before them, and were jostled through the sticky summer evening into a doorway half as large as it should be. David's mind finally caught up with him as his shoes clacked on the gallery floor of the Grand Duke's home: the Palazzo Pitti.

He had stepped into a life-sized jewel box. David stared at the exquisite burgundy floors and marble doorways, all glimmering like a mirror. The ceiling was adorned with gold patterns and figurines in every corner, and *portraits*—there were portraits everywhere. Faces of long-dead Florentine nobility, landscapes, biblical scenes: they bedecked the walls, were nestled into passages, above doorways, even hung thirty feet in the air in the crooks of the ceiling. Every inch of the palace was covered in something beautiful. It was as if David's wildest fantasies as a young man had sprung to life around him, and he was reminded of the opulent homes he'd visited when he was a boy in Scotland. If he hadn't succumbed to his bellirolt, hadn't destroyed Galanforde, might he have one day created his own Palazzo Pitti? Even Cardross—the pragmatic adventurer who lived on his feet—eyed the splendor with a tinge of hunger.

Gallina ushered the bellirolts toward a group of gentlemen who were puffing on short rolls of tobacco. From their number stepped one of the most handsome men David had ever met, whom Gallina introduced as Signor D'Argenio. This Italian bore a face as chiseled and smooth as a sculpture, with a pair of thick, chin-length sideburns. His full lips seemed always upturned in a subtle, confident smile, and his black pardessus cape fluttered about his shoulders as he moved.

"*Signore.*" D'Argenio said the word in a deep voice with care and affection, then bowed to David, as did all the men in his company. David was stunned: this was the home of the Grand Duke of Tuscany, and these gentlemen were deferring to *him?* Former baron from a small town in Scotland?

"Please... recover yourself, sir," David said.

But D'Argenio was intent on doing so in his own time. "As a boy, here in *Firenze*, I heard of your legend, but never once thought I might meet you, *Il nono stregone.* The outposts you built in France, Spain, Portugal... have recruited more knights than we have seen in centuries." He clasped David's hand. "My name is Cesare D'Argenio. I am honored to welcome you to Tuscany."

The warmth of D'Argenio's greeting stirred in David's chest, and spread throughout his body. He was proud of the work he and Cardross had done, but as D'Argenio led the company to another gallery, David felt something beyond pride bloom inside him: *comfort.* For the first time in his life—despite being a bellirolt, despite having turned one hundred seventy-six a few weeks earlier, and knowing he might well live to see D'Argenio's great-grandchildren—he could enjoy a position with other gentlemen that he had earned on his own.

"Tonight," D'Argenio announced as they walked, "we dine as guests of the royal duke. Tomorrow, we begin to rebuild our Tuscan outpost." He guided the men to a table on one side of the golden-walled room, reserved for those who could afford to sit, as most guests were standing. A full band on the other side played the latest European craze called the "waltz," with space for dancing in the middle. David noticed that he and Cardross were the only men with long hair—a blatant violation of

European vogue, but to them it was a matter of pride. Trimming it would take centuries to regrow. He'd begun to appreciate Graven's impressive beard.

"*Non esiste un chianti che lui non conosce!*" Signor Gallina was saying to the rest of the table, throwing his hands around in lieu of his cane. "Signor D'Argenio knows all wine in Tuscany! He makes almost half of it!" D'Argenio smiled as he lit one of the rolled tobacco sticks his friends had been smoking earlier.

"What the de'il is that?" Cardross whispered to David. "It smells awful."

"*DEV-il,*" David said, emphasizing the *v*. "You mustn't drop your consonants, remember."

Cardross shot an icy look at David. He was in no mood to be corrected.

"I beg your pardon, Signore," David turned to D'Argenio, "but that tobacco of yours... is most unusual."

"Oh, you like?" D'Argenio beamed with yellow teeth through the smoke. "It is from France, very new. They call it a '*sigaretta.*' Makes the mouth dry, so I must always have water close!" He patted a glass near his hand. "Bottled, from the mountains."

"Beware the water here in city, Signor Stregone!" Gallina trumpeted. "*È terribile.*"

David smiled. "I shan't need any, though I fear I've been spoiled by the taste of a spring in dear old Scotland. Eh, Cardross?" David turned to his companion, who was absently fingering the full wine glass in front of him. Cardross didn't look angry anymore, just detached, as if his mind were back near that Scottish spring.

David tried to re-engage with his Italian hosts, who were jokingly asking why Scottish men fight in skirts, but he was troubled by Cardross's sudden withdrawal. The men's repartee continued, never discussing any topic more serious than D'Argenio's water, and David began to notice he himself was growing detached—when he suddenly felt he was being watched. A flash of alarm shot through him, but as he turned all he saw was a sea of guests, clad in shiny black and red and cerulean, chattering away over the music. And for an instant, two radiant eyes that stared at him from several tables away.

David blinked and looked again. The eyes belonged to a young woman, who had now focused back on her table. She had obsidian-black hair that was styled into a bun and descended in curls from her temples, framing a face more striking than any David had ever seen. Her lips were full, her cheekbones high and regal, and her eyes a wild blue-green that couldn't exist in any of the waters of the world.

The woman's silk dress draped off her pale shoulders and matched her eyes, and she sat very still as her companions talked. She regarded them all with a soft, amused smile that seemed to say she would rather observe their conversation than partake in it: that she looked the part, but was really an outsider. To David, that smile was so honest, so effortless and elegant, he couldn't help but be captivated by it. He felt, from four tables away in a crowded gallery, he knew exactly what this woman was thinking.

A full-bodied laugh from D'Argenio wrenched David back to his table—the Italians were making fun of Gallina's necktie. He narrowed his eyes and looked back across the gallery. As far as he could tell, the beautiful woman hadn't glanced at him again. He was about to ask D'Argenio for an introduction, when two other young ladies fluttered up to her and whispered excitedly in her ear. She smiled and shook her head, but after more prodding, they coaxed her from her seat and out into the room.

David realized this might be his only chance. He jumped up so fast he almost spilled D'Argenio's wine. The Italians turned to him, perplexed.

"Pardon me, I must... have a look at something," he

muttered. He swept around the table and into the crowd of dancers, musicians, perfumed elite gossiping in clusters... his eyes scanned every face. He had no idea what he'd say when he found the woman. What if she only spoke Italian? What if she were married? All his skills at courting were almost two hundred years old. Today the dances were different, the topics of conversation different...

He rounded the corner to the next gallery and almost choked. *There she is.* The woman had just halted a foot away from him, her chest heaving in the blue-green dress—she'd been in a hurry and had nearly run into him. Her eyes, large in surprise, were even more stunning this close, and the longer David looked into them the less he knew how to speak.

She lowered her gaze and made a small curtsy, smiling in embarrassment.

"*Buona sera, signore,*" she said in a thick accent David couldn't identify. Her two companions—dressed in loud, frilly gowns with bell skirts and leg-of-mutton sleeves—arrived behind her, giggling. They stopped upon seeing David towering over them, and something purple and gloppy slipped from one of their hands onto the floor. He looked more closely and realized the girls had, wrapped in their lace mouchoirs, fist-fulls of jelly from one of the food tables.

"*Buah*—Good evening, madam," he stammered.

She raised her thin, dark eyebrows and looked back at the girls. "*Un homme anglais...*" she said in an intrigued voice. The girls tittered to each other, clutching their sugary prizes closer.

French, then, David realized. They were French, not Italian. This he could handle! The woman said, "Good evening, sir," in her accent, curtsied again, and made to go past him into the main gallery.

"*Je vous prie de m'excuser, Madame...*"

The woman turned, looking relieved he knew the courtly tongue.

"*I was wondering if,*" he continued in French, "*I might have the honor of a dance.*"

The young woman cocked an eyebrow and studied him. Her eyes caught some of the candlelight and seemed to flash provocatively.

"*A lady is not accustomed to dancing with a man she has not met,*" she replied in French.

David's cheeks flared red. How had he forgotten to introduce himself?

"*Mais bien sûr. David Dunbar d'Écosse, pour vous servir.*" He gave a small bow.

"And do you enjoy the dance, Monsieur Dunbar?" the woman asked in unbroken English, her gaze never faltering.

"… On occasion," David replied. What language did she prefer, anyway? "It all depends, of course, upon my partner."

"And what if your partner has *very* tired feet?"

"Then we shall move so swiftly her feet do not touch the ground," David said. She broke into a little smile, looking more amused than impressed. "Although—" he tried to turn the smile into a laugh— "on this floor we might not even have to try. It's so over-waxed we might skate better than dance."

The young woman wrinkled her brow and glanced at her friends, who were following none of this conversation. "You do not care for the palace?" she asked.

"Well, no—of course I do," David backpedaled. Why couldn't they just speak French again? "But you must admit it's rather… *overdone,* a bit, don't you think?" He glanced at the gilded picture frames for support.

The woman, however, gave him a quizzical look, probing as far into his mind as she could. "It is a palace, Monsieur," she said. "Even a palace has beauty sometimes."

"*Viens, Coralie, viens!*" one of the girls broke in. "*Il est temps!*"

David looked at the woman with renewed interest. *Coralie.*

That was her name. Her face seemed to say she knew her friend's error but was unruffled by it, and, for the briefest of moments, the look in her eyes deepened to one of alluring warmth. It was a look David could not translate to words, for a hundred words could not express its meaning, but it penetrated and enlivened him. Then she lowered her eyes, and curtsied one last time before being whisked away into the throng.

David felt as if he'd just been returned to his own body. Never had anyone looked at him that way before. She seemed curious about him, even as she challenged him.

Her name is Coralie. That simple fact alone filled him with wonder and excitement. He floated forward in a reverie, and was halfway across the gallery when a short man appeared in front of him. David tried to sidestep him, but felt a firm hand on his chest. He had to look down before he realized it was Cardross.

"Where the blazes did you go?" the Highlander asked.

"I, uh..." David did his best to blink Coralie from his vision. "I'll tell you later."

Cardross gave him a suspicious look. "D'Argenio says the Grand Duke is about to enter. We've got to line up—you know, look impressive."

All David could do, as they sought out D'Argenio, was replay the encounter with Coralie in his head. Had he been too forward? Too disparaging of Palazzo Pitti? Perhaps she was already engaged to another man. Although, she had been staring at *him* first...

Trumpets blared to David's left. He was standing on one side of an aisle the courtiers had formed, and strolling through the far door was Grand Duke Leopold, his wife on his arm. As the couple passed, David bowed low, following D'Argenio's example, and then his host nudged him.

"We call him *Il Broncio*, Signor Dunbar," D'Argenio said in a low voice, "because of his glum face. Do you see?"

David smiled and nodded. This was the most unfortunate-looking royal pair he could imagine. Leopold had sunken posture and the strange, protruding under-lip that marked the brood of the Austrian court, while his lady was portly and dour. As they strode on, David noticed that several guests at the food tables were taking advantage of the ceremony to slip entire plates of sliced pork and bonbons into their coats and handbags. Apparently leaving Palazzo Pitti empty-handed was something of a disgrace.

David's gaze followed the Grand Duke and Duchess toward the floor where they were about to dance, past more gentleman who made sure Leopold saw them bowing as low as possible, and an ice-blue eye that winked at David from across the aisle.

David stiffened and his skin tingled. This wasn't normal; it was some sort of magic he was feeling—but magic or no, he flashed upon a full head of curly white hair, and the cold face of Claudius Orgeron in the crowd.

Just as David's hand slipped to the dirk hidden in his sleeve, the feeling passed. A veil of cool air lifted from his eyes, and he looked again. The face he'd seen belonged to a sinewy man with tan skin—more Mediterranean than Orgeron's pale countenance—who wasn't staring at David at all. Had he been imagining it?

No. The answer materialized in David's head. *This is a sign.* The Otherworld was trying to tell him something. Orgeron might not be present at that moment, but for the first time since leaving Ireland, David had the distinct feeling that at least his spies were, and that it wouldn't be long before he found himself face to face with them in Florence. Or with the Dark Commander himself.

Chapter Twenty

City of the Flower

" *Sete, belle sete!* Ladies: watered silk, Italian silks, very fine Mantua silks! Lace of Florence and Venice, gentlemen— lace for your ladies?"

David slid past the street vendor waving a yard of red silk before him, and stepped into the orange sunlight on the Piazza della Signoria, in the heart of Florence. Cardross shuffled behind, having followed him through the worn stone streets since their tour of the Renaissance-era Order outpost that morning. David had declared the outpost in barely passable condition as a structure, let alone a command center for the knights of Tuscany. He recommended that D'Argenio secure a place to train new recruits outside the city while the outpost was fortified. The Italian had already summoned his best masons for a meeting that afternoon.

David strode through the bustling square toward the palazzo that towered in the far corner. In his coat he carried a new missive from Graven: the Court of Paladins had returned to Dunadd, as movements of the Dark Legion had become more centered around Scotland. "*Anticipation is ripe,*" Graven wrote, "*that soone the dreade Lair will be found, and our True War to keep the Enemy from it shall commence. Continue your efforts, lads, but do not Tarry overlong: the tyme to begin your*

247

Return is neare at hand." But David wasn't ready to think about returning yet. He would obey that command when it arrived. He still hadn't told anybody about his vision of Orgeron the night before.

Finally he spied what he was looking for in front of the palazzo. He threaded his way between strolling ladies and begging gypsies until he stood beneath the seventeen-foot masterpiece of marble that guarded the entrance: the statue called the *David.*

It was more than just the name of the sculpture that drew David Dunbar. From his private tutor back at Galanforde he'd learned of the statues that lined this piazza, most depicting nude scenes from mythology that could never have been displayed in Scotland. But here was the plain figure of a boy with a slingshot, alert and confident, staring over his shoulder at what David imagined to be a new challenger. His expression was pointed and uncompromising—he was effortless, and he had power.

"Fancy the lad, do you?"

Cardross sounded as rude as he did ignorant. David wheeled on him.

"Have you ever taken the time to *observe* beauty around you, William?"

"Frequently." Cardross was standing with his arms crossed, feet cocked apart, tall hat pulled down at an angle over one eye. "But I don't drool whilst I do it."

David glared at him. "What's your quarrel, then? You've been as sour as a spoiled girl for the past two days. You made horrid company at court last night."

"*Hang the court!*" Cardross stepped forward and growled in David's face. "Hang Gallina, hang D'Argenio—same goes for that pompous nit of a Grand Duke, as well! We are *wastin' time,* Mister Sorcerer, and you know it. Ten years now we've been on this mission, and it's been a mighty fine time, let me tell you; I don't regret a minute. But you read Graven's letter. Orgeron is closin' in on Tor Bellorum. I can *feel* it. I know you can."

David wanted to deny it, but he had felt the anticipation of the bellirolt coiling inside him. He wondered if Cardross had seen the same vision the previous night.

"If it's home you miss, Cardross…" David said, trying a different angle. But Cardross threw back his head and laughed.

"I don't miss Scotland. I miss bein' part of the fight. It's a good thing we've spent ten years buildin' Order outposts where there's hardly any need for the Order, but now we've made it as far as *Tuscany*. Whilst you were indulgin' in your beauty sleep last night, I was lookin' at a map—and you know what I found? We are *fourteen hundred miles* from Dunadd. Can you fathom how long it'll take to return? What if we're needed right away? Is this not the perfect time for Orgeron to strike, whilst we're out here in—" he flung his arm at the *David* statue— "*art land?*"

At that moment, a shrill voice cut through the piazza: "*Signore e signori, venite tutti! Ecco il migliore prestigiatore del mondo! Venite, venite!*"

David glanced down the length of the palazzo, near a statue of Neptune upon a fountain. A large stage had been erected under an awning, with some oddly shaped boxes and full-length mirrors set upon it. A boy dressed in the bright costume of a Renaissance page was gesturing to the stage.

"*Questa non è illusione, signori!* It is not illusion! *È la magia vera!*"

"Real magic?" David raised an eyebrow at Cardross.

"*Signore e signori!*" the boy yelled as loudly as he could. "Ladies and gentlemen! *Vi presento:* the SORCERER SUBINI!"

Right on cue, a burst of blue sparks erupted from the stage with a loud BANG, and in their wake a short magician appeared before the crowd.

Thrilled cheers echoed around the piazza. "Subini" was Cardross's height with fair skin and a neat black beard, dressed in a fanciful imitation of a wizard: a velvety robe shimmering with stars and moons, and a tall conical hat to match. He bowed to his fans.

"A 'sorcerer' indeed?" David glanced at Cardross, and could see that this first trick had caught his friend's attention despite himself. They drifted toward the stage, where Subini commenced an array of illusions. He made birds disappear in one cage and reappear in another. He pulled more birds out of empty bags, had them fly to the far side of the piazza, and then they returned with mates that Subini made vanish and reappear again. In a comical interlude, the conjurer asked a spectator to name a simple object, which Subini then dug through an "empty" bag to look for, tossing out random items before finally producing the object of choice. He even made a glowing crystal ball levitate and dance before him on the stage, at which point David nudged Cardross.

"I think we may have missed our calling, old boy," he said. Cardross grunted.

In between acts, Subini would raise his arms and half a dozen dwarves would rush out from behind the stage like a strange band of minions—all dressed in the same Renaissance attire as the boy—and dart around the audience with pewter tankards for money. Subini proclaimed he would not attempt another illusion unless each dwarf returned with his tankard full to the brim. Surprisingly, this never took long to happen.

"Think if he does this a few times per week," Cardross murmured. "That conjurer is well-breeched, I warrant you."

David nodded. Just then, as Subini began another trick, David cast his eyes through the crowd and felt his heart bound forward. *There is Coralie.* The woman's keen eyes were unmistakable even from the side as she watched the spectacle. She wore a dark gold-patterned gown and rested a parasol over one shoulder, as did the older woman who stood beside her.

David's mind began tripping over itself. Was he going to let her walk away again? How did he know when they might cross paths next? There had to be some way he could get her attention, and Cardross would be no help in his mood...

Then—as if by magic—David found his opportunity.

"For my final act," Subini called out in a thick Italian accent, "I shall require one volunteer! *Solamente uno,* from the audience!"

David's hand shot into the air of its own accord.

"*Ah, perfetto!* The gentleman there! You, Signore, step forward, *prego!*"

David looked around and realized just how emphatic his response had been: not only had he been the first to raise his hand, but he was a head taller than almost everybody else. He ignored Cardross's cautionary look and approached the stage, his stomach lurching as he wondered what he'd gotten himself into. He didn't appreciate how vast the crowd was until he took the stage with the conjurer. For a moment he felt dizzy.

Subini shook his hand warmly. His pointed hat included, the "sorcerer" was still shorter than the actual Sorcerer he'd invited into his show.

"This gentleman has offered to help demonstrate the wonders of an artifact which I have traveled half the known world to procure!" Subini declared. One of his dwarves trotted up and presented a long wooden box. "*Signore e signori,*" he called, "I give you, from the wild, windswept deserts of Persia, the Sword of Tamerlane!"

He drew from the box a long shamshir sword, with a turquoise-encrusted hilt and a radically curved blade. A pair of dwarves ushered David over to a tall box center stage, which, when David was placed within it, covered all sides of his torso with black paper screens and allowed his hands to rest on two wooden arms.

"This sword, after centuries of use, is still a deadly weapon!" Subini slashed the blade through a wooden board stage right. David heard a few impressed murmurs from the audience, and searched for Coralie in their number, but couldn't locate her.

"However!" Subini went on, "the Sorcerer Subini has mastered the essence of this blade! He decides when the Sword of Tamerlane may do harm, and when it may not!"

Without notice, Subini turned and plunged the blade straight through David's belly. There was a collective gasp from the crowd, and suddenly all was silent. David felt as if he'd been split in half. This was no trick—*the conjurer had impaled him.* But his body was covered by the paper screens, so the audience was none the wiser. If he betrayed any sign of injury, they would know he was not mortal.

David clenched his fists and forced his mind from the wrenching, ripping feeling in his gut. He drilled his eyes into Subini. What the hell was this conjurer attempting? Did he really know who David was? Was he trying to kill him? Torture him?

But Subini's exuberant look hadn't changed at all. The consummate performer.

"Do you feel pain, Signore?" the conjurer asked.

David squared his jaw and even let a tinge of a smile bend his lips. "No." In his mind the response was: *Not as much as you'll feel when I'm finished with you, you dog...*

"*Non sente nessun dolore!*" Subini clarified in Italian. Wild cheers erupted from the crowd, and Subini's dwarves rotated the box in which David stood, so everybody could see just how well the Sword of Tamerlane had run him through. When Subini finally retracted the blade, David tried to make a show of checking his garments for damage; really he was hiding the pain of his skin and innards repairing themselves. What he found, however, was that his clothes weren't even torn. It looked as if nothing had touched him. The audience applauded once more.

"Well, *fiorentini e turisti*," Subini called, "either I am a true conjurer, or this man is a demon!" He turned and sent a coy wink in David's direction.

The spectators burst into relieved laughter, but David's face went hot with rage. So Subini did know what he was. A dozen questions pummeled his mind, first and foremost how to catch this conjurer alone, find out who he was... But Subini bade the crowd farewell, smashed a vial on the stage before him, and vanished in a cloud of orange smoke.

"So what was that all about?" Cardross demanded as soon as David found him again. "How did he—"

"Bravo, Monsieur Dunbar!"

Coralie was approaching through the dispersing crowd, her older companion at her side. Something about her golden dress, her radiant eyes, the black ringlets that danced beside her face, lifted David from his troubles for the moment.

"Have you always been a devotee of magic?" Coralie cocked her head at him, again speaking English.

David had no words. *If she only knew.* And what was more, he was astonished she was approaching him in a public square. Casual talk at a ball was one thing, but a young lady never spoke publically to a gentleman unless her parents had made the introduction. Hence the frosty stare David was receiving from Coralie's companion.

"Only in my spare time," he said, in less than a full voice, "Mademoiselle...?"

"De Montagnac," Coralie replied, with a small curtsy. She glanced back at the stage. "That was very brave, Monsieur."

"Well..." David felt tension rise in his body again. "Thank you, Mademoiselle. I must admit I felt emboldened 'til I saw the size of the blade."

Cardross snorted, either at the comment or to remind

David he was still there. David introduced him, and Coralie introduced the woman with her as her chaperone Eugenie. No sooner had she done so than a clock nearby tolled noon, and Coralie said she had to meet her father at their palazzo on the Lungarno. Without thinking, David asked if he and Cardross could escort them.

"That may be well enough for you," Cardross said, "but all this sun is upsettin' my Scottish head. I need a change of scene." Without even a nod to the ladies, he turned on his heel.

David caught him by the shoulder. "What the devil has gotten into you?" he whispered. "If you must go, then find out where that conjurer has gone, and who he—"

Cardross stopped him with a smoldering look. "I am not your spaniel. *Monsieur.*" He shook off David's hand and stalked away.

Anger flamed in David's face, but he swallowed it and turned to Coralie. "Please forgive my friend. He's been poor company lately. Shall we?"

Coralie lifted her eyebrows, and glanced coyly at her chaperone.

"*You may accompany us only to the Lungarno,*" Eugenie declared in French. "*I shan't have Monsieur de Montagnac seeing a strange man converse with his daughter!*"

They strolled out of the piazza toward the Arno River, and talked as best they could while Eugenie hovered behind them. David learned that Coralie's family hailed from Lyon, and her father was a prosperous silk merchant with mills in France, Spain, and Italy. He adored Florence, and brought his wife and only child to spend a quarter of every year in their palazzo overlooking the river. It was Coralie who had requested her own tutor to study English—as well as Spanish and Italian—in order to learn more about the cultures her father dealt with. David was beguiled by how smart and worldly she was.

When Coralie asked about him, David told her the same

cover story he and Cardross had used for a decade. They were gentlemen in the midst of the time-honored Grand Tour of Europe, both of whom had lands in Scotland and Ireland, meaning they didn't have to answer questions about work (as they didn't work), and could excuse themselves as naïve tourists if they got into a difficult situation.

Eugenie brought Coralie and David to an abrupt halt as her eyes landed upon a handsome, three-story building facing the river.

"*That is the palazzo of Monsieur de Montagnac,*" Eugenie stated with finality. "*It has been very stimulating to speak with you, Monsieur Dunbar. We bid you good day.*"

David knew that "good day" meant "goodbye forever." He was an utter stranger to the de Montagnac circle. He noticed Coralie's eyes flash in annoyance at Eugenie, but they both knew the chaperone held the reins.

His spirits plummeting, David extended his hand to Coralie, who laid her fingers overtop his. Her irises sparkled at his show of gallantry, and he'd just lowered his lips to brush her knuckles when she suddenly said in English: "Ah! I thought so."

David paused as his eyes were just coming level with her own. "Thought—?"

"You do not have the hands of a gentleman."

David lifted his eyebrows and straightened himself, letting go of her hand. "And how is that?"

"Yours are too strong. You have not spent your days at a desk, or—" she searched for the words— "twirling a cane. You do not seem like a highbrow on his Grand Tour."

Eugenie cleared her throat so loudly David thought it might echo on the opposite riverbank, whereupon Coralie snapped in French, "*Madame, I am practicing my English with Monsieur Dunbar! My father would be pleased, as you ought to be.*"

The chaperone bristled, seeming to grow half a foot taller as her back stiffened. It was then that David realized this woman likely didn't know a word of English. Why would she? And why should he continue to be so cautious around Coralie, who'd already discerned much more than he'd given her credit for?

He looked at her, drank in the blue-green challenge in her eyes, and leaned closer.

"You are correct, Mademoiselle," he said in a low voice. "I've long been a stranger to the affairs of an estate. My hands can wield a sword, rig a ship, and climb a wall with no rope."

"So you have lied," Coralie responded, the corners of her lips twitching. "This is no Tour for you. You are a pirate in gentleman's clothing."

David smiled, and continued to hold her gaze in his. "I am a man who has seen this whole side of the world. And of all the wonders in it, I am entranced by you."

This time Coralie returned his smile, though it shone far more in her eyes than her lips. It was as if she were saving some part of it, holding it back from public display, and then David knew why:

"*Mademoiselle de Montagnac!*" Eugenie screeched. "*Now your Maman has seen you! She will have my head, Mademoiselle!*"

David looked toward the palazzo and noticed a tall, thin-faced lady standing in a second-floor window. She was wearing a blood-red dress and cradling an aperitif as she stared like a hawk toward them.

Disappointment dimmed Coralie's eyes. Her chaperone grabbed her arm, and she explained to David in rapid French: "*It's not your fault, Monsieur. Maman has been fuming since our phaeton broke down, with her upon it!*"

"*You have a phaeton?*" David loved the sporty, two-person carriages.

Coralie nodded. "*We cannot yet find a craftsman to repair it—*"

"*Now, Mademoiselle!*" Eugenie tugged her charge away, and Coralie managed one last look at David, in which she let out a full, shining smile—with a hint of mischief. As if, for that moment, she didn't care who saw it.

David stood by the river for several moments, gazing at the palazzo, refusing to believe that this was the last time he would see Coralie de Montagnac... until that mischievous glint from her smile sunk in, and a wild idea came with it. *I did tell her I was capable with my hands...* He strode around the back of the palazzo, where he found a stable with two horses and an orange phaeton sitting in pieces on the ground. It seemed its entire front axle had come apart. David remembered how horrible the summer roads had been as he'd ridden into Florence.

A young stable hand materialized from the shadows, and snatched off his cap upon seeing David.

"*Parlez-vous français?*" David asked. The man nodded. David dug a few *quattrini* coins from his waistcoat, which he handed to him.

"*Then bring me the coachman,*" David said. "*Right away.*"

Several days later, Coralie ducked out from a vendor's awning in the Piazza Santa Croce, opening her parasol under the bright sun. Eugenie trotted behind her, as the young woman browsed the stalls of glistening fruits and crisp flowers, closing her eyes and inhaling the aromas. All of a sudden, she spied something at the north end of the square.

"*Eugenie, look!*" she exclaimed.

At the entrance to a side street, just apart from a line of other coaches, stood a bright orange carriage on four giant wheels, drawn by two horses. A black folding top extended to the sides and over the seat, obscuring the driver.

"*It's Papa with the phaeton! May I?*"

Eugenie gave as much of a smile as her tight lips would allow and nodded, saying she wanted to stay and purchase flowers. Coralie dashed across the piazza to the phaeton, and grasped the unusually firm hand that pulled her up into the cushioned alcove.

"*Papa, pourquoi vous ne me l'aviez pas dit—*"

Her voice, and all the excitement in it, frosted over. Seated beside her in the snug carriage, so close their bodies couldn't help but touch, was a man far too tall—and with hair far too long—to be her father.

"*Bonjour, Mademoiselle.*" David tipped his hat.

"Monsieur!" Coralie's face turned crimson, and she backed against the side of the phaeton. "This is my *father's phaeton!* You—repaired it?"

"Alas, I wish I could claim credit. I set the finest wheelwrights in the city on it. Normally they work for a friend of mine, but I was able to borrow their services."

Coralie aimed the end of her closed parasol like a bayonet. "How dare you, Monsieur, lure me into my own father's carriage?"

David twirled his whip over the dash rail in front of him. "Mademoiselle de Montagnac, I did not invite you into this carriage. You ran clear across the piazza and threw yourself upon it, at which point I had no choice but to offer you my hand, lest you fall to the stones and perish." He glanced sideways at her. "A gallant act for a pirate, no?"

Coralie's eyes turned stony. "Flirting in the street is one thing, but you cannot try to abduct me, as if you have no regard for my family name—"

"And without an abduction, how might I have spoken to you again?"

For a full second Coralie was lost for words. Then she shook her head, and gave him a curt "I am leaving."

She turned to dismount, but David swung the whip so it partially blocked her way. Her body went stiff.

"Mademoiselle… Forgive me, but I've seen in your eyes a

yearning for adventure to match my own. And I don't believe I'm mistaken."

Coralie looked back at him. "You *are* mistaken if you think—"

"An afternoon." He lowered the whip and looked at her sincerely. "Give me one afternoon. To take you for a drive. People tell me of a place called Fiesole, in the mountains to the north, with a view of the city that is unparalleled. I shan't take you anywhere else, and I'll deliver you safely back to your palazzo. And if you have a miserable time, you shan't ever see me again."

Coralie's eyes roiled with incredulity. "My father, Monsieur—"

"Is dining with his associates at that hotel on the Tornabuoni. So says the coachman." He paused, and softened his voice. "You may think me a cad, Mademoiselle, but I assure you I've no evil designs. In fact, I promise you this: if an afternoon away from your chaperone doesn't entice you, I'll leave the carriage this instant."

Coralie puffed out a breath, as if she wanted to say something, but then closed her mouth. The spark of indignation in her eyes finally began to appear like a glimmer of intrigue. "I do not know this 'cad,' but you are arrogant, and exceedingly bold."

The corners of David's lips quirked. "I'm not normally so."

She stared at him hard. "Liar."

David leaned his face just a few inches closer. "Be a liar with me."

The fire in Coralie's gaze flared, and she looked away before David could read it. He was convinced, though, that he'd caught a flicker of a smile in her eyes.

"You must keep the top low," she said in a small voice. "If anybody notices me…"

"They'll see the true swashbuckler you are?" David finished. He caught her gaze for an instant and smiled for her, then nudged the horses out of the piazza.

The phaeton rattled its way out of the city and up a winding dirt road, before finally reaching the village of Fiesole. David had brought a picnic blanket with wine, cheese, and bread, and he and Coralie continued on foot to a grove beneath a tall stone embankment, at the edge of a slope. Above them were the sandy, sunbaked walls of an ancient monastery, and below was the sprawling majesty of Florence, glistening in its bed of green hills.

They settled on the blanket, David poured two cups of wine, and they toasted in silence. Coralie looked out over the city, as if waiting for David to speak. The way she tilted her head suggested she wasn't anxious, but was far from at ease.

"So," he said, "tell me of life in Lyon."

She sipped her wine. "I am the daughter of a rich man. What do you want to know?"

"How do spend your hours? What does your mother allow you to do?"

Her dark eyebrows shot up. "My mother, Monsieur?"

David gave a small shrug. "I saw her in that window. She rather resembled a bird of prey."

"Mind what you say, Monsieur Dunbar. Those talons can scratch." She looked down at the picnic blanket. "Maman is very concerned for my future. She is... how do you say... *desperate* for me to marry a man of *noblesse*. My father has the wealth, but if he can marry me to a noble man, then Madame de Montagnac can be the mother of a baroness, or a countess."

David felt a sudden, bitter ache in the pit of his stomach, and he looked out at the Duomo cathedral rising over the center of Florence.

"Fascinating when people put so much stock in something so fleeting, isn't it." He wasn't able to hide the irony in his voice.

But Coralie turned with new appreciation in her eyes. "You are right, Monsieur; it is *fleeting*, thank you. Maman believes just the opposite! She says, 'No, nobility secures your name in the blood, in the history, of your country!'"

David gave a sad smile. "That very notion was ingrained in me from an early age. I believed there were things you could always count on because of your name. And then I grew older and realized... life has a way of changing what you can count on."

"*Ah oui.* But you..." Coralie said, trying to be delicate, "you are not nobility?"

David looked at her, then out at the rosy-roofed city. Somewhere down there was the Order outpost and any number of jobs he ought to be doing, not least of which was tracking down the conjurer who'd attacked him the other day. But somehow all of that melted away in this place with Coralie. She brought him out of himself—not in the exhausting way Graven did, but in a way that thrilled him. For an instant, he longed to break the sacrosanct code of the Order and tell her of when he *had* been a nobleman, that he knew every facet of that life and sorely missed it at times...

"No," he replied. He paused, wrestling with the words. "I had family that was. But... I let my pride destroy my ties to them."

He watched her, and she watched him back, not pressing the issue. And suddenly he realized: with Coralie, he could be free of the nobility. Free of the bellirolt and the Sorcerer. No explanation was needed. He was David Dunbar, *a man,* with this woman.

When the silence grew, he quipped, "Why, is it obvious I'm no aristocrat?"

"Well, you did capture me in my family's carriage. You know, you could try speaking to my father... At least ask his permission to keep company with me."

David smiled ruefully. "Mademoiselle, if it would please you I should be happy to meet your father. But I have nothing to recommend me. No acquaintance, no letter from a man of higher station. I'm not even from his homeland. To him I'm but a tourist."

"But what are you, really?" Coralie said, refusing to be discouraged. "When you are not, eh, *swashbuckling?*" She smiled at the new word, and cocked her head in a somewhat feline way. "What will you do when you return to Scotland?"

David felt the earth slow around him. What would he do if were not a bellirolt, not a Sorcerer, with thousands of men looking to him for salvation?

"I believe I shall... start over." His voice had lowered to a thread of sound. "Have a farm, perhaps. Write..."

Coralie considered him, then smirked. "I do not know that I can picture you behind a plow."

David glanced at her, cocking an eyebrow. "Where *can* you picture me?"

She pursed her lips, appraising him as only a French lady could, and said, "I wonder if you have not yet found what you truly wish to do."

At that moment, a distant peal echoed from the valley. David was considering her words, but he let them rest for the moment. His bellirolt eyes could just make out the swinging bells in the tower beside the Duomo. Coralie grinned—a full, girlish grin that seemed to expand her body—and her fingers brushed his arm.

"You know... my favorite part of France is the Alsace, where there is a church we used to visit when I was a girl. And you must know this about Alsace—" she looked at him with total seriousness— "it has *storks.*"

David laughed out loud.

"The storks sit on the church tower, like that one, and they always forget about the bells! So the bells ring, and all the storks fly off at once. Like they're affronted."

Both David and Coralie smiled. She sipped her wine and rolled her eyes. "As a girl that always delighted me. And if you ride past the vineyards in late afternoon, the sun shines through them, so the grapes look like they are glowing. Like they are filled with... melted gold." Her eyes shimmered with her analogy. "Which I suppose they are! You must see it someday, David."

The recognition flashed between them that she'd just used his first name, but given the tone of the day, an apology didn't seem necessary. Coralie tilted her chin up, shrugged, and looked back out to the city.

David followed her gaze. "I spent two years in France, and I suddenly feel I've seen none of it."

Coralie nodded at the vastness before them. "I feel, right now, as though I have never seen Florence like this."

David felt he ought to respond, but he knew he didn't have to. They could have sat in silence for the rest of the day, leaning close to each other but not quite touching, and watched the sun dance along the crimson crowns of Florence until it set. It didn't matter in the slightest whether or not they spoke.

It was several weeks later when David took to the streets alone after dark, careful to be silent outside Cardross's chamber as he left D'Argenio's palazzo. Coralie had been the one to initiate their next rendezvous, and after that they'd plotted more together: strolls in moonlit piazzas when she could sneak out, "accidental" encounters in markets and shops—any creative way to steal a moment of conversation. But her chaperone Eugenie was growing suspicious, and David was having his own troubles. Two of the stonemasons working at the Florence outpost had been murdered—in the outpost itself. Judging by their Sable Scars, the deed had been done by bellirolts. David wrote straightaway to his new allies in Paris for reinforcements.

As for the shady conjurer Subini, David and Cardross had uncovered no name, story, or whereabouts. The man seemed as elusive as Orgeron.

David crossed the Arno and turned onto Via Maggio, landing in the midst of a cacophonous throng of Italians. He scanned their faces, looking for some flash of those blue-green eyes, then spied Coralie standing against the corner of a building. Beside her stood a older man with bright silvery hair and a neat black mustache. *That must be her father*, David thought. Monsieur de Montagnac was speaking in brisk, animated French with two other businessmen, and David snuck around the group until he was pressed against the adjacent side of the building: next to Coralie, out of view of her father.

His fingers brushed hers, and she gave a little jump. "It is time yet?" he asked.

"No!" she hissed, not turning toward him. "The Duke is not yet—ah, there he is!"

Across the street the tall, awkward figure of Grand Duke Leopold arrived with his retinue to roaring applause. He was dressed in simple street clothes, which seemed to relax him more, but did nothing for his forever-bemused expression. He took his position at the object of interest for the evening: a tall, gas-fed lamppost on the corner of Via Maggio and Borgo San Jacopo. Every corner of the street featured one of these new contraptions. Men with ladders and torches climbed to the glass casings of their respective lampposts, then looked to the Grand Duke.

"This is it!" Coralie danced on her toes as David peered over her shoulder. Leopold seemed to have forgotten the ceremony was waiting on him, as he looked around for a blank moment before giving an over-emphatic nod. The workman nearest him maneuvered his torch inside the lamp, and ignited the gas device inside. The lamp burst to life with a flame several times brighter than the torch.

The crowd exploded. Gentlemen threw their hats into the air and ladies hopped with delight. David hadn't realized how dark the street had been until more lamps were lit on either side of him. Who needed the sun anymore?

"*Dai! Le Gazzette! Le Gazzette!*" somebody called. A string of people formed at the lamppost nearest David and Coralie, each with an arm outstretched from the other in a chain. A spry little boy with long legs and a snaggletooth ran down the line counting them off, until he reached the seventeenth.

"*Ecco il diciassette! Apra la Gazzetta!*" he yelled. The seventeenth man pulled the Florence Gazette from his pocket, donned his glasses, and opened the newspaper. He looked around to make certain all eyes were upon him, then began reading the first page aloud. Again, the crowd roared in approval.

"Isn't it remarkable?" Coralie yelled. "They said you could read at seventeen arms-lengths away! Soon every street in Europe will have the gas lamp." Then she turned her head to David. "I want to see the light on the Arno."

David was about to ask if she was sure, but she took one look at her father—still absorbed with his fellow business-men—and grabbed David's hand. Her dark little curls flew back from her face as she darted around the building and pulled him through a side street, weaving around other cheering Italians until they arrived at the river. A few other avenues had been lit, but for the most part the Arno was still dark: a world apart from the celebration on Via Maggio.

Coralie was smiling breathlessly, reveling in the thrill of escaping her father. She walked to the little wall that separated the street from the river, and leaned over to peer at the light-speckled water.

"I do think the river is much prettier by night, don't you?" she asked. "By day I just find it dirty."

"Certainly," David said as he approached her. Just then, he

heard music behind him, and saw that from a string of open windows a band was playing a slow waltz.

"Don't they know the party is out here?" David looked at Coralie, who'd begun swaying to the music. He snorted. "Well, well. Look who does like to dance, after all."

"Did I ever say I did not?" Coralie stepped the one-two-three beat in place.

David folded his arms. "I believe the last time we ventured upon this topic, Mademoiselle, you complained of tired feet."

"My feet *were* tired."

"And yet you've just run the length of Via Maggio, and you feel fine."

"Perhaps I have sturdier shoes." Coralie twirled herself.

David smiled and looked away. "I don't know if I want to ask you again. I doubt I can bear a second refusal."

Coralie shrugged mid-twirl. "Then I shall never know if you are able to dance."

David held her stare, considering how to respond. Then, like the light of the new gas lamps, another idea kindled in him. It was so absurd—risky, even—he couldn't believe it had crossed his mind. But now that it was there, he couldn't let it go.

He stepped closer to Coralie, and stretched out his left hand. Not missing a beat, she waltzed over to him and laid her hand in his. He placed his other hand on her back, and she shifted as though they were about to step off. But David shook his head.

"This calls for a special kind of dance," he said.

Coralie's brow wrinkled.

"Will you trust me to cast a spell on you?"

Coralie looked taken aback, then narrowed her eyes. "Well, that depends…"

David shook his head again. "Will you trust me?"

Coralie gave him one of her long, prodding looks. Finally, she said, "Why not?"

David nodded. "I need you to close your eyes, and promise me you won't open 'til I say so."

"Your 'spell' will fail otherwise."

"Exactly."

Coralie sighed and closed her eyes. She popped one open to have a quick look at David, but shut it again when he cleared his throat.

"Now then," he said, "I need you to step up on my toes. You won't hurt me."

Coralie's lips parted in bewilderment, but she kept her eyes shut. She placed one small foot on each of David's black leather shoes.

"Right then…" David cast a glance up and down the street. Everybody was either gathered on Via Maggio or heading to it, and took no notice of him and Coralie. He focused his mind, and drew the Sorcerer's word from within his body: *Marghensiù.*

Slowly, gently, he rose into the air, and Coralie with him. He kept the ascension so gradual that she had no sense of movement, and her eyes remained closed. When they had risen five or six feet, David turned his attention to the music cascading from the windows. He kept their bodies hovering in midair, and stepped off.

Coralie's toes stayed connected to his as he led them in a waltz above the dark stones of the street, over its thick wall— and with a bold step across the air, he took them out over the Arno itself. His strides arced wide over the water as the music guided them on, and Coralie seemed to forget that she could hear no sound beneath David's feet, that they should have crashed into a wall or building minutes ago… he felt her grip relax, her back expand with breath. A funny little smile crossed her lips, as if she even suspected what he was doing. They danced on and on, David's magic carrying them with nothing beneath their feet but air and water dappled with light. He sensed the song approaching its end, and spun Coralie around on one toe—then her hand slipped, and he dove forward and caught her as she fell from midair, twenty feet above the Arno.

The rush of the near-fall had forced her eyes open, and she stared up at David in shock and relief. He held onto her, his spell still supporting them both, and prayed she wouldn't look down... but Coralie wasn't interested in what ground might or might not be beneath her. Her brilliant eyes were holding David's, her hand around his neck.

She broke into a smile and gave a single, heartfelt laugh.

"Come here, you fool," she said.

And she kissed him.

Chapter Twenty-One

Santo Spirito

"*You can't be bloody serious.*"

David was sitting in the dining room of D'Argenio's palazzo: a large chamber with paneled walls painted to look like marble, adorned with sculptures and sumptuous paintings. But today the curtains had been drawn and only a few candles gave light to the space.

David leaned forward in his chair at the head of a long table. To his left was D'Argenio, his face grey and gaunt; to his right was Cardross. Sprinkled around the room were a score of other Florentines who had pledged themselves to the Order. David stared at Cardross, whom he'd hardly seen in weeks, since before his dreamlike night over the Arno with Coralie. "How many?" he asked him.

"At least twenty thousand."

David ran a hand over his face. "*All in London?*"

"Mostly. Here, read it yourself." Cardross slid a letter across the glassy tabletop, and David noted the smug look on his face. Yes, things were proceeding just the way he'd warned David they would. Good for him. David saw Graven's scratchy handwriting clawing through the folds of the paper. His fingers approached it, but lost their nerve.

"We can muster ten thousand who are fully trained,

perhaps eleven," David muttered, "but they are scattered. We need time to gather them."

"In London, right now, we have seven thousand at best," Cardross stated. "Graven is with them, as are the Paladins."

David nodded and turned to D'Argenio. "Signore, my mission in coming here was to aid in the rebuilding of your outpost and to secure our ties with Tuscany, and I am still committed to that obligation—"

But D'Argenio shook his head. "I thank you for your words, Signore. A vile serpent has frustrated our efforts here. We know not who, but my men are searching." Several Florentines nodded around the room. D'Argenio's tone was cool and distant, as if his focus were somewhere beyond the table. "Your... guidance has been useful, Signor Stregone, but if Orgeron is gathering his Legion for a fight, then you must fight."

"Now, wait a moment," David said. "We don't know *why* Orgeron is assembling his men in London. True, this is the most tremendous force of bellirolts since the days of Nimarius, but we must first ascertain what—"

"*Open your eyes,* you blitherin' fool!" Cardross flung his arms into the air. "What do you think the Dark Commander is doin' in London? Why do you think he fired a little warnin' shot through those stonemasons here? He's found Tor Bellorum, and he's makin' ready to advance on it. And we're on the wrong side of the continent."

David stiffened in his chair, letting his fury sink into Cardross. Graven would have expelled the little urchin from the meeting for such an insult.

"The Tuscan outpost," he said in a restrained voice, "is in too fragile a state for me to abandon it now. I shall contact Graven myself. Good day, gentlemen."

All the men gave a crisp nod to David, and rose with him as he pushed his chair back and walked from the room. D'Argenio began conversing in swift Italian with his aides, as

Cardross followed David and slammed the door once they were in the hallway. Before the Highlander could say a word, David turned on him.

"If you ever—and I mean *ever*—disrespect my authority like that again, I shall see to it that you never set foot in another conclave or council. Is that clear?"

"The only thing that's clear, *Stregone,* is how far you've wavered from our mission," Cardross spat back at him. "Yes, we came here to build another outpost, but the Legion is gatherin' in London! And not only are you backin' away from a fight, you've lost every bit of control over how these men see you!"

David's resolve began to leak out of him. "What do you mean?"

"'*If Orgeron is gatherin' for a fight, then you must fight*'? Everybody in that room knew what D'Argenio was referrin' to. You've been messin' about like a love-thirsty boy—usin' *our* craftsmen to repair your mistress's coach, sneakin' off for whole afternoons so you can stroke her, all whilst people here are gettin' killed!"

David barely kept his ire from boiling over. "My personal affairs are none of your bloody business, William. Apologize."

Cardross snorted. "Have you told her anythin' about your real life? *Anythin'?*"

"*I demand an apology!*" David was so enraged that he stamped on the floor and sent shudders through the stone tiles. He saw in Cardross's eyes, however, the scalding blue fire that meant the Highlander was ready to bite back before he'd give in. David turned and barreled down the hall and out of the palazzo. Cardross yelled after him:

"*This is not the time to be wanderin' the city alone, you clod! David!*"

David caught something else that sounded like "conjurer," but he was gone before he would give Cardross the chance to say more.

✷

The memory of the meeting, and D'Argenio's disappointment in David, continued to hack through his mind as he sent a hurried letter to Graven via his fastest courier. That afternoon, he sought out Coralie in a darkened corner of the church of Santa Maria Novella. She kissed his shoulder, sending ripples of bliss through his tense body, and told him she'd be able to sneak out of her palazzo and meet him by the river the following night. They planned the rendezvous, though for the first time David felt as apprehensive about it as he did eager.

The next evening, as the sun was drawing in its coral light from the avenues, David was hastening back to D'Argenio's palazzo from the his first meal in a week. He was wondering if he'd hidden the body of the drunken vandal he'd killed well enough, when a short, pillowy man emerged from nowhere and plowed into his chest.

"*What in the bleeding...*" David was about to spew a string of curses when he finally extricated the man's face from his waistcoat, and caught the sharp outline of a neat black beard. Fire swept through his limbs.

In less than a second, David had thrust Subini against the stone wall of the narrow street, his bellirolt hand clamped around the conjurer's throat.

"You're the bloody magician, aren't you? *Aren't you?*" David demanded.

The little man nodded as best he could. "*I... yes, I'm Subini...*"

David ticked his head back, and his grip slackened. There was something very different about the man's voice.

"You're—are you *English?*" David asked.

Subini massaged his throat as he slid away from the wall. "I am not who you might think, Mr. Dunbar," he said, in an accent definitely not Italian, as it had been in the Piazza della Signoria.

The fire in David's limbs frosted over. "If you know who I

am, why did you stab me before an entire crowd?"

Subini smiled, in an "oh-well" sort of way. "I had to get your attention, Sorcerer. Please, I must tell you," he glanced around their secluded avenue, "what dire peril you are in every day that you—"

A harsh CRACK snatched away the rest of Subini's words. David blinked before realizing the sound had come from Cardross's boot colliding with the conjurer's jaw.

Cardross raised himself in front of David and shoved him in the chest.

"I told you to watch your back for this scoundrel!"

Subini whimpered something to David, and Cardross used his bellirolt power to pitch the conjurer into the wall behind him. Blood peppered the round stones.

"Cardross, his jaw is broken!" David said, horrified. "He was trying to tell me—"

"You need to listen to what *I'm* tellin' you, David! That man is no simple street player. He's an agent of Orgeron. He's been followin' me for weeks. Orgeron might well have more humans than bellirolts workin' for him, and this one could have easily slipped into our outpost—"

Subini was clawing his way up the stones behind Cardross, battling to say something, but the Highlander had had enough. In one flash of a bellirolt step, he'd pinned Subini against the wall and pushed a dagger to his throat.

"Hold, Cardross!" David roared. "He was trying to warn me of something!"

Cardross fired a look of incredulity at David. "Warn you? David, he tried to warn me just the other day. Against *you*."

David went still, then shook his head to try to align his thoughts.

"He's a fraudster, David. He can charm his way into anybody's pocket."

But Subini's eyes were blaring behind Cardross, begging

for help, and David couldn't ignore them.

"Then we'll keep him prisoner, and learn from him. But for God's sake—"

Subini was making some sort of gesture that David didn't understand, and it was in that instant, as the conjurer's eyes bulged with his jawbone limp and swollen, that Cardross slashed his throat with the dagger. David caught the crimson flare beneath Cardross's hand that signaled a meal.

David thought he was going to be sick. "*Cardr*— Why did you...?"

"You attend me well, David." Cardross sheathed his dagger and shoved two fingers in David's chest. "We've no more time to mess about. D'Argenio's dead."

David felt as if all his limbs had gone numb. "What do you mean?"

"I mean he's *dead*, David. Killed in his carriage. His men found the body an hour ago. Do you see what I'm tellin' you? Florence is lost. We need to return to Britain."

David's gaze fell upon Subini's grotesque body in the crook of the wall. He forced his eyes shut and groped for answers—yet all he could see, even through the horror, was Coralie's face. All he could think of was the taste of her lips, the sound of her laugh... how could he leave that and go to London now?

"David." Cardross's voice was firm but urgent. "You need to go to your quarters and pack your things. It's time to leave."

David opened his eyes and turned away from the bloody mess before him. It didn't make sense anymore. He looked up to the red eves of this *living* city, this place of music and sunlight and new breath: this world where he could be with Coralie.

"I can't, Cardross."

A silence followed so heavy a gun blast couldn't have broken it. When Cardross finally spoke, his voice was full of measured rage. "*What?*"

David turned to him. "I am home. I cannot leave."

"Is this because of your mistress?"

The word stung David again. "You really have no idea what's been going on between us, do you?"

"No, I don't! Because unlike you, I've been focused on our mission!"

"William, just *think* for a moment," David approached him, his voice tender, "how incredible the coincidence is that, after all these years, I'd meet somebody like her, that we'd meet again—"

"Oh, please! Nothin' is a coincidence, you fool. That's your excuse for this girl? This *mortal?*"

"I love her, William!" It was the first time David had spoken the words, but he felt them to be true. "She has awakened my world. I've never *known* such a thing before, and you expect me to just toss it all behind me?"

"Of course I do! You swore an oath, David. You pledged mind, body, and soul to the Order of Nimarius, and now you're goin' to just walk away—the *Ninth Sorcerer* is goin' to give up the fight for humanity—so you can go to bed with a pretty lass for a few nights of your life? She's not of our world, David! You've known her for, what—how many *weeks,* now? Ha!" Cardross lobbed a wad of spit onto the dirty cobblestones. "You count the number of *decades* you've devoted to our cause."

David ran his hands over his face and looked away as Cardross approached him.

"David, we have the chance to stop Orgeron and his Legion before they reach Tor Bellorum. The future of our world hangs upon your next move. Nobody can stop Orgeron but you; the Augury says so. If you abandon us now, we're lost."

"William…" David shook his head and looked down at his

friend. "This is the first place I've found, in my life, that I've not felt like a bellirolt." A look of deep, disappointed realization crossed Cardross's face. "Yes, we've both fought for more than a century for this, but all that pales in the face of what I feel for Coralie!"

"I expected better from you." Cardross's voice faltered. "You were the one who convinced me not to take my own life when I was turned into a bellirolt. Perhaps I never told you?" A bitter smile fluttered over his face. "You inspired me, you selfish bastard."

Silence spanned the rift between the two men. David felt as if his soul were being torn in two: his chest physically hurt, in a way no bellirolt power could heal. And yet he couldn't change his answer.

"I would hate myself forever if I left now. I cannot—I will not—deny my heart."

"You're only puttin' her in danger. If you commit to her now, somethin' will happen to her. Or her family. D'Argenio's out of the way, which means if we stay here, Orgeron's spies will come after me and you. He'll not rest 'til you're destroyed."

"Then she and I shall have to hide," David said. Cardross choked in disbelief. "I must be with her, William."

"So what the devil have I been doin' this whole time?" Cardross threw his arms wide. "What have I been to you, then? The Ninth Sorcerer's bodyguard, is that all?"

"You know that's not true."

"Do I? You show such respect for all we've been through. What are you goin' to do without me?"

"I am perfectly capable of taking care of myself."

Cardross bellowed with laughter. "How many times have I saved your life, David Dunbar? Though I may be responsible for you bein' a bellirolt, you'd be dead if you weren't one." He gouged David with his icicle-like eyes. "If this is how the life of the Ninth Sorcerer ends, then fine: damn you. Damn you to hell." He spun and charged toward the far end of the street.

"Where are you going?" David called.

"To London!" Cardross yelled over his shoulder. "If you won't stand and face the Legion, then I bloody will!"

Just as Cardross's short frame disappeared around one corner, David heard laughter and high, rhythmic Italian voices approaching from the other. His chest fell as he looked down at Subini's body again—what had the man been trying to tell him? David had trusted Cardross since they'd first set out to find Graven together, but he was certain his friend was mistaken about this conjurer. The least David could do was bury the man's body, maybe clean his blood from the street... and then time ran out. A trio of twig-like Italian boys was rounding the other corner, about to discover Subini's corpse. By the time they did, and their horrified screams stabbed David's ears, he was hiding on a rooftop two streets away.

Half an hour later, as the sun shrank behind the hills, a tiny silhouette appeared at the top of the Duomo. The human beings milling about in the piazza below—the normal, unsullied people of Europe who were to know nothing but the joys and sorrows of seventy-year lives—took no notice. Even if they did happen to glance at the point atop the church, they would have thought the sight a mirage, for what man could scale that giant building?

David leaned back against the warm stone of the pinnacle of Florence, as far removed as he could be from the masses below. He stared the sunset in the face as he reflected on Cardross's words... and how he might have lost his closest friend because he fell in love. Of all the people in his life, shouldn't Cardross understand how important Coralie was? A new possibility had been spread before him: a life of simple, beautiful things like visiting vineyards and watching storks on churches. No more suffering gory battles and humiliating defeat. *For one hundred forty years I have served the Order,* David thought. *But it has taken me one hundred forty years to find somebody like Coralie! Am I to wait that long again to find another? How much time must I devote to my cause before I'm permitted to follow my heart?*

Cardross was right that whatever assassin Orgeron had sent would appear to him or David next. David had to declare his love to Coralie, which meant they'd have to run away together, for there was no way her family would accept him… or he had to leave her and return to Britain. Either way, he had to tell her who he truly was. And the more he thought about it, the less he felt it was fair to ask her to begin a new life with him, forsaking her family, her reputation, all the comforts she knew. And could she—could anybody—really cope with the fact that he was a demon-infected being who had to kill?

But then another thought, an echo from another century, in another country, surfaced in David's mind. *In the end, it is their mission to kill you.* Orgeron's words floated like a ghostly knell through his head. The feeling had arisen in him, now and again since that night in Ireland, that maybe David didn't belong with the Order. That no matter how many missions he attempted, he would never really be one of them. Because he was a bellirolt. And perhaps the only place for a bellirolt like him was somewhere *else,* with no other bellirolts and only oblivious humans. He recalled the challenge she'd put to him at Fiesole: *What was he really? What would he do if he were not the Ninth Sorcerer?* If Coralie would accept him, could they escape together? Make a new life in a quiet corner of Italy?

The last sliver of sun had just disappeared when David stealthily descended from his perch. True, he did feel more at home with Coralie than with the Order, but now he was tired of feeling guilty for keeping the truth from her. If she did love him, she loved only his façade. After all, David's life had been defined by the Order of Nimarius. He couldn't dishonor everything that it, and Graven, had given him. He decided then and there, in mid-stride as he walked away from the Duomo, that he would tell Coralie the complete truth. And then he would find a way to say goodbye.

Darkness had settled by the time he found her on the Lungarno near her palazzo. She wore a blue dress under a hooded cloak, which she parted so she could take his arm.

"Let's walk to Santo Spirito," Coralie whispered before he could say hello. "It's such a beautiful night, and we've not been there yet."

David nodded, unable to speak over the lump in his throat. They crossed the Arno without a word, and he felt the detached, drifting sensation that all this time in Florence had been but a dream, a stolen afternoon in the summer of his life. Was such a thing ever possible to hold onto?

Santo Spirito was a plain-looking church compared to its counterparts in the city. An unadorned white edifice with a single window faced a piazza, which featured a statue and a handsome octagonal fountain. The piazza was almost entirely dark, save one gas lamppost that had just been erected. David and Coralie strolled around the shadows of the perimeter, David's stomach contorting at the thought that this was the last night he would ever speak to her, until Coralie stopped in front of the church.

"You're sure you are well, David?" she asked. David felt his resolve begin to melt before those eyes... *the reflection of Highland mountains in a loch on a clear day.* That was what they reminded him of. He gave a limp smile, and nodded.

"You know we shall be leaving in a week," she said.

David tried to hide his surprise. How had this detail escaped him?

"It will be harder to see each other," she continued, delving into his eyes for clues. "You said your business might be taking you elsewhere..."

"I don't..." David's eyes had fallen—to the bottom of Coralie's dress, to the stones, to anything away from her eyes. "I don't wish to stop seeing you." The words just toppled from his mouth. He wished for the strength to stop them.

"Nor do I." Coralie's voice was firm and steady. He looked up at her.

"I..." She put a hand to his cheek. "I don't really know what we have created. But I'm grateful we have it. Despite your arrogance." She cocked her head, and he smiled. "Despite your buccaneer-like ways. I have known you for so little time, and yet—"

"No." David leaned toward her. "No, darling. I've known you my whole life."

Her lips drew into a smile, eyes glistening with pride—she was *proud* to be with him—and something in those blue-green depths beckoned him. He slid his hands around her waist, leaned in to taste her warm, full lips—and forced himself to halt. *This* was the moment of decision. He could not continue down this road with her.

"Coralie..." David said, his voice shallow, "there is something I absolutely must tell you." Coralie looked mystified, so he glanced into the piazza for inspiration. "When I said I come from Scotland, that is true, but... not in the way you understood. I actually used to be a baron. My castle was in a place called Haddington, where—"

"I am sorry, *mon coeur*," Coralie said, covering her mouth. David looked at her and realized that she was smiling in a puzzled way, gazing past him. "Forgive me, I lost what you were saying."

David was taken aback. Was she not even listening to him?

"There is a man standing on top of that building, behind you." She nodded over David's right shoulder. "He's not even moving; it's very strange!"

Heat surged to David's chest. He spun and looked where

Coralie had been gazing, and saw nothing. Nothing, except a flutter of movement around the eve of the building.

He turned back to her, saw the confusion on her face, and his head erupted. For the first time in ten years, his bellirolt sense was tingling like mad: buzzing through every cavity in his skull, telling him he was moments away from a battle *here, in this place.*

Coralie could see his pain, and she tightened her grip on him, about to speak.

"Stay behind me," David commanded as he forced her around his back. *There's more than one out there,* he sensed; *where are you scoundrels?*

"David, what—"

"No matter what, Coralie, *stay behind me!*" Not a second later, a cloaked figure hurtled out of the darkness to their left—not running, but flying—and David leveled him with a bright blue Disabling Fire to the face.

Coralie screamed. David kept one hand on her, making sure she was still there. Another bellirolt appeared from the opposite direction, and David hurled a second Fire that caught him in the groin. The attacker howled in pain, and David sent him flying into the façade of Santo Spirito with a well-aimed *Marghensiù* spell. Two more bellirolts jumped down from the roof of the church, both armed with sabers, and David knew he would have to abandon Coralie for a moment. He launched himself into the air to meet them, inviting an attack, which one of them gave. He grabbed that bellirolt's sword by the hilt, swung it out of his hand, and in one fluid motion beheaded both men.

David now heard the war cries of advancing bellirolts all around him. He landed back near the terrified Coralie, armed with two sabers, and saw a whole line—at least *ten* bellirolts—running toward them from the far side of the piazza. David was stunned: how many companies of his Legion had Orgeron sent?

Had these fighters already killed Cardross? David realized now his prime concern was to get Coralie out of the piazza. He looked at the lone lamppost, and raised an arm to the flame within it.

"*Fiesum-Cerél!*" Heat burst the glass of the lamp as he pulled a long tongue of fire into the piazza, which he lashed in the faces of the advancing bellirolts. They yelped and shrieked—the wounds would heal soon, but he'd slowed them down. He turned to Coralie, who was trembling against the steps of the church.

"Darling, I need you to *run,*" he said. "I'll hold them off, don't worry about me, but you need to get to safety. Cut through the street there to Palazzo Pitti: it's very close and the Duke has guards. Do you understand?"

Coralie looked at him with a bewildered fear that burned David to the heart. "I'm scared to leave you," she said in a quavering voice.

"You must! Please, go!"

"I love—" she began, but David could already sense another bellirolt approaching.

"*GO!*" he screamed. He turned and shot such a powerful Disabling Fire that the attacker was blown forty feet back into the night.

Coralie leapt up and ran around the far side of the piazza, toward Palazzo Pitti. David turned back to the bellirolts. They seemed to have doubled in number. He roared through his disbelief, vaulting into the air to place his body between them and Coralie, but five were on him before he could get into position. He wielded both his sabers in such lightning-fast fury that even his bellirolt eye lost track of the blades. He sliced the necks of two attackers and was going after the rest when he heard somebody yell:

"*The girl! Aim for the girl first!*"

David froze. He followed the voice and saw, for an instant,

a bellirolt standing on the roof of a building to his right, with straight, shoulder-length hair under a tall hat. The bellirolt smiled—an unnaturally white, many-toothed smile, like a shark—and then flew back behind the building. David looked around wildly for Coralie, fighting off the men before him—and then he heard something break.

A loud CRACK echoed off the walls of the piazza. A faint whiff of smoke reached David's nostrils. Nothing had broken, or cracked... *a gun*. A gun had gone off. The attack ceased for a moment as David looked down the piazza: there, near the fountain, stood Coralie. *Thank God*, he thought, *she's alright...* Then she turned toward him, staggered, and collapsed on the stones.

David didn't know if the cry that rent the air was the roar of the advancing bellirolts or his own anguished scream, but it rattled the very bedrock of the piazza. He lost all sense of everything except the assassins and Coralie. Severed limbs and demonic blood erupted in the wake of his slashing sabers: he ran forward, howled, and beheaded three men in one stroke; he vaulted over their bodies and split the faces of two more. When his swords fell from his hands, he resorted to claws and teeth to wreak havoc. He didn't care at all for his own body anymore. His Sorcerer's power couldn't have mattered less, nor was he in any state to call upon it, as hatred pumped rampantly through his limbs, leaving room for nothing else.

Finally David found himself within yards of Coralie. She was lying, shivering, on the steps of the fountain, a red stain spreading across the back of her cloak. Another bellirolt stepped over her, preparing for a kill, ready to take her soul into his body—and then David saw the pistol tucked into his trousers.

This is the bastard who did it. David sprang forward, seized the bellirolt, and cleaved his neck in two. Jet-black blood stained David's coat and burned his face as the bellirolt crumpled to the stones. David looked around and saw there were no more attackers left. The piazza was littered with dead bellirolts.

He wiped his hands on his torn trousers and knelt by Coralie on the fountain steps. She was shuddering violently. He turned her over, and tears burst down his face. Her soft, elegant skin was stained with mud and dirt, and the ebony curls that had once framed her eyes were now plastered to her cheeks. David smoothed the hair away and looked into those eyes, deep and vivid, that held all the strength he'd ever needed, that now looked at him in agony.

He suddenly released Coralie and jerked his hands back, making sure he was well out of her reach. She moaned and mouthed his name, her fingers fluttering toward him, but he knew what was happening.

"I'm sorry, darling, no…" he said. "No, I can't touch you… *I'm sorry, Coralie…*"

Coralie looked at him with aching desperation. David knew she had no more strength to move, not even to speak, that all she wanted was for him to hold her in these final seconds. Of all the wretched curses of his life, David hated, beyond measure or description, this moment. If he touched her, he would consume her soul.

He gazed at Coralie through cascading tears, and cried his apologies: for not being able to comfort her, for being the cause of her suffering, for ever thinking they could be together… and then he saw through the haze that her eyes were already blank. Her fingers had ceased to move toward him. Coralie was gone.

David seized her body, gathered her into his arms, and wailed to the pitiless sky. He thought if he held her close enough, she just might now feel the power of his love.

※

An hour later, a corner window on the top floor of the de Montagnac palazzo opened, and David sailed into a darkened room carrying Coralie's body. He located her elegant, four-poster bed, and laid her gently in it.

He knew this was the last time he would ever see her face. He'd cleaned the dirt and grime from it, thinking that, of the thousand times he'd seen death, nothing had prepared him for watching the light vanish from these eyes. He tilted her head and kissed her brow and cheeks, gazing at the body he'd once yearned to know, that was now only hollow. Her beauty had escaped to some unseen realm—why could he not venture through the Otherworld and find her? Was that even where souls like hers went?

"*I will always love you,*" he whispered. "*No matter how many centuries I have to live, Coralie, I swear...*"

Just then David heard the voice of Eugenie in the hallway outside. More tears leaked down his face as he looked upon Coralie for one last moment, and squeezed her cold hand.

"*I must leave now, darling. I must, I'm sorry...*"

Seconds later, Eugenie opened the door. At first she seemed relieved that Coralie was lying in her bed, asleep. Then the chaperone saw the open window; the cloak stained with blood; the pale, empty face of her charge... and she screamed. The scream echoed out the window and down the length of the Arno, chilling the ancient stones of Florence and piercing the skull of David Dunbar as he took flight, never to return to that city.

Chapter Twenty-Two

The Blight of Bonnybield

In the hollow seam of a decaying log, a handful of cigarette butts lay discarded. Perched on a moss-covered stone beside David, Percival had only been able to stare at the makeshift ashtray while the bellirolt spoke. He saw now, in the heavy silence, another cigarette had grown cold between David's fingers.

"I..." Percival's voice stuck in his throat. "I'm so sorry, David."

David looked around where they sat in the oak forest above Granny McGugan's house. He had needed a quiet place with a natural surrounding—someplace untroubled. He stood, and gazed at the afternoon sun slanting through the trees as he said, "The next morning, Florentines found the bodies of no less than twenty-five men in the Piazza Santo Spirito. They gossiped about the story for weeks, for it seemed twenty-five angry men, armed with swords and pistols, had met for a battle and all killed one another."

He turned to Percival. "It took twenty-five bellirolts to kill my Coralie. And sometimes I wonder: what if the twenty-fifth had never arrived? Might I have been able to save her?"

Percival opened his mouth as a number of responses tugged at his lips, but he couldn't find a way to begin any of them.

"Oh, Percival…" David smiled sadly as he collected the cigarette butts and stowed them in his coat pocket. He kindled yet another between his lips, and Percival had to remind himself that smoking hardly affected David. A quick rush to the brain, perhaps; nothing more. "How I have wished for old age. Only fools crave the life of an immortal. It's amazing what effect a *mirror* has on age. Amazing not to look as old as you feel. To have no proof of the centuries you've lived." He flicked ash to the ground. "Except to note the true blessings history has given us. Rubber-soled shoes, for instance."

Percival smiled, though a niggling question still pulled at him.

"Toothpaste," David went on, enjoying the lighter moment. "Trousers with zips."

"David… did you really think Coralie would be safe once you started goin' out with her?"

David looked down at Percival, smoke curling around his head. "Did I foresee that a depraved, power-hungry warlord would send two dozen assassins to clear the way so he could advance on Tor Bellorum?" David shook his head and turned toward the slope that led down to Bonnybield. "*Of course* I thought I could keep her safe. But I had no idea the lengths to which Orgeron would go to hunt me down…"

But Percival had stopped listening. David's answer clicked something into motion inside him, and as he followed it point to point, a dire coldness tightened his chest.

He sprang to his feet, already breathless. "Wait—you said, last night, history has patterns. Patterns you've already noticed again here."

David angled his body back toward him. "So I did."

"Does Orgeron have patterns?"

David creased his forehead. "What do you mean?"

"He was tryin' to *clear the way* to Tor Bellorum, and… oh God—the Mochries!"

Percival clutched his head and spun to the sickening greenery of the forest. The truth slithered through him like an icy snake.

"What on earth is the matter, Perciv—"

"I never told you what the Mochries said last night," Percival replied. "They were bein' paid by some 'client' to collect anybody who might recognize these signs you and I are followin'. Somebody wanted to clear the way! For a supernatural battle, with a man named *Dunbar,* where loads o' people could die—even Crannog knew it was somethin' none of us should see!" His chest heaved as he stared at David. "Orgeron is comin' here."

Percival saw the shock in David's eyes—he wanted to challenge the boy, but couldn't.

"That's what all this has been about, hasn't it?" Percival said. "The Mortairian is comin' to Bonnybield. And you're goin' to fight him. You said these omens have only appeared before at some 'disruption in the fabric of nature'? A final showdown between the Ninth Sorcerer and the Mortairian— sounds disruptive enough to me."

David's cigarette hung forgotten from his hand. "I don't… None of our intelligence supports this."

"Ach, to hell with your intelligence! This is what the Mochries told me, when they thought I wouldn't live to tell a soul! Didn't Cardross say Orgeron might have more humans than bellirolts workin' for him? And your ambush, against that field marshal—"

"Orgeron is using him as bait." A whirlwind of fury built in David's eyes. "*He's* going to ambush *me, here.* Tonight!"

He crushed the burning cigarette in his fist and hurled it to the forest floor.

"*Tonight?*" Percival asked.

"Think on it, Percival! If Orgeron is aware of my mission, he knows my knights aren't meeting me here 'til tomorrow morning. He'll want to attack me alone, he only moves by night—he'll be here after sundown."

Percival's head suddenly seemed too light, and he leaned against a moss-coated rock. "This is mad…"

"And yet it's the only way things make sense." David seemed to grow taller as he stood mantled in the afternoon sunlight, as solid as the trees around him. A ready warrior.

"We've got to prepare." Percival stepped forward. "We've got to get everybody out of Bonnybield!"

"We've no time, lad. And once the Order arrives, they'll protect the town if something goes wrong. It's what they're trained for."

Percival shook his head, resolute. "No. I understand you're ready to kill Orgeron, but we don't know what plans he's got. There are people I care about here. I'm not takin' a chance with *my* town."

David glanced away toward the slope, and Percival noticed his hands tense by his sides. "This is rather contrary to Order protocol, but if you're trying to effect an evacuation… a *fright* may be the best course."

Percival nodded. "Aye, like a storm! Can you conjure a storm?"

"That would only serve to drive people inside, Percival. No, we must make them feel as if they have no choice but to leave." David's eyes grew darker, despite the sun upon them. "Come with me."

Feeling tentative, Percival followed David to the edge of the forest, where they looked out over the quilt of berry fields between them and Bonnybield.

David turned to Percival. "This is a town of berry farmers, is it not?"

The iciness Percival had felt began to corkscrew through his gut.

"No, don't…" he said, though his voice lacked the conviction he wanted. There had to be another way… "Berries are the lifeblood here. They're all these people have."

David's voice was low and austere. "Then would the sudden death of their crop not frighten them away? For their own safety?"

Percival gazed at the vibrant green land beneath them, and recognized a cluster of men down to the left, combing through a field. The Prize Bunch Judges.

"It might," he conceded hollowly. "I think… I can make sure it does."

David nodded, and stepped forward onto the slope. He lifted his arms and closed his eyes, and Percival felt, for a moment, that even the air around them paused. Everything was awaiting the Sorcerer's command.

David's eyes opened, their jade glow steady and intense. "*Cayr-ledum, yvechalam,*" he intoned. "*Frantannich carà, mortienem badach-lénes…*"

Percival stared at him, entranced less by the image of a tall, powerful magian shifting elements of earth and air, than by the sound of Sorcerer's Tongue. It was a language he'd never heard, yet he felt he could almost understand it. In some buried place, some shrouded corner of his memory… the words made complete sense.

As David spoke, Percival watched the tragedy unfold. One by one, the long rows of berry bushes crumpled like autumn leaves, vines drooping and fruit blackening. He saw the Prize Bunch Judges recoil, then yell in horror as the magical blight swept past them toward the town. In minutes, the terrible canvas was complete. It looked as if a blanket of coal dust had been thrown over the land.

David relaxed his arms and looked back at Percival. The boy nodded, feeling rotten to his belly, and dug out his mobile phone.

"I've got to make a call."

David fished his sydaeon talisman from under his t-shirt. "As do I."

"You're a bold one, you know that?"

Percival's eyes dropped to the tangled roots at his feet while Abi spoke. They were standing beneath the ridge on Granny's northern field, where they'd raced three days earlier. Abi rammed her bicycle's kickstand into the soil, and turned to him.

"Let's be clear about one thing goin' forward for this..." she flapped her hand between the two of them, "... whatever this is we've got."

Percival furrowed his brow. "Friendship?"

"Can you call it friendship? I don't know, Perce! *Friends* don't say they'll meet after bein' ambushed by thugs, and then not show. Friends don't send *two bloody texts* makin' oblique references to some mystery man they're talkin' to after days o' paranormal psycho-stuff, and then *disappear!* Friends don't turn off their mobile—"

"Abi, I'm sorry." Percival meant it. Seeing her this upset was even worse than watching an entire berry crop die. He had never intended to hurt her. "I know it doesn't seem fair, but I was—"

"I haven't told you what needs to be clear."

Abi's turquoise eyes were firing like pistols at him. Percival shut his mouth.

"I am not a bloody sheep dog who comes to help whenever you call. Got it?"

Percival nodded. "Aye. Certainly."

Abi folded her arms, looking almost impressed with Percival. "Good."

"Now I need your help."

The look in Abi's eyes could have withered any remaining

berry in the field. "*Un-be-lievable.*"

Percival didn't have time to apologize again. "Abi, I know what just happened."

Abi narrowed her eyes at Percival. "The dead berries?"

"Aye. I know *how* it happened. And the Mochries, last night? I know about that, too. I was there."

Abi's face bore a mixture of shock, fear, and even more anger. "Are you serious?"

"I don't have time for details, but the Mochries were killed by a demon. It left me with this." He pulled down his collar to reveal his Sable Scar. Abi gasped, but then leaned closer to inspect it, her scientific eye taking over.

"That's… not like any scar I've ever seen," she said. "With edges like this…"

"Exactly," Percival replied. "And I was rescued by the man I've been talkin' to. He knows all about the supernatural, more even than Grimm. Remember the signs we were followin'? Here's what they mean: more o' these demons will kill everybody else in Bonnybield *tonight*. Unless we get people out."

"And the berries?" Abi asked in a thin, doubtful voice.

"A withered harvest. The final sign." Percival approached her, driving his embellishment deeper. "I know it sounds mad. But people saw how that crop died; it was no act o' nature. They're goin' to want your da' to take samples. And those samples have to show that the soil, and the water, are toxic. Everybody is in danger unless they leave."

Abi's eyes blared with incredulity. "You want me to forge a lab result?"

"Won't your da' trust it?"

"Of course he will! I've never lied to him before!"

"Abi, I'm terrified o' what will happen if you *don't* lie to him!"

Abi blinked and tried to shake the idea from her head. "I can't believe that—"

Percival stepped to within inches of her face. "I don't need you to believe me. I just need you to help me. I'm sorry I couldn't tell you what I was doin', but I didn't think you'd be safe if I did. Please… I just want all o' you to be safe."

Abi ticked her head back. "'All o' you'? You aren't leavin'?"

Percival held her gaze, and shook his head. "I can't."

Abi crossed her arms. "Not good enough. If you can make demands o' *my* safety, I can do the same with yours. There are *demons* comin' here? Then you're leavin' with us."

"Abi…" Percival glanced at the sun that was nearing the tops of the hills. How could he make her understand something he'd never been able to explain to anybody? "This man is *of* the supernatural. He's seen all the things I've ever wanted to know about, since before you and I were friends. He'll protect me, don't worry—I'm safer with him than with anybody else. But I've got to find out more from him. While I have the chance."

Abi watched Percival through pained eyes, her lips parted, as if she were just now seeing her friend in his fullest form. She didn't seem to like all she saw… but she did seem to believe it.

Percival beseeched her, "*Please, Abi.* Your da' is on the town council. People will listen to him. It's the only way we can save them."

She closed her lips, and looked to the ground. "I'll do my best."

Percival let out a shaky breath, and managed a half-smile. "Thank you."

Abi didn't return the smile. "If you're stayin', you ought to look in on Granny."

Percival squinted at her. "Why?"

"I stopped by your house an hour ago to bring your da's book." She lifted a preemptive hand. "It's back in my room now, don't worry. But I found Granny's house all locked up. Didn't see her anywhere. Her car's gone, too."

A cold disquiet trickled through Percival. It had been years since Granny left her farm. He didn't even know that car still ran. What could she possibly be doing?

Abi added, "I also saw a giant motorbike by the bothy—some space-age thing…"

"Oh." Percival peered across the field, as if in surprise. "I'll have a look, then."

Abi gazed at him with a sad, almost lost expression. Then her eyes flitted around the barren earth. "This is all awful. Just a few days ago I was hangin' Festival banners…"

Percival opened his arms before he realized it, and she rushed to him and wrapped him in a powerful hug. He was suddenly aware that they'd never done this before, felt an aching dread that they wouldn't be able to again… and then she whispered fiercely in his ear:

"If anythin' happens to you, I'll kill you."

She pressed her lips—much softer, and wetter, than he'd expected—against his cheek. She turned, mounted her bike, and pedaled onto the road without a glance back.

Percival watched her red ponytail disappear down into the glen. *She'd kissed him.* Nobody had kissed him that he could remember. He felt her absence as fervently as he'd felt her embrace, and he hated that this had become a goodbye he wasn't ready for.

Percival crossed the field to Granny's house. He was half concerned, half annoyed that she was acting oddly enough to warrant his attention. Upon arriving, he found exactly what Abi had described: doors locked, windows shuttered, stoves and electricity switched off. A peek in the garage confirmed that her old Mark 3 Astra was gone, also.

He stared at Granny's front door, bewildered. She'd left the house as if she'd be gone for weeks. Where on earth would she have driven? She had no friends, no other family… And had she just assumed Percival wouldn't need the house in her absence?

Percival drifted up the driveway. What was the point of caring where she'd gone, or why? The woman had always relished hiding things from him. Why should today be any different? As he passed David's motorbike, his eye caught the muddy footprints where Granny had kicked it, and the words "*Vaslor Nimariè*" peeking from underneath them.

Percival stopped at the head of Granny's lane where it met Scobie Road, feeling his mobile buzz in his pocket. He pulled it out and saw a text from Abi: *Council hosting emergency meeting in Town Hall. Dad's going to speak.* Hope flared in Percival's chest as he sent her back an encouraging text, and then watched the wide view of the Bonnybield glen before him.

Not half an hour later came Abi's update, a single word: *Done.* Percival's breath hitched, and he pressed the phone icon to call her, but she didn't pick up. It wasn't long before he spied several cars speeding out of town, making for the A90. Every few minutes, another car followed. Percival closed his eyes amid a warm wave of relief, and thanked his lucky stars for Abi. She had done it.

"Quite a feat, Percival."

Percival didn't turn to face David as the man strode up behind him.

"Are you ready?" Percival asked, catching a whiff of sweet tobacco. He could almost feel David's roguish smile.

"I am always ready for a fight."

"And you contacted the Order?"

"I contacted Cardross, which is enough. He'll make the necessary preparations." David stood beside Percival, puffing smoke from his pipe. "To protect us both, I didn't mention you."

Percival nodded as another, more determined car careened out of Bonnybield. He looked up at David. "Do you think I might be able to... meet the other knights?"

David lifted his eyebrows. "As you're clearly not leaving,

you'll have to. I'm impressed with you, lad. I should like to see how you'd take to life with the Order."

A smile plucked at Percival's lips. *The Order of Nimarius.* Could this be his ticket away from Granny? He'd even stock books for them if—

Just then, something danced across the fringe of his eye, and panic speared through him. *MacBain.* Another vision: the crouching bellirolt, waving and watching him. It felt much closer than before, as if the specter were hovering just over his shoulder.

David noticed the boy's alarm. "Percival?"

Percival glanced at David, remembering his brusque response earlier. "I was wonderin'… have you actually battled Orgeron before?"

David's gaze hardened. "You want to know the rest of the story?"

"I want to know what we're facin' here."

David drew from his pipe in silence, his gaze lengthening beyond Bonnybield. "I battled him once. It was the same time I met the field marshal we're after."

"So then… Coralie was what the marshal took from you."

David shook his head. "Not just Coralie. After Florence, I followed Cardross to London. And I saw why Orgeron had gathered his Legion there."

"Why?" asked Percival.

"Because London, in 1841, was the perfect place to breed an army of darkness."

Chapter Twenty-Three

Valleys
of Brick and Coal

S hoes slapping upon cobblestones punctuated the nighttime
murmurs of Covent Garden. They were the only things
that moved through the dark passages with such purpose, and if
any of the vagabonds huddled in the shadows had looked
closer, they'd have seen the shoes were completely worn
through.

Stall after stall flew past the newcomer as he moved—stalls
that would fill with fruit and vegetable vendors within hours,
but now housed whole families of Londoners. A woman with a
creaking-door voice rasped a warning to his right. A middle-
aged man reeking of gin, fish, and filth thrust out a hand and
wheezed, "Give us a penny, there's a good chap?" But the
newcomer, face hidden under a tall hat and scarf, plowed on.

He sped past a thick oak door, then paused and doubled
back to it. Here was what he'd been looking for: a lock in the
shape of a crooked question mark. No sooner had he stopped
than two sturdy men in black greatcoats appeared on either side
of him.

"What's your business?" one grunted.

"*Sheircanh milur-tyne, Frantanni,*" the new arrival replied.

The other guard furrowed his brow. "*Irbannagh-lluntech?*" he asked.

"*Sho bellech grum-gaird fall'Eralan*," came the response.

The guards started and looked at each other. "*Shulech syne Dunbarech?*" asked one.

The newcomer's reply was to snatch the guard's cravat and hoist him off the ground.

"Of course I am, you halfwit tripe-wife!" David spat into the guard's face. "And who the *hell* taught you to speak Sorcerer's Tongue? *A bloody orangutan?*"

At that moment a bark and a vicious squeal rang out down the street, where David saw a lean dog being chased by a stout grey pig across the cobblestones.

"*Rule number one—*" David growled as the pig snapped at the dog's leg and brought it down— "*never, ever, mention our names on the public street.* Stuff that in the gulf between your ears. Now let me into the damned outpost."

The guard was dropped on his feet, and he fumbled in his coat until he produced a slender iron key, which he traced through the question mark lock. He muttered a few words in Sorcerer's Tongue, and the door made a hissing sound, clicked, and popped open. David glanced over at the starved, brawling animals, shrieking like creatures of the Otherworld as they wrestled to the death. He looked away and stalked into the outpost.

An older guard he remembered from Ireland embraced him like a brother and led him down a hallway, past more guards who saluted him, and opened an iron-framed door. Within was a dining area converted to an Order war room. All the Paladins were standing around a map on a table, and among them—his waist-length silver beard combed and braided, wearing a black suit under a plaid of green tartan—was Doneval Graven.

David hadn't appreciated how much he'd missed his

mentor until that moment. The ten years since Ireland had added no wrinkles to Graven's face. His two Sable Scars still receded like canyons in the gas light of the room, and when he fixed his earthen eyes on David, David crumbled under their weight. His clothes were in tatters, his hair disheveled, his skin filthy. He was the wandering savage arriving at Kintail again.

Graven's eyes lightened upon seeing his Sorcerer, but before he could speak, a higher voice called out: "*David?*"

Cardross stepped forward from behind the Paladins, his face shining with amazement. David locked eyes with him, and all relief at seeing his friend alive evaporated beneath his seething torment.

"David… what happened to you?" Cardross asked.

"What happened?" David's voice came out flat and sunken. He approached Cardross very slowly down the length of the table. "You're a fine one to ask. After you left, Orgeron sent a score of his finest to ambush me and Coralie. They gunned her down on the street. I killed them all, then flew and ran over the rest of Tuscany. I crossed the Alps on foot. I slept in barns, cow-sheds, rail stations, and each time I awoke I was certain this was but a nightmare."

David was now standing so close he could see Cardross's pupils dilate in shock. "And if *you* had but stayed 'til I could talk to her, we could have protected her."

"David, I'm—" Cardross began, but David grabbed him by the chest and shoved him aside. He barreled out of the room without another word.

Hours later, sitting awake in his new chamber, David saw the first beams of dawn peek through his long, thin window. Every morning now was yet another when he would not wake up with the intention of seeing Coralie. Most nights he preferred not to sleep.

He lifted his chin to the feeble orange rays. The one urge

that had propelled him across Europe was the hot ache of revenge. Now, somewhere beneath this same dawn, Coralie's murderer was stirring.

A knock sounded at the door. "Come."

The door creaked open and Graven entered, followed by a tall, severe-looking crow of a man with a frock coat buttoned up to his neck. He had a long face with an oversized nose, lips, and chin, and undersized spectacles beneath glowering eyes. His dark hair lay thin and greasy against his scalp, while two bushy sideburns framed his cheeks. He looked like a dour schoolmaster.

"David," Graven said, "this is Abraham Ortelius, Knight of the Order and dragoman. He knows every street, every door, and every roach that crawls in London."

Ortelius gave a curt nod. "Mr. Dunbar." His lips barely moved as he spoke. "I don't wish to disturb you, sir, but should you require my—"

"I want to know where he is," David said.

Ortelius seemed pleased that David was in no mood for pleasantries.

"I cannot tell you where *he* is, Mr. Dunbar, but I can show you where the Dark Commander has been. And where he is likely to go next."

David nodded. "Very good."

Half an hour later the three men were strolling down the Strand toward Trafalgar Square. The cold grey skies of autumn only allowed specks of light from a faraway sun.

Tall buildings of sooty brick stretched for miles, and the air was thick with coal dust.

"Brooms to buy!" cried a hoarse street hawker. "Knives to whet!"

"Sweet gingerbread!" yelled an old woman ahead of them. "Threepence a loaf!"

David was comforted to be around English speakers again,

but he felt as though he were observing all these people through the wrong end of a telescope. Their lives were so brief, their struggles so simple; there was no centuries-old demon they had to hunt. David looked at Graven, whose face, like tree bark, seemed out of place in this city thick with innovation. *The old man might appear more the misfit*, David thought, *but at least he isn't cursed to kill. He's more like these humans than I am, and they wouldn't look twice at me.*

The three men entered the cluttered, liquor-stinking street of Haymarket, and Ortelius pointed his cane at a narrow alleyway.

"You'd never think it," Ortelius said, a mischievous gleam in his eye, "but this is the first place you ought to look for activity concerning the Dark Legion."

David's senses sharpened right away. He peered into the alley, which was no more than four feet wide, and could only see a few closed doors and three or four rats nosing about in the mud.

"As soon as the gas is lit," Ortelius continued, "this place is teeming with folk of the underworld, for in recent years there has sprung up a new breed of illicit traders and smugglers here." He leaned in a bit too close for David's comfort. "And all their nightly business concerns *magical* goods."

David nodded as he began to understand. A supernatural black market, coming to life in the heart of London. It wasn't difficult to imagine.

"He's been hard at work, hasn't he…" David murmured as his eyes followed the rats in the alleyway. "And all he wants is that bloody crown in Tor Bellorum."

"True, but mind you," Graven joined in, "if Orgeron is to become the Mortairian, he mustn't be the bellirolt who *wants* the Crown the most. He must be the most cunning in how he attains it. The Augury doesn't understate the matter when it says he needs to '*all the Forces of Darkness unite*'—Orgeron's army will have to defy imagination. He must prove himself a leader before Tor Bellorum will open for him. The First Bellirolt intended it that way."

So here is how he proves it, David thought. Uniting bellirolts and smugglers behind closed doors in sunless avenues. Unnoticeable in the teeming throngs of Haymarket. David couldn't wait to return by night to see what Ortelius meant.

But he found that return more difficult than he'd thought.

That evening at the outpost (called a Citadel, as the Court of Paladins was stationed there), Graven insisted upon hearing of David's actions in Florence. He listened with compassion as David recounted the story through his final moments with Coralie, and David prepared for an upbraiding about becoming involved with her.

"David," Graven said somberly, after a minute, "you have been wounded. And you shall be wounded again, many times, in your years. But sadly, wounds do not show on a bellirolt, do they?" He leaned forward, and his Sable Scars were thrown into harsh relief by the candlelight. "Though you don't see them, you *must* learn from them. And one day, I promise, you'll be able to savor your hours of joy with Coralie." Then he stood. "For now, stay within and cool yourself. There's no reason to venture into the nighttime bedlam the Legion feeds upon."

David felt as if his head would explode if he stayed inside. "Graven, I got myself into the heart of this city last night without anybody noticing—"

"I beg to differ." Graven held up a warning finger. "Especially after how many bellirolts you killed in Florence, Orgeron is well aware you're here. You reached us last night because he wanted you to. Now is not the hour to rush out and seek revenge."

And so David found himself sitting at a desk in the Citadel parlor, trying (at Graven's instruction) to put some of his morose thoughts to paper. Graven, meanwhile, was across the room mixing acrid chemicals in an array of beakers and bowls. He'd brought out his music box—the same from his mantle in Kintail—and he reached into it every so often for one of his scientific notes, eliciting a happy tune from the device. Graven announced that he was seeking a way to make the "remarkable foul water" of London drinkable. David retorted that he'd grown too used to drinking from his Kintail spring and was wasting his time. In truth David just couldn't stand the incessant music box.

Finally, David scratched a line through the empty pages taunting him, and declared he was going to rest. Upon reaching his quarters, however, he donned his new tall hat and used his magic to slowly, delicately, unlatch the window in his room.

If nothing else, he thought as a breath of night air chilled him, *the eves of the buildings in this city are comfortably close, as if they were made for bellirolts...*

He made sure the hat was tight upon his head, and leapt out into the night.

From the moment his shoes hit the cobblestones, David knew there was something different about London after dark. His Second Sight sprang to life in a way he hadn't experienced in years, tingling up and down his spine as if trying to alert him to many things at once. It didn't take him long to find the entrance to the Haymarket alley. Two bearded ruffians were brawling on the street before it, a pack of men smoking rank tobacco egging them on. A double-chinned, claw-fingered woman sauntered out of the shadows and said in a croaky voice, "Where you off to in such a hurry, beautiful?"

David kept his head down and plowed through the cramped entrance to the alley, ignoring the warning signs that flared in his head. He ducked through the first door he found, and his stomach forced him to halt. This was a place with no air, where a family of five was huddled around an open fire in a corner, and only a gaping hole at the edge of the ceiling allowed the smoke to exit. Darting around these poor souls were men and women of all ages: some exchanging coins for little leather pouches and envelopes, others receiving whispered messages and then racing from the room. That was when David's blood suddenly iced over. Two men, who had just been told something by an adolescent boy in the corner, turned and disappeared *through the far wall.*

This was why his Second Sight had been so stirred up. Half these people were ghosts. They looked like anybody else in this place, but they'd surpassed the barriers of the physical world. David had had rare, foggy glimpses of these spirits before, but he'd never seen souls of the Otherworld striding so boldly through a human habitat.

At that moment a thought appeared in David's head, like the passing beam of a lighthouse: *The Mortairian is near.* His limbs tensed and his claws lengthened. He whirled as he sought the source. He sped through the dank room to another, threw aside a grimy sheet and found yet another room. The thought blinked by again. *The Mortairian is near.* David finally stumbled out of the dizzying maze onto a back street, using all his mental power to focus his Second Sight. Where was the Mortairian? Was this a trick?

A splash of color on a nearby brick wall snagged his eye. David stepped forward, his senses tuned to their highest degree. A gutter of human and animal filth ran before the building: a rancid moat to guard a tower of squalor. Vulgar shouts of men, women, and children sounded above his head—and then a gasp caught in his throat. *It's Subini.* The bit of color was glittering off the conjurer's sparkling eyes and bright blue costume... but this was only an illustration. A flier, pasted to the wall, with the conjurer's grinning face and an arm extended toward the viewer, and the words: *"Come one, Come all! Learn the Mysteries of the Occult and the treasures of the Black Arts from the world's most Accomplished Conjurer: the Infamous, the One and Only, SUBINI!"*

David was stunned. Subini had been on his way to London? The flier announced the show was one week away; doubtless Londoners hadn't learned of his death. David grimaced as he recalled the scarlet gash left on Subini's throat, his body crumpled in a nameless street... Was London his home? He had turned out to be English, after all. At the very least, somebody here was obsessed with him: David saw more fliers as he walked on, pasted to doors, across windows, on broken carts...

The Mortairian is near. Now the thought possessed David. He needed to move higher, see more. He left the mystery of Subini for the moment. *If I didn't know magic,* he thought, *I might be lost for life in these wretched avenues.* With a firm step off the ground, he propelled himself up through canopies of laundry flapping in the breeze like pinioned spirits, and landed on a rooftop. He saw he was at one end of a vast network of tenements, a festering outgrowth of the building beneath him. Finally he spotted the center of this nighttime frenzy: a courtyard between two buildings nearby. Everybody not leaving the courtyard was moving toward it. David sailed over to a chimney around which he could peer into the space—and his blood turned so cold it burned.

Almost all the figures he saw were bellirolts. He could tell by the protective collars around their necks. There was one who garnered the most attention, speaking authoritatively to one bellirolt after another as he leaned against a barrel at the far side of the courtyard. He was tall and lean, with a hunch in his shoulders and a sheaf of straight ivory hair that hung down beneath his black hat. David thought something about him looked familiar, but he couldn't be sure.

The Mortairian...

Where? David demanded. *Where the hell is he?* He scanned

the courtyard but saw only underling bellirolts inspecting swords on a table. David remembered the one who had killed Coralie, armed with a pistol—a rare choice, as it prevented a bellirolt from being close enough to consume his victim's soul. The assassins' orders that night had been to kill David's love before his eyes. *"Aim for the girl first!"* they'd said. Make him watch her die, then kill him. Anguish lanced through his gut.

"Remarkable, isn't it?" came a familiar voice behind him.

David spun around. Cardross was crouched on the slope of the roof.

"*This* is why Orgeron has come to London," Cardross said. "He can hide his entire army in the same slums where the poor are tucked away. The smallpox, the typhus, the cholera don't plague them. And they have their pick of free, easy meals." He nodded at the rest of the tenements behind them.

David didn't know what to say. He wanted to apologize for his behavior the previous evening, but was still hurt over Cardross's abandoning him in Florence.

"I thought I might find you here," Cardross said in a smaller voice. "And I didn't want you goin' off on your own again." David saw him shaking his head in the darkness. "I'm sorry she's gone, David. I know it's upset you…"

David's face heated with incredulity and pain. Just *"upset"*?

"I'm glad you've come, though," Cardross finished sincerely. "We didn't know what we were goin' to do without you."

David closed his eyes against his anguish. *Poor, dear William*—he didn't know if his friend had any way of understanding what he'd been through. Yes, Cardross had lost his entire family to bellirolts, but he possessed an innocence that made David think he didn't know what romantic love really was.

David opened his eyes and gestured to the courtyard. "Do you know what they're doing?"

Cardross's face brightened now that David had spoken to

him, and he crept closer. "Readyin' for battle. Gatherin' their resources, intelligences—not just from bellirolts, but spirits, too. *Don't move.*"

David had been about to ask if Cardross had seen the Subini fliers. The tall, white-haired bellirolt had walked to the middle of the courtyard to speak with somebody, and was glancing up around the eves of the buildings.

"That one there—" Cardross whispered— "they say he has eyes like a hawk."

"Who is he?"

"Gregor Nathair: Orgeron's field marshal. They call him the 'Snowy Snake' for his look. None of our knights have been able to get close to Orgeron, but we've seen Nathair here for several nights now."

Right then, Nathair smiled at something another bellirolt said, and his face registered in David's memory. That shining grin, with the white, shark-like teeth... the captain of the assassins from Florence.

Rage flamed and sped through David's veins. He raised himself to a standing position atop the roof.

"*David!*" Cardross barked in a harsh whisper. "*GET DOWN!*"

"He was there, William," David said in a quiet, sinister voice. "He was the one who made sure Coralie died in Florence." Nathair was still standing oblivious below.

"*Attackin' him right now is only goin' to get us both killed!*" Cardross scrambled to his feet to grab David.

"*Hold, Cardross,*" a firm voice said from behind the two bellirolts. Cardross froze. David whirled and saw the unmistakable outline of Graven, fixed like an eagle on the peak of the roof, his long hair swaying in the breeze.

"I ordered you not to set foot outside the Citadel, David."

"*Hang your orders,*" David hissed back. His words began to pour from the pulsating fire in his limbs. "And to hell with both of you. You want to keep me locked down, safe, bored, until you deign it appropriate to strike the Legion? I am the Ninth Sorcerer," he said in a voice lighter, calmer than his normal tone. "Last of the line of Eralan, the greatest magical beings to walk this earth. Do you not think that I can summon a wind of retribution to raze every building in this city?"

His hands spread from his body, and he felt the particles of the roofs and chimneys answer to his presence. The angrier he became, the more powerful he felt, and within moments the shingles beneath their feet began to rattle, the bricks of the chimneys loosened in their mortar... David felt that with one flick of his finger, he could send a ripple of power through the city so violent it would rival an earthquake.

"I can make all of London pay for the loss of Coralie," he said. "And I'll destroy the Dark Legion with it." Just then, the chimney that he and Cardross had been using for cover dislodged itself from the roof, and began to fall into the courtyard.

Graven's hand flew out from his side and caught the chimney with his own magic, keeping it balanced over the edge of the building. If any bellirolt beneath them decided to look up, all three Order members would be given away.

"Now you heed me well, David Dunbar," Graven said in a cool, even voice. "If you embark down this road, there will be no turning back for you."

"The road of justice, Doneval?" David asked.

"The road of *vengeance,* my friend. The road of easy, empty punishment. Do you not remember why Coralie loved you?"

David felt his rage, and the power that flowed through it, reach a breaking point. Two shingles snapped beneath the feet of Cardross, who barely caught them before they flew out into the courtyard.

"My love couldn't save her," David said.

"I asked about *her* love for *you,* David."

"Her love is gone." David began to tremble. "It was stolen—"

"Wrong. Her love abides with you. She didn't love you for being a Sorcerer. She loved the *man she knew.* And you would throw that away? Nothing, not even the bellirolt that speaks to you now, can excuse a *loss* of humanity."

David was losing control of the energy coursing around him. *Ignore the old man,* a thought flared in his mind. *The Mortairian is...*

"If you are battling for power, David, you have already lost." Graven's grip on the hovering chimney was as steady as his voice. "Bellirolts feed on enmity. If you grant yours that, if you give in to your lust for blood, then everything of joy in this world—including your chance to love, even again—will be lost to war. Do not sacrifice yourself for the sake of your retribution!"

David had no more power to hold on. His arms fell as if deflated. Everything returned to its previous stillness, and Graven used his magic to silently lay the broken chimney on a nearby roof. Cardross was crouched in terror beside David, and all David wanted to do was crawl inside a hole somewhere and not emerge for another decade. All he ever seemed to do was bring harm to those around him.

Graven glided over to him and took him by the shoulders. "I know it aches, my friend," he said.

"Do you?" David asked bitterly. "Do you know I'd give anything for five more minutes with her? And these beasts who killed her can call upon spirits of the Otherworld to *spy* for them, yet I cannot call upon her so I may explain—"

"Her spirit, wherever it is, does not exist to soothe you, David," Graven replied. "And these ghosts who serve Orgeron are nothing more than restless shadows of our world, forced to move between the realms, seeking an impossible solace. I think your Coralie would have more wisdom than that."

David looked up at Graven. He needed to see certainty in those earthlike eyes.

"You know," Graven said in a quiet voice, "my father the bellirolt, who gave me my name, used to meet my mother in secret. They developed a hidden affair, and loved each other ardently. When she bore me, however, he succumbed to the pressure of his Legion, and tried to kill me." He indicated the two Sable Scars that disfigured his face. "Mother had enlisted the aid of the Order, and they fought my father off. I was raised under the protection of the knights. And my father was killed by his fellow bellirolts."

David forgot his own pain for a moment as he saw the agony his teacher had suffered at such a young age, so many hundreds of years ago. If a stone could bleed, that was the feeling carved on Graven's face.

"You must understand, David: he never found a way to accept and overcome his darker nature. As long as our desires bind us to things of earth and air, we will *never* overcome them. We will never transcend them. Not even in the life hereafter." He looked to the ghosts that weaved among the bellirolts in the shadows below.

※

Two weeks later, David sat on the edge of a roof overlooking the River Thames, holding a pen and journal. He, Cardross, and Graven had just completed their first full map of Orgeron's activities in London. Cardross had taken on the special task of speeding as many knights to the city as possible, while hiding their numbers from bellirolt spies.

David, meanwhile, had learned to value these twilight hours alone, when he could perch on the eves over London and think. The sky stretched over him like a long palette of cracked marble, and he hearkened back to Florence. He had finally sifted through his darker thoughts enough to release them on paper, which he now arranged into a poem—his first attempt at verse. He called it "The Song of the Baron":

We keep no faith in mortal fires,
We know the wind of death:
It feeds us in our covert hearts
And saves the pain of breath.

Through haunted valleys of brick and coal
We trod the screaming streets;
We fill the veins of darkest thought,
And sap the skin of heat.

No sweet epitaphs shall rest on ours;
Our deeds no bards shall sing,
And gloating o'er our unholy heads
The bells of heaven shall ring.

What wondrous end might we expect,
To soothe us as we die?
We all, be just or cruel, are cursed—
And the curse of all am I.

No sooner had he read the last word than a bitter wind blasted up the river, knocking the hat from his head and nearly throwing him from his perch. In the wake of the wind there was nothing but a heavy, charged stillness.

David looked up the river, as if for an explanation, and that was when he saw he wasn't alone. A lanky man was standing on the roof of the building beside him, wearing a black cloak with a tall hat cocked on his head. He was as rigid as a statue, staring straight in David's direction. David laid his journal aside and readied himself for a fight—but then he saw this was no bellirolt.

As if it had lost interest, the Watcher turned away toward the dark Thames, and vanished from sight.

Chapter Twenty-Four

Hounslow Heath

T he next evening, David boarded a horse-drawn omnibus in Cheapside as a distant peal of thunder echoed across the sky. The sun had not set yet, and he wanted to return to the Citadel in time to receive the evening intelligence report. He squeezed into a seat and smoothed out the frock coat he'd just bought, wincing as the top-heavy bus lurched off down the street. As it stopped again to collect a pair of ladies in purple crinoline dresses, a light rain began to trickle outside.

"'Blige a lady, sirs, 'blige a lady!" called the conductor from the front.

A few men stood and climbed to the open bench atop the bus to give the ladies seats. But David was already tired of the cramped vehicle.

"No trouble—I'll walk," he said, and stepped off. A pack of street urchins dashed by with their little coats over their heads, goading each other as they ran. These "racing patterers," as Ortelius called them, were everywhere in London. Sometimes David saw them doing handstands and cartwheels for passersby on the buses, other times rolling up their trousers and wading into the filthy Thames to collect bits of coal and wood to sell.

"*Penny papers!*" a patterer screeched from under an awning

as he caught his breath. He aimed his olive eyes at David. "Penny paper, sir? Keep your neck dry."

Keep your neck dry. That was what caught David's attention. He meandered over to the boy and inspected the paper he held out.

"*The Gallows Confession of Benedict Todd*," David read. "How fresh?"

"As the rain on my nose, sir," the boy replied. He couldn't have been more than eleven—a short eleven at that—and was dressed in a brown fustian coat and vest, an old striped shirt, and a pair of mucky canvas trousers. His face, though smeared with black dust, was sharp and engaging. David decided to take a chance with him.

"What makes you think I'd want to keep my neck dry?"

Half the boy's mouth curled in a smile. "You ain't shiverin' in the rain. Sir."

David returned the semi-smile. So the boy knew what a bellirolt was, and he knew David was one. It was true the weather didn't bother David, though he noticed the boy shudder as the wind kicked rain at his chest.

"I've seen you at Covent Garden, lad," David said, as he fished some coins from his pocket. "Do you have a name?"

The boy shrugged. "Depends 'ow much silver you got."

David laid his heaviest, most austere gaze over the boy.

"Devara," he said. "Geoffrey Devara."

"Well, Mr. Devara. I assume this lurid rag has come by way of Haymarket?"

Devara nodded.

"And who paid you there?" David asked. But Devara was scanning the windows and doors around him, afraid somebody would hear him.

David straightened as if about to walk away. "Well, I'm sure one of the other mudlarks could tell me..." But Devara grabbed his arm, and pulled him down close.

"*The Snowy Snake's man,*" he whispered.

David nodded, satisfied. This penny paper was on the surface an account of appalling affairs and grisly murders, but hidden in its pages were secret messages the Legion sent throughout the city.

David dropped a few pennies in Devara's hand. "This is for your den of thieves." He knew the other patterers would take their cut of the boy's spoils. "And *this* is for you." He slipped a two-pound note into Devara's pocket. "Buy yourself a warm coat."

Devara's eyes bulged with gratitude. David folded the paper inside his suit jacket and walked on.

"Are you gonna kill 'im, sir?" Devara called after him. "The snake."

David stopped and turned back to the boy, who looked hopeful at the idea. "No, Mr. Devara. I'm just going to make him wish I had."

He turned and staggered as a sharp blast of wind hurtled down the street. He wanted to ignore it, but buried in that wind, like a memory drifting through his mind, was the same ghostly moaning he'd heard just before Culloden. Another Wailer.

A terrible battle—or something worse—was near.

No sooner had David slapped the penny paper on the war room table back at the Citadel than Ortelius scooped it up. He planted himself in a chair and scanned with his pen for Orgeron's coded dispatch.

"Straight from Nathair himself," David announced. "So the patterer told me."

"Don't trust everythin' those mudlarks tell you," Cardross said, making notes on a map. "They're professional tricksters, they are."

Graven grunted his assent from where he sat with a message from Dunadd. He'd almost been robbed twice by the patterers. All of a sudden, Ortelius slammed his palm on the table with a triumphant "*Ha!*", and held up the paper for everybody to see.

"Orgeron has found Tor Bellorum."

All movement in the war room froze.

"Are you certain, Abraham?" Graven asked.

Ortelius nodded. "Quite. Look, here's their cipher. He even gives a location: it's in Inverness-shire, near Ben Nevis. And—" he turned to the last page— "they are about to gather."

David, Graven, and Cardross huddled around *The Gallows Confession of Benedict Todd* and read the translation Ortelius had scrawled in the margin: "*Assemble by dawn at MacLaine's Pride.*"

"What the devil is MacLaine's Pride?" David asked.

"James MacLaine," Ortelius said. "The Gentleman Highwayman."

Nobody in the room responded.

"Come now. Really, sirs? He was a celebrity a hundred years ago. Robbed Lord Eglinton on Hounslow Heath."

"*Where?*"

Ortelius rolled his eyes and walked to a hanging map of the London area. "Good God. Thirteen miles west of us. Here." He hit the map with his finger. "Flat, open land. Always a favorite of bandits."

"Explains why the Legion would have a fondness for it," Cardross said.

Ortelius nodded. "They'll gather there, a safe distance from us, and then proceed to Tor Bellorum."

"Not if we're there to meet them!" Cardross replied.

Graven looked at David. "What say you, Sorcerer?"

David cast his eyes around the room, taking in the faces of the men awaiting his assent—men prepared to risk their lives to ensure he would defeat Claudius Orgeron.

"Let's bag the fox."

Cardross squealed with delight. Graven turned to an attendant and gave the order: "Send word to the battalions: assemble, arm yourselves, prepare to move out. We leave in three hours, from diverse locations, to convene at Kensington. MacEwen."

"Sir?" another attendant responded.

"Dismantle the Citadel."

MacEwen nodded smartly and exited the room. Cardross was already out the door and down the hall, crying to all knights within earshot:

"*To arms, lads! To arms!*"

The sunrise the next morning was barely discernable over Hounslow Heath. It had no color, no boldness or energy; the world just got brighter. David sat up in his saddle to get a better view. The heath was a cold, dry place, crisscrossed with paths through the low brown grass, with only a clump of greenery or a stubby tree to add some relief. The sky was as grey as stone, and the air, finally, was still.

He stretched out his legs in his stirrups and tried to ignore how tired they already were. He'd secured a black gelding from the Citadel stables, and he, Graven, Cardross, and the Paladins had spent the night on horseback marshaling all the magia along the western road to Hounslow. They now had a force twelve thousand strong, from men who'd only been knighted a week before to those who'd served the Order for decades. They even had a squadron of bellirolt knights: ten warriors Graven and David had begun recruiting in Ireland, some of whom had defected from the Dark Legion.

A pair of crows cackawed through the biting air, as if impatient for battle, while the rest of nature lay hushed and hidden. David cast his eyes around the other mounted leaders, to the columns of men who bore the Order's standard: a blue shield emblazoned with a tall white star. He saw gentlemen, factory workers, merchants, and servants—some wearing sturdy travel clothes, others in plain shirts and trousers, their faces painted in blue woad like their Pictish forefathers. It had taken David a century and a half, but he finally had his army, of rich and poor men united, ready to charge toward death for a noble cause. And after watching Coralie shudder and slip away, it hardly meant a thing to him. If he were victorious today he would not ride off into her arms. If he died—well, he might. But as he looked out over the somber heath all he could think of were the meaningless lumps of flesh back on Culloden Moor. He was sick, to his guts, of battle.

"Scout returning!" somebody shouted.

A young rider galloped across the heath and halted in front of Graven. He gave a quick Order salute and looked around.

"Have the other riders come back, sir?"

Graven was dressed in his traditional brown robe again with his trusty staff over his shoulder, his hair braided and tied back. The deep, traumatic scars from his childhood were now painted with an ornate woad design that spread over his entire face. His flesh, painful and disfigured, had been transformed into a stunning war mask.

"Not one," he said, glancing at David and Cardross.

"Then I fear the worst!" the scout wailed. "The Legion has arrived—they're forming on the north end of the field. And sirs—" desperation flared in his face— "by my estimate, they have near twenty-four thousand!"

David had no time to react to the news. The next moment, his bellirolt sense began to whine through his head, and that single, sinister thought flared again: *The Mortairian is near.*

A long, deep horn sounded at the far end of the heath. Emerging from a line of trees several hundred yards away, a wave of bellirolts spread like a dark tide onto the field. Every one of them wore the same attire: boots, black trousers, and black coats with gold waistcoats. Some had matching black hats, others let their long hair fly over their collars. Claymores and sabers hung at their sides. For a moment David felt put to shame with his eclectic knights, each with whatever clothing he could provide. *But that's what Orgeron wants you to think*, he reminded himself. *This is part of his game with you.*

David saw then, as he focused his bellirolt eyes, a tall, white-haired officer emerge from the forest at the center of the Legion. *That could only be Nathair*, David thought, because sauntering out behind him on his boar, a new tall shako gleaming upon his head, was Claudius Orgeron.

David's body locked into action. He leapt off his horse and, with a smack to the rump, sent it cantering off to safety. It would only slow him down in a fight against bellirolts. Graven and the other mounted men followed suit, and ordered their battalions into formation. David was to lead the initial charge, while Graven would command the Order from behind where he could use his magic to affect the whole field. David drew his sword and cast his scabbard aside—he didn't plan on sheathing his blade today. His dark hair whipped around his face as he ran to the center of the front line. Cardross's quick steps pattered behind him.

David could make out Orgeron clearly now as he sat, straight and attentive, on his giant boar. *Doesn't that damned creature ever die?* David wondered. The Dark Commander had fashioned for himself a black military uniform with epaulettes and dark gold trim. His ice-blue eyes, curly white hair, and stark features were accentuated by the brightening sky. Coralie's lifeless, grimy face surfaced in David's head, and he raised his sword and let loose a piercing war cry with all his might.

Every Knight of Nimarius joined in. Blades rattled and clanked throughout the army, and as one the men began to chant: "*Vaslor Nimarièl! Vaslor Nimarièl! Vaslor Nimarièl!*" The effect was one of stupendous power, and David felt his soul buoyed.

But the moment was short-lived. The Dark Legion returned the sentiment, with a collective roar that chilled David's flesh. He knew well the power of his own bellirolt cry, which could shred the nerves of any who heard it, but he'd never experienced twenty-four thousand bellirolts howling at the same time. The Order was silenced.

As the roars subsided, Orgeron shouted commands to his officers.

"I want Graven, and I want the Baron!" he said. *"You can have anyone else you please—I want the bloody shadeling and his pet!"*

Both sides now stood silent as they eyed one another across the heath. Not even the crows dared to speak.

Suddenly, in a jarring cacophony, all the bellirolts drew their swords. "There's your breakfast, gentlemen," David heard Orgeron say. *"Have at them."*

With animal swiftness, the entire front line of the Legion took a running start and rocketed into the air. David could feel men on either side of him flinch and hesitate, as the sky was blackened by hundreds of bellirolts flying in a savage arc toward them.

"HOLD STEADY, MEN!" David cried, his sword aloft. *"MAKE READY!"*

Every man except Cardross uttered the incantation *"Loách-Tirnó!"* They each stepped back into battle posture as a shining blue ball of Disabling Fire appeared in one hand, while they clenched their swords in the other. The Disabling Fires hovered there, shimmering, as the bellirolts closed in from above.

"TAKE AIM!" David yelled, his eyes fixed on a cluster of five—or was it ten?—attackers. When they were within thirty feet, he brought his sword down.

"FIRE!"

A thousand flashes of blue exploded in the morning air, as each knight's Disabling Fire brought down several bellirolts over him. David and the knights beside him dove under the rain of stunned attackers, who had hardly hit the ground before their Black Swells were slashed. In a gruesome minute, the first line of the Legion was vanquished.

David and Cardross raised their swords and launched another battle cry through the ranks of the Order. All the knights responded again, with twice the energy, and then David brought down his blade in the signal to charge.

Hundreds of pounding boots shook the ground. The Legion responded in kind, and sent their next line powering down the heath to meet the Order. Violent cries shrieked from both sides, a few men tripped and sprawled beneath the stampede, but the sprint to destruction only accelerated as the lines drew closer. As David saw the mass of bellirolts speeding toward him, their eyes hot with bloodlust, he drew the single most powerful word he could from his body and let it fly before him:

"*CORALIE!*"

He channeled a *Marghensiù* spell through his pumping legs, sending him soaring above the bellirolts so fast he nearly lost control. He spread his arms like a hawk and took down two as he descended, and the lines of warriors collided in a tumult of bloodcurdling cries. The battle had begun in earnest.

David launched himself into the melee, all his instincts firing at once to outpace these super-warriors. Black Swells burst and sprayed before him, but there was no end to the Legion's numbers. He used his magic to propel himself up and around in the air, hurling Disabling Fires while swinging his blade, flipping over bellirolts to catch more than one in the same stroke. His limbs and chest stung as the beasts wounded him, but he fought on, even though ten more appeared for every one he killed.

David looked back and saw that Graven had ordered the next battalion to begin a flanking move to Orgeron's right, as planned. He spun and saw the Dark Commander still on the Legion's side of the field, sitting in pompous defiance atop his boar, observing the battle as if for entertainment.

Furious, David hacked off the head of a bellirolt captain near him, and looked around for Cardross. With his help, David could reach Orgeron... but the Highlander was nowhere to be seen. *Has he fallen already?* Cardross was several times the warrior of these Legion foot soldiers.

Suddenly an excruciating pain burst in David's belly, and he saw that one of the bellirolts had run him through with a barbed spear. He collapsed to one knee as he struggled to free himself, but three more were already upon him, sticking him again and disarming him. It was then that David heard the same horn blast from the Legion, but now it came from two different locations—*behind him.* Fighting the searing pain in his abdomen, David turned to the Order's side of the field, and felt his blood ice over.

Graven's flanking movement, if it had gone anywhere, had been all but obliterated. His remaining battalions were now being charged on both sides by troops of the Dark Legion. *This is all wrong,* David thought; *where are these bellirolts coming from? This is almost a thousand more Orgeron was hiding from us!*

The full reality slammed into David like a blunt iron. The Order's reconnaissance had failed them again, and now it would cost them their army. Not only had they underestimated how many men Orgeron could bring to the field, but they'd been unaware of his reserves that were now crushing them like a fist. David's stomach twisted as he saw Graven and the Paladins summoning their mightiest spells to keep the bellirolts at bay, but they wouldn't hold for long. He needed to get to Orgeron, fast.

David set his eyes on a discarded sword near him and summoned it to his hand. With a barrage of Disabling Fires that racked his torso with pain, he forced the bellirolts back and sliced the shaft of the spear six inches from his body. He could feel its barbs latched into him like fish hooks—this was a weapon designed to hold him in place—but he'd have to extract it later. He sprang into the air, new sword raised, and locked eyes with Claudius Orgeron. The Dark Commander held his gaze with menacing coolness, daring David to act as he sat unsullied by the battle. David cried out: "*Ventum-Cerél!*"

A tempest-like wind rocketed toward Orgeron. There was nothing he could do but brace himself as he was thrown twenty yards from his precious boar, and the animal, Nathair, and the rest of Orgeron's officers were scattered around the edge of the heath like leaves. David landed hard on the ground and watched as Orgeron scrambled to his feet, his proud shako gone, and drew his diamond-hilted saber. Both men took a running start toward each other, and for a charged moment, the Ninth Sorcerer and the Mortairian moved in perfect unison, flying through the air with swords raised and voices howling. But David didn't see Orgeron's face—he saw Coralie's, soft and tear-streaked with pain she should never have had to endure. This death would be for her.

The two bellirolts grappled in midair and crashed to the earth in a tangled heap. As fast as David could swing his blade, Orgeron could dodge it and return an attack. As fast as David could parry and shoot a Disabling Fire, Orgeron could duck that, as well, leap over David, and nearly behead him. David's agility hardly made a difference here; he needed to use every resource at his disposal to wear the Mortairian down. And he was suddenly terrified—as pain continued to smart in his belly and his muscles begged for mercy—that he didn't have the stamina to beat Orgeron.

But he wasn't out of ideas. He dove under Orgeron's blade and summoned a claymore from the ground to his free hand. Orgeron had an answer to that, and used his bellirolt power to send another fallen sword flying at David's face. No sooner had

David parried it than yet another was speeding at his chest. David could only fight off the flying weapons as fast they came, and in between them Orgeron was still attacking him. Finally, a well-aimed cuttoe hit home, piercing David above his spear wound and sending him twisting back onto the ground. He gritted his teeth and saw Orgeron stalk toward him, ready for the kill. Just as Orgeron raised his glistening saber, David slashed one of his claymores straight through the Dark Commander's thigh, nearly severing his leg. Orgeron screamed and fell back, but managed with his good leg to kick the broken spear even deeper into David's torso. David felt as though his body had been sliced in two.

"*Aiiiiii!*" A shrill cry rang in David's ears. He turned and saw Cardross—*Thank God he's alive!*—running up the battlefield toward David and Orgeron. Burning in the Highlander's face was a wrath David had never seen: a focused, hungry fierceness like a springing tiger. Cardross leapt and raised his claymore to impale Orgeron behind David—and then a black shadow cut him off. Brocklesby, Orgeron's mammoth boar, had slammed Cardross to the ground and was trying to spear him with his falchion-like tusks. But Cardross had the advantage of agility and rolled under the boar, stabbing him several times with his claymore. Brocklesby's hoof landed in the side of Cardross's head, sending him sprawling as the boar collapsed in a squealing heap. Before Cardross could rise, Nathair had pinned him to the heath with another barbed spear.

David bellowed in pain for his friend, but Nathair seemed intent only on keeping Cardross where he'd trapped him. David pushed himself from the ground, his every muscle wracked with fatigue—and then looked to the heath again. As he focused his eyes, he saw far more black uniforms than the mismatched outfits of knights... but something was changing in the tone of the battle. The knights were taking down three or four bellirolts for every one of them. In some places, whole groups of bellirolts were being scattered by deft strokes of magic. Then David saw the standard bearers with the blue shields of Nimarius calling and pointing toward his end of the field. *They know I'm still alive*, he thought. The Order was still tragically outnumbered—they knew they would all die this day… but could they take the Legion with them? Spurred on by the courage of his men, David rose, despite the spear and debris embedded in him, and let out a mighty roar for every knight on the field.

He turned and cut down a line of Orgeron's guards. He summoned spell after spell and brought dozens of bellirolts to their knees, and then Orgeron tackled him from the side. David focused all his energy on the center of Orgeron's body and shot forth a colossal Disabling Fire. The spell slammed into the front of Orgeron's neck, knocking him boot-over-head onto the rough grass. He lay still, sputtering and hacking. Against any other bellirolt, such a spell at point-blank range would have exploded his Black Swell. But Orgeron was strong, his Swell very protected, and he croaked a furious cry and lunged back toward David, whereupon they knocked each other to the ground. They wrestled, biting and scratching with their claws, until Orgeron threw David off and lay stunned and fatigued on the dirt. David felt innumerable Sable Scars begin to heal themselves on his body, but the process was slow; he had so little strength left… He tried to move, to yell Coralie's name again and rally, but no words would escape his throat. He and Orgeron had worn each other to pieces.

David felt himself being lifted from the ground. He saw several bellirolts tending to Orgeron, who was writhing nearby. David turned his head, having to blink to focus his swimming eyes, and saw Cardross being pulled from the ground by the barbed spear, hands and feet shackled with helmonite. And then, halfway down the heath, he spotted Graven. The old man was bound hand and foot as well, squirming on a rough iron stretcher as the bellirolts carried him from the field. He didn't appear injured, but the sight of him in such a state—helpless and struggling, like a captured wild animal—shattered David's heart. *Where are you taking him?* he tried to ask. *What have you done to him?* Still no words came.

David faded out of consciousness. When he came to again, he was in a dark, dank room of stone, with a lone torch in the corner, and felt as though his intestines were being ripped from his body. A second later he saw a bellirolt handling the barbed spearhead that had been stuck in him, and toss it away. He blacked out again.

The next time he awoke, Nathair was slapping him hard in the face.

"I said *listen* tae me, ye Sorcerer filth," Nathair barked. "Ye an' yer bellirolt traitors—the lackey an' yer special recruits—are remainin' here in our prison 'til His Lordship is fit tae fight again. As for the shadeling bastard, we're takin' him someplace special. I'll return when His Lordship is ready tae kill ye proper. 'Til then…"

Nathair kicked David in the gut, sending stars bursting over his world. He doubled over in the corner of the room with the single torch, in nothing but his shredded trousers, torn boots, and mangled shirt. He had no weapon, and no idea where he was. And he realized there wasn't another soul in the room with him as a heavy stone door boomed shut. After that, there was nothing.

Chapter Twenty-Five

The Cell
Beneath the City

O ne chink in the wall above David's head.

That was the only source of light in his prison cell once the torch died away. Somewhere above the chink there were people—free people—who walked and chatted and sang and bought things, but David could only hear muffled echoes of their lives. The chink came from a thin crack in what must have been a solid block of stone, for David only saw light through it in random intervals, on what he imagined were the brightest, most glorious days. It didn't take him long to realize that this cell lay beneath a street, and that street was somewhere in London. He and the other noble bellirolts had been imprisoned beneath the very avenues they'd walked only days before.

The cell was about ten feet by fifteen, and the ceiling rose barely six feet over a stone floor, so David couldn't stand fully straight. He could move, but not actually *do* anything. At the end of the cell opposite the chink was a door of carved stone that had no window, eyehole, or even a lock visible on David's side. This was a prison designed by bellirolts, for bellirolts. There was no way any of David's strength or powers could free him, especially not while he was so weak and had no food.

There were no irons to affix David to the wall, and no pillow or blanket to comfort him. All he found was a wooden tray in a corner by the door, with a dozen small bottles of Moora-Juice. This, then, had been Orgeron's back-up plan: if he couldn't defeat the Sorcerer in battle, he'd lock him up and keep him alive, but feeble, until he could kill him personally.

The moment he noticed the Moora-Juice, David snatched a bottle, uncorked it, and downed it in seconds. The nebulous liquid dissolved in his throat, spreading to every corner of his body and giving the blissful illusion that he was satiated. But the feeling lasted only moments, and then he was sitting in a tense crouch again, staring at the eleven remaining bottles with delirious hunger. When would the Mortairian, or his henchman Nathair, come to retrieve him? Would it take months? Years? *Decades?* David moaned as he realized the torture to which Orgeron had subjected him. He, David himself, had to measure out how long it would take him to rot. A bellirolt was only supposed to be killed with a blow to his Black Swell, but given time, he could starve. Perhaps Orgeron would just let him waste away in this cell, rebuild the Dark Legion, and march on Tor Bellorum. Then the Crown of the Mortairian would be his, and bellirolts would have untold powers over the dark forces of the world. Maybe all of mankind would descend into bloody war, and the Legion would have the feast of its life. There was no more David, no more Cardross, and no more Graven—wherever he might be—to stop them.

Cardross... David didn't know how long he'd been lying on the freezing stone floor, clutching his empty bottle as if to absorb a little more nourishment from it, when he remembered that Nathair had said his friend was in this same prison. He staggered, trembling, to his knees and pounded on the walls of the cell.

"Cardross! Are you there? Answer me!" he cried in a cracking

voice. He pummeled his fists on every side of his cell for hours before he finally heard a distant response. It was a horrible, gut-wrenching wail, emanating from somewhere beyond the door, and David recognized the clear, high voice. He couldn't discern Cardross's words, but he heard sobs and cries unlike anything he'd ever known from the man. Were they torturing him? Why would they torture him and not David?

This muffled communication went on for days—or weeks; David had lost sense of time. He grasped the sydaeon talisman beneath his frayed shirt—the one possession his captors had neglected to steal, likely out of ignorance—and whispered summonings in Sorcerer's Tongue. He called to Graven, to Ortelius, to the various Paladins, even to Cardross across the way, but received no response. Had the Legion also devised a way to block summonings in this prison? David downed another bottle of Moora-Juice, tried the sydaeon again, and gave up. He didn't have the energy to carve his way out of this cell with his claws... given time, he could probably do it, but what was the point? The war between the bellirolts and the Order of Nimarius was over. The Ninth Sorcerer had fallen.

David lay for ages on the stone floor. The sounds flowing through the chink above his head began to shift. They grew louder, more metallic, and he began to hear growling beasts rumble by several times per day. They sounded almost mechanical, but what sort of machine could create such a sound?

The one thought that eclipsed the outside world, that brought a glimmer of warmth to his freezing body, was the sight of Coralie. He looked for her every time he closed his eyes. He recalled the long afternoon at Fiesole, with the possibility of Florence, of *life*, shining beneath them. He recalled the freedom of dancing with her over the Arno, the joy of kissing her... and he saw that she had been the one flash of true happiness in his long life. He'd failed to avenge her, he'd walked with the false hope that he could use his bellirolt demon to make some difference in the world, but at least he'd been blessed with her presence. *If I weren't a bellirolt, I'd never have known her*, he thought. *Those handful of weeks were worth a hundred fifty years.*

It was all David could do to keep his mind active so it didn't give out. *Starvation is a terrible thing when it takes years to die.* Finally, as he found the last bottle of Moora-Juice in his hands, he realized the game was up. He had endured this cruel world long enough. He clutched the vial of green liquid in his fist, curled up in a corner by the door, and waited to die.

Somewhere through the heavy grey storm in David's mind, a dream broke through. He was staring at the chink, through which the rumbling beasts had been joined by loud blaring horns, and voices amplified as though speaking through a long metal tube. Then David saw the bit of light through the chink become brighter, then blinding, then suddenly the whole crack itself exploded in a burst of white-hot energy that deafened him. His day of judgment had now arrived, and maybe some angel was breaking through his torturous cell to set him free... and then something cool and startling hit his legs. *Water... cold water. Does it rain in the afterlife?* It was then that he realized he was balled up with his hands over his ears, his eyes screwed shut. He slowly opened them, and uncovered himself.

Half the ceiling of his cell had collapsed. David was still huddled in the corner by the door, still had the last bottle of Moora-Juice locked in his cramped hand, but the entire other side of his prison was destroyed. He felt a flare of exhilaration: maybe he hadn't been dreaming, after all. Maybe this was still his life... and he was free.

Another sprinkle of water ran across his legs. Miraculously, he was uninjured from the falling debris, but he still couldn't move from his corner. He squinted through a haze of dust and smoke and saw, twenty feet above him, figures moving and calling out on the street. A few were spraying above him with a long hose. Tears erupted and sat in his dry eyes as he felt a wave of fresh air—soft and beautiful like music—greet his face.

"*Ahoy down there!*" an English voice called out. Somebody silhouetted against a white early evening sky waved at him from above.

"Yeah, I just saw a bloke down there," the voice said to somebody else. "*Can you hear me, mate?*"

"*Ye—*" David's voice snagged in his throat. He felt as if he were tearing his neck apart. Shaking, he uncorked the final bottle of Moora-Juice and drank it, trying not to gag.

"*Yes, hello!*" he croaked. "*Hello, I'm here...*" His voice died as he said it. Was this all real? After so long, was there anything left of him to rescue?

"*You just stay right there, mate, and don't move! We're with the Army; we'll get you out!*"

Alarm flashed in David's head—it was murky in his clouded state, but still there. He arched his neck and strained to be heard: "*The* English *Army?*"

"*No, the bloody Hun army! Who do you think? Don't move; we're gonna gather some chaps and move this building off o' you!*" A flurry of activity commenced above.

A wave of uneasiness crept over David as he remembered the redcoats singing drunken songs and torturing Scottish peasants after Culloden, not to mention the soldiers he'd attacked at Killiecrankie years before, even Orgeron in his colonel's uniform... now he was going to be *rescued* by English soldiers?

It took the men nearly an hour to clear enough rubble away that they could help David out of his cell. The sharp scent of smoke attacked his nostrils as he was raised to the street, still clutching his last empty vial of Moora-Juice—his hand seemed locked around it. It was when his ragged boots finally touched the street, and he leaned on the shoulder of a stocky young soldier, that he realized something was very wrong. This was not the world he'd left when Orgeron had imprisoned him.

He was surrounded by shouting, crying people, all dressed in suits, uniforms, and gowns he'd never seen before in his life. The men had short hair and clean, trimmed faces, with strange angular hats and wide, droopy outfits. The soldiers who were helping him wore round helmets like tortoise shells, and simple olive-colored uniforms that spoke nothing to the dignity of a warrior. The ladies wore their hair down and had slim dresses that exposed their ankles, with no crinolines or hoops to add shape to their figures. David suddenly didn't feel as out of place with his threadbare shirt, trousers, and riding boots that hung in pieces off his emaciated legs. As far as he was concerned, these people looked less clothed than he.

Yet everything else David saw was far more striking. The buildings rose twice as high as he remembered, and seemed to be made of just as much metal as brick or stone. The street wasn't covered in mud or cobblestones, but was coated in a smooth, black surface. And the vehicles had no horses to pull them! He saw one speed down a side avenue, spewing filthy smoke and emitting the same horrid rumbling sound he remembered from his cell... and it was moving of its own accord.

"Sir, what is the date?" David asked the soldier he leaned upon. "Please, I must know the date."

The soldier stared at him in concern. "You must've had a nasty knock on the head down there, eh, old boy? It's September the seventh."

"*What year?*" David pleaded.

"1940, mate! Look, we've got to get you to the medics, otherwise..."

The soldier's voice was lost amid a torrent of sound in David's head. The world was sliding in waves around him.

1940, he thought... *Great God. I've been underground, in the same cell, for ninety-nine years.*

David suddenly realized that the barrage of sound between his ears wasn't his brain struggling to make sense of everything. It was an earth-shaking roar that was coming from *above,* and David heard people scream as he saw, in a moment that chilled every bone in his body, a swarm of angry metal birds shoot across the sky.

There were hundreds of them—so many he couldn't see a beginning or end. They streaked through the air with a terrible, mechanical grinding, and as they advanced over London each one began to drop large black objects from its belly. Explosions sounded with a jarring *BOOM,* CRUMP, CRUMP from across the city, and David felt the street tremble beneath his feet. *Bombs,* he thought. *Is this what has come from cannon fire and grenadoes?* Not only had man found a way to propel himself through the air by machine, but he'd used it to obliterate entire cities. David had seen too much now, had come too far from fist fighting and swordplay at his quiet castle in Haddington.

Suddenly David spun back to the crumbling building behind him.

"Sir, wait—" he grabbed his rescuer's arm again— "there are still men alive beneath that building!"

The soldier narrowed his eyes at him. "Are you sure, mate?"

David nodded frantically. "Yes. Just have a look at the area around my ce—... around where you found me. Quickly."

As great columns of smoke billowed up around the city, and the cracks of what sounded like rapid-fire guns filled the sky, a team of soldiers dug through the rubble around his cell. Night was coming on now, but the bombing continued across London.

And then a voice rang out from the rubble: *"Here's one!"*

David stumbled toward the ruined crater of the building.

The soldiers had just uncovered another cell from a pile of loose stones, and curled up in its corner was a shriveled man with long, matted black hair, in dark trousers and boots like David's.

David's heart bounded up into his throat, and he clambered across the rubble to see if the man was alive. "*Cardross!*" he cried. "*Cardross, answer me!*"

In a movement so gradual it was like something from a nightmare, the shrunken man in the stone pit raised his head to look at David. David leapt back at what he saw. This man—this *thing*—couldn't be Cardross. He was pale, and unbelievably gaunt. David had thought he himself had grown scrawny and withered, as he could feel the curve of his own ribcage, but this figure was nothing more than a skeleton with skin. However, it wasn't even how emaciated the man was that haunted David; it was the look in his face. There were Cardross's wide blue eyes, but they possessed none of the brightness David had known for so many years. They were ashen, empty, and lost. The Highlander seemed already dead.

The soldiers lifted the waiflike Cardross from his dirty lair. They continued to hunt in the rubble for the other men that David swore were trapped beneath the building and found two more, both dead. The bellirolts who'd charged into battle all those years ago on David's side, not Orgeron's, deserved better than to waste away like this. A pair of medics arrived but David waved them off, insisting he knew where he and his friend could find treatment. They needed real food—bellirolt food—and fast.

David draped Cardross over his back and staggered off through these new London streets. Weak as he was, David felt more able-bodied upon seeing Cardross's condition: he had to be strong for his friend, otherwise they were both finished. He slogged through the ringing, smoke-laden avenues, Cardross all-too-light on his shoulders, as he searched for food in the way that only bellirolts knew. Finally David came upon three kitchen workers—wounded and delirious—lying outside a hotel. This would have to do for him and his friend. They had no other options.

They built up enough strength to keep moving, and David decided to try for the slim chance that somebody from the Order was close by and able to help. He put out a call through his sydaeon talisman: David Dunbar, the Ninth Sorcerer, was alive and in dire need of assistance. For several minutes he received no response, then suddenly the little stone began to burn against his chest. His trembling fingers closed around it and he heard the answer in Sorcerer's Tongue in his head: "*We are here, My Lord. Can you get to a safe location and we will find you? Tell us your position.*"

David reeled with joy. He sputtered the good news to Cardross, who registered none of it, and hobbled to the nearest recognizable street he could find. He collapsed against a rough stone building, arms wrapped around his friend, and sent another message. It was night, and these vicious enemies who flew overhead hadn't ceased their bombing for more than a few hours at a time. David watched the horizon come alive with dozens upon dozens of fires, filling the sky with angry clouds of smoke that buried the moon and all the stars, as five men stepped from the darkness around him. He looked at them for a tense moment, and they stared back at the two bellirolts. If he and Cardross had been tricked, this was the end for them. Neither could defend himself. Finally, one of the men drew his index finger slowly down his forehead and around his eye in the salute of the Order, and dropped to one knee. His four companions did the same.

David tried to breathe, to steady himself, but all the air got caught in his chest. *The Order is not dead, thank all the powers!* he thought. *We are not finished yet...*

"*Shulech syne Dunbarech?*" the first man asked in a halting voice. David couldn't help closing his eyes and smiling. When he opened them, they were glassy and hot. He swallowed the bubble in his throat and nodded.

"Yes," he said. "Yes, I am."

Chapter Twenty-Six

Crannog's View

Percival closed his coat more tightly as the cold of early evening settled around him. He and David were sitting on a sagging stoop at the end of the bothy, facing up Granny's lane. They leaned back in two wicker chairs they'd pulled from inside the building, as David cradled his empty pipe against his chest. Percival had polished off a sandwich, thrown together from what remained in Granny's kitchen, and now he set the finished plate on the stoop.

"So what happened next?" he asked.

David raised his eyebrows. "Next, I came here."

Percival stared at him. "But that was back in 1940, and the Germans were bombin'—"

David smiled. "What happened next was we rebuilt the Order. Brick by brick. There were only a handful of knights who survived Hounslow Heath, and fortunately they had the tenacity to continue recruiting, to keep our cause alive. However, their numbers remained low, and they could no longer engage the Legion in open combat. So they did the most prudent thing: they studied, they trained, and they waited. They waited for some sign of me, for otherwise they had no hope—"

"Of defeatin' Orgeron," Percival finished. "But did you

ever find out how he got so many men past you? You said he had, what, *twenty-five thousand* at Hounslow?"

David shook his head. "To this day we are uncertain. He was very cunning in his organization."

Anxiety wormed through Percival as he thought of how Orgeron had almost outsmarted David again. "Maybe there were spies within the Order," he suggested. "Like that Ortelius. I didn't trust him."

David shook his head. "Ortelius was a good man. And we discovered no spies."

"So you've not seen Orgeron since then?"

"Not face to face. He survived the battle, and whilst he nearly annihilated the Order, he almost lost all *his* men, as well. What I didn't know all those years in his prison was that I had singlehandedly destroyed the flower of his army. And the magia continued fighting even after Graven, Cardross, and I were captured. After that day there was no more Legion, only bands of bellirolts that Orgeron has been trying to cobble together into another army. He spent centuries creating that force, and should have wiped us from the face of the earth. Instead, they lost faith in him, and he nearly lost his life." David swung one booted leg over the other. "A troop of twelve thousand knights took on a bellirolt army more than twice their size. We destroyed their morale, crippled their leader, and damn near won. *That* is the legacy of Hounslow Heath."

"And Graven?" Percival asked. "What happened to him?"

David's face took on the mournful, faraway look to which Percival had become accustomed. "I don't know. We've searched for years for Graven, but found nothing. He could very well be alive right now if Orgeron has chosen to keep him so, though I fear he may be tortured and long dead. But we seek him still."

Percival was crestfallen. He'd grown to love the rugged old magian. "And Orgeron still hasn't claimed the Crown of the Mortairian?"

"No, he has not. We wrecked his army at Hounslow, and without a similar force he won't be able to open Tor Bellorum. To our knowledge he is approaching such numbers now, but we also are ready. For, as peace settled over Europe after the Second World War, we began to recruit again. And we recruited from everywhere.

"You see, what I hadn't realized, in addition to the damage we'd inflicted on the Dark Legion, was that an intimidating legend had taken shape around my name. Or, luckily, not my name, but my former title."

"The Tercentennial Baron," Percival murmured.

"Precisely. There's the folk story you've read, of course, but I speak of one that grew among the people who know the Otherworld. Tales of the Battle of Hounslow Heath were whispered everywhere. The Legion did all they could to hush it up, but several thousand bodies had to be cleared from that field. The tales spread like a flood through the London underworld, through distant branches of the Order, of how 'the Baron' had taken on Claudius Orgeron again and again, 'til he outlasted the Dark Commander himself. The saga enchanted people, and so when I emerged from captivity, hope was rekindled. Families who only knew the Order from the stories of their grandfathers flocked to us in droves. By 1950, we had reconnected with every foreign outpost I had visited in my time abroad. By 1970, we had an army again. We now have more knights, in more places, and they're better equipped than at any time in history. We even have our motorbikes." He nodded to where Maggie sat around the corner of the bothy.

"Which run on magic?" Percival asked.

"In essence, yes." David smiled. "With any luck, later I can show you how she works. For now," he rose to his feet, "I have a duel to prepare for."

Percival stood with him. "Wait—what happened to Cardross? He recovered, right?"

"Cardross is fine, lad. He was sullen for a long time after we were rescued, but he soon returned to himself. He personally reshaped our spy network, so we shan't be caught unawares again. I'm meeting him outside town after sunset, in advance of our battalions."

"So, this evening…" Percival's heart quickened as he thought of the battle to come. "What's our plan?"

David paused in the process of stowing his pipe in his coat. His eyes deepened in sympathy. "Percival, my plan, from this moment forward, cannot include you."

A sharp, cold sensation plunged through Percival. He stammered, "What… are you serious?"

"Dear boy, I am about to battle the Mortairian—"

"I know what you're about to do. I figured it out." Percival stared incredulously at David. "After all this—all we've been through in the last twenty-four hours—you're goin' to shut me out?"

"For your own safety, yes. I'll send a detachment of knights to guard you, but that's only on the condition that you remain here, away from the fray. I cannot afford to be worried for your safety."

"You are completely maddening!" Percival jumped off the stoop. "I accepted the danger o' what we're doin' every step o' the way. Now that's no longer good enough? You said you needed my Second Sight!"

"Percival." David stepped down to approach the boy. "The world will be well-served by your Second Sight. You are a gifted lad. But yes, things changed when—"

"What about the Watcher?" Percival demanded, crossing his arms. "Not once in your whole story did you mention a Watcher who *spoke*. Do we know what he was tryin' to tell us?"

David's eyes softened for a moment. "No. That's one riddle we may only guess at. Watchers don't speak, Percival. They never have. Until now."

Percival shook his head and let out a sharp, resentful laugh. He charged away to Granny's house.

"*Percival.*"

It was the pervasive, magical power of David's voice that stopped Percival long enough to look back. David had followed him around the bothy, his eyes glowing in the meaningful yet mysterious way Percival had first seen the night before.

"No matter what happens," David said, "I want to tell you that I'm glad I know you. I've not said that enough over the years. And I'm proud of you. You searched beyond the myth. You know the truth. Most people never look closely enough to learn the truth." He gave a brief smile—encouraging, full of confidence—then stepped inside the bothy and shut the door.

Percival stood for a moment, feeling the warmth in David's words but not comforted by it, before turning back to Granny's door. He paused just as his hand skimmed the doorknob—why was he retreating to Granny's hovel? He needed space to think, to process. He turned and, hearing David packing inside the bothy, crept past the building and up Granny's lane. He continued walking in agitation, and didn't stop until he found himself on the High Street, as the sun was beginning to sink behind the hills.

The street bore the leaden emptiness of a ghost town. All the shops were locked, the cars were gone, and the blue and red Berry Festival ribbons hung like the mismatched trappings of a funeral from the mercat cross. Traditionally, this would have been the evening of the Festival Ceilidh: a night of dancing and music in the Town Hall where the crowd toasted (and roasted) the winner of the Prize Bunch. Not so this year.

Percival drifted toward Crannog's bench, feeling the cold ache of solitude. He supposed it was a small price to pay if it meant Bonnybielders were safe. He sank into the smooth wood of the bench and leaned back, hearing a board creak beneath him. He shifted his weight, and the board creaked again. He looked down at it in annoyance and saw, to his surprise, a small red tassel caught under the board at the end of the bench. Percival cocked his head and pulled the tassel toward him. An entire bookmark from Barclay's Books and Inks came with it.

Percival furrowed his brow in amusement. He flipped the cardboard strip over to see if he could sign his name, as he did with all his bookmarks—and saw somebody else had already written something. A scratchy, uneven hand had left what looked like a message, and Percival squinted to make it out:

FOR PERCIVAL: ORTELIUS 257

Percival's heart began to pound. For *him?* He searched the length of the bench for another clue, but found none. How long had this been sitting here? Some aspect of the handwriting seemed familiar, but he knew there was only one person who would have left such a note in this place: Old Man Crannog.

Ortelius... Percival thought. The same man from David's London story?

It's a book, he realized. *A book, and a page number.* The idea was mad, and yet Percival had learned in the past three days that the maddest ideas often led to the truth. He leapt from the bench and sprinted over to Barclay's.

Crannog never just watched the Old Steeple, or Balloch Hill behind it, Percival thought as he ran; *he saw all of us out of his periphery for over a decade. He knew very well where I worked; he knew I would understand this...*

Percival found the hole in the windowsill where Barclay hid his spare key, and let himself into the shop, easing the door shut behind him. Every sound was amplified now on the High Street. He stood on the doormat beside his counter, surveying the dark store.

If this is the same Ortelius, it would be an older book, MUCH older...

Percival darted around the stacks to Barclay's most treasured section: Bonnybield of Bygone Days. He scanned the authors' names on the book spines, until his eye fell upon a thin hardcover halfway down: *Notable Scottish Churches of the Early Nineteenth Century*, by A. Ortelius.

Percival felt as if time had ceased to move. He drew the book into his hands. It was an old edition, from the mid-1900's, and the pages were brittle and faintly stained. To be certain he was right about the author, Percival flipped to the back inside cover and saw, to his delight: *"Abraham Ortelius, 1787 - 1899."* There was even a picture of the man, matching the description David had given. A dour Dickensian schoolmaster.

Apparently you were an expert on more than just London, Percival thought as he flipped to page 257. He found himself in a chapter called "Hambledon Trinity Church, Bonnybield," and nodded with comprehension. What had he been told as a child? The Old Steeple at which Crannog stared had been ruined by lightning in the early nineteenth century, and the church was built soon after—while Ortelius was alive. Percival scanned down the page, and his breathing halted when he read:

> *When the foundations for this Neo-Gothic church were laid, a poem was found etched into a large stone on the very spot the builder wished to begin. No man or machine was able to remove said stone, and so it remains buried beneath the nave of the church. As an item of interest, the text of the poem was as follows:*

> *As the Sun draws in its dragon Breath,*
> *Just beyond the burning Heath,*
> *And writes the Sign of knights alight,*
> *Holding the pregnant whisper of the night,*
> *Behold: in arms there come two Beasts,*
> *One from South and one from East,*
> *To end a battle with Blood and Flame,*
> *And raise from its ashes the Devil's Bane.*

There the page ended. Percival looked back at the book-mark and its shaky writing. So this was what Crannog wanted him to have. The poem—the same verses the old man had been repeating for Percival's entire life—was written here in a book. It had been sitting under his nose every day he'd been sweeping the floors and stocking the shelves around it. And it seemed to describe the Order of Nimarius.

Percival ripped the page from the book and ran out of the shop. He planted himself on the bench, directly in front of the church and that stone beneath it, and fixed his eyes on the Old Steeple.

He was looking northwest, toward the sunset-bathed Balloch Hill to the left of the tower. He saw nothing remarkable there, so he glanced back at the poem.

"'*As the Sun draws in its dragon Breath*' —well that could be the sunset," he muttered. "'*Just beyond the burning Heath*' — I'm lookin' at the heath on Balloch Hill now— '*And writes the Sign of knights alight...*'" Here Percival stopped. The sign of knights? Was it really referring to the Knights of Nimarius?

Percival looked up at the ruined Steeple. There was some image that seemed to be pulling at his mind, something he knew he was almost seeing but couldn't quite grasp. He kept staring at the Steeple, taking in its shape, its orange and pink hues in the setting sun... *Crannog sat here for years and years*, Percival thought. *Whatever he saw could have been a very small change; he knew the view perfectly...*

All of a sudden Percival realized he was neglecting one detail: Crannog's posture. He hunched his back, mimicking the way Crannog had sat, the angle of his head... and then it happened. The sun sank to a position between two hills in the west, sending a stray shaft of light toward the tower. A form appeared before Percival: the head of a large horse, framed in the broken outline of the Steeple, and the new beam of light sprouted from the animal's head like a gleaming horn.

The Unicorn! That was the sign of the knights. That was the signal Crannog had been waiting for all these years, that had sent him dancing around the High Street like a boy at Christmas—it had just appeared today. Percival's eyes shot back to the poem. Everything else seemed to fit. *"Holding the pregnant whisper of the night"*: that had to be the air, which was flat and calm without a trace of a Wailer; the *"two Beasts"*: Orgeron and David, both bellirolts; *"One from South and one from East..."*

"Their origins," Percival said aloud. David was born in Haddington, in southern Scotland, and the Mortairian was heir to the First Bellirolt. What was it the Augury had said? The bellirolts *"rose and ravaged our homes from the East."*

Percival read the last two lines of the poem, but then he stopped again. David and Orgeron might have come to *"end a battle with Blood and Flame,"* but how would that battle *"raise from its ashes the Devil's Bane"*? Something was out of place. *"The Devil's Bane"* should be the Ninth Sorcerer. The only one who could defeat the Mortairian and his Dark Legion—his devil's army. But hadn't David already risen as the Devil's Bane? Everybody knew he was the Ninth. Perhaps he still had to prove himself?

Percival looked up and estimated he had less than half an hour of daylight left. A sinister feeling was burrowing through him the more he thought about the page in his hand. The poem, like a second Augury, had to be predicting this last battle between the Ninth Sorcerer and the Mortairian, but why those final lines?

David is missing something, Percival thought. *There's something he doesn't know, and he may be in more danger than he thinks.* Percival closed his eyes, feeling as if the bench were a giant precipice on which he was teetering. He stuffed the page into his coat pocket, and as he rose to leave, he remembered standing opposite this very spot a few hours earlier, puzzling

over the location with David—

And wondering how the Watcher and Crannog were connected.

The Watcher had been gazing from Balloch Hill toward Crannog and the Steeple. Crannog had been looking up toward Balloch Hill. Percival pictured the hill in his mind: a tall, barren summit, covered in heather up to a sharp rim…

Percival cried out, clutching his head as he remembered. Above that rim was an old, abandoned barn.

The image rose to life in him again: *a burning barn, atop a hill, in the dead of night with nobody around…* If Percival had learned one thing from his day with David, it was to pay attention to his dreams. The battle was going to occur at the Balloch barn, and David might be in trouble.

He took a deep breath, turned up the High Street, and ran toward Granny's.

David examined the length of his blade by the single light he'd switched on in the bothy. The edge was still fine, no sign of fractures or breaks. He watched the light play upon the words inscribed along the bottom of the steel: *"Dunbarech-magiel-gaird fall'Eralan."* Dunbar, Sorcerer of Eralan.

It was the task of every knight to forge his own sword after completing training; David had had to remake his after returning from captivity in 1940. He felt the familiar worn grip in his palm, and let his senses connect to its weight and balance. It moved like a continuation of his arm, a whole other presence complementing his own. He slid it into the sheath hidden on his back beneath his brown coat.

The sun had dissolved from the sky by the time he crested Balloch Hill on his motorbike and was greeted by a giant stone barn. Before arriving in Bonnybield, he and his fellow knights had chosen the barn as their rendezvous point. He parked and approached the building, looking left into the silent town, and right into a deep, dark glen. He sensed nobody else. Only a vast full moon kept watch over the stillness.

David pulled the sydaeon talisman from beneath his shirt and grasped it, muttering a few summonings in Sorcerer's Tongue. He received no response. He cocked his head, and tried again. Still no answer. His first battalion should be close by now, and it was unlike them—and very unlike Cardross—not to answer a summoning.

The barn loomed over David like a silent, sleeping beast. He decided he might as well make himself comfortable while he waited. He placed one hand on his sword hilt, and ducked into the building.

The balls of Percival's feet were aching, and his sides splitting with cramps, by the time he limped up Balloch Hill. He'd made it as far as Scobie Road before realizing that David had already left the bothy, and he was going to have to continue on foot all the way up to the barn. He collapsed on his knees to catch his breath at the hill's rim, several yards from the barn. When he finally looked up, he noticed a healthy glow was emanating from the building. Through a row of windows he spied David seated inside, stoking a small campfire. He appeared to be alone.

Percival straightened, and was about to call David's name when he heard soft footsteps to his right. He dropped down beneath the rim, and spied a short man with a thick tangle of black hair gliding past David's motorbike. The man wore a sleek leather jacket, jeans, and boots, and moved as swiftly as a fox through the shadows. *William Cardross*, he thought, with a mixture of excitement and frustration. The only way he could warn David now would be to reveal to Cardross how much David had told him. To Percival, that felt like breaking a bond. He knew how much David valued his secrecy.

And still, Percival had to know the truth of what Crannog

had spent over a decade waiting for. He wasn't about to leave the scene yet. He crouched at the rim to watch.

The heavy oak door groaned open and Cardross peeked inside. David was sitting on a wooden crate, tending a fire he'd lit from loose straw and fallen beams. As he heard the door his eyes flashed up, and his face brightened.

"You're late," he said.

"Got held up," was Cardross's reply.

Cardross entered the cavernous barn and lifted himself through the air until he landed before David, embracing him like a brother.

"Have the others reported?" Cardross asked.

"No. And I've heard no answer to my summonings."

"You know, the same bloody thing happened to me!" Cardross paced around the hay-strewn floor as David turned back to his fire. "Does this place have some sort of magical property I'm not aware of?"

"It very well might," David said. "But I can't begin to work it out."

"Hm." Cardross inspected the corners of the building. "Well thank God you worked out that this is where Orgeron's comin'."

David stared into the flames for a moment, as memories of the last twenty-four hours flickered through him. He hadn't begun to puzzle through his nephew's remarkable gifts, or his strange, determined character. But despite how they'd clashed, he was immensely grateful he'd met the boy. "It was... quite the endeavor," he murmured.

Suddenly, the tingling sensation exploded in David's head, and for a moment it was so overpowering his eyes watered and he couldn't see straight. Then the thought, like a recurring nightmare, reared up in his mind: *The Mortairian is near.*

He rose to his feet and leapt over the fire. Cardross looked at him.

"What is it?"

"The Mortairian approaches." David's eyes were fixed like gun barrels on the door of the barn. Something was happening out there, and he couldn't tell what...

"Where the *hell* are the other knights?" Cardross demanded.

"I wish I knew." David threw an urgent look at Cardross, whose indignant face reshaped into one of readiness.

"Glad I have you, old friend," David said, clasping Cardross's hand. The tingling in his head was building to a fierce climax.

"*Vaslor Nimarièl*," Cardross replied, his sapphire eyes shining.

"*Vaslor Nimarièl.*"

Both men drew their swords and stood ready in front of the fire. Something began to hammer, steadily, on the barn door. The door bowed inward once, twice, three times—and on the fourth it burst open. David strained his eyes but saw nobody in the blackness beyond. Instead, a vicious wind barreled into his face, slinging pebbles and dirt. He shielded his head, and was about to use the *Ventum-Cerél* incantation to stop this strange attack, when something flew toward him out of the night. It was a sword—no, *two* swords, one right behind the other, and David was just able to parry the ruby-encrusted hilt of one, when the diamond-laden hilt of the other smashed into his forehead and knocked him on his back.

He could now feel that a new presence had entered the barn, and he shook his head as he felt his skull repairing itself. He raised his sword and looked up to the entrance.

Hovering there above him was William Cardross.

Chapter Twenty-Seven

The Battle
of Balloch Hill

"*W*illiam?"
David's head still ached from the blow he'd taken. Something had to be wrong with his vision—this was some illusion, some untold power of Orgeron's. But there, indeed, was Cardross, floating on his bellirolt power twenty feet away, sword hanging in his hand. This was not the Cardross David was used to. His keen expression had now taken on a quality of ease—even delight—as his eyes shone with sinister coolness.

"What on earth are you doing?" David asked.

"Enjoyin' the view," Cardross crooned in his high, boyish voice.

David clambered to his feet. The wind was gone, and the two swords that had flown at him now rested in the straw on the barn floor. A ruby-hilted claymore and a diamond-hilted saber... then they clicked in David's memory. Deuchar's sword from three hundred years ago, and Orgeron's blade that had nearly killed David on Hounslow Heath. But what were they doing here?

"William... where is Orgeron?" David could still feel the

warning blaring in his mind: *The Mortairian...*

A bright smile spread over Cardross's face, and he chuckled. "You really don't understand, do you, David?" He descended to the ground. "You won't be seein' Orgeron tonight. Or any night again, for that matter."

David was becoming fed up. He pointed his sword at Cardross. "You need to stop toying around and tell me what the hell is going on."

"You think your match is Claudius Orgeron? The oldest, mightiest living bellirolt! Heir to the Crown of the Mortairian. Oh, David..." Cardross's mouth quivered in jubilation. "I've waited such a long time to tell you this. I am older than Orgeron—older even than your dear Doneval Graven. For over seven hundred years I've practiced my powers. *I am the Mortairian.*"

Shards of ice stabbed into David's body. Several yards away, outside the barn, Percival clapped a hand to his mouth in shock. He wanted to scream, to help David, but was rooted where he knelt.

"That's impossible," David choked, but something in his Second Sight told him it wasn't. "I saw you turned, saw you go through demortisation just as I had—"

Cardross sniggered. "You never saw a thing, David! You saw me *after* I had made believe I was turned. All I had to do was kill that bellirolt at Kintail and have him latch onto me. I couldn't very well meet the great Doneval Graven as you knew me—he would've seen right away I was already a bellirolt. I should say I put on a fine show all those years at his outpost, didn't I?" He did a rude imitation of himself shuddering and moaning as a new bellirolt, then laughed again. David was repulsed.

"You're telling me you were a bellirolt when I met you?"

"I'd been a bellirolt for over four hundred years when you met me, David. I was turned as I began my twelfth year—a wee birthday present I sought out for myself."

"So that entire story about your family being killed by bellirolts, your reason for joining our fight…"

"Oh, my family *was* killed by bellirolts." Cardross nodded matter-of-factly. "But I was the one who led the attack. Once I realized I wanted nothin' more from them, I trapped them. And killed them. But that was a fine story to win your pity, wasn't it? I was delighted how readily you took to it."

"*Delighted?*" David doubled over as if the word had kicked him in the gut. "Has this all been a game to you? For three hundred years, you've *pretended* to be my friend?"

Cardross's expression shifted to one of dire solemnity. "Oh no, David. No, I wouldn't call it a game. It was a *plan*. I've had a plan for you since before I met you."

David felt as if he were being hollowed out. "What?"

The sapphire flame in Cardross's eyes burned brighter as he spoke. "Do you really think it was an accident that we met how we did at Craigvaran? I had discovered the Augury when I was a young bellirolt, back in the 1200's. It didn't take me long to decide that *I* was to be the Mortairian, that I wouldn't suffer any other fool to claim the Crown in my place. But I'd heard the tales of bellirolts who'd tried and failed. I wouldn't let that happen to me—not I, not William Cardross. I knew the key was *you*." He grinned at David. "I had to find the Ninth Sorcerer. I had to make certain I could defeat him, because he was all that would ever stand between me and the Crown. So, I tracked the bloodline of Eralan, watched it unfold, and I waited. And waited. And *waited.* I needed a man born of that line, in Haddington where the Seventh Sorcerer lies, who could be scarred by a bellirolt before he was turned. Finally, after four hundred years, you came along. You fit all the criteria—you even had a penchant for battle to boot—but of course you weren't a bellirolt yet. That was where MacBain came in."

David fought a shiver as he remembered the eyes he'd felt

watching him in his gardens at Galanforde. "You sent him after me."

Cardross shrugged. "Didn't take much. He was a bit delusional—I think you could tell—so I just had to convince him you ought to be his next target. I knew he would nab you at Craigvaran, so I was there waitin' for you both."

A dark weight settled into David as he realized the full extent of Cardross's powers. There was something that had never made sense to him about that day he was turned, about the feeling he'd had as he fell toward the water…

"You made him catch up to me in mid-air," David said. "You're the reason I slowed down *as I fell…*"

Cardross grinned again. "I'm the reason my shots hit home in the first place! You don't live as a bellirolt for four centuries and not learn how to control movin' objects. No matter how fast they're movin'."

David shook his head, as if he could throw Cardross's words from it. "So all those years, then… *everything* you ever said was a lie. You pledged your life to me! I put all my trust in you!"

"I needed you to be the Ninth, David." Cardross scanned David from his boots to his head. "And look at you! You've done remarkably well. Far better than I'd even hoped. Like when you volunteered to show Graven your water trick, all to cheer me up! Even I hadn't thought of that!"

David swallowed the shame of being made to look like a puppet. "You can't be the Mortairian without an army behind you. I don't care how clever you think you are, *duplicity* does not make—"

"I've been raisin' an army for centuries, David; save your breath. What do you think I was doin' every time I ran off from an outpost lookin' for food? I can smell a meal in the next county. I was spyin' on Orgeron, and recruitin' for myself. Most of my men never saw my face; they thought they were workin' for Orgeron. But when I presented myself to them, they knew who to follow."

David clutched his head as more horrid truths bombarded him. "Good God, that's it, then! I let you be our liaison—I let *you* conduct our espionage! Every time Orgeron slipped out of our grasp, every time we thought we knew his abilities and our intelligence failed us, that was *your* doing?"

A small, satisfied laugh escaped Cardross's lips. "It's what I do best."

"Why?" David pressed him. "Why toy with us and let us stumble into his clutches again and again?"

"I knew when you needed a good fight, laddie! You had to test yourself. And oh, how I *wish* that old pillock Graven was here to see this." David could see a hundred ways of murdering Graven flash over Cardross's eyes. "His precious Order intelligence, his *plans* for you—all strewn to pieces by the wee squire who was supposed to be submissive to *him:* a rank shadeling. For over a hundred years I had to bend my knee to a *shadeling!*" He spat on the straw. "If I knew what Orgeron did with him I'd have happily brought him here for this. Just to see the look on his face."

David's heart ached for Graven. And for what he'd thought he had with Cardross... he wanted to scream as he remembered who had brought the Order to Naas that night the rebellion began, who had been so eager to get him out of Florence and back to London where Orgeron was, who had found him first above the maze of London tenements—and especially, who had been close by, prepared to finally reveal the sinister truth, every time David's Second Sight had whispered the Mortairian was near...

"So it was you who killed those workers in Florence. And D'Argenio. What about Subini, the poor conjurer? Why him?"

"Subini was trackin' me, like I told you. He was on to me from our arrival there—I don't how, but he was a slippery little eel. Good thing I got to him in time."

"So where is Orgeron, then? Has he been a follower of yours all these centuries?"

This time Cardross let out an uproarious laugh that rang through the barn. "Orgeron follow *me?* That self-lovin' gull would never follow anybody! I was feedin' his men information the same time I was feedin' it to you, see? He and his white weasel Nathair never knew, but I had both sides in my pocket. Finally, I needed control of his army, so he had to go. I ambushed him outside his hideout and killed him months ago. The Legion answers to me now."

David swayed where he stood, and had to lean on his sword. *Cardross* had been able to kill Orgeron? The very thing to which David had devoted his life, and failed to do on Hounslow Heath?

"I suppose you're also the reason the sydaeons aren't working?"

Cardross spread his arms as if welcoming guests to dinner. "I enlisted the help of some of our Otherworld friends to... *muffle* your summonings. And I made sure the Order thinks they're meetin' you on the other side of the country, by the way."

A bitter laugh burst out of David. He was alone, then. No Knight of Nimarius would arrive to help him. Or to protect Percival.

"So Orgeron never intended to face me here."

"He never knew you'd be here. And you would've laughed to see him, David. After Hounslow he lost his... touch, you might say. He was a pitiful sight, really, far from the formidable commander he once was. I rightly think I did him a favor."

"That look in your eyes, then..." David realized, "when you charged at the end of the battle on the heath, that was for me, wasn't it? Not Orgeron." *No wonder, then, Cardross had vanished right after the battle had begun...*

A heavy, seething shadow passed over Cardross's face. "Hounslow Heath…" he murmured, "was supposed to be the end of you, and the Order. I had prepared everything for that day. I'd recruited the lion's share of Orgeron's army, without him or his officers catchin' on. And I'd made sure you thought he had a fraction of the men he truly did. *I,* not he, had masterminded that battle. The plan was simple. You would kill *him,* then I would kill *you* in full view of the Legion, and take my place as Dark Commander. My followers would recognize me, and any bellirolts who didn't would be killed. We would obliterate the Order, and march on Tor Bellorum."

He cocked his head, quiet anger glinting in his eye. "But you mucked that up, didn't you? You kept on fightin', tough wee tyke. You killed too many bellirolts, but not Orgeron. And by the time his officers nabbed us, my followers were too scattered to save me. The Crown could have been mine a hundred and seventy years ago. That was when I knew, after Hounslow Heath, that next time I'd have to face you alone."

David spun and laughed in agony. "For *three hundred years,*" he cried, "all I ever believed was that you were so committed to destroying the bellirolts that you thought of nothing but finding and killing Orgeron. And this was the reason? You wanted me to do your dirty work so you could snatch up his army?"

A sour smile creased Cardross's lips, and he looked away. "It's a bloody shame it didn't work. The underworld in London was ripe for the pickin' then…"

"You look at me, you dog." David stood beside the fire and waited until Cardross peered at him in curiosity. "Was there a scrap of truth in anything you ever said to me?"

Cardross's only response was a look of mirthful satisfaction.

"What of your face when I pulled you from the rubble in London?" David demanded. "You were not yourself. I'm the reason you're standing here right now."

"Oh, aye…" Cardross's eyes took on a faraway look, and his face softened for a moment. "Aye, I was quite depressed then, wasn't I? I thought, for all those years, writhin' and cryin' in that cell, that my life was over. That I'd failed. Luckily—" his face returned to its youthful eagerness— "it inspired me to work twice as hard afterward."

David caught himself in a moment of empathy. *He means he failed to kill you*, he thought, *not failed to vanquish the Legion.*

"Answer me this, then," David ordered, his voice beginning to waver. "Did you have anything to do with Coralie?"

A wide, condescending smile crept over Cardross's face. "Oh, David… No, no, David, that was you. Did I not warn you somethin' would happen to her if you didn't leave? How many times did I tell you we ought to be in London?"

"*Did you send those men after us?*" David roared.

"Those were Orgeron's minions, you cretin! He wanted to kill her, so you would face him in battle! I knew they were comin', but you'd already refused to leave!"

"So you let us be attacked? You let her die?"

"I saved myself, David." Cardross aimed his sword point at him. "The same as you should have done. Don't you see? Nobody is responsible for her death but you."

David's rage was building like a volcano. He'd done everything he could to save her that day.

"We are bellirolts, David," Cardross went on softly. "Killing is our nature. If people we care about die, we can take them into us, so they're always there."

David recoiled in horror. "*You think I took Coralie's soul?*"

Cardross looked puzzled. "You didn't?"

Hot tears began to pound the surface of David's face, but he held them back. "I *loved* her. You ignorant pig."

Disappointment fell over Cardross's features. "Ah, yes. You did, didn't you? Odd thing, love. Makes people quite unpredictable. I'll admit it inflamed your temper on Hounslow Heath. You accomplished *feats* that day. Though you didn't win."

"No single man could defeat that army."

"No single man *should* have been able to defeat that army, yet you nearly did!" Cardross screamed in fury. He raised his sword. "I'd like to show you, if I might, a force stronger than love. It's called *true destiny.*"

David finally felt a tear break through his face as he raised his own blade. Never, in his darkest dreams, did he imagine he would be doing so against this man.

"You have caused me grievous injury, William."

Cardross's eyes only glistened with pride.

"You almost caused me the same, darling David. I must say, I believe I owe you my thanks before I kill you. On the whole, the last three hundred years have been *mighty entertainin'.*"

Cardross let out a lion-like roar, and sprang toward David. A cry burst from David's inmost soul as he met his adversary in midair, and the ringing of their blades awakened the stillness of Balloch Hill.

From where he crouched behind the rim of the hill, Percival could barely follow the savage fight. David and Cardross were flying around the barn, battling like hawks in the air. Every heartbeat was a gunshot in his ears, and rage and despair crashed through him in waves. His instinct after reading Crannog's poem had been more prescient than he'd thought possible. He looked down the hill behind him and prayed that everybody had made it out of Bonnybield. There would be no Order to protect them.

Inside the barn, the battle grew fiercer every minute. In all his centuries of knowing Cardross, David had never seen the man fight like this. This *animal* moved like a tiger with wings. He pounced, tore, slashed, and flew around David, so fast that

David thought for a minute there was something wrong with his vision. But then he realized that, with every stroke he made, tears were pouring from his eyes. He *hated* this. For the whole of David's life as a bellirolt, Cardross had been his anchor of loyalty, the companion he never questioned—and it was all a lie. How had he built his life on a lie? He'd loved this man like a brother, and now he hacked and stabbed through his anger and denial that *this* was the final enemy of the Ninth Sorcerer: his best friend.

David finally decided to call upon the one skill he had that Cardross didn't: his magic. If he really had to kill the man, then so be it. He hurled Disabling Fires that Cardross dodged. He conjured wind around Cardross to throw him off-balance. He even whipped up a tongue of flame from the campfire and lashed it at the Highlander. But Cardross was too agile, and let the flame curve past him to a dry bed of hay by the far wall. In seconds, the blaze was streaming across the barn.

Bits of roof thatching began to fall in a slow, fiery rain around the warriors. David, nearing exhaustion, summoned a flaming bullet that threw Cardross back against the wall. They perched above opposite windows, the blaze growing around them.

"You're gettin' winded, old man!" Cardross goaded David, who recalled torturously the days when such words were said in jest, not cruelty. "I know your weakness when I see it!"

"*Curse you for a warrior!*" David howled back, his hair plastered to his face. "What in God's name makes you think you have the measure of me?"

"*I MADE YOU, David Dunbar!*" Cardross bellowed as a flaming beam crashed down between them. "*I made you!* Everythin' you are, you owe to me! You'd never have known Graven or life as a Sorcerer without me! And I can rend you to pieces just as easily as I put you together!"

Cardross flew out from the wall, sword aimed at David's

neck. David felt his heart surge into his throat at Cardross's words, but he blasted forward nonetheless, in a collision course with certain death… then he realized that the two swords from the ground were speeding up toward him. He fixed his eye on one, caught it, and hit the other out into space. Cardross, however, snatched it from the air, and now both men were doubly armed as they met, swords wheeling, thirty feet above the barn floor. David made two powerful slashes that sent Cardross tumbling away in midair, and then another falling rafter caught them both and sent them plummeting to the ground.

One of David's swords went flying. He extricated himself from the rafter just as Cardross struck his remaining sword and sent it spinning into a vertical beam, where the blade lodged itself. David conjured a Disabling Fire before Cardross could land another blow, and blasted the Highlander into the stone wall behind him. Turning, David set his eyes on the sword in the beam, stuck beside a south-facing window, and decided it was the one weapon he could reach. The blade was only a few yards away, and David lunged, arm outstretched, fingers about to grasp the hilt… then he heard a bloodthirsty howl behind him. Cardross was already on his heels, and before David could respond, he felt five claws like shards of glass latch into the back of his neck. A sharp sting convulsed his veins, and for a moment he thought it was the shock of five Sable Scars at once. Then he felt a thick, hot liquid form a slow trail down his neck. His Black Swell had been pierced.

David tried to scream, but his tongue had ceased to work. He only stared at the sword hilt inches from his fingertips—was salvation really that close?—and his eyes fell on a form outside the window. A tall boy had suddenly risen out of the night, and stood staring in horror. A desperate cry welled up inside David, and he tried to give some signal to Percival to hide—but Cardross had already released his grip, and dropped David to the ground. He didn't see what David had been looking at outside.

Percival dove back beneath the rim so quickly he slid ten yards down the steep hill. He latched onto the grass as an anchor, curled in a ball, and felt, rather than heard, David hit the barn floor. The impact—the fall of the Ninth Sorcerer—sent a gut-wrenching spasm through Percival's body. He even thought the earth shuddered beneath him. *No, this can't be real,* he tried to tell himself; *David can't be dead...*

Inside the barn, Cardross loomed in triumph over David, admiring the inky blood that now stained his hand. David lay half on his back on the floor, one leg trapped under him. Try as he might, he couldn't seem to move it. He could feel, with every passing moment, life leaking out of him.

Cardross's blue eyes flared through the swelling heat above David.

"Goodnight, David Dunbar," he sang. He stepped over David, summoned his sword to his hand, and soared out of the burning barn.

Percival held himself as tightly as he could, not daring to breathe or move a muscle, as he heard Cardross's feet land on the ground before the barn. The Mortairian raised his face to the sky and trumpeted, "*LEGION!*" A hundred figures flew up from the glen on the other side of Balloch Hill and landed in a circle around Cardross. Percival heard them roar in adulation, and the short Highlander cried, with the same boyish glee David had always described: "*The Ninth Sorcerer has fallen!*" Earth-rending cheers shook the night.

"*Onto the town, lads,*" Cardross called, "*where there's ten souls for each of you to honor our victory this night! Then we meet our army and march to Tor Bellorum, and our prize!*"

With howls of assent, the bellirolts rose as one mass and glided over Percival's unmoving form down into Bonnybield. He heard windows shattering and doors breaking, as his nightmare came true: as these monsters pillaged his hometown.

Percival listened, and heard only two—maybe three—human cries as the bellirolts tore through Bonnybield. He felt sick to think who might still be down there, but at least Cardross and his henchmen wouldn't receive the feast they'd planned on. He uncurled himself and clawed his shaking hands up the face of the hill, fighting to reach the top before David died, if he wasn't dead already... His knees found the hold he needed and he wrenched his body onto the crest, then stood and faced the glowing red barn beneath the full moon.

It was a premonition, he thought. This was everything he'd seen before, in his first dream at Granny's. And now, like then, he had to see if David was still alive.

He took a deep breath, steeled himself against the heat, and ran forward. But as he did, just like in the dream, he saw David's silhouette begin to rise inside the building. It was a slow, desperate climb out of the scorching heat.

Elation bloomed in Percival's chest. *He's not finished yet! The Devil's Bane is rising from the ashes!* He saw David lean on a long, diamond-hilted saber, raise his eyes to Percival's—but the look on his face displayed anything but triumph.

David stumbled, reached toward the gaping entrance—and fell. Percival wailed and ran closer, but saw no sign of David getting back up. *No*, he thought, *this isn't right; this can't happen...* He took one look at the hole where the door had been, that now spouted torrid heat, and knew he couldn't leave David. He ran inside.

It was like diving headlong into an oven. The heat stole Percival's breath, and he shielded his face with his coat to get a fix of oxygen. Fire raged everywhere, and the building only had minutes before it collapsed on top of him. He staggered forward and located David: crumpled on his back beside half a burning crossbeam.

Percival ran to David's side and kicked the beam away.

The sight of David Dunbar—his great-uncle, the Sorcerer, the warrior—lying so helpless ripped through his chest. David was smeared with black blood, his long hair clung to his face, and his body was tangled in the same brown coat he'd worn to save Percival from the Mochries. How could this be the end? Three hundred years, from Scotland to Florence to London and back, and now this?

Percival wanted to carry David from the building, but knew he didn't have the strength. The most he could do would be to drag him, and there were too many obstacles in the way. His body poured sweat and begged him to leave, but then he connected with David's jade-green eyes. They looked mournful, resigned—but not dark yet.

Percival made his decision so quickly there was no thought involved. He stretched out his hand to David.

David squinted at the boy. *Are you mad?* he wanted to cry. *Get out and save yourself; I can't grab hold of you!* But then, with an awful plunge in his stomach, David realized what Percival was saying.

He tried to shake his head, but the muscles wouldn't work. All he could do was plead with his eyes, use his remaining strength to say: *NO. No, I cannot, I will not—*

But Percival shoved his hand forward again. He knew what was at stake. He had listened to the entire story. The Ninth Sorcerer had fallen. The Mortairian had won. But even if Cardross succeeded in marching to Tor Bellorum and claiming the Crown, there was still a chance to bring him down. The Order was stronger than ever, David had said. If he passed his bellirolt on to Percival, then maybe—just *maybe*—with what Percival now knew, he could challenge Cardross.

This, Percival realized, was what the omens in Bonnybield had been foretelling. Not just that the Mortairian was coming, but that the Ninth Sorcerer was going to battle him, and lose. The Wailer had been preparing for the death of the Sorcerer and those left in Bonnybield, the vision of MacBain—the beginning of Cardross's deceit—had dogged Percival for days, and the Watcher had known that some sort of connection was about to pass between two men named *Dunbar*. Percival had done his best to save Bonnybield, but now he was facing the destruction of other towns, countries—multitudes of innocent people. He thought of Abi… thank God she'd left already. And Granny. Was she safe? Could she even care for herself without Percival?

She's going to have to, he told himself. *This is more important.*

He stretched out his fingers to David.

David rolled his head away and peered through the crackling flames as he felt the last drops of energy seep from his body. He didn't know where he would go in a few moments, nor did he care; his thoughts were of Percival. He longed for the boy to leave, to have a life, to grow old as a man and not a monster…

In all David's pleading and silent moving of his lips, Percival caught one word: *Coralie*. He didn't know whether it was a call for companionship or guidance. But as Percival stood there with his hand outstretched, David rolled his head back to face him, and locked eyes with him in one final, dire look.

David grunted, his eyelids fluttered, and with his last burst of strength, he threw his hand up to meet Percival's. Their fingers grazed in a split second of contact, and David's hand collapsed on the barn floor. He moved no more.

An instant of peace passed, and then a burning spear shot from Percival's fingers through his veins. His limbs screamed with a pain hotter than the fire around him, and his stomach caved as the new bellirolt presence spread through his body. The pain dropped him to his knees, and as he writhed and wailed beside his dead uncle, the final support beams of the barn began to collapse.

A grinding cacophony of stone and wood tumbled down over the two Dunbars. The night all around had grown cold and silent, and only the pallid moon watched, with tranquil fascination, as a new bellirolt was born in the fiery spectacle.

Over three hundred twenty years earlier, under the same full moon, a figure glided down like a bird from a castle window. In its place, a frantic, terrified baron ran to the opening and cried, "*WATCH! DOUGLAS! Call the damned watch!*"

Beneath the window of Galanforde, a short, wild-haired bellirolt landed in a crouch on the grass. He raised himself and glanced up the wall of the castle, smiling with pride. His sapphire eyes gleamed for a moment in the moonlight.

William Cardross replaced the hood of the cloak he'd borrowed from MacBain, and strode off into the night.

He had an inkling, as he walked, of the wheels of providence he'd just set in motion. His great plan had only just begun, but if the moon that watched him that night could speak, tones of subtle laughter might have echoed across the centuries.

END OF BOOK ONE

ACKNOWLEDGEMENTS

It takes one person to write a book, but an army to support that person. Thank you, first and foremost, to my family. To my mother, who always read to me as a child, instilled in me a true love for words and the Romantic writers, and was instrumental in the completion of this book. To my father and stepfather, who read the manuscript multiple times and helped provide for me as this book was written. To Mollie, my number one editor, who has read and responded to more drafts of the Baron's story than anyone. To Katie and Frank, whose knowledge of Scotland and the French language were invaluable to my research. To my grandmother, Carter Catlett Williams—the first independently published author in our family—and my grandfather, Dr. T. Franklin Williams, for making the production of this book possible. To *all* my family together, for listening to and commenting on the early drafts, and continuing to believe in this story for eight years.

Thank you to the friends and acquaintances who gave me feedback on the early drafts: Julia Whelan, John Stephens, Bill Thomas, Wendy Lustbader and Barry Grosskopf, Amaree Cluff, JC Herz, Will Blythe, Jared Rosenberg, Shannon O'Brien, and Janet Johnson.

Thank you to whose who were so generous with their knowledge of Scotland, England, and Europe as I researched this book. First, to Stephen Watson, whose stories of growing up in Northeast Scotland served as the inspiration for Bonnybield. To Simon Vance, Eileen Gary, and Katie Woltz, for providing a perspective on English and Scottish day-to-day life and customs. To Austen Saunders, for reading the whole book and offering vital historical assistance. To Dr. Nicole Robinson, for her expertise on the Italian language. And finally, to the McClures: Ewan, for your perspective as a native Aberdonian; and Derrick, for straightening out the Scottish dialects in the book, and deepening my understanding and love of Scottish history. You two were the heroes at the end of this journey.

Thank you to my young beta readers: Jack Streed and Alyssa Ortiz. Your honesty and perspective have helped make this book what it is.

Thank you to those who also offered their assistance in submitting the manuscript to agents and editors: Dick Couch, Anne Marshall, Steve Bennett, and Kate Hollander.

Thank you to all those who said no. You made me a better writer.

Thank you to all who were involved in the final production of this book. First, to Geof Prysirr, whose training and guidance have given me the tools to be a truer artist and more astute businessman at every step of this journey. To Chris McGrath, for being such a wonderful collaborator on the cover illustration (and for producing a beautiful piece of art in the process). To Dane and the folks at Ebook Launch, for working with me on the final book design. To Keidy Moreno, for making me look like a professional on the back cover.

And thank you to Rachel, my fiancée and partner in all things. You have not only supported me throughout the writing and completion of this book, but challenged me to grow even more as I've pursued it. I am a better writer, and a better man, with you beside me.

Lastly, thank *you* for reading this book. Nothing brings me joy like being able to share this story with you. Remember, this is only the beginning of Percival's journey…

Connect with Will Damron

Thank you for reading. Now don't hesitate to say hello!

Find me on Facebook: Facebook.com/Damron.Stories

On Twitter: @jwdamron

On Instagram: @jwdamron

Or on my website: www.willdamron.com